Clerical Errors

A NOVEL

Alan Isler

SCRIBNER

NEW YORK LONDON TORONTO SYDNEY SINGAPORE

SCRIBNER
1230 Avenue of the Americas
New York, NY 10020

Designed by Kyoko Watanabe
Text set in Aldine

Manufactured in the United States of America

1 3 5 7 9 10 8 6 4 2

Library of Congress Cataloging-in-Publication Data

Isler, Alan, 1934–
Clerical errors: a novel/Alan Isler.
p. cm.
I. Title.

PS3559.S52 C58 2001
813'.54—dc21
00–048488

ISBN 0-7432-1060-3

For Adam and Ethan Gahtan

The End of the World

Quite unexpectedly as Vasserot
The armless ambidextrian was lighting
A match between his great and second toe,
And Ralph the lion was engaged in biting
The neck of Madame Sossman while the drum
Pointed, and Teeny was about to cough
In waltz-time swinging Jocko by the thumb—
Quite unexpectedly the top blew off:

And there, there overhead, there, there hung over
Those thousands of white faces, those dazed eyes,
There in the starless dark the poise, the hover,
There with vast wings across the canceled skies,
There in the sudden blackness the black pall
Of nothing, nothing, nothing—nothing at all.

—Archibald MacLeish

Part One

A story should be taken with a grain of salt. Salt improves the flavour . . . And a little pepper doesn't hurt, either.

—The Ba'al Shem of Ludlow,
Table-Talk, 1768

$\int$ ipping a Calvados in a bar in the rue de Malengin and reading an English newspaper left on the seat by its previous occupant, I discovered to my surprise that I had just died. It appeared that I had driven my car, a modest Morris Minor of a certain age, into the famous Stuart Oak of the Beale estate, the oak so named because planted to commemorate the death of the unfortunate James II. The Stuart Oak had sustained little damage; the Morris Minor was now a twisted, tortured tangle of metal, from which had been extracted a pulped human body supposed to be mine. Our local constable, Timothy "Tubby" Whiting, had identified the car and its owner. Tubby has a palate for local ale and bitter than which there is surely none more refined. He is, moreover, as am I, a Catholic, he rather more persuasively than I. But he is no Sherlock Holmes, or, for that matter, Father Brown.

First I phoned Maude back at the Hall. She, foolish soul, supposed, or pretended to suppose, I was phoning from the Other Side.

"God be praised! *Deo gratias!* Oh, sweet Jesus! Oh! Oh! Oh!"

"Maude, my love, I'm all right."

"All right, is it? Of *course* you're all right, there with the Holy Virgin and the blessed angels. Is that the heavenly choir I hear?"

From the jukebox at the back of the bar the late Edith Piaf sang "Milord."

"I mean that I'm not dead."

"Not dead, is it? Of course you're not dead! Everlasting life, that's what He promised us, that's why He bled upon the Cross. Oh, I must tell Father Bastien immediately. Oh, Edmond, I miss you so. Be patient, my love. I'll be with you as soon as I'm allowed." And she hung up.

The silly old woman! It's extraordinary how *any* sort of excitement brings back the brogue she otherwise abandoned with her youth. She was jesting, surely. Her relief must have found its outlet in hysteria. And, no doubt, mother's ruin has played its part, too. Yes, gin has long been her favorite tipple, and lots of it—but in a pinch she will make do with whatever's on offer. She likes to pretend that I am the one who has "a little drinking problem"; as for her, why, she drinks merely to be sociable or because she finds herself without company, or because she feels cheerful or because she is bored, or because she is worried or because she's not. We don't talk about it.

Ah, but to remember what she was like when first I knew her, Maude Moriarty, the keeper of my house and my flesh, lo these many years! Ah, the swish of her hips, the rustle of her skirts, the slender shape of her arched above me! And yet to see and hear what she has become as Time's wingèd chariot rattles behind us, nearer and nearer! Gone—or, at any rate, usually hidden nowadays—are the wit and the sharp intelligence. She has played an Irish washerwoman for so long, she has at last become one. Too much television, perhaps.

> O she had not these ways
> When all the wild summer was in her gaze.

Next I phoned Tubby, assuring him that I was as good as on my way home. His shock at hearing my voice was somewhat mitigated by his acceptance of the glad tidings: I was still alive. "But who *was* it, then, Father," he said almost accusingly, "we squeezed and scraped out of the car? He must've been doing a hundred down the drive." The drive is curved and dangerously steep as it plunges toward the Stuart Oak.

"D'you suppose it was poor Trevor? As I remember, I'd asked him to pick up the car over the weekend. The hand brake had given out, and the foot brake was sluggish." Trevor Stuffins was our local odd-job man, a fellow of my own age and girth.

"Hmmm," said Tubby noncommittally.

"We must pray for his soul."

"He was a Protestant, Father."

"All the more reason."

"If it *was* Trevor." Tubby was capable of learning from his mistakes.

"Do me a favor, Tubby, go and have a word with Maude. Explain to her I'm still alive—alive, that is, in the *this*-worldly sense. Do it gently."

Before leaving the rue de Malengin, I ordered another Calvados and sipped it slowly. My trip to Paris had been a failure, but I felt somehow like one recalled to life.

ᠭ᠎

Could it be that Castignac was right? He had telephoned me a month before, getting to a phone who-knew-how, and warned that Vatican assassins were after me. "Watch out, Edmond, pay attention! They want you dead!" This was followed by a mad cackle. "They will stop at nothing! Nothing!" And then the line went suddenly silent.

But poor Castignac is a lunatic. Why should I have paid attention?

Well, perhaps because of the historical record. *Parva*, as we say, *componere magnis*, to compare small things with big, the popes themselves have not been safe from their coreligionists, even as their coreligionists have not been safe from the popes. In the tenth century fully one in three popes died in (nudge-nudge) "suspicious circumstances." Pope Stephen VI was deposed and strangled in prison. And as for murderous corruption, poisonous intrigue, and the savage pursuit of power, why, everyone knows that the popes of the High Renaissance—the Borgias and their like—wrote the book, created the template. To step a little closer to our own time, what of John Paul I, who died in 1978 after only thirty-four days on the throne, eh? I point only to the fact, nothing more. Dear me, no. But if so magnificent a beast as a lion may be cruelly slain in his lair, what hope for compassion has a mere flea?

Still, a sense of proportion is a wonderful thing. I cannot truly believe that what I might call the upper hierarchy is after my blood, much as they would like to see me out of a job. No, but rather lower down, though. Father Fred Twombly, say, chairman of the Department of English at Holyrood College, Joliet, Illinois, my undoubted enemy since we were graduate students together in Paris, the wretch who wants my job, the fact that I have it and that he does not gnawing at his vitals like a poisonous mineral. He, I think, if all else failed him, could interfere with the brakes of my car.

But all else has not yet failed him. He thinks he has me by the hip, and it may be that he has. I shall tell you about him anon, and about his latest letter to me, the occasion of my trip to Paris.

Perhaps I should pray.

Perhaps not.

At what moment, I wonder, did I lose my faith? It is a question that has no answer, a semantic dilemma. Have you stopped beating your wife? To lose something—virginity, say, or a gold watch—one must first have possessed it. But I put it on, this faith, because it was offered me, it *suited* me, it was a habit, in both senses of the word. It was at once an ecclesiastical vestment, an outward sign of belief, and a way of life to which I became comfortably—well, perhaps that word needs modification, but, for the moment, let it stand—comfortably accustomed.

Which brings the young Castignac's joke to mind. He rose to

the exalted rank of papal nuncio, traveled the world—Guatemala, Lebanon, Hawaii, wherever the Holy See had need of him—a spy, after his fashion, yes, one of God's spies, gazing into the mystery of things. But he also learned at firsthand the intricacies of the Vatican's inner workings, what the Protestant Milton calls its secret conclaves. And where is he now? As I have said, stark staring mad, terminally bonkers, or so designated, and in the merciful hands of the Sisters of the Five Wounds, a hospice in Cambridge, Massachusetts. Well, he always liked America, did Castignac.

But why do I mention him? Ah, yes, the joke. We were seminarians then, you see, the old Adam not quite squeezed out of us. Not out of Castignac, in particular. What a rogue he was! He possessed the blue-black, curly hair, black eyes, and olive skin of the true Corsican, a young Napoleon, but well endowed, hugely endowed. In the dormitory, he slapped away at it. "Down, wicked fellow, down!" and thus revealed himself, grandly tumescent, to our secret envy. "Look," he said one early morning, pointing through the window grille to the courtyard, where an ancient van idled and out of which stepped a young woman. She opened the van's back door and took out a basket. "That's Véronique," he said. "She's the laundress. Every fortnight, she picks up the monks' dirty habits." He looked at us slyly, and then he roared with laughter. And so we understood we had been told a joke.

But to get back to the question of faith. In those early days, I gloried in the words of Tertullian. *Certum est quia absurdum est.* Those words had—to use the modern idiom—a certain in-your-face quality that appealed to the adolescent that I was. To believe in something because it is absurd! Oh, yes. Yes, indeed. But I had in any case reasons enough to be grateful to them, to the Church, I mean. (Notice that "them." What an astonishing irruption after all these years!) I was taken in, given shelter, occasionally shown kindness. Those were terrifying times, quite terrifying. The saintly fathers saved my life, and—so they believed—my immortal soul.

Still, I had an early taste for it, I must admit, the incense, the chanting, one's breath during Mass of a winter's morning rising like mist to the cathedral's vault. I enjoyed, not piety, but the spectacle of piety and, to the burgeoning visionary imagination, myself as pious. I could see myself on my knees, dragging myself over the cruel stones, to throw my broken body, bloodied, prostrate before the Cross. Of course, I never did any such thing. Self-flagellation, outside of the visionary imagination, was not my style. Perhaps I felt a little of what moved Edward Gibbon (who was to show with devastating irony in his *Decline and Fall* the utter nonsense and demonstrable cruelty of Christianity) to embrace Roman Catholicism in his impressionable youth:

> The marvellous tales that are so boldly attested by the Basils and Chrysostoms, the Austins and Jeromes, compelled me to embrace the superior merits of celibacy, the institutions of the monastic life, the use of the sign of the Cross, of holy oil, and even of images, the invocation of saints, the worship of relics, the rudiments of purgatory in prayers for the dead, and the tremendous mystery of the sacrifice and the body and blood of Christ, which insensibly swelled into the prodigy of Transubstantiation.

Thus Gibbon in his *Autobiography*, writing of the follies of his youth. Well, I was not (and am not) a Gibbon, but it is clear enough to me now that what I possessed as a youth was a painterly inner eye, if not a painter's ability. I saw, as it were, a Catholicism as it might exist in a Platonic realm of Ideas, and to *that* I responded, a victory of frosty sensuality over pulsating reason.

But to return to Tertullian, to know, intellectually, that the whole rigamarole was *absurdum* and therefore to believe . . . well, really. Suppose I had put it to the faithful as follows: "Know that the world and all that inhabits it—all of you, my dear little brothers and sisters, and even I myself—we are actually resident in the mind of a monstrous carp swimming languidly in the warm waters of Eternity. *Certum est quia absurdum est.*" You see what I mean. It is not for nothing that the phrase "hocus-pocus" derives from the words of consecration in the Mass, *"Hoc est enim corpus meum,"* and in turn gives birth to the word "hoax."

And yet here I am in black suit and dog collar, and, of course, my color-coordinated black-and-white trainers (my bunions, you see), back home from Paris, mission unaccomplished, awaiting a courtesy call from the German ambassador. The pious, thankfully few in number in my neck of the woods, bow and scrape before me— or would, perhaps, if I spent more time among them. Bastien appeared at my side. "Our Côte de Gherlaine is quite used up, Father, but we have an untroubled Coeur de Languedoc, 1963, a gift of Colonel Fulke-Greville, grateful for your kindness on his recent visit. May I tempt you?" *"Retro me, Satana,"* I said sternly. But then I saw his crestfallen face: "But of course, my dear Bastien. What luck! A Coeur de Languedoc! The colonel is too kind. You will not only convey to him my gratitude, noting that nothing we were able to do for him could match his generosity, but you will pour a glass of it for yourself."

It is so easy to be gracious.

Bastien, the donkey, has been with me, appropriately, for donkey's years. He has grown old in my service, my factotum. How would I get on without him? Slippered indoors and out, curved like a question mark, wisps of white hair attached untidily to an almost bald pate, he stands in his stained cassock, knees bent and splayed, bouncing gently as if he were an exhausted spring. He is another to whom Time has not been kind. Odd he has long been, for reasons I shall no doubt divulge, but he also possesses a kind of peasant shrewdness and a honed intelligence that show themselves when least expected. That I keep him on in so privileged a position rather than arrange for his retirement is regarded as a unique sign of my inviolable charity. But I have known him since our schooldays. We were orphans together. He would be lost without me—I say it in all modesty—and I suspect that I would be lost without him.

His joy at my recent resurrection was unfeigned. He spared not a tear for poor Trevor—yes, Trevor it was who had died in my place—or for Trevor's distraught sister-in-law from Wigan, now conferring with her solicitors, for, as Tubby told me lugubriously, using language appropriate to a sexually distraught maiden aunt, it was likely that the brakes, hand and foot, "had been *interfered* with." I, he was happy to report, was "not in the frame." But somebody had been out to get Trevor. I did not tell Tubby that I was myself a likelier target.

Bastien placed two glasses on the table beside me. I was in my study, the Music Room, on my cushioned chair, my poor feet on a yielding stool. He retired momentarily but returned with the bottle of Coeur de Languedoc. Around his neck, where his Cross should be, hung a corkscrew on a string. Bouncing gently, he held the bottle before my eyes, label toward me; and, as if in the hands of a drunken sommelier, the bottle bounced with him. I could not have read it if I would.

"That's it," I said, "the very thing. No cork-sniffing, Bastien, no preliminaries. Let's to it."

I held the filled glass up to the light. "Stand off a little," I said, waving with my free hand. He has in these his last years acquired an unpleasant smell, has Father Bastien, not strong, to be sure, not unwholesome, but rather like the aroma of turned-over compost that, on a damp day, reaches one from a distance. "I want to see the famous Coeur de Languedoc ruby." What I saw, in fact, were his greasy finger smudges on the glass. But no matter. Bastien was now at a safe distance, bouncing after his fashion, his wine in danger of slopping over the glass's rim. He would not, honest fellow, drink before his master. I sipped. "Aah!" I smacked my lips. I sipped again. This was his signal to drink.

Why, you may wonder, do I keep him on? In part, as I have said, because his continuing presence here is a visible *earnest* of my charitable disposition. All to the good, that, all to the good. Besides, there is no more discreet man than he. Pincers to his tongue would not draw from him my secrets. And oh, I have a secret or two. In some, we are complicit, he and I.

"A short nap, I think, before the arrival of the German ambassador. We'll offer him one of our sherries, good Bastien." I wink at him. "He need not know we have a Coeur de Languedoc, 1963."

"*Sale boche!*" he grumbled.

I reproved him gently, as was my fashion. "Love is the lesson that the Lord us taught."

⌒

How on earth did I get myself into such a pickle? Are the agents of the Vatican after me in England, now, virtually at the end of the millennium, simply because almost six decades earlier the Wehrmacht marched triumphantly into Paris, that time, you may remember, when Hitler gave his little hop of delight? It's hard to believe. History, even personal history, has its problems. Leopold von Ranke blithely advises us to write history "*wie es eigentlich gewesen ist,*" as it *actually* was. But how *was* it, actually? However much I try to re-create the past, I necessarily view it through the unreliable eyes of the present. No, Croce had it right: "All history is contemporary history." Nor was Hobbes far off the mark: "Imagination and memory are but one thing." And further complicating my difficulty, I have always felt a certain sympathy with what is essentially a Marxist stance vis-à-vis the role of accident, chance, and contingency in history—as compared, I mean, with the role of underlying, ineluctable social patterns. For example, I believe it unlikely European history would have been much different in the thirties and forties had Hitler died in 1928. But I find myself, for all that, increasingly of the opinion that accident, chance, and contingency rule individual lives, mine in particular.

I really ought to explain what two Frenchmen, Bastien and I, are doing here in England in the first place. Before that, I ought to reveal that I am in fact a Jew—well, that I arrived in this world a Jew. My parents were born not in France but in Hungary, in Dunaharaszti, to be exact, a townlet south of Budapest, and went to Paris, a young married couple, in 1923, a mere five years before my birth.

Curiously (and coincidentally), Dunaharaszti was also the birthplace of Solomon Reuben Hayyim Falsch, 1720(?)–1796, kabbalist, sorcerer, scallywag, and sometime adventurer, who, reformed (or, perhaps like Shakespeare's Prince Hal, choosing the moment to reveal to the world his true self), became known to his disciples as פּיש, the Pish, a word formed from the acronym of his supposed attributes: פּוסק יועץ שגיא—roughly, Exalted and Prudent Adviser and Giver of Judgment. Falsch in his time blossomed into the Ba'al Shem of Ludlow. Now here is a figure who, for all sorts of reasons, appeals to me. I shall have rather more to say of him anon.

My father, Konrad Musič, was something of a *schlimazel*, a born loser, a fact that may have saved his life. He was a sallow man, inclined to embonpoint, and he usually wore, apart from a thick serge suit and a shirt with celluloid collars, a meaningless scowl. In the Marais, he opened a small shop, dark, dank, selling buttons of various sorts, threads, needles, and, on occasion, Jewish artifacts, prayer shawls, decorative yarmulkes, the odd Hanukkah dreidel, that sort of thing. I do not remember that the shop was much peopled by customers. Nevertheless, from this unlikely enterprise, he eked out a living. Beyond this, or perhaps allied with this, my father fidgeted a lot, was never still. Even when seated in an easy chair, he would twitch a leg and twirl a small pillow between his hands. You'd have thought that so much nervous activity would have whittled him down. Not at all. We lived in a small flat immediately above the shop.

I look nothing like him, my father, I might add, and have often doubted my paternity. On the other hand, honesty compels me to say that in old age I look rather anomalous in my priestly costume.

The truth is, I look like an old Jew of Middle European origin, which of course I am, unmistakable to those who know. Not the stereotype promulgated by the Nazis and those who think like them, not quite, but unquestionably Jewish, just the same. (Yet, in what does this "Jewishness" reside? I wonder. The particular rounding of the back, what in middle-aged Jewish women is known as "Hadassah hump"? The sudden assertive fullness of the nose? Could that be it? The lengthening ears? The wholly unexpected but sudden omnipresence of the shrug? In all these, at least, I resemble my father in his final years.) Damn it all, I *do* begin to sound like one of the anti-Semites! Still, nowadays, as I look at myself in the mirror and view my rotund priestly self, I seem to see a species of mountebank, at the very least an actor in the Yiddish theater, a Jew dressed up to represent the enemy.

But where was I? Ah, yes, my parents. My mother was a beauty, that needs saying. I have photographs of her that corroborate memory. How to describe her? She was taller than my father, and slim, wonderfully shapely, with the kind of tubular, pliant figure so admired in the thirties. Her beauty was that of the eternally pure American film star Claudette Colbert, but crossed with that of the more recent, passionately earthy, French Jeanne Moreau, but Jeanne Moreau in her prime. How extraordinary that she should have been married to my father! But I suppose that, of all her suitors in Dunaharaszti, it was he alone who promised to take her to Paris. Paris was where she belonged. Her French name was Hélène, née Shayna Blum. When my father called her *"la belle Hélène,"* which he was wont to do, she would reward him with a bored and weary smile. I adored her. Alas, I am not sure that she cared much for me. I don't really know.

On the other hand, I shared her bed until my tenth year. By then my hapless father had long accepted the notion of satisfying his bestial passions elsewhere. (Whether he *did* satisfy them elsewhere is a matter for pointless and distasteful conjecture. He slept on a pallet that he arranged nightly on the shop's countertop. As a small child, I imagined him below bravely protecting us from villains.) My mother's ruse of having me in her bed should not be understood to mean that she herself was not of a passionate nature. She was, and she entertained her lovers in the afternoons. Her chief occupation was the cosmetic preservation of her complexion, and she sought to maintain her beauty sleep unbroken by lying through the long mornings absolutely motionless in the bed. My earliest memories are of lying beside her, already knowing I must not say a word.

It was one of her lovers who betrayed her in the end, the butch-bitch Madeleine Dormeuil, whose brother was a *flic* in the local gendarmerie. We had fled as a family to Orléans at the beginning of the war. "Why Orléans?" you ask. I have no idea. Perhaps my parents had friends there; perhaps my father had heard of work. It was a move that for me had the most serious consequences. Paris, in any case, was in panic. The important thing, it seemed to my parents, was to save *l'enfant* from the bombardment Paris was certain to suffer, the falling buildings, the poison gas, and so on. My father was mobilized, to be sure—I remember him in uniform—but it was not the fate of the French army to require his services for long. In 1941 he made his first secret foray into the ZNO, the Unoccupied Zone.

Orléans was no safer for us than Paris. Jews, for example, were required to register qua Jews with the police, a terrifying requirement my parents were able to ignore by assuring one another that their proper place of registration was not Orléans but Paris. The plan was for Papa to find work and shelter somewhere south of the Massif Central and then send for Maman and me. Whenever Papa slipped south, Maman slipped north—to Paris, ostensibly to keep an eye on the shop and the flat above it but actually to lie in the arms of her adored Madeleine. While she was gone I was to be obedient to "Tante" Louise, our elderly, austerely Catholic landlady, who, for an extra few francs, agreed to keep a motherly eye on a refugee child.

On July 16, 1942, a scribbled note from my father was delivered into the hands of Tante Louise, once more acting *in loco matris*: he was in St-Pons, not far from Béziers, in the Hérault department, whither we should make our way with cautious haste. But also on July 16, 1942, with the kind of symmetrical neatness that almost makes one believe in a purposeful deity, my mother was arrested, betrayed, rounded up with thousands of her coreligionists by the police of Paris and their eager helpers and dumped in the Vel d'Hiv, where she spent a week in conditions that Dante himself might have balked at describing. This intelligence came to Tante Louise in yet another scribbled note. This time my *tante de convenance* was acting *in loco patris*. From the Vel d'Hiv my mother was sent to Drancy, where she languished in misery for five months, managing, my beautiful mother, to bribe a policeman—one dare not decently ask how, for she had no money—to deliver to us (via Tante Louise) her letters. From Drancy she was dispatched to Auschwitz, from which she was dispatched. As for Madeleine Dormeuil, may she burn forever in the deepest circle of Hell—were there only such a place! *Du calme, du calme.* I get ahead of myself.

⌒

Beale Hall is situated atop a long and gentle rise in the Corve Dales and thus commands magnificent views over its own park and woodlands. On the northern boundary of the estate, a tributary to the river Corve itself meanders by; to the distant south may just be seen, when in winter months a stand of beech has shed all foliage, a portion of Ludlow Castle's ruined keep. The Hall was designed by Sir John Vanbrugh for Sir Peregrine Beale in 1693, a *jeu d'esprit* in whose magnificence one can easily read *in piccolo*, as it were, the lineaments of the yet undreamed-of Castle Howard. What caused this successful playwright to undertake architectural design—we say nothing at the moment of his unexpected architectural genius—may never be known. We *do* know, however, that

Sir Peregrine and he were boozing and wenching companions and
that both took fencing lessons under Gaston Lefeu in his academy
in Piddle Lane. Perhaps that is explanation enough. The surprise
of Vanbrugh's contemporaries in his new venture is preserved in
an execrable couplet ascribed by tradition to none other than
Jonathan Swift:

> 'Tis claim'd in Town that quondam *Scribbler* Van
> Has quit the Stage and turn'd a *Buildings* Man!

If some of the above sounds to you like the effusions of a guide-
book, take heart: you have an ear for prose. Most of it comes from
Beale Hall, A History and a Guide, an illustrated pamphlet for
visitors that sold when it first appeared in 1957 for fourpence, Old
Style, and now may be had for ninety pence, New Style,
unchanged in content if not in appearance—we now print on
glossy paper. I have not used inverted commas for my quotations
because—yes, laugh if you must—I myself am the author of *Beale
Hall, A History and a Guide,* and so there is no question of plagia-
rism. But if you have, as I posited at the beginning of this para-
graph, an ear for prose, then I trust you have recognized that even
in 1957 my English was sufficiently fluent to parody guidebook-
ese, if I may so term it. By now, of course, I use the language as if
it were my first, the instrument of all my thoughts, even of my
dreams. I am far more comfortable with it than I am with my
native French, whose finer points of grammar and more arcane
vocabulary tend little by little to slip from me. On my recent visit
to Paris, a taxi driver actually answered me in English, a sure sign
that he thought me a foreigner, one probably from across the
Channel!

Of course, my spoken English is still marked by a slight
French accent, one which fifty years ago seems to have pleased the
ear (and other parts) of the female Anglophone. The young Kiki,
for example, described it as "sexy"; the young Maude said that it

had from the first "dampened her knickers." Well, well, I have no wish to boast. In any case, these pages will either reveal my command of the language or my ignorance of it. As for the pamphlet, I shall certainly quote from it again, but you should understand why. It is in Beale Hall that Bastien and I live and, thanks to Kiki, *have* lived for almost half a century now.

⌒

There is so much to tell and perhaps only a little time. Where to begin? I emancipated two gnomes this morning. Is that relevant? I got the idea from the French, of all people. The young over there are so much *better* than they were in my day. At any rate, a group of them are in secret—they wear bright balaclavas for their photographs, their flashing eyes and perfect teeth alone visible, gnomes under protective arms—removing the fairy folk from bourgeois gardens and setting them free in the forests, "their natural habitat." This morning, moments before sunrise, I liberated two of them from the front garden of Benghazi, Major Catchpole's cottage—one gnome, *couchant,* with a languidly held fishing pole and another sitting, finger along his nose, on a pseudo-toadstool—and let them loose in Tetley Wood.

Tetley Wood, once part of the Beale estate, now borders it. The woods had been sold off by the last of Sir Peregrine's descendants, Squadron Leader Sir Ferdinando Beale, to help pay the death duties imposed on his inheritance by the victorious, postwar Labor government. He died without issue in 1955, hanging himself from the lower branches of the Stuart Oak, a homosexual victim of blackmailers. His heir was Lady Violet Devlin, my very own Kiki, and she, already into New Age living *avant la lettre,* albeit, in that far-off time, Catholic in hue, had no interest in the property. She gave it to the Church, specifically to the Vatican, but with certain provisos: Beale Hall, its accommodations, peerless library, and grounds were to become a scholarly Catholic retreat, maintained by the Devlin Trust, to be created for the purpose. Its first director general was to be Father Edmond Music, yours truly, whose tenure was for life, unless at some point, having given due notice to the trust, he chose to retire, or it came to the attention of the trust, buttressed by irrefutable medical evidence, that his health seriously impaired the fulfillment of his duties. The director general, short of selling the estate, had absolute control over Beale Hall and its grounds. Not bad, eh?

That was Kiki, my well-loved Kiki, responding magnificently to my plea to her in 1956 that if I had to suffer another parish I would perish, that I could bear no longer to cast artificial pearls before real swine. She was then in Big Sur, California. An alert surfer having spotted the Blessed Virgin Mary rising Venus-like from a large half-shell, thousands of the faithful had duly assembled on the wonder-working beach, Kiki among them. But she took time out from her BVM vigil to arrange my future. (By 1960 Kiki, inspired by Aldous Huxley, had moved on to the sacred mushroom and other natural psychedelic routes to mystical truths; in 1975, having lived by then for some years in Sausalito, she had overdosed on a powerful cocktail of mind-bending pills. In Beale Hall, I conducted a special Mass. For me, she was *fidelitas ipse*, Loyalty writ large. Ever since her death, the Church has been trying to oust me.)

The road through the estate begins at the massive iron gates, now permanently open, that pierce the high park wall along the southern perimeter. It passes the gatekeeper's cottage, thatched and built in late Victorian days of the local stone, unoccupied now but for our local lads and lasses, who use it for their amorous pursuits, and begins immediately to curve around a lake that is pinched in its center as if to accommodate its balustraded bridge. Duck and moorhen dabble among the reeds. The road begins to rise now, and quite sharply, past the Stuart Oak, where once Sir Ferdinando and latterly poor old Trevor met their deaths, and under arching trees, ancient oak and chestnut, through which one catches occasional glimpses in the distance of the column erected by Sir Humphrey Beale to celebrate Nelson's famous victory at Trafalgar. Now the road divides, one arm branching off to the stable block on the right, with its central archway and clock tower, converted under my direction more than thirty years ago into administrative office, kitchen, refectory, all-purpose lounge, and small bed-sitters for our visiting scholars. The presence of so many dog collars, Jesuits for the most part, in Beale Hall itself and at all hours, I soon found irksome. The conversion of the stable block was the obvious answer. Of course, I can't keep them out of the library or the chapel, but I can and do restrict library hours and I have Bastien put them on some sort of a rota for taking services. In fact, they are greeted by slippered Bastien upon arrival, fêted by slippered Bastien during their stay, and fare-thee-welled by slippered Bastien upon departure. I seldom see any of them anymore. (The seculars are another matter. I vet the list of applicants myself and limit admissions to those who seem interesting.)

The other branch of the road now widens and soon Beale Hall itself, this magnificent baroque mansion, comes into sight. One notices first—but I can't burble on like this! If you're interested in such matters, I urge you to read *Beale Hall, A History and a Guide.* Find out there, for example, about the Great Hall, its extraordinary chimneypiece, the even more extraordinary painting by Giovanni Malocchio in its dome: Aphrodite, Britomartis, and Ellen Scrim-Pitt of Drury Lane, all largely starkers, all ascending to the empyrean while winged amoretti, puffy-cheeked, blow trumpets, and all offering a most unexpected view of their rotund beauties, a masterpiece of erotic perspective. In my *History and a Guide,* which bears the *Nihil Obstat,* I identify the ladies, discreetly, as Faith, Hope, and Charity and suggest that they are descending *from,* not ascending *to,* heaven. Whether the greatest of these ladies is Charity (i.e., Ellen Scrim-Pitt) is bound to be a matter of taste. She certainly has the greatest bum and is, of the three, the one upon whom my gaze has always lingered. At any rate, I shall speak of the Library, the Tapestry Room, the Long Galleries, the

splendid collection of pictures and furniture, the paintings by
Rubens, Domenico Feti, Holbein, Van Dyck, Lely, Kneller,
Hogarth, Stubbs, Turner, and so on, only as and if they come up.
So too with the chapel, altered in 1875 by Charles Ogilvie Beale,
who had deserted Rome for Canterbury (until he lay dying), that
boasts a bas-relief by Mantovani and stained glass by Morris and
Burne-Jones. But the Music Room is another matter. I have made
the Music Room my own, my private domain, where I have spent
most of my waking hours (and not a few hours in slumber) for
almost fifty years. With this room I was beguiled from the first, by
its beauties, its elegant proportions, and, of course, by its name. It
once was and now again is the *Music* Room.

∽

Major William Clive ("Call me 'W.C.,' old boy!") Catchpole,
O.B.E., had been a Desert Rat who had served with distinction
under Montgomery in North Africa. What he had seen there of
human suffering, folly, wickedness, and, yes, heroism had caused
him to lose his faith. He had entered the war a Roman Catholic,
"idiotically devout, old chap"; he had emerged a confirmed atheist. No priest, not even His Holiness—"*your* master, not mine, old
son"—could fob him off with pietistic apologia for ubiquitous,
gratuitous evil. He had been sprayed with the blood and brains,
pierced by the splintered bones, of comrades blown up before his
eyes; he had heard the screams of men burning alive in their
tanks, smelled the rank odor of the spilled guts their shocked own-
ers strove in vain to stuff back into gurgling cavities. And he knew
that whatever murderous evil the Germans were wreaking on English lads, English lads were striving to wreak on them. "Where was
your God while all that was going on, that tiny part, I mean, of a
far greater atrocity stretching back through time beyond the Crucifixion—although doctrinally, perhaps, the Crucifixion is far
back enough—and from there forward to today? Where, Father,
was your gentle Jesus then?"

No Contest.

For Catchpole, though, once that card had been removed, the whole house of cards fell apart. His former faith lay in ruins about him. He became, if I may so term it, a *crusading* atheist. He put on the glistening armor of Truth and took up the razor-sharp weapons of Reason. Put less fancifully, Catholicism-bashing became his avocation. And since we are neighbors—indeed, have been neighbors for almost half a century now—and I am conveniently to hand, I have long been the recipient of his anti-Catholic attacks.

Let me say at once that I like the major, I like him very much indeed, and he, I think, likes me. We are, and have long been, friends. It is in this context that my theft of his garden gnomes must be seen. It is a move in a long-standing contest. The contest is normally verbal, and he has all the best lines. The theft will, I hope, shift our ongoing, friendly arguments to less familiar territory.

We play chess once a week, alternating between the Music Room at Beale Hall and the parlor of Benghazi, the major's cottage on the edge of Tetley Wood, once the gamekeeper's cottage on the original estate. We are not very good at chess, but we are, at least, equally bad. Of course, chess is merely an excuse for regular meetings. At Beale Hall, Maude has for decades brought to the chess players their refreshments—sandwiches, seed cake or lemon tart, a pot of tea. The major has long known—I am sure of it—that Maude and I share a bed, but he has pretended otherwise. He would not use that knowledge in his attack on Catholic hypocrisy; he was and is a gentleman.

Of course, I have never spoken to him of his stream of cousins, nieces, and housekeepers, a stream, of late, drying up. But then, how could I? He had married shortly after the war a woman whose postnatal depression could be traced back, seemingly, to her birth. Imogen carried about with her an unfailing suggestion of bleakness, of a gray overcast made filthier with stains of yellow and black. "She cast me down, old chap. Not her fault, poor soul, but she cast me down." She had seemed always on the point of tears, the tip of her nose red, as if with a perpetual cold. He was Patience on a monument, and she was Grief; only, he could not smile. They lived together for twelve miserable years. "Bit of luck at that point. Her doctor-chappie, probably sick and tired of her whinging on, suggested a month or two in Brighton, bracing sea air, do her the world of good, take her out of herself, that sort of thing. Well, in Brighton she met this Spanish dancer, Blasco Mendoza, ever heard of him? No matter. Not Spanish, actually. Came from Brooklyn, New York. They fell in love, perfect mesh of temperaments, for all I know. Ran off with him, don't know where—don't care, to be honest. Perhaps Brooklyn."

I have heard this story many times. The major, bless him, has long forgotten that I was a witness to the events.

This evening the major came to Beale Hall—it was my turn to be host at chess—and he congratulated me on my "miraculous"—he loved to use such words—"resurrection." W.C. is now eighty and somewhat feeble. His current lady is—he no longer pretends otherwise—a private nurse. But he bubbled with excitement. Inwardly, I groaned. He had a new argument. I was going to have to defend once more, God help me, not only the existence but also the integrity of the triune God. I tried to arrange my face in an expression of eager anticipation.

Casually, as if to increase his pleasure by deferring the moment of triumph, he picked up a leatherbound book that lay on my desk. "What have we here?" he said, turning to the title page.

"As you see, a Coleridge first edition, 1816. 'Christabel,' 'Kubla Khan,' 'The Pains of Sleep.' What's particularly noteworthy, though, is the fact that Scott's 'Field of Waterloo' is bound in at the end. Here, let me show you."

"Yes, yes, most interesting."

But, of course, he wasn't in the least interested. It is a beautiful little volume, and it is one of those that I keep in here as my private stock, so to speak. Nor was he interested in the skull, the *memento mori,* that sat on my desk beside it. The skull presumably belonged to the Pish, the Ba'al Shem of Ludlow, although I can find no reference to it in his papers. Still, inscribed across the crown are the Hebrew characters יוריק, Yorick, a reliable clue, as perhaps I shall later reveal, to the Pish. W.C. could contain himself no longer. He sat down on his side of the chess table, carefully pinched his trouser legs above his knees in what has become since the advent of blue jeans a charmingly old-fashioned gesture, and pulled on his left earlobe. It was, he said, possible to prove the presence in the world of gratuitous, and therefore God-denying, evil by a mathematical formula, by Bayes's Theorem. "Look at this," he said, and he removed from his breast pocket a folded piece of paper. I opened it:

$$P(H/e\&k) = \frac{P(H/k) \times P(e/H\&k)}{P(e/k)}$$

This was the moment that Maude chose to knock. Is it possible to know a person by the knock? I would, I swear, be able to distinguish Maude's knock from no matter how many others. (Of course, who else but Maude might have knocked at that moment? I want to be fair about this. Is not the truth the truth? asks Falstaff.)

"Come," I said, using an English verbal expression that for Maude and me had a salacious meaning going back to the days of our earliest sexual raptures.

No wonder she blushed when she entered, bearing a tray on which were sandwich fingers (smoked salmon, ham and cheese, tomato and cucumber), slices of chocolate cake, plates and cutlery, a pot of tea, a jug of milk, and cups and saucers.

"A feast, Maude! Splendid. You are far too kind," said Catchpole. "What d'you say to our friend here's rising from the dead? *Non nobis*, eh what? Still, we're grateful, aren't we?"

Maude has become quite stout as she inches toward seventy—limps, I should say, for her left hip pains her dreadfully. Her face has a myriad of crosshatches now, but when she smiles—and

Catchpole was granted a smile—all her heart-stopping beauty still shines forth. Her green eyes beckon still. When she smiles, ah . . .

> No spring nor summer beauties have such grace
> As I have seen in one autumnal face.

Her hair is still red, too, perhaps even redder than it was when she was young, but for this small miracle thanks are perhaps due to Angie Mackletwist, proud proprietrix of Snippety-Snip in Ludlow, who comes as friend and "professional" and spends an hour or two with Maude on alternate Thursday evenings.

Like me, Maude has a soft spot for W.C. She arranged her offerings before us with practiced efficiency. "I admit it's good to have the rascal back," she said. "But to speak true, I thought him in a better place."

"If you ever get a car again," said W.C., a mischievous twinkle in his eye, "I do hope you'll do the sensible thing and take it first to Copacabana in Bolivia."

It would have been cruel not to ask the question. Besides, I wondered what he was on about. "Why would I do that?"

"Why, to get it blessed of course. People drive up there from all over South America, all the way up to Lake Titicaca. They jam the central plaza, especially on so-called holy days. Your Church, old man, has six Franciscan priests—count 'em: *six!*—all happy to sprinkle your car with holy water and say the appropriate mumbo jumbo."

"Come now, Major."

"It's true, I give you my word. Far, far better than ordinary motor insurance, you see. The priests will protect you and your car from earthquakes, drink-drivers, broken axles, misleading directions, bad brakes, petrol shortages, you name it. Why, man, the economy of the town depends upon it. The very banks stay open on Sundays to accommodate the pilgrims. The Church and the banks are in collusion, you see. And yet your Savior, you may recall, threw the money changers out of the Temple. You can buy from the Indian women all the paraphernalia you need to decorate your car for its blessing."

"It's a miracle," said Maude.

"It's a scandal!" said W.C.

"Franciscan priests, you say?" said Maude.

"Yes. Six of 'em."

"Well, that's all right, then."

"Strength in numbers, eh?" said W.C., winking at me. "Your pope is not slow to learn from example, I'll say that for him. He's actually invoked protection for an underground parking garage, the new one at the Vatican. The building, the motorcars, and all the people who park there will be perfectly safe from now on. What a blessing, so to speak. The Church has formally entered the Automotive Age, with special attention to parking garages. How maddening for the Yanks that His Holiness didn't recognize this needful new arena for his expertise in time to save the New York World Trade Center."

Maude's sense of humor tends to desert her in matters pertaining to faith. The major's sarcasm distressed her, much as she liked the man himself. "Who's to say what a papal blessing might have achieved?" she said sharply. But then she softened her tone: "I've always wanted to go to New York, never had the chance. There's cousins there on my mother's side, the Dowds. They've a pub in a place called Queens." She turned to me. "Did you know, Father, no sooner had word come of your horrible death than the major dashed over to comfort me? He was more in need of comfort than I, poor damned pagan that he is, sighing and blubbering and beating his poor heart with his fist."

She made for the door, leaving behind her a vacuum that men who are ashamed of their emotions abhor. To fill the silence, I refolded the paper he had given me and then with rustling deliberation reopened it, thrusting out my lip pensively as I gazed at the formula. "Hmm."

"Got you this time, what?" said the major eagerly. He has a way of twitching the corners of his mouth as if to suggest that he is much amused by your folly, is, indeed, on the point of laughing at it, but is making a valiant and polite effort to restrain himself. "We begin as always with God, who is by definition omnipotent, omniscient, and, of course, good." The major twitched rapidly, momentarily covering his mouth with his hand. "Now, suffering is assuredly not good. You with me so far?"

I shook my head at him, smiling the while, as who should say, "Ah, W.C., you jolly rogue, there you go again!" Aloud, I said, "What of these sandwiches, which will begin to curl if we're not careful? And shall we not have some of Maude's excellent tea?"

The twitches at the corners of the major's mouth accelerated. "You be mother, Father." This is one of his favorite jokes and I regularly set it up for him.

I poured. "One lump or two?"

"'Two for me, and three for you,'" he sang, and then intoned:

> You the Trinity illustrate
> Drinking orange pekoe tea—
> With three lumps the Arian frustrate,
> While the Devil smiles at me.

"Sound man, Browning. Knew hypocrisy when he saw it." This too was a favorite joke, seldom missing from our sessions. He bit into a sandwich. "Someone's nicked my garden gnomes."

"I can't believe it," I said. "Your garden gnomes? What kind of degenerate would do something like that? The Devil himself must be in it."

"The Devil, eh? If so, I'm grateful to him. Couldn't stand the bloody things, myself. Imogen put them there. Betrayed her origins more than anything else about her, I'd say. Meant to get rid of them for yonks. Bloody inertia."

I sighed.

W.C. took another sandwich and waved it at the paper in my hand. "You see the point?" he said eventually. "Gratuitous suffering is evil. That's self-evident. If God permits it, he's not good; if not good, he's not God. That's where the theorem comes in."

I tossed his piece of paper onto the table. "Come now, Major. You can do better than this."

"You know it, then?" No twitching now.

"I try to keep up, do the best I can, you know. I can't claim to be much of a philosopher anymore. Still, I'll have a whack. It's probability theory, right? A way of testing a hypothesis?"

"Well, yes. If you'll grant that your so-called New Testament is improbability theory. But can you answer it?"

"I think so. Still, I may've forgotten the elements in the equation. You may have to remind me. *H* is the hypothesis, of course; *e* is . . . evidence; *k*, let me see, yes, *k* is background knowledge or justified beliefs. Not bad, not bad. Well, W.C., what now?"

He had been masking his disappointment by staring intently at the chess pieces ranged between us. Now he noisily sipped his tea. "Suppose *H*, my hypothesis, is that there is no point to certain instances or patterns of suffering; *e* equals the statement that even after careful reflection we see no point to that suffering; and *k* equals whatever justified background beliefs we have."

"But we can only test your hypothesis by putting it alongside its opposite, the theist's belief: there *is* a reason for that suffering, but the reason is beyond our ken. Let's call *my* hypothesis *T*." And beneath his equation, I scribbled my own:

$$P(T/e\&k) = \frac{P(T/k) \times P(e/T\&k)}{P(e/k)}$$

Now it was my turn to sip my tea noisily. "Now, is it more reasonable to accept *H* or *T* on *e* and *k*? The answer to that is which of the right sides of the two equations is the greater, you agree? Surely P(e/T and k) is greater than P(e/H and k). If there is a reason for the suffering, but the reason is beyond our ken, then of course we won't know that reason, even after the most careful reflection."

"So you say," he said grumpily.

"I'll go further. Even if we found a reason, that reason might be wrong, a mere illusion, since my hypothesis states that the reason is beyond our ken."

W.C. concentrated on the chess pieces.

"Any religion that's worth its salt should challenge its adherent to an uphill battle of belief. Come, come, old friend. I have not convinced *you*, and you have not convinced *me*. We scarcely needed Bayes's Theorem to end up where we began."

"True, true."

And with that, we turned to our game.

If it were still possible to believe in Freud, another God That Failed, I would say that W.C. is desperate to believe once more, that more than anything else he wishes he could prostrate himself before the Cross.

How can any rational creature believe the absurdities of Christianity? How can he not see in the story of Christ the pattern of countless pagan myths, the universal romance of the sacrificial god, his apotheosis, and his rebirth? How can contemporary man give credence to the accretions of early, of medieval, of subsequent superstitions? It is a puzzle. It is not modesty but obvious, simple honesty for me to acknowledge that there have been throughout Catholic history and also today believing men and women of far, far greater intellectual reach and mental acumen than I can lay claim to. The Bishop of Hippo or Thomas Aquinas or Thomas More or, perhaps more appropriately for my argument, one of the newest saints, the Holocaust martyr Edith Stein, could rip my poor objections to shreds. And as for the major, even *I* can overcome his weak triumphs.

Can it be that belief and doubt are genetically determined? Is there a switch that at conception or in the developing fetus may be turned on or off? I don't profess to know. Proofs *for* religious truth are full of holes; proofs *against* are useless. Some seem predisposed to believe, and others not. I only know that what is plainly nonsense to me is an incontrovertible article of faith to another.

ᐁ

The Pish, as I have told you, became known as the Ba'al Shem of Ludlow. Ba'al Shem means something like "Master of the Divine Name," a title once given to those who possessed the secret knowledge of the tetragrammaton and the other "Holy Names" of God and who could work miracles by the names' power. I have long felt an affinity with this Falsch and have devoted many an idle hour to finding out what I could about him. (Well, the word "idle" is a bit disingenuous. My research reacquainted me with Hebrew and broadened and deepened my knowledge of it. I found myself delving into the Talmud, into kabbalistic texts, into rabbinical and magical works. I became, albeit modestly, something of an Hebraist.) Luckily for my interest in the Pish, there is material aplenty on him here at Beale Hall. He and Sir Percival, the Beale of Falsch's day, were very thick, very thick indeed.

In fact, I once thought to write Falsch's biography, and over the years I have written quite a lot of it, more than 350 pages, but I doubt that I shall finish it now. This is a pity since all that the world today knows of the Pish is to be found in Lester Bradley's foreword to Horace Winstanley's collection, *Tales of the Ba'al Shem of Ludlow* (1936). Bradley, a devout member of a Hasidic sect, innocently supposed that the biographical details appearing in the tales were authentic. Winstanley, for his part, seems unaware that the tales themselves were mere adaptions of and variations on the earliest legends of Rabbi Israel ben Eliezer (1700–1760), the Ba'al Shem Tov, the founder of Hasidism. It is clear that these tales of the Pish are attempts by succeeding generations of the devout to make the life of their first teacher, the Ba'al Shem of

Ludlow, conform to an acceptable pattern of rabbinical heroism, the wonder-workings of a first-rank Hebrew sage. But while events taking place in Zornisziza or Chechelnik or Polonnoye or, indeed, anywhere within the Pale of Settlement in the eighteenth century may be granted a certain credence if only because of the strange music these faraway place-names create, they become little short of ludicrous when the "holy community" is Wigan or Chepstow or Harrogate or Tunbridge Wells, a fact to which Winstanley seems quite oblivious.

Here, for example, is an excerpt from a letter that appears in full as an appendix to the *Tales*. It is somewhat grandly called "The Annunciation" and purports to be written by Jaime Pardo, one of a circle of mystically inclined students drawn to Rabbi Falsch. It was addressed to Daniel Ruback, a wealthy businessman living in Amsterdam, learned himself and a patron of learning. Why Pardo chose Ruback to be the conduit to European Jewry of Falsch's interactions with a divine spirit is unclear.

From His great storehouse of treasures, the Holy One, blessed be He, has endowed us with one of His richest jewels, His most brilliant gems. I mean that holy lamp and man of G-d, my noble master, my incomparable teacher, his honor Rabbi Solomon Reuben Hayyim Falsch. A great and powerful angel, a *maggid,* has revealed himself to this holy man, and for two years and more has been discovering to him supernal mysteries.

Let me speak now of wonders. The angel speaks out of Rabbi Falsch's mouth, but we, his disciples, hear nothing! And yet the angel is revealing to the rabbi sacred mysteries! The rabbi's mouth moves; he seems to be addressing us, his disciples, but silently. Meanwhile, his saintly body expands as if filled with air, grows round like the blown-up bladder of the unclean beast that rough gentile boys (and men, too!) kick through the town of a winter's day. At first, we feared our rabbi would burst, but as we approached him, he rose slowly into the air and, leaning forward as if bowing before the Ark, bounced gently on the ceiling. All the while, he spoke to us silently. To our joy, we are now accustomed to these holy visitations and are no longer alarmed by them.

The angel has discovered unto our teacher many mysteries of the Torah. Even now, my master knows the incarnations of all men and the healing tasks, the *tikkunim,* they are allotted. He knows the hidden medicinal virtues of all plants and the languages of the beasts. The science of reading the lines in the faces and hands of men is as open to him as the *Aleph-Bet.* He can look at the skies by night or by day and find written thereon what is to befall us, the Jews, whether good, God willing, or bad, God forbid. He knows all the events of the past and the causes and roots of all things. In short, the *maggid* has revealed everything to him.

But what must you think of me, your honor! I have left our rabbi bouncing on the ceiling, God forbid! I shall tell you now what follows upon the *maggid*'s visit. There is a loud noise—*barrr-aakk! barrr-aakk!*—like the passing of wind. And as the angelic afflatus leaves, my master is returned slowly to his proper size and to his chair. In the air there lingers for a short while the delightful aroma of burnt sugar.

Well, I daresay these *Tales* have a certain charm. The truth is, I rather like them. A few of them are even useful, like the parables in the Gospels. Yet the actual life of the man who became the Pish was far more interesting than the travesty of a life Bradley and Winstanley have given us. But this is my hobbyhorse, and I should dismount.

~

As, in the spring of 1942, the time of Passover approached, my father began to get itchy. We had not as a family much pursued our Judaism in Paris. To be sure, we had lived among Jews, my father's business had brought us in daily contact with Jews, and we had observed in however desultory a fashion the feasts, the fasts, and the doctrinal dates that punctuate the Jewish year. But we were not devout, not in the least. As for me, I had from age six been sent to a nearby *cheder,* where I had learned to read and write and eventually speak biblical Hebrew and Aramaic and where grooming had begun for an expected bar mitzvah. Needless to say, these studies were in addition to those undertaken in the normal way at local schools. My father had been impelled by some atavistic imperative to insist I attend *cheder;* my mother had not much cared. I remember he called me his *kaddishl,* the son who would say kaddish, the mourner's prayer, for him when he died. My mother thought him ghoulish.

But now we were in Orléans, in Occupied France, and while we made no secret of our Jewish origins to our landlady, we lived among Christians under the constant threat of exposure and could not, especially with so strong a German presence in the city, live as Jews. My father's Judaism was, so to speak, a viral infection that had lain quiescent during most of his married life but that flared up in Orléans in the absence of any palliative whenever an occasion in the Jewish calendar rolled round. "There'll be no matzos," he said, "no *charoset.* We don't even have a Haggadah. Edmond will forget the Four Questions."

"No, I won't, Papa. I still know them."

"Well, I'll forget the four answers."

"For God's sake, stop the nonsense, Konrad," said my mother in disgust. "Is that all you can worry about, the Four Questions? Sentimental rubbish! Here's a question for you. Pay attention. Are you going to find work today? Here's another, even better. How long d'you think our few francs will last? You want questions? I've got questions. All the questions you can use."

My once plump father had become quite gaunt. The stubble on his face grew dark where his cheeks caved in. His trousers, held up by braces, flapped around his middle like the costume of a clown. He was not responding well to this crisis in our lives. True, he went out every morning, ostensibly to look for work, achieving thereby the appearance, at least, of responsibility. How he filled his days, I cannot say. Once, out on some errand or other, I saw him sitting on the rim of the fountain in the Place de la Victoire, idly swinging his legs, for his feet did not reach the step. The fountain was not playing, but he contrived to get soaked anyway: the rain was pelting down. Shocked, I turned from the sight and ran down the rue des Capuchins. No, he was not coping well. He had developed certain new mannerisms that made him appear if not quite mad then not quite sane. For example, if he met with disagreement of whatever degree, he would lower his bristly chin onto his chest, look up with hungry eyes, and enunciate deliberately, "Tee-hee-hee." Crushed by my mother's response, he did this now. "Tee-hee-hee."

My mother turned from him abruptly. Terrified by our plight, longing, no doubt, to be with her beloved Madeleine, she took out her frustration on me. "Edmond, what are you staring at? Do your homework."

"I've finished it, Maman."

"Do some more. There's always more. Study your Latin declensions, your Greek verbs. You want to grow up like him?" She jerked a thumb behind her, where stood her hapless husband.

"But it's Sunday, Maman."

"Your day of rest?" she said sarcastically. But then she bethought herself and turned to my father. "Edmond must become a Christian."

My conversion, temporary, of course, was becoming an ever more frequent topic of conversation between them. They believed that at worst the Nazis would have no reason to bother a Christian boy whose Jewish origins were hidden from them and that at best they would spare the Jewish parents of a Christian boy, should his origins become known. I cannot say if my parents at this time knew what fate the Nazis proposed for them, for all of us, and in the case of my beautiful mother would actually achieve. They knew that the Germans had instituted in France as elsewhere in Europe a new Reign of Terror and that many French descendants of the earlier reign stood ready to assist them in its implementation.

"I said, Konrad, that we must get him converted."

"Yes, yes, we must, no question."

"I mean now. We can't put it off any longer. We must have a word with Madame Goupil." Madame Goupil was our landlady, my so-called Tante Louise. "She'll speak to her priest, set up an appointment."

We were living in a seedy, working-class area on the outskirts of Orléans, an area long blighted by unemployment—gray, slimily cobbled, decorated with broken glass, rusted tin, and other rubbish, the flotsam and jetsam of the poor; peopled with desperate men who drunkenly fought one another to uphold their honor and, losing it, clobbered their wives and women. Here, Madame Goupil was something of an anomaly. She was the widow of a railroad signalman who had died *pour la patrie* in 1917; she was living on a small pension and the income from renting the larger of the two bedrooms in her neatly kept house. Poor she certainly was; her cleanliness was a habit of mind, a companion of her godliness, and a prerequisite, as she saw it, in the entertaining for tea and biscuits of a succession of priests, incumbents at the long-neglected, ever-damp, always cold church a mere five minutes' walk from her home.

"But Edmond is almost fourteen," said my father. "This is the time he should have his bar mitzvah."

"So what? We're talking about survival, not about life as it should be."

"Well, all right, but still, don't you think he should be bar mitzvah before he's converted? A matter of precedent. Of protocol, you might say."

"You think that before they spritz him with holy water he should read his portion in a synagogue?"

"Right, right, you've got it. That's it."

"Here in Orléans, where we haven't even bothered to register, where we're outlaws?"

"Well, for a bar mitzvah, for a *simcha* like that, we could go back to Paris."

"Are you crazy?"

My father pressed his stubbled chin into his chest. He looked up at Mother with bloodshot eyes. "Tee-hee-hee," he said.

꒳

W.C.'s casual picking up of the Coleridge first edition on my desk the other evening has reminded me of my enemy Twombly and his recent letter. I must do something about him, and quickly. In two short months he will descend upon Beale Hall for his annual six-week stint in the library. He has the goods on me this time, he thinks. I suspect he's right. My recent trip to Paris had proved useless. Aristide Popescu was in Budapest, according to his wretched son. No, there was no knowing when he'd be back. *Was* Aristide in Budapest? I doubt it. I think he is avoiding me.

I first met Twombly when we were both graduate students, as I have said. Why we should have been sent to Paris, of all places, to study English literature—he from a working-class parish in Philadelphia and I from South Kensington, where my parishioners had been, for the most part, members of the French diplomatic corps and their families—is a question that only the Church in its abiding wisdom can answer. It may be that some lowly, priestly clerk "cut our orders," to use a military expression for an obvious cock-up, an expression that also has a charmingly churchly aroma ("orders," I mean, not "cock-up"), out of incompetence or boredom or spite—or all three. We wanted out, after all; we wanted the ivied academic life, with its meerschaum pipes, its wit at high table, and its many manly pleasures. Perhaps he, my imaginary clerk, envied us.

We priestly students formed a coterie of our own, excluded by our calling from easy integration with the "civilians" and their heterosexual jollity. As for the intellectuals among them, they were all communists and sneered openly at us. We used to meet in a student hangout, La Grenouille Farcie, sitting at our table like a congery of crows, beer or cheap wine before us. Castignac, my old seminary friend, was of our number, although he was reading not English but political philosophy; Bastien, too, whom I had first met at the orphanage in Orléans, whither the Church had sent me after Tante Louise's consultation with her priest, my father never returning from St-Pons (Bastien, in fact, was not himself a student. He ran a soup kitchen for the indigent out of a lean-to in a rubbish-strewn alley not five minutes' walk from where we all met); Twombly, of course; and I. We formed the hard core, the regulars. Others drifted in from time to time, only to drop from sight.

We strove as best we could to match the high spirits, the laughter and bravado, of the other tables, the civilian tables. Castignac was particularly good at telling anticlerical jokes, *insider* jokes— he had an inexhaustible fund of them—"allowed," so to speak, because a cleric was telling them to clerics. He caused the few genuine roars of laughter that emanated from our table. Twombly, though, never managed more than a tight-lipped, reluctant smile, and not because he failed to understand them, at least not in the linguistic sense: his French, if vilely accented, was utterly fluent. No, he wanted to register sophisticated amusement, but he seemed instead to be making mental notes, taking evidence.

It was at one such occasion at La Grenouille Farcie that he became my enemy, although to this day I don't understand why. Bastien and I were entertaining the company with tales of our orphanage experience, the cruelty we suffered at the hands of the nuns. It's true, "cruelty" is the word, or "sadism." These were bitter old women, viciously punishing helpless children for the barren wasteland of their own lost lives. They thrashed us mercilessly, humiliated us before our fellows, kept us thirsty lest we wet our beds and inadequately clad lest we forget the sufferings of Our Savior. At any rate, Bastien and I were going on about this, not complainingly, truly, but as if vying with one another in a television game of "Can You Top This?" or like retired soldiers of the Foreign Legion recalling in retrospective amusement their sufferings under a particularly brutal sergeant major.

"They would come into the dormitory at night," said Bastien. "If they found you asleep with your hands anywhere but crossed on your chest, they would thrash you awake. Then they would thrash your hands. Sister Angélique, in particular, she of the wen and the drooping eye, she used a meter length of bamboo. She'd not stop until your hands bled."

Twombly, slim and pale, not yet bald but already possessing a natural tonsure, pursed his lips and showed us momentarily his perfect American teeth. "At least," he said, "you learned early to keep your hands off your genitals."

"Perhaps," I said. "But that didn't keep Father Damien's hands off our genitals."

That was all I said, and it was greeted by general, knowing laughter at the table. But the expression on Twombly's face was one of murderous hatred. He rose to his feet, his jaw clenched, large veins visibly throbbing at his temples. He said not a word but turned from us and strode away.

Now, why should what I said have earned his lifelong enmity? You tell me.

Part Two

Our extremest pleasure has some air of groaning and complaining in it. Would you not say that it is dying of pain?

—Montaigne, Essays, 1580–1588

Christianity has done a great deal for love by making a sin of it.

—Anatole France,
The Garden of Epicurus, 1894

Lady Violet Devlin, my very own Kiki, was a descendant of old Yorkshire "brass," her grandfather the owner of coal mines and mills and whatnot, her father a philanthropist, the founder of hospitals, patron of museums, restorer of churches, and so forth, elevated by his grateful Parliamentary party to the lowest rung of the peerage and by his pope to a knighthood. Kiki's mother, Lady Diana, was herself born to wealth and to a rather older name. She was, in fact, sister to the unfortunate Sir Ferdinando Beale, who hanged himself, you may remember, from the Stuart Oak and in doing so uncoiled the string of circumstances that brought me here.

Kiki and I fell in love the instant we set eyes on each other, an explosion in our breasts of passion and yearning, a roiling and raging in our still innocent groins, a melting, a seething of hormones, to a degree of which only the young are capable. Not that this delicious turmoil could have been visible to the outside world, that is to say to other visitors to the Louvre on that fateful day, for it was in the Louvre that we met. I found her examining Gustave Tournier's sculpture of the stricken Adonis, bending over in an effort to see what, if anything, lay beneath his tunic.

"There's nothing there, mademoiselle," I said.

She turned toward me, frowning at first, peering shortsightedly, and then she smiled. We knew already and forever what we knew.

"Let's see," she said. She winked mischievously and put her hand beneath the tunic. Across the room a guard coughed and pointed to a sign on the wall, *"Ne touchez pas les oeuvres."* "You're right," she said. "Nothing, nothing at all. Alas, poor fellow, the boar must have eaten it."

She was in the Louvre with her class and Sister Marie-Joséphine, the nun in charge of their cultural well-being. Sister Marie-Joséphine's idea of art was of paintings of persons in mute adoration of Jesus at various points in his career, principally his birth and death, of saints and martyrs, especially martyrs undergoing martyrdom, and of popes. "Boring" was not the word for it. Kiki could bear it no longer and had excused herself, pleading necessary obedience to a call of nature. But now her class would be assembling on the pavement outside; the bus would even now be drawing to the curb. She must rejoin them soon or she would get into trouble, severe trouble. She must go.

As for me, I was supposed to have spent the afternoon in meditation in some shaded nook or other on the seminary grounds, one of those spots where some poorly executed bit of vapid Christian statuary, piety or severe abdominal cramps contorting its stony face, peeps out from behind the bushes, a poor substitute for satyr or dryad or, for that matter, garden gnome. A few francs in the doorkeeper's hand, a wink and a finger to the lips, and I was on the road to the station and Paris. And so I met Kiki, and so I am here in Beale Hall all these years later. But what if, as I ought, I had remained on the seminary grounds that afternoon? What if Kiki had not broken away from her class and Sister Marie-Joséphine? What if I had gone to Paris but not to the Louvre? What if in that vast building we had not encountered one another? As I have already suggested, accident, chance, contingency, these rule individual lives. But I too now had to leave, and quickly if I was to catch my train and return, my absence-without-leave unnoticed.

Hastily, Kiki tore paper from her exercise book. "We must write to one another," she said. "We must meet. Here. Give me your address; I'll give you mine. Best pretend to be my brother. I think they steam open our letters, so be discreet, my darling."

～

For the better part of a year we met whenever we could, the nuns innocently complicit in our bliss. Hitherto regarded as somewhat wayward but indulged because of her family's great wealth, Kiki was now granted special dispensation for absence from the schoolrooms and from her devotions. Her sisterly adoration of a brother who would ere long become a priest could only hasten her reformation. Once, after a picnic among the haystacks, where Kiki and I had achieved the glorious languor that follows upon multiple erotic exercises, I returned in the late summer afternoon with my beloved to her convent, reluctant as ever to leave her but helpless to change our fate.

At the Porte de Pudicité I was told that the mother superior wished to see me. I supposed that the jig was up and, trembling, as you may imagine, I was ushered into her holy presence. But no, she wished only to offer me tea and tell me how beneficial to my dear little sister was the blessing of my presence. Lady Violet's demeanor was much improved since my arrival, her—dare one say it?—her *fractiousness* was a thing of the past, her innate humility was clearly winning the battle over her innate pride, a *psychomachia* of whose conduct Prudentius himself would have approved.

Pink-cheeked and plump, her eyes glistening with sincerity, the mother superior poured me my tea. "One lump or two?"

"No sugar, thank you." I had not yet developed a sweet tooth. That would wait upon Maude, who, laughing to think that the French could know anything about how true tea should taste, corrected my ignorance.

"Ah." The mother superior nodded as if she understood. Doing without sugar in one's tea was, in her view, the pious equivalent of donning a hair shirt. "In your presence, I will myself do without."

"Je vous en prie, Mère, do not deny yourself on my account."

"Pouf!" She winked flirtatiously at me and with her silver tongs dropped three lumps into her cup. "Your French is almost impeccable for an Englishman," she told me. "You have only the slightest trace of an accent."

"You flatter me, of course. I fear that it is appalling."

"In chapel, Lady Violet now falls eagerly to her knees; she gazes at the image of our bleeding Lord with tearful longing. It has been noticed. Who can doubt that where we have failed to impart the spiritual dimension, you, her brother, have succeeded?"

I bowed my head in appropriate self-deprecation.

How Kiki laughed the following week when I, seated in our sunlit room in the station hotel of Mantes-la-Jolie, told her of this! She fell eagerly to her knees between my legs, took me, swollen, between her lips, and gazed, if not tearfully then saucily, into my eyes.

Over the almost-year we met for afternoons, for whole days, for weekends—once, during Lenten *vacances,* when her family were in India, for seventeen inexpressibly wonderful days. We made love in fields, in woods, by babbling brooks, in country inns and the hotels of provincial towns, outdoors or in, according to the weather and the season, wherever we could or would, in Oise and Eure and Seine-et-Marne and Somme. We explored each other's bodies, each other's tastes and smells. We made love in every position we could think of, she being far more inventive than I. I sucked a melting champagne chocolate truffle out of her; she licked slathers of whipped cream and raspberry coulis from me.

Of course, such happiness could not last. At length, she returned to England and I, ordained, was sent to the parish in South Kensington I have already spoken of. There I languished. In England it was, ironically, more difficult for us to meet than it had been in France. To be sure, when we met, we made love, but the fire was gone, at least it was for her, perhaps not extinguished but banked. England took her over, her wealth embraced her. And then she went to America. Our love never died, but was, as the poet Donne says, "like gold to airy thinness beat." In America she found other imperatives. We corresponded. She found me my place here at Beale Hall. But we had once been, albeit unnoticed by the greater world, like unto Héloïse and Abélard—except, of course, that I had at least emerged from the affair physically unscathed.

⌒

I first met Aristide Popescu during our days as graduate students in Paris. Like Twombly and me, Popescu was reading English literature; unlike us, he was not a priest. In fact, he was already dealing in secondhand books and had his own fair-weather stall on one of the quais. He was specializing then in Victorian erotica, which he was able to sell at a handsome profit to an ever-growing clientele of visiting postwar Englishmen. He banged out his catalogs on an old Underwood typewriter, one that produced broken, smudged, and uneven letters, and posted these catalogs "cold" not only to the librarians of all the gentlemen's clubs in Pall Mall and St. James's Street but also to every tenth clergyman listed in the Anglican Church Directory. "Rosy bums and bamboo rods, that's literature to the well-born Englishman," he used to say, shaking his head in wonder.

In those days he would sometimes join us crows at La Grenouille Farcie, a jolly rogue, what the English once called "fly," but in appearance sickly. His long, thin, hairless face was pale and had a waxen sheen. His eyes bulged glassily, red-rimmed. He was forever clearing his throat. He would turn up with his mistress in tow, Yvette, a sweet-tempered, fat girl with a pimply face and thick round glasses, who owned, so far as I could judge, only one dress. "She's good," he would say, and he gave her a gentle poke in the stomach. "On that a man could bounce all night. Why not try her?" He cleared his throat and winked. *"Quel salaud!"* she said lovingly and pinched his pale cheek. "These fellows are priests, *alors!*" Twombly narrowed his lips in disgust. Castignac looked her over speculatively.

With the passage of time, Aristide prospered. He had become an antiquarian bookseller with premises on the rue du Faubourg St-Honoré, acquired a slim, snooty wife of impeccable ancestry who had many dresses and who provided him with an heir, his son, Gabriel. Now Aristide wintered in Gstaad and Santa Monica, summered in Cetona and Amagansett. But, as I have said, he was not in Paris when I went looking for him. According to Gabriel, his father had gone to Budapest. Perhaps. Budapest, for heaven's sake! How romantic! If the young Aristide had looked fly, Gabriel, sitting behind his father's desk in the rue du Faubourg St-Honoré, looked guilty and shifty-eyed.

Aristide, perhaps without intending it—I *hope* without intending it—had delivered me up to Twombly. Together, though, they were cooking my goose.

The house of Popescu still published its catalogs on ordinary foolscap clipped together with staples, an affectation designed to suggest not only the firm's humble beginnings but its owner's rough honesty as well. The very font had been specially designed to suggest the botched and exhausted work of the original Underwood, bleeding, crooked, and chipped. Never mind the family Popescu's long current *modus vivendi*, never mind the elegant premises of Aristide Popescu & Fils in the most distinguished shopping street in Paris: the catalog, in appearance, at least, might have been printed when my old acquaintance was selling books in plain brown wrappers to blushing, snorting Englishmen.

Twombly had bumped into Popescu at the New York International Book Fair. They had never had any use for each other, but the pull of the past was strong, and Aristide invited him to dinner at Mon Truc in Madison Avenue near the corner of Sixty-third Street. It was far easier to get into the Oval Office than to be granted a table at Mon Truc. Twombly admitted he was impressed;

Aristide cleared his throat. Over an exploratory Pomerol of supernal smoothness, Twombly told his host that he was working on a biography of Shakespeare. Between a *topinambour aux cervettes rouges émincées* and a *potage à la tortue Valencienne,* Aristide produced from his breast pocket what he called his "private" catalog, one intended for discreet high rollers only.

It was a photocopy of a sheet torn from this catalog that Twombly had sent me with his recent letter. He had circled with the bright red ink of a marker pen the following:

S[hakespeare?], W[illiam?]. *Dyuers and Sondry Sonettes /* Written By *W.S.* / Neuer before Imprinted. / AT LONDON / By G. Fynes for E.E. and are / to be solde by Wm. Askey. / 1600.

> Sm. 4to, dampstaining to lower inner portions not affecting legibility, bottom fore corner of penultimate leaf restored, hole repaired in blank outer margin of final leaf. Nineteenth-century black morocco, scuffed. T.-p. stamped "Library. Beale Hall."

The bright red ink of the same marker pen had underlined "Library. Beale Hall." Alongside, in the margin, were two bright red exclamation marks and three question marks.

᷅ℒ

Well, after what I have said above, you no doubt think you have understood or guessed my crime. Let us suppose you right. What course of action should I follow? I know very well what in my priestly capacity I would be expected to advise one of the faithful in like circumstances, "Satisfy both God and Caesar. Go to the police; throw yourself on the mercy of the court; if Caesar so determines it, languish awhile in gaol. Go to the Church; confess; repent; amend your life—and be certain that mercy in heaven is far more sure than is justice in the courts of man."

In America, if what we are told is true, criminals of the highest social order have found their Jesus in the federal prisons, have been washed clean in the Blood of the Lamb, have even written books in a pious desire to warn the unwary: "I lived high on the hog and was almost shut out of the Kingdom of Heaven." As Shakespeare himself puts it in one of his lesser sonnets, "Within be fed, without be rich no more." True, they were for the most part reborn into the wilder purlieus of Protestantism. But what of that? Catholics—as Protestants must know in the Freudian parts of their guts—are the *original* Christians, the *echt* Christians (apart from the first-century Jewish New Agers, of course). For a millennium and a half Catholics wrote the book, for pity's sake. Hence, Protestants have always killed Catholics with a betraying nervousness. Catholics kill Protestants confident of their Lord.

Luckily, I'm not stupid.

As Christianity struggles to catch up with that time in which most of us live and breathe, there has emerged in the Church, still muted but growing ever more audible, a school of what may be called "proportionalism." This school holds that there are only a few acts that are illicit or immoral in themselves—and besides, much depends upon circumstances. I am myself not a proportionalist. Moreover, one can know one has done wrong without reference to the pope—or, so far as that goes, to the rabbis or the mullahs. But I *do* believe that much depends upon circumstances.

In the matter of the rare edition—*how* rare, I shall make clear anon—it may seem that I have done wrong, very wrong indeed. But if there is no acceptable excuse for the deed, there is an explanation. That, I propose to give you.

"Once upon a time," I am tempted to write, "there was a beautiful young woman from Donegal called Maude Moriarty. She had abundant red hair that, when it was not caught up in pins and bright ribbons, fell gloriously about her and reached to her waist. Her eyes were green, with flecks of teal, and they were large and impudent. Her shapeliness might have inspired the dreams of a Praxiteles . . ."

Let me start again, prosaically. Maude and I arrived at Beale Hall on the same day, she in the morning, I in the afternoon. The frequent showers of an English late summer had given place to the frequent rains of an English early autumn. Bastien, my donkey, was to follow me the next day, together with our luggage, a box of our religious paraphernalia, and two trunks that contained my books, papers, and prints, many obscene, urged upon me by my friend Aristide, not, I am now convinced, because he supposed me prurient but because he wished to secure my financial future.

The Church, recognizing the innate, simpleminded goodness of Bastien, his potential saintliness, had given him those tasks to perform on earth that might guarantee his reward in heaven. He worked in squalor amid the dispossessed, vilified by the very wretches whose miserable lot he sought to alleviate. One day, attempting to administer the last rites to a hoodlum shot amid the rubbish bins of a greasily cobbled alley by a member of a rival gang, he was himself beaten to purple jelly by that gang, who were, to a man, believers in the efficacy of last-minute confession and who wished to prevent their dying enemy the possibility of salvation. Bastien was never quite the same after that. In time he recovered, to be sure—physically, at any rate—but there was now something odd about him. Nevertheless, the Church in its compassionate wisdom sent him back to his soup kitchen and its related duties.

But Bastien and I had shared our wartime schooldays, had suffered the wickedness of the nuns together, the cruelty resulting from their displaced sexual frustration; we had both heard the excited, rattling phlegm of Father Damien's heavy breathing and been the victims of his eager fingers. I said that I would not accept the posting unless Bastien were to join me as my majordomo. The trustees were willing; the Church, wanting the property, agreed. And so I saved Bastien from sainthood.

Maude came to the Beale estate from her native Ballymagh in Donegal, recommended for the post of housekeeper by one of our trustees, who had property athwart the river Finn and who was her godfather, and by Father Timothy Tierney, author of the pamphlet "Christ Knows," who was her parish priest. Both felt that she was bright and capable and would benefit from seeing a little more of the world than Ballymagh. As a schoolgirl, she had won many an honor, especially the coveted county Latin prize, the first girl to do so. She might have gone on to the university, were it not, Father Tierney darkly hinted, for certain intractable family problems. ("Poppycock!" Maude told me one day gaily. "My da' did not think it fitting that I shame my ignorant brothers, let alone himself. Ma, by custom long established, did not oppose him. But by the time my da,' boozed to the gills in Jamieson's, fell off the Tyrone Bridge into the Finn and cracked his head open on an inconvenient boulder, I had lost the desire to go. The hope is," she added, "that he squeaked into Purgatory and not the worser place, but not even Father Tierney could be sure.") Beale Hall, far from the corrupting influences of town and city and safely within the purview of the Church, would provide a young woman who, admittedly, had no spiritual vocation but who, thankfully, was otherwise devout with, in the words of Father Tierney, "scope aplenty to show her stuff."

Is it not amazing how attractive to certain women is a man, a priest, who has chosen the celibate life? Can it be that he is, so to speak, a species of forbidden fruit? Does she regard him as a challenge? On the very first day—and on the late-Georgian watered-silk chaise in the Music Room—Maude had, with many a hypocritical tear and many a happy sigh, "shown me her stuff."

We had spent the first hour or so after my arrival wandering through the house, getting a first look at what was to be our future home. She was to gather together as soon as possible a household staff. Mr. and Mrs. Parfitt, who had served the Beales since 1902, when, little more than children, he had been taken on as bootboy and she as third tweeny, were anxious to retire to their cottage in Combpyne, halfway between Seaton and Lyme Regis. They had handed Maude the keys, shown her the kitchen, which they supposed her proper place, and took off, tootling down the drive in their ancient Triumph. As for me, I was to meet formally with the trustees in London the following week, when *inter alia* I would be given a rough inventory of the contents. Meanwhile, Maude and I wandered, pretending that such surroundings as we now found ourselves in were the ordinary stuff of our lives. By the time we reached the Music Room we could play the game no longer. We looked at each other and doubled over in laughter.

"A drink is what we want, Father," she said.

"Try the cabinet over there, the japanned one. It looks promising."

It fulfilled its promise.

We drank to future happiness. We drank again. And then again.

She looked at me and pulled the ribbon from her hair; she eyed me from top to toe.

I raised an eyebrow.

"I feel quite faint," she said. "It must be the drink." She sank onto the chaise and placed the back of her left hand against her brow.

I knew where I was at once. I was in the seduction scene of an eighteenth-century novel. Accordingly, I rushed over to her. "Is there any way I can do you ease?" I said.

"What?" she said. "What?" Distractedly, she reached out. Distractedly, she cupped in her hand the bulge in my trousers. "What?" she said again.

And so, as they say in holiest Scripture, I went in unto her.

That night we shared the four-poster bed that we have shared ever since.

"We have sinned," she said. "We shall roast forever in hell." She began to blubber.

"Not a bit of it. You have only to confess, and here am I ready to hear your confession."

"No, but," she said. "You're a priest, you've taken a vow."

"Bastien will be here tomorrow. He'll hear my confession."

"But you're a priest, after all." She took me gently in hand and gently squeezed my balls.

"By now, it is akin to a tradition." I tickled her nipples with the tip of my tongue. "Just consider, my love, the abbé Sade d'Ebreuil, a Roman Catholic priest, uncle of the Marquis de Sade, a writer, a friend of Voltaire. Here is a priest who lived with *two* women, no less, a mother and daughter, and openly patronized local prostitutes."

"You want my mother too, you filthy man?"

"Of course not. Only you. Another example: In 1456 a Carmelite friar, a chaplain to a convent in Prato, Italy, a man you have surely heard of, Fra Filippo Lippi, ran off with a nun who was half his age, the beauteous Lucrezia Buti, both of them eager, like us, to taste forbidden joys. They ran off, mind you, while most of Prato was busy celebrating the feast of the Girdle of Our Lady."

"Oh, no!"

"Oh, yes! Not only that, their scandalous union bore fruit, a boy they called Filippino. But, as the poet Donne puts it, 'this, alas, is more than we would do.' Well, what do you suppose the Church did about it? Not a blessed thing. The Church overlooked their sinful lives. They lived together, and together they brought up their son. Perhaps it helped that Fra Filippo Lippi was already a famous painter, a great man. The Church even entrusted commissions to him and made payments to father and son."

"Priests have done it before, you mean? Diddled and fiddled, is that it?"

"Exactly. There is none so righteous on earth that they do only good and never sin."

"Ecclesiastes?"

"Chapter Seven."

"Well, then." She tickled my scrotum.

"I shall in all my best obey you, madam."

"Is that the Bard?"

"It is."

"I've always admired a poetical fellow."

She rolled me over onto my back and straddled me. I gazed upon her as she rose majestically above me, awed by her disheveled beauty and the splendid tumult of her flaming passion.

In those lusty days, I often wished I possessed the strength of the male ladybird, a member of the family Coccinellidae, which, according to the entomologists, are able to enjoy multiple orgasms, three of them, one after the other, and each of them lasting about one and a half hours. She was Milton's Eve, but after the Fall, and I was, if not Adam, then Satan, already preparing to slink guiltily away.

However, not yet. While we still were "in our prime," we enjoyed— as the old poet pleasingly put it—what seemed to be "the harmless folly of the time." And then, alas, the harm of it made itself known. Six weeks into our raptures and Maude came red-eyed to bed. She was well past the due date of her monthlies, she said—she, who had always been so regular, she added, you could know from her bleeding the phase of the moon on a cloudy night.

I confess to a certain squeamishness about the physical aspects of the female menstrual cycle, a certain distaste, perhaps rooted in Judaic and biblical soil, but more likely attributable to the moment I saw the bloody stain on the back of my mother's skirt. We were in Orléans; I was then thirteen, without reference to the Nazis an anxious, pimply age. Mme Goupil had been visiting Maman in our room. The two of them had sipped mineral water and nibbled biscuits, chatting daintily of the difficult times. I sat in a corner, apart from the ladies, reading. At length, my mother broke in upon my concentration.

"Edmond, where are your manners? Mme Goupil is leaving."

"Do not disturb the child, Mme Musič."

"He is absorbed in *The Golden Legend: The Lives of the Saints,* madame," said my mother cunningly. "Nevertheless, he would be desolate to learn he had been impolite, especially to you."

"*The Golden Legend,* to be sure. It can only do him good."

"He reads it at *your* suggestion, after all, madame."

Mme Goupil scrunched her nose over her massive teeth like a pleased rabbit.

"Edmond, say thank you to Mme Goupil! Ah, these children, madame, ill-mannered, like the times."

I stood and bowed. "Thank you, madame; *au revoir,* madame." In fact, I had been reading for the umpteenth time Verne's *Voyage au centre de la terre,* one of the few books I had been allowed to bring from Paris. I hated, even as I understood, the sycophancy with which my parents dealt with Mme Goupil. Our safety depended upon her discretion, which meant, of course, her good-will. But to say that they toadied up to her is to risk a class-action suit by the world's toads.

At any rate, it was when she accompanied Mme Goupil to the door that I saw the glistening, bright red smear on the back of my mother's skirt. How I knew what it was, I cannot say. Certainly, I had received no instruction on the subject. But this visible sign of my mother's biological *esse* disgusted me, yes, even *this* mother, whom I adored, and whose memory I still revere. I averted my gaze to the chair on which she had sat and saw there the recipro-cal stain. As quickly as I reasonably could, I said I wanted to go out for some fresh air. Of course, I wanted to give her time to dis-cover her condition, to wash the blood from her self, her skirt, her chair. And, happily, by the time I returned, all was once more well.

How I have digressed! It is a function, no doubt, of my advanc-ing years. Expect to encounter further examples of an old man's weakness.

One might have thought that Maude, given her somewhat

sheltered upbringing in rural Ireland and given, in the Larkinian sense, the pre-Beatles' time of the revelatory moment, would not have spoken quite so baldly. As a matter of fact, she has been all her life something of a prude, somewhat reticent in her verbal sexual expression. Except before me. Since I had, in *her* formulation, *had* her, she spoke to me, from the start, in a way that she might have hesitated to use before her closest female friend. And so she evoked, via her blubbering, that hateful image of my mother, if only because Maude had *failed* to bleed, a kind of *absence-présence*.

But in that pre-Beatles' time, imagine the scandal! Roman Catholic Priest Maintains Secret Love Nest! Father Music, Director General of Beale Hall, to Become "Father"! (See "Making a New Music Together" by Pieter de Pawl, p. 7; and Editorial: "The Betrayal of Trust," p. 13.) No fear of that, actually. It would be more than a quarter century before the dam would burst, before the public marriages of former priests and nuns became commonplace; before the revelations of the most appalling hankypanky perpetrated by "men of the cloth" on children, boys and girls, became so yawningly unstartling as to appear just before the sports pages at the back of the newspaper; before the Church, finding no hiding place down here, stopped hushing up the crimes and misdemeanors of both its officer class and its front line cadre, confessed to the odd rotten apple in the priestly barrel, and sought to deflect universal opprobrium by translating the natural, human revulsion from evident hypocrisy into, oh, dear, one more example of villainous "Catholic bashing." Catholic bashing, indeed! How can we explain that our laity have been forced into a posture of self-defense against the clergy, establishing an organization called S.N.A.P., Survivors Network of Those Abused by Priests? The pedophiles among us have given a whole new meaning to "Suffer the little children to come unto me."

It may seem that I have not devoted much space or concern to poor Maude in all of this. True, but I wish to be honest. At the time, I thought only of myself. I hardly knew Maude. The Church

would have hushed up my peccadillo, of that I felt sure. No doubt
I would have suffered a severe twigging from my bishop. That
didn't bother me. Confession, penance, amendment of life, the
usual rigmarole. But I would surely have lost Beale Hall. They would
have moved me on somewhere, probably somewhere mosquito-
ridden, Colombia, Guyana, that sort of impossible place.

Maude's *grossesse* was Maude's fault. Yes, yes, I know how that
comment sounds nowadays. Appalling! It appalls me, especially
in view of the years that she and I have been together. But that's
what I thought then. And I am not at all sure that it's not what she
thought too. I knew what lay before her, and it seemed to me to be
not too bad, compassionate even, in a cold, Catholic sort of way.
When her pregnancy was on the brink of becoming apparent, she
would be sent back to Ireland, and there she would become a
Magdalen, looked after with loving disapproval by the nuns, until
she gave birth to a baby that would be taken from her for adop-
tion; and then she would be required to work, as if she were a
slave, in a laundry or whatever, until the moment that she wised
up to the fact that she had only to walk away, childless, to be sure,
but free.

On the other hand, this was *my* child who was on his way. I
shook my finger with mock anger at my equipment even as I
exulted in its accomplishment. *My* child would not join the secret
traffic in newborn babies to unknown homes of which the Church
for her own mysterious reasons approved. *My* child would be
brought up by his mother in comfortable surroundings under-
written by his father—clandestinely, to be sure, since no child
brought up a Catholic could take pride in knowing he had a priest
for a father.

But how was this goal to be achieved? I was penniless person-
ally, however comfortably I was to live in Beale Hall. It was a
puzzle.

Meanwhile, Maude thought we should no longer share a bed,
let alone engage in those activities that had precipitated the

present crisis. "But, Maude," I said, anxious not to be deprived of her, "the horse has bolted. It is already too late to shut the stable door."

My apothegm was ill chosen. How she howled! "Is that what you think of me? Was that the means of entry? Did I offer you no more than an unbarred stable door? Or am I perhaps a mare, fit only for breeding?"

"Be calm, dear Maude. It's just an expression. Perhaps it was ill chosen. Perhaps my English is not so good as I thought." I took her in my arms, caressed her, kissed the tears from her eyes. "After all, you are already with child. By sharing my bed, you cannot become either more or less *enceinte*."

"We must not persist in this wickedness," she said, and smoothed her flat belly with her well-shaped hand. *"Ecce signum."*

"Look here," I said, pointing to the bulge in my trousers. *"Ecce signum."*

She smiled in spite of herself, but turned from me with a sniff. "Have I not shriven you?"

"What can that be worth, *your* shriving, and yourself a sinner, no better than me, perhaps worse? I think I should betake myself to Father Bastien." She pouted and flounced.

"Sinners are we all, not just you and I; that is the human condition. Into sin we are born. But, Maude, my love, wicked though I may be, I retain the Power and the Glory. My absolution is as good as the pope's himself. And, in the matter of the flesh, I point you in the direction of Saint Augustine, who prayed to Christ to be saved from his sexual profligacy—but not yet."

"When it comes to the gab, you're more Irish than French."

"Confess to Father Bastien, if you wish. Do what is best for you."

"Well, we shall see." She shrugged and left me. But she made herself up a bed in the East Wing.

It seemed to me wise to have an anticipatory word with Bastien myself. Who knew what Maude might say to him?

Bastien, odd though he is, surprised me. First, he welcomed the arrival of a new little Music into the world, a stock that could only be improved by Maude's contribution. Second, he addressed himself to my need to provide for my offspring. He suggested that I begin by exploring the limits of my power at Beale Hall; thereafter, I should get in touch with Popescu, the only person known to us who had some business acumen. "After all, Edmond," he said, "our realm is the spiritual, not the practical." He patted me on the back in a comradely fashion. "Meanwhile, I have been exploring the cellar again. Not bad, not at all bad. I have brought up a couple of bottles of Puligny-Montrachet 1937. We shall see."

"Maude might come to you for confession."

"Let her do so. She has nothing to fear from me."

"Of course not, no, that's not what I meant. I just didn't want you to be shocked."

"Edmond!"

"Well, well, *mon vieux,* you know what I mean."

"I know."

൧

Popescu drove up from Heathrow in a rented sports car, a snappy little model in yolk yellow that squealed to a stop before the Great Door. He remained in the car, honking peremptorily until, from several directions, Maude, Bastien, two gardeners (one with a pitchfork), the charwoman, and I appeared, expressing, variously, alarm, curiosity, anger, and puzzlement. Then Aristide leapt from his car, exulting, "Here I am!" He placed a hand over his heart. "Ah, it is madness driving in this country, suicidal! It is a wonder I am still alive. You should offer a special Mass of thanksgiving." He embraced Bastien and me. "My friends, my good friends." Before Maude, he clicked his heels together and, smiling ironically, executed an abrupt Germanic bow, gazing up at her from his lowered brow, his eyes bulging. "A visiting film star, perhaps? Or merely the *dea loci?*" Maude giggled, delighted. "Got it in two. The *dea loci,* actually," she said. With an aristocratic, backhanded wave, Aristide dismissed the gardeners and the charwoman. He was much changed in the few years since last I had seen him. No longer gaunt, his body had a pantherlike sleekness. He spoke in the elevated accents of Charles de Gaulle. His dark suit was of an elegant cut, his shirt gleamed white, his silk tie was carefully knotted. He was neatly barbered; you would call him well groomed. Only his eyes were unchanged, bulging, roguish as ever. He folded Maude's arm in his and led her into the Hall. "What is your name, you vision? At what shrine shall I worship?" He looked over his shoulder at Bastien and me. "Come along, don't dawdle. There isn't much time. We have quite a lot to talk about."

Aristide readily admitted being impressed by Beale Hall, but he cut short the tour. "You've landed softly," he said to me. "Good for you." But he asked to be taken to the Library. "About the value of books, I can speak as an authority."

I left him to roam by himself the open shelves and the locked cabinets, to which I gave him the keys. I sat in a comfortable chair before the fire and read once more Byron's *Don Juan,* cantos I and II, in the 1819 edition, the very first, published by Thomas Davison, Whitefriars, and to be found here in Beale Hall from that splendid year. From time to time I heard him whistle, or cry *"Merde, alors!"* or "I don't believe it!" or "Magnificent!" Time passed. Maude brought in tea and crumpets and a Swiss roll, but Aristide would not stop his work. Bastien looked in, saw the piles of books on the long library table, saw Aristide in shirtsleeves, his hair tousled, his face smudged with errant dust, and shook his head at me before withdrawing. It grew dark; I switched on the lamps.

"I will have to stay the night," he said. "There is more here, much more, than I could have imagined."

I got up. "My pleasure," I said. "Maude will prepare a bed for you. She will set an extra place at table."

"Something simple," he said. "The English are vile cooks. A

bowl of soup, some bread, a glass of wine. But in here, with the books. I must go on."

I found him the following morning, fast asleep, slumped over the library table, his head in his arms, pages of notes scattered about him. The bottle of wine was empty; the soup and bread were untouched. I shook him awake. He looked awful, his bulging eyes red-rimmed and bloodshot, but curiously more familiar, more his old self.

"Coffee, for the love of God," he croaked. "But first, where can I take a piss? My bladder's bursting."

When next he appeared in the Library, he looked a little more like the dapper Aristide of the day before. He had bathed, shaved, and generally neatened himself. Bastien and I greeted him. He sat and poured coffee for himself. He gulped greedily. "Ech! What is this? Tea?" He broke a breakfast roll and buttered it. "So, Bastien," he said, looking at his watch, "*ça va, mon gars?*" He turned to me. "Perhaps you would prefer a private conference, *hein?*"

"I have no secrets from Bastien. He is my oldest friend. Besides, it was he who suggested I turn to you for help."

What I have called Bastien's oddness, quiescent most of the time, manifested itself at that moment in his making the sign of the Cross over the coffeepot.

"Wonderful, yes, we are all friends, I hope," said Aristide smoothly. "Well, as I understand it, Edmond, you wish to create a fund to benefit your child and its mother?"

"Precisely."

"And at this moment you possess nothing, am I right?"

"I've managed to save a few pounds. Most of my needs here are taken care of. But no, nothing with which to create a fund."

"But you have the authority here at Beale Hall, especially with regard to the Library, to buy and sell?"

"Well, yes. Thanks to Bastien, I've looked into it. I don't think the trustees expected much in the way of selling, unless perhaps of duplicates, and then only as a means of further acquisition."

"But you have the authority, nevertheless, to sell as well as buy?"

"Yes, I have."

Aristide closed his eyes and sighed. "What you must do first is sell to Beale Hall those books and prints you had from me and brought with you. I will recommend a price that is generous to you but not outrageous. This is a sum that you will deposit in Switzerland in favor of your beneficiary, the interest, or part of it, to pay for life insurance, again in favor of your beneficiary." Aristide poured another cup of coffee. "But that's only a beginning. This is an extraordinary library, the finest, so far as I can judge, still in private hands. It possesses many, many rarities, among them the Caxton edition of *Morte d'Arthur* and the ten-book first edition of *Paradise Lost.* There are many boxed, unsorted papers besides, a potential treasure trove. The cataloging is primitive, incomplete, and in disarray. But, my friends, I have found two works here that are unknown to the bibliographers, one a medieval Psalter, the other a work possibly by Shakespeare that, I happen to know, appears in a slightly different form in the Stationers' Register." Aristide broke off another piece of roll and buttered it. "I will need to do a thorough check, of course, but I am willing, right now, to buy either or both."

"Tell me about the Psalter."

"Well," said Aristide casually, consulting his notes, "it was made for Bodo de l'Île Amoureuse, who was the grand prior of the Order of the Knights Hospitaller of Saint Iago. Bodo led the defense of Acre in 1291, you know, and he died on Cyprus. The Psalter is the work of the Villefranche Master, a court artist in Paris. Bodo took it with him to the Holy Land. Take a look at it, *mon cher,* when you have a moment. It is surely the Master's finest work, page after page of illumination, shimmering with gold and colors. A wonder."

"And the other?"

"It too is an unknown. It may be an edition of Shakespeare

until now unrecorded. In either case, I'll give you what I think is a fair price. You need the money now, but I must tell you that their value will jump year by year. In a manner of speaking, I've got you by the balls."

"How much?"

Aristide mentioned a price for each that made both Bastien and me gasp.

"But the money will belong to Beale Hall. How does that help me?"

Aristide looked at me as if I were a half-wit; even Bastien chuckled in his sleeve and averted his eyes. Aristide poured a little more coffee fastidiously into his cup, raising the pot with a questioning gesture at us before putting it down.

"Of course, you will furnish me with an authentic bill of sale, signed by you, the director general. Everything aboveboard. I, for my part, will pay you in cash. What happens to that cash is no affair of mine. Perhaps it, or some of it, will end up in Switzerland in the account of a certain beneficiary."

Bastien was nodding his head in his bouncing way. "Sell him the Shakespeare, not the Psalter," he said to me. "We are, after all, a Catholic institution."

"A hearteningly pious choice," said Aristide, winking.

"Piety has nothing to do with it," said Bastien sharply. "Clerical scholars have been using this library for years. The Bodo Psalter is more likely to have been noted than the Shakespeare, even if its value has gone unrecognized."

It is always surprising when Bastien's intelligence bursts through his oddness. He was still bouncing his head up and down, after all, and once more he made the sign of the Cross over the coffeepot.

"But once you put it on the market, Aristide," I said, "the game is up."

"He will not put it on the market until after you are dead. Meanwhile, it will only accumulate in value, a tidy little something for his old age or for his heirs."

"I can't keep so much money tied up for so long. As it is, I don't know where I'll find the sum I spoke of."

"You'll find it, you'll find it. Meanwhile, to make the search easier, Edmond will knock fifty thousand off the price." Bounce, bounce, bounce went Bastien's head.

Aristide laughed. "Done!" he said. "If you ever want a job in the book trade, Bastien, come and see me."

I watched the two of them, my own head going back and forth as if at a tennis match.

Aristide reached across the table to shake Bastien's hand, but Bastien backed off, shocked. "First you must shake Edmond's hand," he said. "He is the director general, after all, the boss."

"Well," I said, "you've had your fun. Now we must be serious. You cannot truly mean that I become a common criminal."

"Not so common," said Aristide, winking at Bastien. "What sort of crime is it to take from an unknowing, overendowed institution an abstract, bloodless *thing,* in order to help the needy and innocent? Think of yourself as a gentleman thief, as Robin Hood or Raffles. This is a great opportunity, my friend. It may not come again."

"I cannot do it."

"But, Edmond!" said Bastien. "Aristide has come all this way."

"Let me reason with him, Bastien." Aristide turned to me. "All I ask is that you think about it. I'm offering you a fortune. Think of the mother of your unborn child, think of the child himself."

"What I *will* do is sell my books and prints to the Beale Hall Library at the price you recommend. And I shall invest the proceeds as you advise. But that is all."

Bastien sighed. Aristide shrugged.

At that moment, Maude knocked and popped her lovely head around the door. She wanted to know if the gentleman wished to stay to lunch.

Aristide's eyes lit up when he saw her. If there was any sign of her pregnancy it was in a new splendor that emanated from her like a halo. "Lunch? Ah, but, yes, of course, it will be my great pleasure. And after lunch, perhaps, this goddess will accompany me to Ludlow, show me all the sights that should detain the visitor. There is a castle, yes?"

"There is, yes, it's a beautiful ruin, but I'm not sure that I . . ."

"Ah, do not trifle with me, ma'm'selle. I am desolate."

Maude laughed, and sunshine entered the room. She quite fancied herself alongside this elegant foreigner in his little yellow sports car. "Well, I can offer you an hour, if that's any use to you," she said. "Then I must be back."

In the event, she was gone all afternoon.

⌒〜

Within a fortnight of my opening the Swiss account, the proceeds from the sale of my books and prints to the Library, Maude came once more to my room. She wore one of those old-fashioned flannel nightgowns that speak of innocence but hint at erotic delight. Her glorious red hair tumbled about her shoulders. She got demurely into bed beside me. I put my book on the bedside table.

"You're very welcome," I said, "but what can have changed your mind?"

"'The curse is come upon me,' cried the Lady of Shalott." It had never happened to her before, missing her monthlies. What was she to think? She hoped she hadn't worried me. She had been dreadfully worried herself. "It's not a curse at all," she said. "It's a benison." She placed my hand on her breast. "I've been praying to Mary the Virgin for weeks and weeks."

I was, of course, greatly relieved by the news. "Ah, well, then," I said, "that's the answer. Still, the experience of the BVM was somewhat different."

"Heretic! Oh, you wicked man!" She took my hand from her breast and kissed my palm.

"Did you know that the Church once considered requiring women to cover their ears for modesty's sake?"

"You're making it up!"

"Not at all, I assure you. They reasoned that God must have inseminated the BVM by way of the ear, gave her an earful, as it were. The Word, you know, which was in the beginning. The Annunciation, that sort of thing. At any rate, it was reasonable to assume the female ear a bodily part suited to pudency. Even Satan, after all, phallically serpentine, spat his seminal poison into the ear of Eve."

"Ah, and is himself revealed as one of the women-haters, a fellow traveler?"

"Not me," I said. "I'm not like the wicked old buggers of former times. 'Every day is Ladies' Day for me.'"

"You're the wickedest old bugger of them all."

"And are you still, as it were, in the throes?"

"I know your peculiarities," she said. "No, I waited until it was over. You have nothing to fear, you silly, finicky fellow."

I fell upon her. *"Da mi basia mille, deinde centum!"*

She held me off. "Never mind counting kisses. From now on, you'll wear one of these. I'm not going through such terror again." She took from the pocket at the stomach of her nightgown a box of condoms, Durex, as I remember.

"Sin upon sin," I said. "Would you doom us to the deepest pit of Hell?"

"We're headed there already," she said seriously. "Like Paolo and Francesca. I don't have to tell you what you already know."

I took the box from her. "But where did you get them? Weren't you horribly embarrassed?"

"At a chemist's in Ludlow, Bellamy's, in Bridgewater Close. 'We Dispense with Accuracy.' And, yes, I *was* embarrassed. But *you* could hardly go and get them. I said to the man that my father needed them, which was not much of a fib, if you think of it."

Later that night, she whispered that she had a confession to make.

"Te absolvo," I said.

She dug me sharply in the ribs. "It's not a formal confession I'm after. This is different. I have to say the words to somebody, somebody who won't want to harm me. Somebody who'll forgive me without reference to his dog collar. That's you." She grasped my hand but turned her head away from me. "I've sold an old Shakespeare book from the Library to your friend Aristide." I sat up in the bed. "You've *what?*"

And out came the story, haltingly, amid sighs and tears and utterly unavailing attempts to return my interests to matters libidinous. It was while they were walking in the gardens of Ludlow Castle that this particular avatar of Satan spat his poison into the ear of my Maude. He had heard of her "fortunate misfortune," he told her, and she looked radiant withal, a walking testament to the glory of God's chosen means of propagation. But, to be practical, she would surely want the best of what the world had to offer for her baby. That would require money, a lot of money. Where was she to obtain it? Obviously not from the child's father, who was relatively penniless and who, in any case, could not even acknowledge his paternity. She found herself in (how could he put it?) *delicate* circumstances. A priest, after all. He had suggested to Edmond the solution to the financial problem, but Edmond was too—as an old friend he felt he had the right to say it—too *bourgeois* to accept the obvious, too quick to sanctify property before the just demands of compassion. But *she* could take the reins into her own hands. She could secure her own and her unborn child's future, and perhaps, in the end, help Edmond himself. Had she sufficient generosity of spirit? He did not doubt her. She had only to sell him a certain book from the Beale Hall Library. He would tell her what it was and precisely where it was to be found. As soon as she gave him the book and a bill of sale (which she would sign with Edmond's signature), he would give her, cash in hand, the enormous sum agreed upon in advance, or he would place that sum for her in an account in any bank in the world she designated. (In fairness to Aristide, he offered her the very sum and the very terms he had offered me.) Well, she hemmed and hawed. She mustn't, she wouldn't, she couldn't, she shouldn't. But in the end, over tea and crumpets in a shop near Butter Cross, the fiend prevailed. "But you're not even pregnant," I said. "Not that that would be an excuse. You must give him back his money and get back the book."

"I tried," she wailed. "I phoned him this morning. He just laughed. 'Forget it,' he said. 'Enjoy the money.' Oh, Edmond, whatever am I to do? How could I have done such a thing?"

"I'll phone him," I said. And phone him I did.

"Sue me," he said. "Take me to court."

"You know I can't do that. I might endanger Maude."

Aristide sighed. "Why not enjoy life a little, Edmond? Spend a little money. Thanks to me, both of you have plenty. Try again to make babies. You obviously know how." And he hung up.

I tried to reach him again, but there was no reply.

All that was decades ago. I did not really believe that he would hold on to the book for very long. He already had in mind, I supposed, some private punter into whose collection it would silently go. And yet I was wrong. Until now he had kept his promise to Maude. What can have prompted him to betray his trust? Why after all this time? And now the wretched Twombly is asking his dangerous questions. Well, as the Bard puts it somewhere, somewhat we must do.

◌2◌

Curiously, one of the *Tales of the Ba'al Shem of Ludlow*, "The Pish and the Unjust Philanthropist," touches at a tangent or with a glancing blow upon this wretched issue. The tale is told by Rabbi Ivor Connick of the holy community of Roehampton, who claims to have heard it from Rabbi Aubrey Lubert of the holy community of Manchester. The Pish, it seems, was once a guest in the house of the Manchester community's wealthiest congregant, a great philanthropist. Of course, the Pish was treated according to his worth, which is to say, as a distinguished member of a royal house. The table groaned beneath dishes of silver and gold and goblets and flagons of crystal; there was an abundance of food and drink, a rich variety to tempt the most jaded palate.

That night the Pish had a dream. In his dream, he entered a glorious palace in paradise where a court of justice was in session. Satan entered in the form of a toad and informed against a member of the Manchester community: "It is true that his deeds of charity are without number, that he brings help to the indigent and to the halt and the lame, to the widow and the orphan, that he provides dowries for the penniless bride and support for the impoverished student. It is true, moreover, that he devotes many hours of each day to his own study of the Torah. But he has been in business in Manchester for many, many years, and in each of those years he has robbed the gentiles. Here is the bill, the grand total of his theft." And Satan presented the court with the sum.

The court rumbled its displeasure and would have had the bailiffs remove the Accuser forthwith. But Satan stood his ground. "Masters of Justice," he said, "I have brought a serious charge into this court. You must heed my words or Justice dies."

There came then a thunderclap from on high: "Issue a verdict!"

The court wrote down its verdict, which was this: the Accused must choose either to return all his wealth to those gentiles whom he had robbed over many years or accept the conversion of his sons and daughters to Christianity. *You shall have one standard for stranger and citizen alike* (Leviticus 24:22). Be fearful lest *your sons and daughters be given to another people, while your eyes look on and fail with longing for them all the day* (Deuteronomy 28:32). Satan took the written verdict in his mouth and hopped away.

Needless to say, the philanthropist rent his garments and cried, "Woe is me!" But he decided to return to the gentiles as much as he could of what he had robbed them, and then, with his wife and babes, betook himself to debtors' prison. Better to live in cruel want, he reasoned, than to see even one of his children abandon his religion. As Rabbi Connick comments, citing Deuteronomy 25:16, *"All who act dishonestly are an abomination to the Lord."*

What am I to make of this? How am I to act upon it?

⌒

Yes, if you must know, I suppose I still love Maude, whom I think of, sentimentally, as my old Dutch, but how to connect this fat old woman, she of the thinning hair and aches and pains, especially from her poor hip, with the witty, sensual beauty that won from me a lifetime's devotion, I cannot possibly say. (Can she actually have believed I had phoned her from heaven? Of course not. It must have been the tipple talking.) Mind you, time has not been particularly kind to me, either.

We used those horrid things, the condoms, for a while, but the use tapered off. Neither of us liked them. Nor did she ever become pregnant. Do you see the hand of God in that?

⌒

Meanwhile, on the wall before me here in the Music Room hangs the beautifully illuminated curse composed and inscribed by Solomon Falsch, the Pish, in 1760 at the behest of Sir Percival Beale, the antiquarian and collector:

For him that stealeth a Book from this Library, let it change into a burning Brand in his Hand and there blister him. Let him be struck with the sweating Sickness and let his Organs of Generation wither. Let him languish in indescribable Pain, crying in vain for Mercy; and in Misery let his Cup run over. Let there be no surcease to his Misery, even unto the final Moment of Dissolution. Meanwhile, let Bookworms gnaw with sharp teeth perpetually at his living Entrails, an Earnest of the Worm that lost us Eden and, dying not, lords it over the Unrighteous. And when at last he goeth to his final Abode, to his Punishment in the Vale of Sheol, let him be visited there by the pitiless Flames of Gehenna and consumed forever and aye.

I reminded Maude of this dreadful curse, the curse that hangs ever before me, a reminder and a goad, the one dissonant note in the harmony of my well-loved Music Room. "Are you not dreadfully afraid?" I asked her.

"It's only words," she said, but she grew pale.

"Words, yes, but composed by a holy man."

"Get away, he was just an old Jew."

I must say, *that* gave me pause.

I have often thought of taking the curse down, for it bothers me, it makes me uncomfortable. But I am not superstitious, truly I'm not, and I would not wish to appear so, even to myself. Visitors often ask why the curse does not hang in the Library, for which it was surely intended. I have no answer, other than to say that it occupied its present place when first I came to the Hall. I *could* move it to the Library, of course, if I would. But I am just neurotic (or do I mean Catholic? Or perhaps I mean Jewish?) enough to believe that the guilt it induces is good for me.

Some months later, Maude asked me whether I thought the curse was only potent as a whole or if each of its parts had the ability to wreak its own harm without reference to the rest. She had begun to worry about her "organs of generation."

Part Three

Memento, homo, quia pulvis es, et in pulverem reverteris.

—Priestly exhortation to the faithful before the beginning of Mass on Ash Wednesday, the *dies cinerum* of the Latin Missal

Religion is an insult to human dignity. With or without it, you'd have good people doing good things and evil people doing evil things. But for good people to do evil things, it takes religion.

—Dr. Steven Weinberg, physicist, Nobel laureate, at a meeting of the American Association for the Advancement of Science, April 1999

Twombly's letter was addressed, as always, to "Father Edmond Music, S.J." No, I am not a Jesuit, nor does Twombly suppose me to be one. He first used the "S.J." years ago on a postcard he sent me one summer from Rome, at a time when we were both still graduate students. Back in Paris that autumn, at our table at La Grenouille Farcie, he explained what he had meant.

"It's a joke, don't you get it?" he said. Against the pallor of his lank cheeks, his ruby lips essayed a grimace. "S.J. means Secret Jew!" His laugh, in him something of a rarity, was a high-pitched, girlish titter.

"That's a joke?" said Bastien.

"Look at the picture," said Twombly.

It was a detail from Versace's *Christ Throwing the Money Changers Out of the Temple,* the only persuasive reason to visit S. Simpliciano Maggiore in the via degli Specchi in Rome, where, in an abiding gloom, it hangs. One of the money changers, notoriously, has a monkey on his shoulder, a jeering, ugly monkey who, somewhat shockingly, urinates in a glittering arc onto the coins scattered on the ground. On his head, the creature has a sequined turban that sports a Star of David. The painting would deserve a prominent place in any exhibition devoted to anti-Semitism in art. The monkey, of course, was the detail on the postcard.

"Look at its eyes," said Twombly, tittering nervously. "It made me think of you, Edmond."

"A remarkable resemblance," I said dryly.

Since then, Twombly has used the "S.J." in all his correspondence with me, as if it were an endearing reminder of our jolly student days. In fact, he knows it is an insult that rankles like an endlessly suppurating sore. He also knows that I can say nothing to him about it, lest he imply, humbly to be sure, that so exaggerated a response to his pleasantry is a sign that I have a chip on my shoulder, a Hebraic predisposition to find offense in overtures of Christian fellowship, like all my tribe. And thus, by another route, I would confirm his use of "S.J."

Early in his academic career, Twombly had shifted his attention from what was then the substance of literary studies—classical and other influences, the tracing of themes, the sources and iteration and patterns of poetic imagery and metaphor, Christian symbolism and sexual significance in unexpected places, the close readings of texts—to literary biography. He was already the author of slim, largely unread biographies of Hilaire Belloc, G. K Chesterton, and Graham Greene. He had for many years now been at work on a Shakespeare biography, a comically ambitious project for so pedestrian a brain, seeking to demonstrate Shakespeare's Catholic origins and recusancy. Well, the best of British luck to him, as we say over here.

It was this "new" interest that had caused him to mention Shakespeare to Aristide Popescu, as they sat dining together, extravagantly, in the trendy New York restaurant, the glowing Pomerol generously flowing. But I've already told you all about that. What I have not told you yet—or rather not yet told you in detail—is the threat, scarcely veiled, that his letter contained.

Twombly had done his homework. The closest he had come to finding an entry in the Stationers' Register for the "mystery" volume was one for January 3, 1599, Old Style (that is, 1600, New). It reads as follows: "Eleazar Edgar. Entred for his copye under the handes of the Wardens / A booke called Amours by J.D. with / certain other sonnetes by W.S." Twombly's letter assured me that there is no copy extant of this book. "Imagine if there were," he went on musingly.

What if J.D. were John Donne. What if W.S. were indeed William Shakespeare. What a combo, Edmond! The two greatest love poets of the turning century coming together between covers. Gosh! The possibilities make the mind boggle!

(Twombly offers the American academy's best example of an epistolary style for which the term "banal" carries too much of a sense of vigor and bite. His double entendre is rendered hilarious largely because he doesn't know it's there. "Coming together between the covers," indeed. Oh, dearie me! The mind really does "boggle.")

The book Popescu's catalog offers is utterly unknown to scholarship! I mention it in connection with the entry in the Stationers' Register only because it shares the year, 1600, and because the latter was entered by Eleazar Edgar. Is Eleazar Edgar the "E.E." on Popescu's title page? I'd bet my last dollar he is. And I also think that Popescu's book is a kind of prequel or sequel, if you will, to the one in the Stationers' Register, the one that brings together J.D. and W.S.

("Prequel!" "Sequel!" God save the mark! He never lets a buzzword escape him. Tell me, "if you will," how do such fellows as this 'scape whipping?)

What I can't understand, Edmond, is how come the title page, according to the catalog, is stamped "Library. Beale Hall"? Hey, I know you, for pete's sake! Golly, you wouldn't have sold a treasure like that from a collection whose ultimate owner is the Church, which is to say, Christ. No, not you. Never. You'd have flung those who came fawning with money in their hands away from the Temple. But isn't it amazing that Popescu, the pornographer, the least salubrious of your many insalubrious friends who, in our salad days, haunted La Grenouille Farcie, should have on his shelf a book whose rightful place is that very library it's your honor, *inter alia,* to administer!

Well, we shall have our work cut out this summer, S.J., trying to trace the journey undertaken by this unique volume from Beale Hall to the catalog of that immoral tradesman—a man, I might add, who seems to have disappeared from the face of the earth. He is, I am repeatedly told on the phone, amid muttered background instructions, "unavailable at the moment," "out of the country." Oh, sure. You bet.

As I have told you, Aristide's "unavailability" has created something of a problem for me too. In vain I looked for him in Paris. For Twombly, in spite of himself, had offered me an out. As he said with ill-concealed sarcasm, I could most certainly *not* have sold so rare a book to Aristide, abso-*lute*-ly not. It was unthinkable. Very well, then. It must have been sold before I took up my post, perhaps by the financially strapped Ferdinando Beale, the suicide. What I had wanted to suggest to Aristide was that he sequester the bill of sale Maude had so foolishly given him and create a provenance for the book that was complicated by wartime chicanery and deaths, a murkiness that might explain how it had turned up at his stall years before, at a time when he was young and new to the trade and unaware of its value.

The real threat in Twombly's letter was slipped in casually. He had "just happened to mention" in a courtesy letter to Bishop McGonagle the extraordinary entry in Aristide's catalog, and the bishop, "good, good soul," had expressed an interest in Twombly's researches and had promised to visit Beale Hall during the American scholar's stay. "The game's afoot!" the dear man had condescended to convey to Twombly, no doubt aware of the latter's enthusiasm for Holmesian inductive reasoning.

But Bishop McGonagle, as the slimy Twombly certainly knew, was not merely the local hierarchical bigwig, he was also an ex officio member of Beale Hall's board of trustees. It seemed to me, as I looked about me for advice, as I looked for a reasonable ear into which I could pour my present problem, that the major was my best bet, that dear old W.C. might have something useful to offer. Accordingly, I tried in anticipation to formulate Maude's theft into terms that a hero of the North African campaign might find sympathetic.

ᢙ

I took the familiar, pleasant walk through the estate toward Tetley Wood and Benghazi. It was his turn to host our chess evening. Off in the distance, Sir Humphrey Beale's victory column on the brow of Trafalgar Hill caught at its summit the rays of the setting sun, a golden lance quixotically defying the advancing night. Unseen birds twittered their melodious diapason. Enraptured, I listened, pausing for a moment before the wood's verdurous glooms. Meanwhile, back at the Hall, Angie Mackletwist was wreaking her red magic on Maude's thinning hair. Soon the ladies would settle down to the social part of the evening, cups of tea and slices of cake at first, and then, with a fortifying bottle of gin and two tumblers at the ready, a delicious consideration of the gossip that had this week swept through the doors of Snippety-Snip and swirled about its domed, space-age hair dryers.

Whenever possible, I dress for comfort, which is to say, slacks, open-necked shirt, woolly cardigan, and, of course, my black-and-white trainers. In my role as director—when I am forced, that is, to mingle with the priestly crew or greet visiting dignitaries—I wear, except for the necessary trainers, the expected outfit: black suit, black bib, and shiny if yellowing dog collar. But on chess nights I am in full fig (once more, I except my trainers), the better to sharpen the major's wit. And thus I stood knocking at his door, my cassock reaching to my ankles, around my neck a necklace of black beads from which depended a whopping great ebony Cross sporting a squirming, ivory Jesus, and on my head a biretta. I had bought the biretta years and years ago for a lark. I had found it in a shop in a smelly, cobbled alley not far from St. Peter's, a shop devoted to ecclesiastical needments and the sort of ghastly trinkets and souvenirs the pious tourist might buy to distribute among loved ones at home. I had been summoned to Rome at the time by the chief librarian of the Vatican Library, ostensibly to be offered a position as, well, not quite curator, but as one of the three assistant curators of the Vatican's unrivaled collection of Hebraica, unblushingly "liberated" from Jewish hands over the centuries. (Was there a subtle allusion in this offer to my origins? A reminder, perhaps, of my reasons for gratitude? Edmond Music, S.J.? Or was this concern of mine evidence of the Hebraic chip whose weight used to cause one of my shoulders to sag?) I was taken on a tour of the library; I was wined and dined amid youthful, witty clerical company. After three days, I was called to the office of Father Rocco Marinaccio, first secretary to the second assistant to the chief librarian. Father Marinaccio, sitting behind his imposing desk, ancient volumes piled around him, golden dust motes dancing in rays of sunlight streaming through the windows, leaned forward on his elbows and brought the flat of his palms together beneath his chin, an attitude suggestive of Christopher Robin at prayer. "Think well, Father." He sniffed. "For a young man at the beginning of his career, here is an opportunity to leap several rungs up the ladder in one bound." He hinted that the honorific "Monsignor" would follow soon upon the appointment.

I had not needed my old friend Castignac to warn me off. It was clear from the beginning that all the Church wanted was to pry me loose from Beale Hall. But it was good to encounter an old friend in this labyrinth of policy and chicanery. He was then private secretary to the bishop of Nîmes, who had detoured through Rome on his way to the Dolomites and a clinic run by the Cistercians, where it was hoped he would dry out. "In Nîmes," said Castignac with a wink, "we can scarcely keep him in brandy." We stood in the gloom of S. Simpliciano Maggiore, peering at Versace's painting. Castignac abruptly turned his back on it. "That so sublime an artist should curry favor with the Church by painting such an abomination! We've a lot to answer for," he said. "Be careful, Edmond. Once you're voluntarily out of Beale Hall, how long do you think they'll keep you in Rome? You'll find yourself in some Central African village doling out rotted rice and ducking bullets." He shook his head and laughed ruefully. "I myself have a lot to answer for, my friend. The world pulls like an irresistible magnet. What would Our Lord say to me? 'Castignac, get thee to a Central African village.' Oh, Dante would have a choice spot for me, perhaps among the trimmers."

Well, I thanked Father Marinaccio for laying before me so unexpected an honor, of which I was surely unworthy. I begged leave to return to England, where, in the quiet sanctuary of Beale Hall's private chapel, I would have the necessary peace to reflect upon unmerited preferment and to pray humbly for guidance. Father Marinaccio regarded me with ill-disguised distaste. He lit a cigarette, forgetting that he had one still smoking in the choked ashtray before him. One of his irritable thoughts hung, unspoken, with the smoke in the air: Had he not himself just expended valuable time in offering me "guidance"? What need had I of more? He sniffed, then waved his cigarette dismissively at me, turning his attention to the documents on his desk. I crept from the audience, secretly exulting.

Two nights later I was back in my own bedroom. When Maude came in, she was wearing a cotton nightie, Empire in style, her delightful bosom outlined in pink satin ribbons that gathered in a small rosette at the center of the low-cut neckline. For my part, I was sitting up on the bed, starkers, but for my new biretta tilted at a rakish angle on my head. At first, she gasped, but then she put both her hands over her mouth to muffle her laughter. Still, she would not come to bed until I had taken it off. Her faith was played on a field where the goalposts were never settled in a single place. But those were ancient times. It is difficult to convey today the danger that we ran. And so, even now, my mind returns to it. Besides, old men repeat themselves. I repeat, then: what we were engaged in was worse than a sin; if it had become public knowledge, it would have been a major scandal, confusing the faithful even as it delighted the Protestants. Most probably, open scandal would have been avoided. The matter would have been hushed up. I would have been sent off, as I have said, to some remote retreat, there to do penance and to be straightened out. Maude would have been paid off in some fashion, bribed into silence by money or fear or both.

Ironically, the Western world's view of the Catholic Church, both within and without, had been molded in that far-off time—as I believe a scholar has recently argued about the twentieth-century American's sense of himself, his history and his values—by the immigrant Jews of Hollywood, the moguls of celluloid. If you were a "man of the cloth" in those years, you were almost certainly a Catholic priest. If the film was set in America, you were either Irish or Mexican. The Irish priest might be something of a leprechaun, canny, comical, his eyes atwinkle, spreading cheer, solving problems, finding fundamental good even in sinners. If he was a manly fellow, he might be good at boxing, winning delinquent boys' admiration and wooing them off the mean streets and into his gym. The Mexican priest, on the other hand, was motivated by his concern for the wretched of the earth and placed his own body between the cringing peon and the tyrant's wrath. He was apt to die a martyr's death.

But what the Catholic priest most certainly did not possess in that halcyon time was a cock.

Nowadays, of course, he possesses rather too much. So common has it become to read of priests running off with their female parishioners, single or married, of priests tried before judges and juries, found guilty, and imprisoned for sexually abusing children, boys usually but sometimes girls, that the layman may be forgiven if he begins to wonder whether the anticlerical pornography of revolutionary France had some basis in fact.

What would have been a major scandal when Maude and I, still young, were most besotted with each other today would scarcely raise an eyebrow. Only my friend the major, like many an atheist a true believer, dines with a hearty appetite on reports of the Church's wrongdoings.

᠙

Good grief, the major! How I have digressed!

᠙

Dressed, as I have said, in my cassock and biretta, I knocked at the door of Benghazi. I knocked again, then again. No one came to let me in. The door, when I tried it, was locked. I put my ear to its polished surface. Silence. Where was the romantically named Belinda Scudamour, the major's nurse, the squeezable, jolly young lady who now "did" for him? Her evening off? But perhaps I could get in through the scullery. As I made my way past the living-room windows, I peered in. There was dear old W.C., frailer than ever, hunched forward in his favorite chair and rubbing his hands together before an empty grate. Between his chair and the one I would soon occupy was his chess table, the chess pieces already in place. (It was our rule that the visitor begin with white.)

I rapped sharply on the glass. W.C., oblivious, leaned back in his chair and weakly waved a finger to and fro. It was then that I saw his earphones. Of course. He must be listening to opera. He had told me only last week that he thought Belinda not too keen on opera. "What's that screeching?" she had once said, placing his tiffin before him. "'That screeching,' old chum, was the divine Regina Resnik singing *'Chanson bohème'* from *Carmen.* Still, she's a cheerful, willing sort, is Belinda. She must be permitted her cultural ignorance." So the dear man was wearing earphones to spare a young lady the miseries of operatic screeching.

I made my way around the cottage and through the unlocked scullery door. Once inside, I paused to allow my eyes to adjust to the dimness. Twilight was rapidly giving way to night. Outside, above the lawn, a bat twittered and whistled and flew in demented circles. The scullery was tiny, little more than an anteroom to the small kitchen beyond, from which, I now became aware, curious sounds were emerging, groans and gasps and small shrieks, as of one in the throes of the most severe abdominal cramps.

I made my way quickly to the kitchen door, which stood ajar, and peeped in. All I could see in the near-darkness were two figures struggling in the vicinity of what I knew to be the kitchen table, one of the figures, I sensed rather than saw, a woman. Belinda was being attacked! But what could a man crippled by age and bunions do to help her? I would turn on the light, startle her . assailant, stand before him in the glory of my priestly vestments, perhaps thrust toward him my heavy Cross with its twisted Jesus, intone a few words in Latin.

I reached for the switch beside the door and flipped it on. *"Lux et veritas,"* I said severely. What I saw, though, made me turn off the light as quickly as I had put it on. "Sorry," I said. "So sorry. Excuse me. Just passing through." And I fled across the kitchen and into the living room, hopping on my poor bunions, closing the door decisively behind me.

What I had seen in that brief flash of light was an extraordinary *tableau vivant,* one that has imprinted itself in my brain like a fixed photograph, inexpungible. There, balanced daringly on her coccyx at the edge of the kitchen table, her shapely legs aloft and resting on the shoulders of Tubby Whiting, her arms encircling the constable's neck, was Belinda Scudamour. Her skirts were around her waist. Tubby stood between her legs, his hands clutching her breasts. His policeman's trousers girdled his ankles; his membrum virile was, so to speak, invaginated. In brief, I had caught them at it. On Tubby's face was a look of comic horror. Belinda's brow was beaded with perspiration. Her blue eyes stared wildly at me. Her upper teeth had captured her lower lip, perhaps to muffle a scream, perhaps to suppress laughter. At the other end of the table, somewhat forlornly, stood Tubby's helmet.

Well, I never! Such goings-on! And thus we see, as the Bard so feelingly puts it, how the world wags.

The major, meanwhile, had fallen asleep. I sat for a few minutes, silently, in the chair prepared for me, collecting myself. Old as I am, I must say that the scene I had just witnessed stirred me, not out of absolute lust, you understand, but out of warm, sadly ineffectual memory—and hence, perhaps, a little out of envy. Poor Maude, who desperately needs a hip replacement, the NHS willing! Poor me, who can no longer stand to, not like Tubby, at any rate, not up against the kitchen table! *Lacrimae rerum,* and all that. *Où sont les neiges d'antan,* eh? Never mind, never mind.

I sat and stared at the major. He was still wearing his earphones. How vulnerable he looked, how old age had in recent months reduced him! Thanks to Angie Mackletwist, who dropped in on him once a fortnight, his white hair and military mustache were neatly clipped. But his face had grown painfully narrow and long, its skin crosshatched and desiccated. His head lolled against the wing of his chair as if the thin stalk of his scraggy neck were not strong enough to support it. His upper teeth had slipped a little, producing a death's-head grin. From the corner of his mouth issued weak, bubbly snores. He was dressed like an army officer in civvies: a knotted silk scarf tucked neatly into the open neck of a cream-colored, small-checked shirt, an old tweed jacket with leather patches at the elbows and leather strips at the cuffs, well-worn corduroy trousers, brown leather desert boots. But alas, his clothes were now too big for him.

"Major," I said, and then more loudly, "Major!" I reached over and touched his knee.

He opened his eyes quite suddenly, his gnarled and spotted fingers crawling along the armrests of his chair until they grasped their ends like talons. "Where were we?" he said. "My move, what?" He leaned toward the board, saw the chess pieces still in their initial positions. "I must have dropped off. Dreadfully sorry. How long have you been here?"

"Not long. Perhaps five minutes."

He looked at me, puzzled. "Can't hear a word you say. Lips moving, but no sound. Have to speak up, old man. Think my damned hearing's going, like everything else."

I mimed the removal of earphones.

"Aha!" He removed them, grinning almost boyishly. "Well done, Edmond. Full marks for alertness." He pointed at my head. "Two kinds of men in the world, just two. Those who wear funny hats and those who don't."

I had completely forgotten about my biretta. "There are two kinds of men in the world. Those who divide everything into two and those who don't." I got up and placed my biretta squarely on the head of a bust of Voltaire, which stood on the sideboard beneath the window. "Serves the old atheist right." I sat down again.

"What would you say to a drink, Father?" W.C. picked up a small silver bell from the floor beside his chair and rang it sharply. "Wedding present, I think. Imogen left it behind when she ran off. Ludicrous little item, actually. Still, comes in useful nowadays, eh?"

Belinda entered with such promptness she might have been waiting patiently outside the door for his summons. There was not the least hint in her appearance and manner of her recent activity. She was carrying a small tray on which stood the whiskey decanter, two tumblers, and a pitcher of water. "Good evening, Father. I didn't hear you come in."

I pointed to my feet. "Trainers."

She put the tray down on a small table just out of comfortable reach. "I'll pour you your first ones. After that it's up to the two of you. Just so you know, Father, for Major Catchpole, it's one part whiskey, three parts water. Doctor's orders." She gave each of us a modest measure of whiskey, holding the major's tumbler up to eye level as she diluted it. "How's Father Bastien?"

I nodded.

"And Maude?"

"Well. Both well."

"Tell them I asked after them." She stood now behind W.C.'s chair, where he could not see her, winked at me, grinned, and put an exquisitely slender finger to her lips. "I shall be gone for two hours or so. When you wicked men have had enough of that horrid poison and want some nice tea and biscuits, you'll find it all waiting for you in the kitchen. You've only to boil the water." She paused for a moment at the door. "And may the better man win."

"Not bad, eh?" said W.C., meaning Belinda's lusciousness, not her grammatical acuity. "There was nothing like that about when I was young, more's the pity. Envy the chap who's shagging her." He chugalugged his diluted drink and thrust his empty tumbler toward me. "Bloody piss," he said. "Here, Edmond, you're closer. Get me a real drink, there's a good fellow."

"But the doctor—"

"Bollocks to the doctor!" His grin for a split second revealed the young man lurking within this wizened exterior. "Saving Your Reverence, of course."

I poured him a stiff drink.

"Mud in your eye," he said.

"Cheers."

We sipped in companionable silence for a while.

"Your bish is even more of an ass than I supposed." W.C. twitched the corners of his lips, repressing amusement.

"Bishop McGonagle is a devout Christian and an able admin-

istrator, if as yet no obvious candidate for sainthood. It does you
no credit, W.C., to speak ill of him."

"Bollocks to that, too," he said.

"What's the poor man done to offend you?"

"Bugger all," he said, and grinned slyly. "No pun intended, of
course. He can't offend me. I don't give a pig's fart for him. But he
collapses faith into farce. It's you who should be offended. I heard
his latest on the wireless this afternoon. Thinks he's invulnerable,
soppy arse. Superman has nothing on him. No need to dodge bullets. Convinced that the Lord has some special, as yet unrevealed
mission for him. Until he fulfills it, he can't be touched. And this
truth manifested itself, mind you, on the golf course!"

"No doubt he was talking of Providence. Free will is no con-
tradiction of Providence. The Lord has a plan for each of us. As
old Lear says, 'The ripeness is all.'"

"Oh, stuff it, Edmond. It's got nothing to do with that musty
old paradox." He thrust his empty tumbler at me once more and
eyed mine. "Top us up, all right?"

I did his bidding.

He was right, of course. McGonagle is an ass—and to me,
thanks to the interfering Twombly, potentially a dangerous one.

"You know your bish is a keen golfer, I suppose? Member of
CAGE? Clerical Association of Golfing Enthusiasts? Well, their
annual competition began this morning at a course near Culloden,
a mile or two from the Moray Firth. Began and ended, I should
say." W.C. took a swig of whiskey, swished it around his mouth
appreciatively, and then swallowed. "No sooner had McGonagle
arrived at the fifth green than the heavens opened up, a second
deluge, water, water, everywhere. Well, you can see why the heavens were pissed. All those dog collars, each with a direct line to the
Almighty, each praying for personal victory! Confusion on the
highest level. *Sturm und Drang*, don't y'know."

"I don't quite see how this makes the bishop an ass, a soppy
arse, or an arsehole." I savored the words, enjoying the freedom

afforded me by quotation to apply them, in seeming denial, to the bishop.

"Wait for it. The officials sounded the siren that was supposed to clear the course. It was so dark you could scarcely tell your niblick from your mashie. Everyone but McGonagle ran for the clubhouse. McGonagle putted out and opened his umbrella. A bolt of lightning struck the tip, and the shock so jangled his arm that he dropped the umbrella and dashed for the shelter of a tree. Within minutes another bolt struck the tree, splitting it and throwing McGonagle onto his knees in the mud. You'd've thought he'd have the message by then. Not a bit of it. Pulled himself to his feet and slogged on, finishing the course at the eighteenth—'a very gallant gentleman,' as the wireless wallah fatuously put it. Claimed to have his best score ever, seventy-two, despite the sheets of driving rain, the poor visibility, the thunder and lightning, but of course he had no witnesses, and besides, the competition had been canceled. Then the wireless fellow asked him whether he would like to tell us what the experience had meant to him. 'My faith has been much strengthened,' he said. 'It's clear enough that He's looking out for me. I believe that He must have some special purpose for me in this life.' Now tell me, Edmond, is this man an arsehole, or is he perhaps an arsehole?"

"I can only marvel at the miracle of his deliverance," I said pacifically—in character, as always, for the major. "And I'm prompted to offer up thanks for it."

He eyed me keenly for a moment before finding in my words the meaning he evidently wanted to find there. "You're a sly old dog, Father Music, a sly old dog. I'm ashamed sometimes to acknowledge you my friend." He chuckled and pointed to the decanter. "Come, let's drink to friendship."

∿

We played no chess that night. The major got quietly and decently squiffy. I made no attempt to match him drink for drink, not caring to lose control of my tongue. There was no point, I soon saw, in telling my problems to the major. How could I ask that man of integrity to advise me in the covering up of a crime? Besides, I would only diminish Maude in his eyes, and perhaps myself, an outcome I could not bear to contemplate. I walked back to Beale Hall slowly, relying on the bright moon to mark my way, and found that Maude had stayed up for me. I stood at the open door of the Music Room and looked at the elderly, dumpy woman with her thin, flaming-red hair, her rouged cheeks, and her bloodred, manicured fingernails. She turned her head this way and that, comically striving for naturalness, willing me to notice and comment on the wonders that Angie Mackletwist had wrought. I could not disappoint her.

"You are beautiful, Maude, truly beautiful—no less so than when I first fell in love with you. And how splendid your hair looks! 'Lustrous,' 'rich,' as they say on the telly. Is the style new? There's something different about it. What can it be?"

She smiled modestly. "The fringe."

"Of course, the fringe. That's it."

Her own eyes bloodshot and teary, she looked at me critically where I stood in the doorway. "Have you and W.C. been drinking?"

"A bit."

"You're slouching, Edmond. You used to have such a lovely straight back."

I tried to straighten myself but succeeded only in tottering backward a step or two. "Whoops!" I said, giggling foolishly for her benefit and ending with a nicely contrived hiccup.

And so we played our game. Maude does not care to have me drinking, for she remembers the violent sot her father was and what became of him. Men are susceptible, she knows. As for herself, a drop now and then did her no harm, whether as a social courtesy in the company of others or as a pick-me-up at the end of a tiring day. She rewarded me now with a sniff of disapproval and a bitter laugh. "The cassock and that biretta! On you, they're a joke, a mockery of better men who've proudly worn them, holy men among them. You spend too much time with the major. He means no harm, but his influence is wicked. And please don't wear that costume again. I don't think it suits you anymore."

She's right. I don't think it suits me either. But I nevertheless recognized the liquor talking, not Maude, for after half a bottle or so she becomes irritable. I wondered how much she had knocked back that evening, with and after Angie.

Still and all, something has happened between Maude and me, something has driven a wedge between us. But what? And when did it happen? We live together like a married couple who have long since agreed to live separate lives, maintaining only for public show a convivial mutuality. (Even in this formulation, the complexity of our lives together is manifest. After all, the public show has always been the aseptic one of priest and housekeeper, where distant agreeableness is easy to manage. It is only really in the private show, if I may so term it, that our loss of mutuality is manifest.) And yet we still love each other. At least, I think we do.

She has not lost the intelligence and wit that, along with her beauty, first drew me to her, bound me to her, let me admit, with hoops of steel. But at some point (when, precisely, and, more important, why?) she took upon herself the role of an uneducated, superstitious, plebeian Irishwoman, a gross caricature such as once appeared in nineteenth-century *Punch* cartoons or in provincial Christmas pantos. I suspect that she plays the role for me alone.

Certainly, her mind cannot have atrophied. She still manages Beale Hall, no small task with its myriad duties, the great house itself, the grounds, the converted stable block, the mundane needs of the visiting scholars, the small army of employees, some daily, some brought in when needed. Her office is behind the old kitchen, a spacious room that once was the butler's pantry. There she is to be found on most weekdays between the hours of 8 A.M. and 1 P.M.; sometimes she puts in full days, holding court in matters of employee disgruntlement or dispute, say, or when accounts are due, or when Bastien and I need help in preparing quarterly or annual reports for the board. In all these tasks, she works with efficiency and dispatch, intelligence and wit.

It is only in her dealings with me—when she is being, so to speak, "herself"—that she plays the foolish old woman, her chosen role. It is almost more than I can bear. I think sometimes that I am going mad. Perhaps that's why she does it.

Of late, she has been writing her memoirs, chapter by chapter, but she won't vouchsafe me even a glimpse. She told me of the undertaking one wobbly evening after she had exhausted her supply of gin and had begun on the cognac. But she bridled when I asked if I might see a passage or two. "It is no affair of yours," she said, and sniffed in disdain. "You're not even in it." As for the theft she made to secure her future, it has proved unnecessary. For the last several years, Maude has been accumulating a sizable sum of money, the income from a series of romances, bodice rippers, all still in print. She writes under the names of Penelope Traherne for Melmoth Press and Lorna Devereux for Ardor Books. She is exceedingly modest about her work and will not talk about it, not to me, certainly. She taps busily away at her old Olympia portable behind the locked door of her office; no novel of hers is to be found at Beale Hall, not officially, at any rate. I have read them all, buying my copies on the sly. But her success may be judged from her bank balance and her portfolio of investments.

I would date the change in her to the menopause, not to its onset, the fearsome mood swings, the colds and heats that filled her veins, the physical and mental aches, the sense that she no longer had a purpose as a woman, whether in her ability to attract a male or to bring forth a child, but to its establishment, to the total disappearance of a monthly flow. Some women fight the ineluctable march of time, devoting their remaining years, energy, and wealth to reversing (or attempting to reverse) its effects, pursuing fleeing youth to the cosmetics counter and the surgeon's table. Maude was one of those who give up, who "let themselves go." Her one remaining vanity was her hair, so glorious in her youth and in her young womanhood, so much a part of her self-definition. Hence Angie Mackletwist. But giving up, growing fat, and the rest did not bring with it relief. To the contrary. Maude, I think, had come to despise herself as a barren woman, one whose barrenness was not the curse of nature but the curse of God. And I was a cause in her punishment, I, a so-called priest, who for his own lewd satisfaction had perverted a God-given libido intended for the chaste bringing forth of children within the sacrament of marriage. And so her giving up was translated into her revenge on me. Her body she allowed to become slack and unsightly because it was the body alongside which *I* must lie. Her wit and her intellect, in which I had so much delighted, were to disappear, at least in my presence; I was to be mocked by a bubble-brain.

But for all that, I do not believe Maude hates me. We are Francesca da Rimini and Paolo grown old; we must be punished for our sins. The fire of our first passion has long since burned out. She thinks it right that we swallow the cold ashes.

ᘓ

I must change the mood. Let's talk about sex. The priestly vestments Maude wants me to discard served a useful purpose, I must say, early in my career, fig leaves to cover a frequently burgeoning embarrassment. I was then in my parish in South Kensington, at L'Église des Heureuses Martyres Sanglantes in Belvoir Street, just off the Old Brompton Road. I say "my parish," but in fact I was a mere dogsbody for the then incumbent, one Father Zbigniew Kalabinski, a stout Pole with a lecherous gap between his teeth, an insatiable appetite for beet soup and kielbasa, and violently repellent breath, who left to me such undesirable tasks as early-morning Mass, hospital visits to the impoverished among his parishioners, and creative accounting in the matter of an astonishing sacramental-wine consumption. At any rate, imagine the effect upon a young

priest who, when trying to administer the host, sees before him on
her knees a desirable woman, her eyes closed, her mouth open
receptively, her head tilted just so, all at the approximate height of
his inevitably swelling Scallywag, his fiercely independent Cock
Robin. Imagine that effect multiplied when the senior class of
St. Bridget's queue up to drop thus invitingly before our young
priest, nubile creatures all. He would be glad enough then for his
all-concealing skirts, I can assure you.

I read what I have written above and think to strike it out, not
because it is false or shames me as one who is less than human, but
because its intended purpose, to strike a lighter tone, fails. What it
shows is that I, like Maude, am "letting myself go." Be as digusted
as you want, the passage says, I deserve it. Well, to hell with that!
Like Othello, whose condition as the Other in Venice and Cyprus
accords well with my own in the Church—without, in my case, the
attendant heroism—I ask only that you "speak of me as I am.
Nothing extenuate, nor set down aught in malice." I know that
among those, especially the young, who place the host upon a
tempting tongue, I was not alone. Let the passage stand.

⌒𝔔⌒

Here is a tale of the Pish told by Rabbi Alisdair Klatzkin of West
Hampstead, who as a young man was present at the Beth ha-
Midrash in Ludlow. It was the evening of Yom Kippur, moments
before Kol Nidre, and the congregation waited for the Pish to pray.
He rose to his feet, but he did not begin. What was wrong? The
congregation murmured in distress.

> But then the Pish looked out of the window and saw, walking
> past the Beth ha-Midrash, an elderly priest, one of those
> whom gentiles call "a man of God." The Pish went out to
> him, and they began to talk. The priest quickly understood
> that he was talking to no ordinary man. So engrossed were

they in their conversation that they found themselves as if by magic at a large inn, which was the goal of the priest's journey. Of course, the Pish could not enter, especially on Yom Kippur. The two men stood outside and continued their conversation. The Pish asked the priest why he did not take a wife. *The Lord,* he said, *did not create the world in a chaos; He formed it to be inhabited* (Isaiah 45:18). The priest explained that he was not permitted to marry. "Well, then, leave the priesthood," said the Pish. "You're old now. Perform the mitzvah of propagation before you die. *Be fertile, then, and increase; abound on the earth and increase on it"* (Genesis 9:7; cf. 1:28). The priest said he was descended of a respectable family. Even if he wished to, he could not marry beneath him. And besides, who at his own social level would marry an old man who had taken such unequivocal vows? "The Lady Una," said the Pish, "who is the daughter of Sir Thomas Cuny. Do you know her?" The priest said he did not, for he was merely a visitor newly arrived in the neighborhood and had yet to meet the local gentry. So then the Pish described the woman Una in great detail, his voice seeming to caress especially those parts of the female form that most lure the student from his study. So vivid was the image of loveliness that the Pish shaped out of words in the air that the priest had an accidental emission. Immediately, the Pish returned to the Beth ha-Midrash and began to pray Kol Nidre.

Afterward, his followers came to him and he explained what had just occurred. He told them that there had been a blockage in heaven, preventing the ascent of prayers to the Most High, blessed be He. The reason for the blockage was this priest, who had never spent his seed, even unwittingly in his sleep. With the help of the Most Merciful, blessed be He, the Pish had been able to dissolve the blockage by bringing about the accidental emission. The heavens resounded with shouts of joy.

"But, Rabbi, how could you know that he had an accidental emission?"

"When it became impossible for me to stand near him, on that instant I knew."

And Rabbi Klatzkin said in wonder: *"Aaron shall put all the transgressions of the Israelites upon the head of a goat, and it shall be sent off to the wilderness through a designated man"* (Leviticus 16:21).

In what by now are decades of relative ease, I have become rather too lax, rather too soft and vulnerable. It behooves me to defend myself, to gird my loins, to man the battlements, and so forth, for in the sky at the horizon I behold a little cloud, at present no bigger than a man's hand. Vigilance, vigilance. The hour cometh and now is. Bastien, too, must be reined in. Last night, W.C., his mouth twitching with seeming mirth, alluded to Pax Tecum!, warning me thereby that I might be attacked from any direction.

Let me explain. Pax Tecum! started innocently enough. A parishioner, so to speak—a gypsy, a middle-aged woman of the easiest virtue, whose passionate favors Bastien had twice or thrice enjoyed—had departed the district for her native Ballymena, county Antrim, but not before expressing her regret that he would no longer be able to hear her confession. (She got off, probably, less from the humdrum physical act than from telling Bastien her sexual fantasies.) Bastien, of course, confessed his venial sin to me. And as for me, I enjoyed our sessions in the confessional, I suspect, almost as much as the country copulatives enjoyed their sessions in bed. Such tricks hath strong imagination, as the poet says.

"Well," I told him jokingly, "if she'll miss you so much, you should tell her to phone her confession in." Believe it or not, she did. And ere long, so did some of her friends. Word spread. Bastien was receiving calls from both sides of the Irish Sea. Dear old Bastien. He is, I suppose, like Chaucer's Friar, "an esy man to yive penaunce." It suddenly occurred to him, as it had long before to the jovial Friar, that there was money in this, "a good pitaunce." Bastien has never lost his peasant shrewdness, you know. And so was born Pax Tecum! his premium-charge telephone ministry.

In the ensuing years, Pax Tecum! made money, not much, as money is reckoned nowadays, but enough to keep Bastien in Gauloises, enough to stuff the poor box and buy votive candles, enough to provide a modest dowry for his niece, his sister's child, in Artois.

But rumors are beginning to be heard not only in the environs of Beale and neighboring Ludlow but, according to W.C., may have already reached distant Shrewsbury and Kidderminster, rumors of a priest who claims to have a direct telephone line to God and who is bilking the credulous with a "dial-a-confession" gimmick. These rumors are circulating, if that is not too strong a word, only among Protestants at the moment, who reportedly express amusement at new evidence of Roman ignorance and superstition. But the vicar of St. Botolph's in nearby Dimthorpe Abbas referred sneeringly in his sermon last Sunday to "Roman travesties of faith," the "easy and conscienceless" acceptance of commercial technology, as illustrated by "our very good friends at Beale Hall." Luckily, the vicar addressed only three worshipers that day, his wife, his mistress, and his mistress's husband, the verger. On the other hand, the verger works for the *Kidderminster Guardian*. Still, his post is merely that of advertising manager. But the danger of newspaper interference is too great. All that's required is an ironical word at the tea trolley and, as the British once said, Bob's your uncle.

I considered only briefly engaging in a counteroffensive. "Our very good friend" at St. Botolph's, after all, is, with his shameless mistress, not himself the finest example of moral rectitude. I say nothing of his scandalous predecessor, who made frequent visits to the Tassel and Feather Club in Soho's well-named Dean Street, where he met Bella Cosabella, an artiste or *sui ipsius nudator,* also known as Joanie Dixon. Within five years he had left his wife and three children, his living, and his Church, fetching up in Luton, where he and Bella started a poodle-clipping business.

But alas, I am too old and tired to enter the arena. Besides, I would only draw to myself additional fire from Bishop McGonagle and Twombly, his wretched toady. No, I must order Bastien to cancel his telephone service, and quickly.

Pox take 'em!

⌒⌒

I sometimes think that, as a Catholic, I am more comfortable in England than in my native France, and for the very reason that I know what it is to be a Jew. That is to say, England, a formally Protestant but increasingly irreligious country, views Jew and Catholic with equal suspicion. Both are outsiders, unable thoroughly to merge with the majority. Both seem enigmas, probably up to no good, perhaps owing primary allegiance elsewhere. In France, the Jew is despised, in brief; it is to this day a land half in the darkness cast by the shadow of poor, wronged Dreyfus. In England, the word "despised" is too strong; what most Englishmen feel is a mild distaste, a distaste which they bestow indifferently on Jew and Catholic alike. For a Jew from France, English evenhandedness is a refreshing change. For a Jew in the trappings of Catholicism, it is a blessed relief.

If, as the old (Jewish) joke goes, an anti-Semite is one who dislikes the Jews more than is strictly necessary, the Englishman tends to stay within the appropriate bounds.

But what becomes of a Catholic Jew in the land of Israel?

I became an orphan in the spring of 1942, as I have told you. My mother had followed her heart to Paris and betrayal; my father had disappeared into the ZNO, from which only one brief note emerged, the note urging my mother and me to follow him south to St-Pons. But whether he had ever tried again to reach us in

Orléans or had learned of his wife's fate or had shown concern for his son's, the pages of my (metaphorical until now) personal history yielded no clues. *"Pauvre enfant,"* said Madame Goupil, my Tante Louise, patting me on the head, *"pauvre p'tit gars."* Within a month she had me standing before abbé Dindan, my few belongings in a brown-paper parcel beneath my arm, my knees scrubbed clean, my hair clipped and glued down. Two days after that, I was in the orphanage.

Eventually, I went looking for him, for my father, I an unlikely Telemachus in search of an even less likely Odysseus. In the interim between saying farewell to Father Kalabinski in South Kensington and beginning my graduate studies in Paris, I traveled by train and bus to Béziers and St-Pons. Of my father there was no trace. I made what inquiries I could: the gendarmerie, the post office, the waiter at the local bistro, the proprietor of the gloomy bar in the minuscule Place de la Victoire. No one remembered Konrad Musič, no one had even heard of him. They did not warm to strangers in dusty, sun-blasted St-Pons; they viewed strangers with considerable suspicion. My father could not have spent a very happy time there. Only the madame of the local brothel listened to my tale with interest and sympathy. She put aside the book by Camus she had been reading—*L'Étranger,* I believe it was—and served me tea and a delicious, cream-filled pastry called *pet-de-nonne.* Alas, she could not help me either, but her compassionate nature prompted her to offer me either of her two girls for half price or, if I was as heroic as I looked, both eager beauties for the price of one.

I found my father long after I had ceased looking for him, quite by chance, and in Tel Aviv, of all places. It happened like this. The library at Beale Hall has three early copies of the complete Talmud, one printed in Ancona in 1534, another in Venice in 1538, and a third in Avignon in 1541. They had been acquired in 1778 by Sir Percival Beale, the collector of oddities and curiosities, and they had arrived in a single shipment along with a tiny, mummified merbaby, the giant toe of some ancient statue, a stoppered glass vial containing the actual tears of the BVM, and, of course, the infamous Beale whale's pizzle, suspended to this day from the chandelier of what had been Sir Percival's bedchamber. In 1963 the curators of the Tabakman Museum in Tel Aviv were planning an exhibition of Hebrew incunabula, and they invited me to Israel, all expenses paid, for preliminary discussions leading, they hoped, to the loan of the Beale Hall Talmuds. Of course, I accepted. Why not? I had never been to Israel.

I was put up at the Hotel Paradiso in Zamenhof Street, a street named after the inventor of Esperanto. Zamenhof Street began well enough, at Dizengoff Square, the Étoile of Tel Aviv, but, like Esperanto, it led nowhere. As for the Hotel Paradiso, it were better called Inferno. A narrow building squeezed between two faceless blocks of flats, it welcomed the sweltering August heat of Tel Aviv during the day and pitilessly circulated it throughout the night. I lay sleepless, naked, and miserable upon sweat-soaked sheets. On my first morning I bought myself what was then the native costume, khaki shorts, short-sleeved white shirt, sandals, and a khaki idiot hat, rather like Pinocchio's in the Disney film, and called a *kova tembl*. During my stay, I drank gallons of orange juice, iced coffee, and iced tea.

It is clear that I am putting off the telling of my encounter with my father. After all these years, I still find it difficult to contemplate. But how foolish! I am older now than he was then. In a somewhat different sense from what the poet Wordsworth had in mind, "the child is father of the man." What have I to fear? Very well, then. To it at once.

I had more or less concluded negotiations with my hosts at the Tabakman Museum, genial chaps all, three cultured Europeans complete with numbers on their wrists, and I still had three days remaining before my return to England. I thought I might hop over to Jerusalem, visit a few Christian sites, walk along the Via Dolorosa, see the Galilee, equip myself with the sort of pilgrim's viewpoint my bishop and other of my coreligionists might expect me to acquire. "Thou hast conquered, O pale Galilean, / The world has grown grey from thy breath." Well, maybe. There's not much actual gray in Mediterranean lands.

At any rate, I was pondering these matters on Friday afternoon, sitting at a table at the Café Vered in Dizengoff Street, "the main drag," as American Jews there call it. Dizengoff was crowded at this pre-Sabbath hour. Couples sauntered arm in arm, the old and the young; whole families promenaded back and forth, seeing and being seen; people greeted one another, hailed friends or acquaintances. The many cafés along the street were crowded, the tables spilling over with people in animated conversation, laughing, gesticulating. Despite what for me was still oppressive heat, the scene on Dizengoff was charged with jollity and excitement.

Two tables away from me sat an overweight man in a black suit and a black hat whose very posture suggested the deepest gloom. His elbows were on the table; his fists supported his pale face. From his lips hung a straw with which he made idle circles in the bottom of an empty glass. There was something about him I seemed to recognize, something familiar about the eyes, their expression of weary defeat. He looks, I thought, rather like my father—never supposing for a moment that he was. Still, so strong was the resemblance, I thought he might be a relative, a cousin, perhaps. Nothing venture, nothing gain. I walked over to his table. Slowly, he raised his red-rimmed eyes to me; slowly he lifted his cheeks from his fists, the straw now dangling from his lips in the empty air. He badly needed a shave.

I spoke to him in French. "Please excuse the intrusion," I said, "but are you by any chance related to Konrad Musič of Dunaharaszti?"

He narrowed his eyes suspiciously at me; the straw dropped from his lips and landed neatly in his glass. "Who wants to know?"

"I thought we might be relatives. My name is Edmond Musič,

or Music, nowadays. I myself was born in France, but my parents came from Hungary, from a town called Dunaharaszti." A look of sheer terror came over his face. He half rose from his seat and then fell back heavily into it. "Edmond? Oh, my God, oh, my God! I knew it! Didn't I always say? I knew it!" He lowered his head into his arms; his shoulders heaved; he sobbed.

So I had found him! I looked about me in some embarrassment, but no one was paying much attention to us. For all I knew, such scenes as this were common in Israel. I sat down opposite him. "It's all right, Father. It's all right." But was it all right? This was a major recognition scene, after all, the stuff of which romantic fiction is made. Still, what had I to do with this blubbering figure before me? It pains me to say so, it fills me with shame, but if at that moment I felt anything at all for my father, it was a certain distaste.

He lifted his head from his arms. "I couldn't come for you. There were spies everywhere. It wasn't my fault." His voice had quavered at first but it was now accusatory. "What did you want of me? What? I should walk into the arms of the Gestapo? It wasn't safe. What could I do?"

"I understand. Of course I understand. You mustn't apologize. No need, no need at all." I put out a comforting hand to his arm.

"Apologize? Who's apologizing?" He tore his arm away. "It was all *her* fault. If she hadn't gone off to Paris to play the whore, to indulge in what filthiness I cannot even imagine, we'd have all been together, safe, a family. But no, off she went, abandoning her child, her husband, her sacred duty. Well, she got what she deserved!" His head dropped once more to his arms, and his shoulders heaved.

I looked at him and saw what one sees squirming when one lifts a stone.

He raised his head, dry-eyed. "I registered her death at Yad Vashem, you know," he said matter-of-factly. "I filled out the form. It was the least I could do for her, the whore."

"She was my mother!"

"You've a better mother now."

For the life of me, I thought he meant our Holy Mother, the Church! "That may be," I said, "but why didn't you come looking for me *after* the war?"

"You've no idea what things were like then. Everything was upside-down, chaos, tumult. Everybody was looking for everybody. It was impossible." He looked at his watch. "You've a new brother, and a sister, too."

And then I understood. He had married again.

"I've got to go," he said. "It's Friday night. Come to dinner, meet your new family." He took a piece of paper from a wallet bulging with similar scraps and scribbled an address on it. "Take the number five bus right there." He pointed to a bus stop. "Ask the driver where to let you off. We've a lot to talk about." He got up. "For me," he said flatly, "this is a very happy day, a day, as Reb Nachman calls it, to remember. I hope for you too. Eight-thirty." He looked at me in my shorts and *kova tembl.* "Get dressed. It's shabbos." And off he lumbered, a Jewish Oliver Hardy, a clown, soon disappearing in the crowd.

What prompted me to go? Some imp of the perverse, no doubt. Having found my father, I wished only to lose him again. Better the father of memory, smoothed over, burnished, improved by the warm glow of nostalgia, than the father who had just now sat before me, wretched, self-pitying, unforgiving, callous, and all too real. And yet I went.

The address he had given me proved to be a four-story concrete block squatting on four concrete pillars, an ugly, utilitarian structure amid identical others. I had taken a taxi there, not the number 5 bus, and it was as well I had, for I would otherwise never have found it. I looked about me. There was no hint in the oncoming darkness that not far off the Mediterranean rolled, no sound, no sight whatever to tell me where I was, save for the ubiquitous sand that seeped up through the paving cracks and gathered at the margins of road.

The feeble light that had guided me to the third floor went out as I stood before my father's door. An argument was going on within. I could hear the shriek of a woman's voice, the guttural mumble of a man's. I knocked. Immediate silence. I knocked again. The door opened, flooding me with sudden light. Before me stood a little girl of perhaps six or seven, her face scrubbed to greet the Sabbath, a cast in one eye and teeth missing from her grin. She had obviously rehearsed what she intended to say, beginning with delight and ending with shock. "*Shabbat shalom,* Edmond." It was while she was saying this that she got a good look at me. It was what she saw that caused her to turn on her heel and run for another room, crying, "Abba, Abba, come quickly!"

My father had told me to dress for the Sabbath meal. The only formal wear I had with me was clerical, my black suit and dog collar. I could have bought a white shirt and worn it open-necked, I suppose; in fact, I should have done so. But I had put the dog collar on with a certain malicious satisfaction, hoping it might at the very least irritate him. After all those years, I still wanted my revenge. And what for? Surely I already understood that this weak, benighted man could not have done other than he did. The past is like a fly frozen in amber; we can view it, but we can't change it. For all I knew, he had long wished he had behaved differently. How else explain his unprovoked attack on me?

What I had not thought was that my dog collar might also upset others. A woman of perhaps forty peeked around the door through which the girl had fled. She was deeply tanned; her hair, frizzed and long, hung to her shoulders and framed her face. She too had a cast in her eye; and when she opened her mouth to speak, she revealed gold-capped canine teeth. "One moment, please. Stay where you are." A hand reached around the door and dangled from the knob a filigree chain holding a large, flat, circular eye.

Two could play at that game. From my pocket I took a plain silver Cross and hung it from my neck. From the next room came the woman's shrieks. Then I heard my father's voice. "Stop it, Nurit! Nothing will happen, he won't harm you or the children, you have my word. It's me he's after. Take Moshe and Daphna into the kitchen. Light the shabbos candles, do something useful."

By then I had moved into the small foyer and closed the front door behind me. My father stormed in to confront me, the veins at his temples throbbing, his finger pointing to denounce me. "*Apikoros!* How dare you defile a Jewish home with that Cross? Get out, I can't bear to look at you! I can't bear the shame! Have you forgotten already who taught the Nazis how to burn Jews? A lesson well learned that included putting your own mother in the oven? Never mind what she was, she was also a human being." He raised his eyes to the ceiling. "Tell me, God, what have I done, what have I done that you should punish me with this?" He intended, no doubt, to look and sound like an Old Testament prophet. But he was too plump, too soft, for the role; and his voice, like that of many a weak man, whined, when what he wanted was an angry snarl.

"Don't worry, I shan't stay. I'm on my way. Just remember, though, that it was you who invited me here. 'Meet your new family,' you said. Oh, yes: and remember, too, Father, it was you who agreed with Maman that I should be baptized."

"That was to save your life!" he screamed. "*Pikuach nefesh!* To save a life. It was for the time being, not forever."

From the next room came the sound of a slap and the wail of a child. My father's color was turning bright red; sweat beaded his brow. With his right fist he beat at his heart.

"Calm down," I said, alarmed. "I'm going."

He fought to control his breath. "Wicked, wicked!" He pounded his heart.

I reached blindly behind me for the doorknob. "See, I'm going."

"Nobody said you had to become a priest. Who told you that? Did I say that?" He dropped into a chair against the wall, this fat

man, this clown, my father, the weight of his descent causing the
floor beneath us to judder and a heavy glass mirror above him to
swing off true. "A Cross! He's wearing a Cross! In my house, my
son is wearing a Cross!" He laughed harshly, bitterly. "No son of
mine! Go back to your *goyim, apikoros!* Wallow like a *chazer,* like a
pig, in your treachery. Don't you know that Hitler has been dead
for almost twenty years? I thank God for it, I thank the Almighty,
baruch hu. And what does that mean for you, twenty years? I'll tell
you. It means you've had all that time to set things right, to turn
your back on this wickedness, this apostasy. 'If I forget thee, O
Jerusalem . . .' Look to your right hand, *apikoros*"—he pointed at
it, choking out his words—"it will shrivel up; it will wither away."
From where he sat, he reached for the amulet his wife had left
hanging on its chain. He held it, dangling, before me, his head
bowed, as if contemplating his knees, his shoulders bouncing
while he caught his breath.

The flat disk turned this way and that, recto and verso; on both
sides, the identical eye bore into me. I ran from my father's house.
I fled into the darkness. But I could not escape the eye.

ᕲ

The eye still follows me, although, after so many, many years, no
longer with quite so piercing a gaze. Hitler has been dead for more
than half a century now, so long, in fact, that for most of those
alive today who have at least heard of him he belongs in that
amorphous past that contains, higgledy-piggledy, the likes of
Genghis Khan, Napoleon, Caligula, Judge Jeffreys, and Grendel's
dam. The Jews remember him, of course, and they strive—we
strive?—to keep his crimes alive in the minds of non-Jews, an
uphill battle against the armies of Holocaust deniers and the
heavy artillery of time. From London, a young Jew can fly to
Poland nowadays for a quickie visit to Auschwitz, kosher box
lunch included. But even for the young Jew, I sometimes think,
Hitler has already taken his place in the mythic land of Pharaoh

and Titus, of Ferdinand and Isabella, of a conclave of popes and a knout of czars. I, of course, remember Hitler. And yet my father's question still rankles. Why did I not at the end of the war throw off the nonsense? My archenemy dead, why did I not cast off the disguise assumed only for my survival? And more to the point, why on earth did I take on another layer of disguise, the priesthood, when disguise was no longer needful?

I don't have the answers. Sometimes, I think that, like Macbeth crossing his river of blood, I had already stepped so far into the flood of Romanism, returning would have been "as tedious as [going] o'er." A good word that, "tedious," the precise word. It has an appropriately leaden sound, hinting at a yawn. The real horror of getting rather more than one's feet wet, for Macbeth and for me, is the ennui.

To accuse me of hypocrisy is too simple. It explains everything and explains nothing. Hypocrisy is a constant of the human condition, unavoidable, as necessary to our well-being as meat and drink. For me, the priesthood was a job, like any other. Which is to say, mostly it has been "tedious." Once in a while in the early days, I was caught up in the details or felt an intellectual challenge. Sometimes I even felt a species of excitement. But that was rare. What made it tolerable, I suppose, was (and is) the art and the music, but to enjoy these one need not be a priest. That is why, thanks to my darling Kiki, I got out of it as soon as I could, choosing administering here at Beale Hall and leaving ministering, whenever possible, to Bastien and our visiting brethren. By and large, what had early in my career seemed at the very least interesting turned out to be the very opposite. How long was I supposed to find satisfaction, like Socrates' Sophists, in making the worse appear the better case? I was soon burned out, unable to feel sympathy any more for the naïveté of those who *believed* the nonsense it was my task to have them believe. It was the children that bothered me most, the innocents upon whose backs I was to pile the mischief of centuries.

At the end of the second millennium, it is not easy to have faith in a benevolent, active God. In the West, in Western Europe at least, we think those who profess to possess it deluded or lacking a few pence in the pound. The tide is out for the Sea of Faith; nowadays, we can, with Matthew Arnold,

> only hear
> Its melancholy, long, withdrawing roar,
> Retreating, to the breath
> Of the night-wind, down to the vast edges drear
> And naked shingles of the world.

Paradoxically, the very recrudescence of fundamentalism in the world's major religions points to the diminution of faith, for the fundamentalist, in the view of the enlightened majority, is a kook and a menace, prepared to impose his vision of the godly life on the rest of us with all the coercive power of modern weaponry. (In America, I am given to understand, the reverse is true.)

Most of us who care about such things, I daresay, have long since effected a divorce between faith and God. God has become something of an embarrassment, a paper tiger, a bug with which to frighten babes. What we have faith in today is universal evil, a harsh faith suited to grown-ups. We look about us and we see a world riddled with evil, a world in which all power is corrupt and all humanity is debased. We know, moreover, that we can do nothing about any of it. Belief in universal evil saves us from despair. Once more, we are able to perceive a horizon of ultimate meaning. Ultimate meaning, after all, is what we as a species yearn for. With faith in universal, ineluctable evil, we recover something of what was lost to mankind with the disappearance of God from our daily lives. Grown up now, we can acknowledge that we live in the worst and most chaotic of times, that all is in pieces, all coherence gone, that Sod's Law, not God's Law, rules our lives, that hope is the cruelest of the many cruel jokes we are born to suffer. The only words in the New Testament that have the ring of authenticity, I sometimes think, are "My God, my God, why hast Thou forsaken me?" The ancients believed in four Ages—Gold, Silver, Bronze, and Iron. The world has long been in the Iron Age, and, as the poet Donne remarked, "it's rusty, too." What this new faith offers us is epistemological certainty; we feel in our bones that we possess the truth.

What I betrayed, therefore, was not the God of the Jews, not the ancient faith, but the Jews themselves, my own people. When, at first to save my life, I joined the enemy, hung the Cross about my neck, genuflected before painted idols, ingested and imbibed like a cannibal what I was told were the real body and blood of the Jew Jesus, I betrayed the six million, and the millions before them, and the many since. It doesn't matter that I believed none of it. The Jesuit principle of *reservatio mentalis* helps not a whit. I knew myself to be a traitor. That is why I still see the eye dangling from the chain held before me by my father.

∽

The Oedipus complex is, as I understand it, undergoing a revision nowadays, Freud's bourgeois Viennese interpretation of the myth being turned on its head. I saw a wonderful cartoon many years ago in *The New Yorker*, a magazine through whose pages I was idly leafing one afternoon, having arrived early at the Reform in Pall Mall, whither I had been invited, flatteringly, to address interested members on "Sir Percival Beale and the Rarest of the Rare." The cartoon showed an irate lady dragging a small boy from the office of a child psychiatrist. "Oedipus, Schmoedipus!" she is saying. "As long as he loves his mommy!" It now appears, however, that rather than kill his father, it was his "mommy" Oedipus thought he *really* wanted to kill. The point of the tragedy no longer is that he surrendered to unconscious desires and killed his father in order to roger his mother; no, his horror at incest is a species of displacement, a means of not confronting unbearable issues of childhood abandonment. For his mother Jocasta failed to succor him when he was crippled by his father and left on a mountain to die. We cannot hope to understand the meaning of Oedipus, the new wisdom has it, if we continue to think of the hero as Oedipal.

༄

Before leaving Israel, I took an Egged bus to Jerusalem, and from there a taxi to Yad Vashem, a Monument and a Name, atop Har Hazikaron, the Mount of Remembrance. In the Hall of Names, I found my mother's name. My reaction was as violent as it was unexpected. I doubled up, as if I had received a blow to the stomach, and fell to my knees. Twenty years had passed since my mother rose as motes of ash, dancing in the pitiless skies above Auschwitz. Twenty years, and until now her son had failed to mourn her. For me, she had been dead/not-dead, occupying a place between what the mind knows and the heart feels. But now I knew her dead, I knew it as a certainty, and the knowledge of it felled me. There, on the floor before her name, I took great gulps of air, I strove to breathe, and, breathing at last, rocked and keened.

Later, in the Hall of Remembrance, I sat for several hours, fasting, praying, meditating. What I was experiencing was a kind of dissociation, an alienation from the self. Who or what was I? I was a Jew, I was a Catholic priest, I was a child bereft of his mother. I was and was not Edmond Music.

The Jewish martyrs pointed skeletal fingers at me. "He has betrayed us, he has left us, he is one with Them."

"No," I answered them, "in my soul I remain free."

"Leave them, then. Why do you not leave them? Join us, come to us."

"But you are dead. How can I join you?"

"Die."

Perhaps I looked like a madman. A caretaker came up to me where I sat rocking, for all the world like an Orthodox Jew in the synagogue. He wore an orthopedic shoe with a sole at least a foot high. The clump-clump of his approach shook me from my daze. Beneath his left eye was a shocking disfigurement, a large, purple birthmark shaped like a spider.

"God doesn't want you to destroy yourself in sorrow," he said. He handed me a printed sheet. "Here. Say kaddish, and go home." I recited the kaddish and left.

Whom was I to thank for this intrusion? The caretaker, whose simple compassion had granted me status as a human being? Assuredly, not the God in whom I had never believed. Nevertheless, the caretaker had recalled me to life, even as the angel had comforted Elijah in the desert.

Part Four

Any activity after a meal, whether physical exercise or copulation or bathing or mental gymnastics, interferes with digestion.

—Moses Maimonides,
Treatise on Hemorrhoids

Deliver my soul, O Lord, from lying lips and a deceitful tongue.

—Psalms 120:2

I had not replaced my ancient Morris Minor and consequently was feeling a trifle housebound. It was not that I had anywhere in particular to go; it was that my old bones and my poor bunions made walking any decent distance painful. The major's cottage was about my limit. In fact, I had taken to wandering the corridors and many rooms of Beale Hall, seeing their wonders as if for the first time, sitting in each of them and looking about me. How fortunate I had been in Kiki!

The Morris Minor was a write-off. Even before it ran into the Stuart Oak, it had long since been without book value. Tubby dropped in to see me last week, ostensibly to tell me that "the boys at forensics" no longer suspected foul play, that Trevor had only himself to blame for driving at reckless speed a car whose brakes he knew to be faulty, and that Trevor's sister-in-law had been persuaded by her solicitors in Wigan not to pursue a losing case. In his concern, Tubby is reminiscent of the brave meerkat of the Kalahari, seemingly nature's true altruist, standing bolt upright, selflessly scanning the skies and the surrounding desert for hawks and other predators while his fellows scour safely for delicious scorpions and plump mice.

But, as naturalists now know, no meerkat stands on sentry duty before he has a full stomach. And even then, his altruism is suspect. As the first to spot danger, he is either the first down a bolt-hole or else the one most coolly able to disappear into the pandemonium his warning screams and whistles create.

Altruism, if it exists, is a human invention. But it probably doesn't exist.

Tubby had come to see me because he wanted to find out what, if anything, would follow upon his indiscretion with the lubricious Belinda on the kitchen table at Benghazi. This was not a subject that he could broach directly. I was at my desk in the Music Room. He stood at attention before me, his helmet secured beneath his left arm, and gazed fixedly above my head at the wonderful de Kuyk portrait of the Ba'al Shem of Ludlow.

"I've put in for promotion to sergeant, Father."

"That last infirmity of noble mind. Good for you, my dear fellow."

"The exam's next Saturday. Kidderminster. The town hall."

"Ah."

"I was never much of a lad for exams, Father. I'll not pretend otherwise. But surely the exam isn't everything, is it? There's my record on the force to consider. That should count for something. At least, as long as no one speaks ill of me."

"Why should anyone do that? You'll do brilliantly, Tubby. I've every faith in you."

He breathed in sharply and audibly through his nostrils. His chest expanded. "Tubby" he was most certainly not. There wasn't an unnecessary ounce of flesh on him. A fine-looking fellow he was, too. Like Paris, he might have been a shepherd upon Mount Ida.

"Stand at ease, I beg of you. I'm not your commanding officer."

Tubby placed first his helmet and then his fists on my desk, bumping aside my *memento mori*. He leaned toward me, his eyes no longer on the de Kuyk portrait. This meerkat was on the lookout for danger. "About the other night at the major's, Belinda is, well . . . what happened is . . . I mean, I wouldn't want you to think, Father, that—"

"The major and I spent a perfectly pleasant and utterly ordinary evening. Nothing happened that's worth a mention. As for

Miss Scudamour, well, Major Catchpole praised her highly, and, so far as I can see, he is lucky to have her looking after him."

Tubby, obviously relieved, stood up. In a gesture I had only read about but never seen—except on one of W.C.'s emancipated gnomes—he placed his finger alongside his nose and winked. "All's well, then," he said, grinning.

"If it ends well. Is there something you want to confess, Tubby, some ungainly gobbet your conscience cannot quite swallow? If so, I recommend you betake yourself to Father Bastien. As for me, I'm in a fierce mood and might require you to march on your knees to your exam in Kidderminster."

Tubby picked up his helmet, waved it at me in clumsy farewell, and turned for the door.

Can it be that such innocence still exists—even at such a time as this, when one utterly wretched, cruel, and cynical century ends and another, no doubt eager to prove worse, begins? Why, yes, it exists—if we understand "innocent" in its etymological sense of nonhurtful, noninjurious. Tubby may seem like a comic policeman from a Gilbert and Sullivan operetta, but he has his psychological complexities, I suppose. It is just that they are irrelevant to the world's concerns. The world will go on very well without knowing of him. A Tolstoy or, to step down a rung or two, an Updike might make something of him. But, failing such exalters of the commonplace, Tubby, like most of us, was born to be a supernumerary. And has the supernumerary an inner life? A foolish question. Of course he has. The trouble is, nobody cares.

～

Yesterday, just before lunch, Maude came to the Music Room.

"An unexpected pleasure," I said.

"Happy birthday! Many happy returns of the day!"

"It's not my birthday, as you very well know. What can you mean?"

"Let's pretend it is," she said, and she took me by the hand. "Come. Let's look out the window."

Maude has been staying out of my way of late, keeping to the old butler's pantry, where she has even been taking her meals. At night, she comes to bed only when she supposes me already asleep. It is a kindness in her. I recognize the signs. She has been "going cold turkey," trying once more to "dry out," to escape at last from "mother's ruin." At such times, she suffers cramps and fever; she becomes moody, irritable, and argumentative: she will blackly dispute the cost of a one-penny stamp. All this she wishes to spare me. But, meerkat that she is, she wishes also to spare herself my unbearable gestures of patient understanding. And if (or rather when) she falls once more from grace, she will be spared the open acknowledgment of failure.

Now, she stood beside me at the window, clear-eyed, holding my hand, transmitting her excitement. In the forecourt was a shiny black car. A wide blue ribbon ran around and under it, ending in a gigantic bow on the roof.

"What on earth is that?"

"It's a Rover 75, to be precise," she said gaily. "Apart from a seemly exterior of clerical black, it has a dove-gray leather interior and all mod cons. It is a car for the millennium, and, more importantly, it is yours."

"It must have cost a fortune!"

"And what of that? It's not as if we're wanting. There's plenty where that came from." She meant her savings from her writing and from a salary she had scarcely ever used, of course. Of the obscene sum Aristide had given her for the stolen book of poems she never spoke. "There's no need to worry, not about a thing." She looked at me with peculiar intensity. "I'm on top of things, I promise you. I'm watching out." She laughed, and poked me almost painfully in the ribs. "Is it to be the richest nobs in the cemetery we're after? You needed a car. There it is, down below."

I felt—I still feel—like a child surprised with a longed-for toy. "You mean it's really mine?"

"Let's take it for a spin." And she dropped the car keys into my hand.

There was, it seemed to me, something desperate in her mood, a devil-m'care attitude like that of the gambler who, after sustained losses, throws the dice on the table and turns away, his mind already tallying the complications of utter ruin.

Still, what a pleasure it is to drive without screech or rattle, without holding the gear stick in place lest it leap into neutral, a powerful car possessed of all mod cons! It was a revelation. We swooped through the countryside, heading, as if by instinct, for the Long Mynd.

It was to the moorland ridge of the Long Mynd that we used to cycle in the early years of our passion, abandoning our bikes and tramping the turf, devouring our cheese-and-tomato sandwiches atop a prehistoric barrow, gulping the tea from our thermos, heady with the delight of the windswept views, the glory of so miraculously cultivated a wilderness.

On one such excursion, Maude ran from me, downhill, through wildflowers and purple gorse, her arms aloft, her fists aimed at the roiling, threatening clouds, crying, "Alas! Alas! Is there no one will save me?"

I ran after her, caught her in my arms, and we fell laughing to the springy turf.

"Oh, sir, I am undone."

"Indeed, I hope so."

"Alas, you do me wrong."

"Give me but a moment, and I'll do you right."

And there we made love as the birds wheeled above us and the stark white sheep munched and baaed nearby.

(Was my command of the language as good as this even in those early times? I believe it was. Of *course* it was. Perhaps my accent was a little stronger then than now. But even Kiki had praised my command of English.)

"Are you my Heathcliff?" she whispered in my ear.

"A better man, I trust," I said.

"Ah, but," she said. "Every girl needs her Heathcliff."

The drive through the Long Mynd must have stirred similar memories in Maude. That night in bed she actually strove to arouse me. And because she was patient and skillful, to my astonished delight she succeeded. Ah, but then she tried to heave her bulk above me, stretching her leg to straddle me, seeking the position she had always most enjoyed—and collapsed on her side, poor soul, screaming in her pain. "Damn the hip! Damn and blast it! Oh, dear Christ, it hurts so!"

I held her in my arms, caressed her. "You'll have a new hip, Maude, my love. We'll soon have you dancing all the newest dances at the Palais in Ludlow. You'll see. The young chaps will be standing in line to lead you to the floor."

"There's an eighteen-month wait on the National Health, and rising." She sniffed. "As for the Palais, it closed down fifteen years ago."

"Who spoke of the National Health? Can you have forgotten already what you said to me? We're spending money now. You'll be a private patient in a room of your own. No waiting then. We'll get the top surgeon, the one who fixed the Queen Mum, why not? Why on earth didn't we think of it before?"

"Yes, we will, we will!" She reached for me and found me crestfallen. "Oh, Edmond, we wasted it!" And that set her off blubbering.

"There, there. Never mind. There'll be other times."

She sniffed. "Oh, to be sure," she said sarcastically.

All that my mind overheard was the sound of a door clanging shut. I held her until she fell asleep, her puffs and tiny snorts tickling the hair on my upper arm. For the entire day she seemed to have forgotten her self-imposed scatterbrain role. We had slipped, thanks to her effort, into our old ease. Is this the benefit of her sobriety? And will it last? Of course not. Only when I could bear the ache in my arm no longer did I shift her.

ᢙ

Twombly phoned this morning. He had been in London for a little over a week, he said, spending most of his time, of course, in the British Library, but some of it, he admitted, in the galleries and at the theater. "All work and no play, Edmond," he began to intone.

"Yes, quite," I said.

But he was not to be stopped. "Makes Jack a dull boy."

"Oh, jolly good!" I said. "Give me a second, I want to jot that down."

His tone changed. "While you're at it, you can jot this down, too, wise guy. I'm taking the bus from Victoria tomorrow morning. It arrives in Ludlow just after noon, twelve-oh-three or oh-four. I've only got the one valise—and my laptop, of course—but I could use a ride out to the Hall." The voice admitted a grain of politeness. "Hey, sorry for the short notice. Any takers at your end?"

Was I not the proud owner of a new Rover? "I'll come and get you myself."

"Great. We'll do lunch, maybe. My treat."

"No need."

"There's this place I remember, the end of Broad Street, near the Butter Cross. Know where I mean?"

"The G and T?"

"Could be," said Twombly doubtfully. "I'll know it when I see it."

"Noon at the bus station, then?"

"Give or take a couple of minutes. Oh, and thanks, S.J."

"My pleasure."

Damn, I say! Damn and blast him!

ᐖ

The de Kuyk portrait on the wall behind my desk captures the Pish in old age, long-haired, white-bearded, a circular fur hat upon his head. Still, his cheeks are rosy and his eyes are bright. The artist has captured the hint of a smile, the suggestion of the charm and deviltry that made the Ba'al Shem of Ludlow so charismatic a figure. In his right hand he holds a compass whose point pierces the sign for infinity—drawn on a sheet of papyrus draped over the edge of a Shakespeare first folio on the table beside him—at the place where the line crosses over itself. His left hand indicates a chart, affixed to the wall, of the ten kabbalistic *Sefirot*, the complex images of God in His process of creation; the Pish's forefinger points specifically to the second of these, *hochmah*, wisdom. The Pish looks directly at the viewer, and the smile I spoke of seems ironic.

The Library here at Beale Hall has all of Falsch's published and much of his unpublished writing, a fascinating collection, including a notebook, scribbled in his own hand, of his alchemical experiments. I mention this only as an indication of my desperation in the last weeks as the day of Twombly's arrival drew ever closer. For Falsch includes in his crabbed Hebrew lettering "an unfailing recipe for the transmutation of base metal into gold," which I set about transliterating. Yes, I actually thought to take some of the lead from the Hall's many roofs, not enough to cause real damage, and make gold of it. With that gold I would buy back the book Maude had foolishly sold to Popescu all those years ago. How I, in my feeble and hoary eld, was to clamber about on the rooftops and strip them of lead without doing grievous harm to myself was a problem I had not yet addressed:

The Only True and Infallible Method

Let him [who would create the Philosopher's Stone] first purify himself after the Seven Ways of Leon Ebreo of Padua, in order and omitting none. Then let him range before him upon a smooth and polished board of ash the following simples: one pound of white ammoniac salt, in which there is no spot of blackness; the whites of thirteen two-day-old hard boiled eggs, cut into the finest of particles; six scruples of inaqit; two pounds of quicksilver of the very best, pounded into a powder so fine that the merest zephyr might blow it away; two fintuqs of tarishu, no more and no less; and the pure white vinegar of Girona, as much as may be needed . . .

And so on and on through fifteen pages of instruction.

Judge if you will of my madness: I cursed my ignorance of Leon Ebreo of Padua and of his seven ways of purification; I all but wept when I could not discover the meaning of such substances as "inaqit" or "tarishu" or such quantities as a "fintuq." "The Only True and Infallible Method" was useless to me. And so I raged as though it might have otherwise been possible, perhaps in one of the garden sheds with the help of a gardener or two and the special knowledge of Bellamy, Ludlow's premier chemist, to transmute lead into gold!

~

What I forget about Twombly in the times between our meetings is the fact that he too has grown old. Somehow, I remember only the smooth, sleek, slightly balding fellow I knew in Paris in our student days, an athlete of a sort, hinting modestly then at his glory days of high-school basketball, lettered, it seems, and jogging in the Jardin du Luxembourg in those far-off years before jogging became an identifiable American disease. But what got off the bus at Ludlow was a man as old as I—not so fat, to be sure, perhaps even scrawny, a man a trifle bent with the weight of years, bald but for a skimpy fringe of white hair, his face deeply lined and seemingly powdered, his lips, still red, prissily pursed. Well, and why should he not grow old? The bastard was not, after all, the

Devil himself, not immune to the terrible depredations of time. Diabolic, perhaps, but like us one who had felt the ache between his shoulders. In short, he creaked with the accumulation of years and his breath was stale, even if he was far more spry than I.

"Nice car," said Twombly, strapping himself into the Rover and sniffing at its leathery smell. "New?"

"Not a week old yet."

"Lucky you."

The G and T was no more, gone the way of the Palais, no doubt, and Twombly could not find the restaurant he remembered so well.

"Never mind," he said. "Let's have something typically English. My treat, remember."

"A pub lunch?" I suggested.

"A fish-and-chippery. There's always one about somewhere."

We found Bless My Sole in an alley off the Market Square, perhaps twenty feet this side of the public urinals. The name and location augured ill. And in fact it was the worst kind of fish-and-chippery, one in which the stench of fried foods hung, almost visible, in the humid air. The fish, when it came, was bubbled o'er with fried but pale and still slimy batter; the chips were sodden; the weak tea in the discolored plastic mugs was already provided with milk and sugar.

"*Deo gratias,*" said Twombly without a trace of irony. He made the sign of the Cross and set to hungrily. I followed at a somewhat slower rate. "Come along, Edmond," he said. "Eat it while it's hot." His plate soon empty, he swilled tea in his mouth and swallowed with evident relish. "Not finishing those french fries?" His fork crossed the table and speared a few limp chips from my abandoned plate.

"We'll need to bathe right away and send our clothes to the cleaners, or we'll never be rid of the stench of this place," I said. "It clings, you know."

Twombly thrust his forearm at me and nodded toward his

sleeve, on which could be seen two small white spots. "Know what that is?" he said eagerly.

"Not semen, then? Whatever it is, I'm sure the cleaners will be able to get it out."

"Get it out?" he all but screamed. "Get it out? This jacket will never be cleaned, never again. What you're looking at, my boy . . ." He glanced about him suspiciously, as if Special Branch itself were perhaps listening in, and lowered his voice to a whisper. "What you're looking at is the Holy Father's saliva."

"The pope spat at you?"

"Don't be ridiculous, Edmond. You can't have forgotten I was in Rome before coming to London. I briefed you. I was attending a conference of American academics: 'Christ, the Millennium, and the Classroom.' His Holiness was gracious enough to grant us an audience. Oh, Edmond, if you could only know what it means to see him in the flesh, to hear his voice! His goodness was an emanation that filled the chamber, a halo that shimmered over us all. Every one of us felt touched by the compassionate fingers, so to speak, of his great soul. And then he condescended to walk among us, feeble of movement though he is, and his smile was a radiance, and he blessed us as he passed by. For a split second, he stood before me, and he was saying *'Pace'*—not to me alone, of course, but generally. And as he said that wonderful, wonderful word, the word *'Pace,'* two tiny drops of saliva flew from his lips to my sleeve. And here they are!"

"You are very fortunate," I said, recoiling a bit from the forearm he held demonstratively before me. I am not much of a one, you see, for dried spittle, even if it is the Holy Father's. "No wonder you won't have the jacket cleaned."

"One day, in the very next pontificate, I shouldn't wonder, this man will be beatified and soon proclaimed a saint. What I have here is a genuine relic, *in potentia* if not yet *in actu.* It will be venerated. I venerate it now. Is it not wonderful? Should I not rejoice? Have you no appetite, Edmond?" And the sanctified forearm descended, its clawing fingers scooping up a few more chips from my plate. He chewed them speculatively, a faraway look in his eye. In my conceit, he saw as if through a glass, darkly, long lines of the faithful, come from the four corners of the earth, eager only to fall to their knees and worship the sleeve of his black polyester jacket. The crippled would throw away their crutches, the blind would see; hosannas would rise to the empyrean. Then he wiped his greasy fingers and his prissy mouth fastidiously with the thin strip of paper the café provided for the purpose. "Well, old friend"— and he pointed to the bill the waitress had just brought, unasked, to our table—"your treat or mine?"

Do you begin to see what I mean about Twombly?

Not much is known about the early years of the Ba'al Shem, not even with certainty the year of his birth, although the available clues point to 1720. In fact, we only have his word for it that he was born in Dunaharaszti ("I dropped from my mother's womb in Dunaharaszti in the third week of the Great Freeze, when starving wolves roamed the Town Square. That was the Year of Ill-Fortune, the cursèd year when the ancient church of St. Stephen's succumbed to the flames and the innocent Jews were accused of incendiary wickedness . . ." [*Table-Talk*, 1768]). Well, in addition to his word, we have that of his embittered contemporary Jacob Emden, who denounced him as a Sabbatian heretic and a fraud and, in the vigorous, no-holds-barred religious polemics of the time, "the *Dummkopf* of Dunaharaszti." Besides, why should Falsch lie about such a thing? What glory attaches itself to birth in such a place? It is not exactly Paris, or Prague, or Vienna. It's not a manger, either.

He early became known as a magician and sorcerer, escaping burning for his shenanigans in Westphalia only through the interference of Oskar Leopold, Ritter von Schweindorf, whose sexual impotence Falsch had allegedly cured. Certainly, the old knight's young wife had brought forth a lusty boy-child with curly black hair and a humped little nose, an event provoking a local tavern poet to quip, *"Sein oder nicht sein? ist hier die Frage,"* a pun on the opening line of Hamlet's most famous soliloquy, for in German *sein* may mean either "to be" or "his." Falsch, according to the archbishop elector of Cologne, was leading astray the young wives and maidens of Christendom with his odious charms and philters, imperiling their immortal souls with a species of carnal Jewish diabolism. If he was prevented from burning Falsch, so be it. The Ritter and his cronies would one day face their God. But the archbishop elector could at least banish the Jew, and so banish him he did. In Cologne and throughout Westphalia and the Rhineland, Falsch tells us in his *Table-Talk,* the news of his banishment was met with a general (and especially female) moan.

From Cologne he made his way to Amsterdam in the Low Countries, where he seems to have put aside for a while his alchemical experiments and his delvings into what today would be called holistic medicine. In Amsterdam, instead, he immersed himself deeply in the sacred mysteries of kabbala, studying under the Kotziner Rebbe, Michal Itzhak ben Eli Zvi, also known as the Gaon of Kotzin. It was in Amsterdam, too, that he acquired the first of his three wives, Leah, the daughter of Menassah Halevi, a wealthy spice merchant with dealings in the New World. He seems genuinely to have loved Leah, she of the dark eyes and impudent breasts. Her death and that of their baby in childbirth sent him spinning downward into a depression from which, according to the Gaon and reported in *Table-Talk* by Falsch himself, he could hope to emerge only in the Holy Land, most likely in Safed but perhaps also in Jerusalem. The Kotziner Rebbe prevailed upon Falsch's father-in-law to underwrite a trip for the widower to Palestine. (In the service of completeness, I should note that a prewar English fascist, Neville fflyte-Dacres, suggested in *The International Jew and Racial Pollution: The Record in Europe* [Little England Press, 1937] that Falsch fled Amsterdam because eleven Aryan women attacked him with paternity suits.)

Falsch, in fact, curtailed his eastward pilgrimage in Alexandria, whose climate and cosmopolitanism appealed to him, and sojourned there for five years, a disciple of the great Arabic scholar Abu Ali ibn Osana ("Avisana"). It was with Avisana that he studied the medical works of Moses Maimonides, the renowned medieval philosopher and codifier of Jewish law, especially Maimonides' *Treatise on Cohabitation*, written at the request of a Syrian sultan.

Among the remedies for various kinds of sexual dysfunction noted in the *Treatise* was one that was to endear Falsch to Sir Percival Beale, who, in the spring of 1748, was in Egypt on one of his earliest searches for antiquities and curiosities. Sir Percival had heard from an English consul in Naples of a wonder-working "medical chappie" in Alexandria, "a dark-skinned, white-bearded heathen sitting on silken cushions"—"Feller can cure anything, my dear sir, from bleeding gums and poxy sweats to syrupy wounds and swollen goolies"—and once settled in the city sought an audience.

It is a measure of Falsch's charm that Avisana had come to regard his disciple as a favorite, if wayward, son, one whose intellectual brilliance outweighed his religious stubbornness and occasional peccadillos. At any rate, he thought to put a bit of business in his disciple's way, and sent Sir Percival to consult Falsch, whom he described as a master of the erotic arts. The record of this consultation is preserved in Falsch's own hand among a bundle of papers in the Beale Library that were, perhaps, to have formed part of an autobiography or a selective collection of memoirs.

"Not impotence, Doctor," Sir Percival told Falsch, "not that at all, d'you see? Can get it up all right, stands firm, the naughty fellow, at the drop of a hat—or should I say lift of a shift, eh what? Not bad that. 'Lift of a shift,' d'you see? Point is, I die too soon, expire in a rush, lose all my 'pearly liquid treasure,' as the poet says, usually before I can sheathe my sword. Wench lies panting.

'La, sir, what's to become of me? Alas, alas. Why do you tease me so?' No good, that. Terrible thing, d'you see? Can you help me, Doctor?"

Thanks to Maimonides, the answer was yes. But of course Falsch did not say so right away. Instead, he looked grave and stroked his beard. "Be so good, honored sir, as to show me the offending member."

"Reveal all?"

"Aye, sir."

"Ahem." Sir Percival unbuttoned his breeches, dropped the flap, and encouraged his member and its attachments to appear. "At rest now, d'you see?"

Falsch took a silver pointer from the low table beside him and with it lifted Sir Percival's flaccid penis, allowed it to fall, lifted it and let it fall once more. "Yes, honored sir, I believe I can help you. My fee is one thousand guineas. If you wish to remedy your misfortune, return one week from today with half of that sum. If not, it was for me in any case a great honor to meet you."

Sir Percival returned the following week.

Falsch handed him a flask containing an amber liquid. "Massage your cheeky fellow herewith for two hours before you approach the fortunate lady. Then wash him in warm water. He will remain upstanding for two hours before he releases his pulsating 'pearly liquid treasure' and for two hours after."

"And if the balm fails to work its magic?"

"Fear not. It will not fail. You, Sir Percival, are an Englishman and a gentleman. Accordingly, I trust you. You, for your part, must trust me. Trust between physician and patient is nine-tenths of the cure. My fee is one thousand guineas, but I will accept today the half I asked you to bring with you. If the balm fails, you will tell me so and I will return to you your five hundred guineas. Otherwise, you will pay me the half still owing, and I will give you three further fintuqs of your cure."

Within a week, Sir Percival paid the balance.

For those who are curious, here is the recipe Maimonides gives in his *Treatise on Cohabitation*:

> 1 liter carrot oil
> 1 liter radish oil
> 250 ml mustard oil
> 500 ml live saffron-colored ants

1. In a large pot, combine the carrot oil, radish oil, and mustard oil. Add the live ants.
2. Set the mixture in the sun for 7 days.
3. Massage the penis with the mixture for 2 hours; then, wash the penis in warm water.
4. Repeat when necessary.

It is not known why Falsch left Alexandria, where life for him had been rather good, but leave it he did, hastily, and under something of a cloud. He hints at the backbiting of others, envious of his successes and of the favors Avisana had showered upon him. It may be that Sir Percival, once more in Alexandria, assisted in Falsch's escape. There is an expense notation and an accompanying remark in the Englishman's accounts book for 1750 that are otherwise inexplicable: "£250.12s.7d in compensa[tn] to the girl Ayeesha's father." Against this sum is scribbled in the margin, "F. a jolly rogue!" At any rate, in the very month and year Sir Percival left Alexandria for Athens, April 1750, Falsch turned up in Bamberg, a penniless scholar.

⌒

I have been thinking of Solomon Falsch rather a lot of late; in fact, ever since the wretched Twombly's arrival. For Falsch, not limited to Moses Maimonides and a specific against premature ejaculation, had scribbled down many remedies, charms, spells, and simples. These are now to be found here in the Music Room, in the cabinet behind me to which I alone have the key. For example, you can take an ordinary lemon and name it after your enemy; thereafter, "as the lemon dries and decays, so will your enemy waste away." This process takes time. And so Falsch has added a useful refinement for more immediate results. "With an entire new knife, one that has been whetted at the first glimmering of the new moon, cut the lemon asunder, using words expressive of hatred and contumely. Your enemy will on the instant feel a certain inexpressible and cutting anguish of the heart, together with an agued chilliness and failure throughout the body."

On my desk sits a lemon bought this morning at the Greenpeace Gourmet Greengrocers' in Pepper Lane in Ludlow. It sits here between the teeth of my *memento mori;* it is plump and juicy, bitterly yellow and dimpled. Before it lies a silver dagger, a letter opener, a gift as yet unused to "Edmond Music, S.J., from the Knights of Columbus, Joliet, Illinois," who this year were the sponsors of Twombly's visit. They knew that I would "extend every courtesy to Father Twombly."

As yet, the lemon has no name.

To be fair to Twombly, he has stayed out of my way, dining in the refectory and trading banalities in the lounge with the other visiting fellows, like them sleeping and perhaps masturbating in his own room—all facilities located by my cunning in the former stable block. But his very presence on the grounds throws me off-balance. The real threat he poses to me by his chance meeting in New York with Aristide Popescu cannot be doubted. People like Twombly never let go. They worry the bone, despoiling dogs, dimly aware that merely by chomping they bring trouble to others. Whenever I hear a footfall outside the sanctuary of the Music Room, I expect a knock on the door. Yesterday, I actually went to the door, put my ear against it, then opened it carefully. At the end of the corridor, to the left of the Library doors, stood Twombly, his back to me, one hand in his trouser pocket, gazing at Lemuel O'Toole's painting of naked boys leaping into one of Hampstead Heath's ponds. You know the one. It shocked the art world in 1932, the Royal Academy bowing to moralistic pressure during the annual exhibition and removing it from its walls. An old man now, Twombly stood before the painting, his back curved, his shoulders shaking.

෫ଠ—

"Let's get it over with," said Maude, meaning the one dinner in Beale Hall proper to which we invite Twombly on his annual visits, thus extending to him at least one of the courtesies the Knights of Columbus were confident he would receive. "Let's have him in tonight. Old McGonagle arrives this afternoon, remember. Like it or not, we'll have to feed his bishophood. In for a penny, in for a pound. Let's kill the two birds with the one stone."

"You're bursting with gnomic wisdom, Maude."

I had told her nothing of Twombly's "discovery" in New York, his suspicions about me, or his implied accusation. She seemed to have entirely forgotten her crime, a massive triumph of the will. But she had not really forgotten it, of course. She had swallowed her guilt, an ill-digested meal, but it stayed with her, she could not eliminate it. What she remembered from that time was the sale of my own collection of erotica to the Beale Hall Library—although she could not fathom what an avowedly Catholic institution would want with all that "shameful filthiness." ("Research, Maude," I had told her. "Research. The holier the priest, the more he need learn about human depravity and sin. How otherwise can he inveigh against them?" "You must be the holiest of the holy, then," she told me tartly.) And she certainly did not know of the present danger posed by the confluence of Twombly and Bishop McGonagle.

"But all right, let's have 'em to dinner, and let's have W.C. along, too. Shake things up a bit, lighten the atmosphere, reduce the piety." It was my use of the word "gnomic" that had reminded me of the major. In his presence, they would not—they could not—raise the matter of Popescu's catalog.

"Are you sure, Edmond? An atheist at the bishop's table?"

"It's not the bishop's table, it's mine. Besides, the major's an ideal dinner guest. He'll have us roaring with laughter. You know how he is."

"Indeed I do. That's why I wonder."

"Will you dine with us? Will you preside?"

"No. I'll serve the meal, demonstrating a proper humility. Your friend Twombly always makes me feel unclean. He shrinks from me, of course, because I'm a woman. Perhaps he's heard too many confessions. He thinks he understands women, and what he understands he doesn't much like, no, not at all, at all. I sometimes wonder whether he suspects the truth about us, you and me; or, at any rate, what the truth once was." Here she paused and crossed herself, mumbling something inaudible. "No one could accuse him of Mariolatry," she went on. "That's quite certain. He prays to the Mother of God only because the Church certifies her a virgin. By what particular gate Christ entered the world he must choose not to think."

"I'm astonished. You don't like him, then?"

She looked at me, puzzled at first, and then she laughed.

"Well, if I can't have you there, I'll have Bastien. He shall preside."

She sniffed the air meaningfully.

"You're right. Bishop McGonagle will preside. Twombly will sit at the bishop's right hand, as is fitting, and Bastien will sit next to Twombly, well upwind. At the bishop's left hand will sit W.C., and I'll sit next to him." And then I thought again of Solomon Falsch. "What will you serve? What d'you say to a sheep's heart?"

"What d'you say to a lamb curry? Sheep's heart! Where would I get one? Besides, how d'you cook a sheep's heart?"

"Stick pins in it. Then roast it over a slow fire strewn with salt. Say the following:

From this sheep's heart you will learn
'Tis Twombly's heart I mean to burn.

Let him have no peace, no rest,
Until he's dead. I mean no jest.

"That should do it. Roast potatoes, I think, along with the sheep's heart, and cauliflower."

"Lamb curry it is, then," she said, and she looked at me most peculiarly. "You're not to worry, Edmond. I've promised you, everything's in hand."

∽∂⁓

Of course, I could not accommodate McGonagle in the converted stable block where I house the clerical plebs, Twombly among them. No, the bishop when he visits must stay in the Hall. He fancies the Garsington Room above all others for its spaciousness, its rich furnishings, and the magnificent view it offers over the dales, and he has come to think of it as his own. "Have them air out the Garsington, there's a good chap. I shall be at the Hall on Friday"—or whenever. He is not a particularly well-read man. I wonder whether he would be pleased or displeased to learn that his favorite room is called Garsington because Lady Ottoline Morrell and Bertie Russell are rumored to have had it off there one summer weekend in the heady, gloriously illicit days of their early middle age.

That evening, I answered the major's ring at the Rose Garden door, his nearest entrance on the walk from Benghazi, hung his mac and cap for him on a convenient pike in Armorer's Hall, and led him to the smaller dining room, the former Gun Room. There stood the bishop and Twombly before the sideboard, clad in their customary suits of solemn black, stark in view like the cutout silhouettes that amused an earlier era, and examining the bottles of spirits and wine that Maude had arrayed there for us.

"Och," said the major in an execrable Scottish accent when he saw them, "the twa corbies."

"It's Major Catchpole, isn't it?" said McGonagle and smiled a

McGonagle smile. The truth is, the bishop looks very like the late W. C. Fields, the American film actor, whom I remember in his stellar role as Mr. Micawber, and his voice, like the actor's, is flat and gravelly. "What a pleasure!" His nose is pocked and red and shaped like a potato.

"'God save thy Grace.'"

"Flatterer. I am as yet only a bishop."

"Bishop, 'I should say, for grace thou wilt have none.' *Henry IV*, you know, the first part."

"Major Catchpole is one of our lost sheep, Bishop," said Twombly ingratiatingly. "He has strayed, but we pray that he may once more find the fold."

"Baa-aa, baa-aa!" said dear old W.C.

Hastily, I went to the sideboard and offered drinks. "What's your poison, Bishop? Major?"

"Seltzer for me," said Twombly primly. "What you Brits call fizzy water, right?"

"Edmond is not exactly a true Brit," said McGonagle, grinning as if his witticism had the polish of Restoration comedy. "Edmond is a bundle of not-exactlies. I'll take the single malt, whatever it is, my dear fellow."

"Sheep Dip?"

"Why not?"

"Black Label for me," said W.C., "and a splash, Edmond."

The door opened, and there stood slippered Bastien, stooping, his hair in its customary disorder. From his neck hung and swung his corkscrew. Very solemnly, he made the sign of the Cross before us and then shuffled in.

"Father Bastien, is it not?" said McGonagle genially to a man he had met many times before.

"I believe it is, yes," said Bastien, nodding. "Yes, I'm sure it is. But why do you ask?" He smiled sweetly and made once more the sign of the Cross.

Bastien, I fear, is teetering on the very edge.

Twombly turned from him in disgust. "But I've been longing to tell you, Bishop," he said, rubbing his hands together, a living, breathing Uriah Heep, "of my recent encounter with the Holy Father."

"Ah, yes," chortled the major, "Father Music was telling me all about it. Absolutely ripping yarn. The pope spat at you, am I right? Go on, Father."

Twombly shot me a venomous look.

From the kitchen came a loud metallic clatter and clang followed by a cry of "Jesus, Mary, and Joseph!" Then Maude's red face appeared around the door, her eyes wet. "I've had what you might call a bit of an accident with the canapés. You'll have to make do with the peanuts over there on the sideboard. Dinner's very soon now, anyway. You could even sit down if you wanted."

Her latest period of abstinence had not lasted long. Well, she had tried, after all.

"It's her hip, poor soul," said Bastien sorrowfully. "Every now and then, it betrays her." He shuffled over to the sideboard. "Ah, look, Father," he said to me, picking up a bottle of wine and rocking with it. "It's a Castello Armani '96. If it's a Chianti Classico with dinner, Maude must be making one of her curries. You see, my dear bishop, she'd never make a good French wine do battle with those ethnic spices. Amen."

I poured drinks for W.C. and the bishop and urged Twombly to help himself to fizzy water. "You'll find lumps of ice in the bucket there," I told him. "What you Yanks call rocks, right?"

"*Touché,*" said W.C.

McGonagle grasped his rotundity with open hands. "I must say, Shropshire air does wonders for the appetite."

"Shall we sit down, then," I said. "We can take our drinks with us. Ah, good, I see you have the bottle of wine with you, Bastien." I led the way to the table. "You sit here, of course, Bishop, at the head." I pointed the others to their places.

Like W.C., I had taken a blended whiskey. I raised my glass.

"To Faith, Hope, and Charity," I said, thinking deliberately of Malocchio's painting on the dome of the Great Hall, thinking most particularly of Ellen Scrim-Pitt of Drury Lane. We drank.

Our "appetizers" already awaited us. McGonagle viewed his with suspicion and dismay. "And what have we here?"

It was, in fact, sushi from Waitrose that Maude had tumbled higgledy-piggledy from the original containers onto untidy beds of lamb's lettuce.

"It's Japanese," I said. "Rice, chopped raw fish, and so on, all neatly compressed—wonderfully healthy, I'm told. It's called sushi. In the thimble glass you'll find some sort of Oriental liqueur; it goes well with it."

"But isn't Mrs. Moriarty Irish?"

"*Miss* Moriarty. Yes, from Ballymagh in Donegal."

"*Ms.* Moriarty," said W.C.

"Amazing what we eat nowadays! Sushi, you say? Bless my soul!" The bishop shifted from his plummy to his chummy voice, the voice that signaled him a man of the people. "When I was a lad growing up in working-class Preston we ate only simple, British food: fish and chips, of course; bangers and mash; roast beef and Yorkshire on a Sunday if we were lucky, roast lamb else. And we were none the worse for it. When I got back from school or choir practice on a raw winter's day, what I wanted was a mug of Bovril and, if I was very good, a slab of bread smeared with dripping. I even amended the Lord's Prayer (and got a clout round the ear from my dad for it): 'Give us this day our daily bread and dripping.' And now sushi. Well, well, well." He forked a piece and held it very dubiously before his eyes.

"Don't you like the look of it, Bishop?" said W.C., pursing his lips as if suppressing laughter. "Come, come. Eat up, do. Think of Catherine of Siena."

"Did she like Japanese food?" said McGonagle jovially, eager to steer the conversation elsewhere.

But W.C. was not to be stopped. "Saint Catherine," he said,

"filled a cup with the suppurating filth of an old woman's sore and drank it down heartily."

"My dear fellow," said McGonagle, scanning the ceiling as if seeking succor there.

"A saint, forsooth," said W.C. amiably. "She was tending the old woman and recoiled from the stench of the sore. She realized immediately, saint that she was, that her recoil was the work of the Devil, whose malice she found this clever way to overcome."

"Yes, indeed," said McGonagle.

W.C. and Bastien exchanged chuckles.

"But that was long ago, the fourteenth century, I think," said Twombly. "It was an age of innocence, after all, that witnessed many acts of piety—supernal piety, I might add—that later times might find a trifle extravagant."

"What of Father Picard, then—not even a saint, mind you— hardly more than a hundred years ago?" said W.C.

"To be sure," said McGonagle weakly.

"This was at Lourdes, of course, locus of countless miracles. Picard asked for a glass of water from a pool already filled with the infected blood and scabs of sick pilgrims. He drank it down, smacked his lips, and pronounced it excellent—as how could the water of the Mother of Heaven not be?" W.C. twitched his lips. "And will you balk at a bit of sushi, Bishop? True believers should be made of sterner stuff."

Twombly cleared his throat. His fingers were interlaced in an attitude of prayer. He glanced meaningfully at the piece of sushi at the end of the bishop's fork.

"Oh, right," said McGonagle. He put down his fork and gratefully pushed aside his plate. "Go ahead, Father Twombly."

Twombly closed his eyes the better to concentrate—or perhaps the better to see the Occupant of the Heavenly Throne—and strove painfully to make each syllable meaningful. "Bless us. O Lord. And these . . . thy gifts. Which we are. About to receive. From thy bounty. Through Christ. Our Lord. Amen." From his bowed head he opened one eye and glanced at the bishop for approval.

"Amen," said McGonagle heartily and took a roll from the basket. "Tuck in, chaps."

We tucked in.

Through the swinging kitchen door came Maude staggering beneath the weight of a laden tray, a face red from hob heat, exertion, and gin, puffing in vain at a strand of hair that fell before her eyes. Gallantly, Bastien sprang to help her. (Well, his intention was, no doubt, to spring. What he managed was to pull himself to his feet and half shuffle, half totter to the rescue.) Together, they wrestled the tray to the sideboard and distributed there the covered dishes—lamb curry, rice, lentils—and a variety of condiments.

"It's Mrs. Moriarty, isn't it?" said McGonagle cheerfully. (He must have learned this method of greeting people from some primer on social niceties: "Show them you remember the name. It suggests caring and interest.")

"It is, Bishop. Maude Moriarty."

"I had hoped, Maude, you would be joining us at table. All these elderly men and no female leavening. I remember a few years ago we had a lively discussion on the Troubles, you and I." He winked fetchingly.

"That we did. But the staff, you see, won't work late anymore, not without crippling overtime. That's why I'm needed in the kitchen. Would you mind treating the main course as a buffet? Just help yourselves, do." She limped over to the table and began to collect the first plates. "You don't care for sushi, Bishop?"

"Love it, Maude. A favorite food. But Dr. Cronin says no. 'No raw fish for you, McGonagle, me lad!' A rare gastric condition, I'm told."

Maude left us, and we took what we wanted from the sideboard. McGonagle made do with rice, only slightly burned, and lentils.

Bastien opened the Castello Armani, sniffed the cork disdainfully, and began to pour. Twombly placed his hand over his wineglass. "I'll stick with fizzy water," he said primly.

"Drink no longer fizzy water," I said, "but use a little wine for thy stomach's sake."

"1 Timothy 5:23," said McGonagle, delighted. "That was my father's favorite biblical passage. I heard it oft and anon."

"What shall we talk about?" said W.C., who had evidently primed himself for the evening. "The Shroud of Turin? Vatican help to fleeing Nazis? The raising of Lazarus? The pederasty of Archbishop Turpin of Wigan?"

A hectic blush rose to Twombly's pale cheeks as he looked first with distaste at W.C. and then with a show of exasperation at the ceiling. "Father, forgive him, for he knows not what he says."

"What have you accomplished, Father Twombly," said W.C. acidly, "that entitles you to talk like Christ? At your age, Christ was long since dead."

There was a moment's shocked silence.

"I shall always treasure that anecdote of your boyhood, Bishop," said Twombly, glancing significantly at me and from me to the major, running his forefinger across his throat. "'Give us this day our daily bread and dripping.' Fabulous!"

McGonagle ignored him and turned to W.C. "Your topics are most, most interesting, no doubt of it whatever, not a bit. But no shop this evening, Major, no shop. I'd rather talk about golf." He chuckled to show a certain bonhomie. "D'you play?"

"Golf!" said W.C., delighted. "Golf! Yes, yes, I've heard about the most recent Battle of Culloden, a battle with the elements, and the miracle that attended your game. Why, my dear Bishop, you are an immortal! Twice struck by lightning and yet going on to the best score the course has ever known! You need a poet, my dear sir, a Robbie Burns, at the least. Your deeds outdo those of Beowulf himself."

"You are too kind."

"I heard you on the wireless."

"Ah."

"Who can doubt that the Lord has some special mission for you?"

"That was my understanding of the miracle at the time. I said as much."

"It was a miracle, then?"

"In my view, yes." McGonagle smiled warmly, craving our indulgence. "Of course, I was using the vernacular."

"I'm glad you said that," said the major, sniffing the air joyfully like the hound who has caught a whiff of his prey. "It raises the whole question of so-called miracles and the Catholic Church."

But McGonagle is a wily fox. "You heard me on the 'wireless,' you say. How wonderful! Wireless. That takes me back. One hardly ever encounters the word anymore, have you noticed? The young probably have no idea what it means. 'Radio' is all the rage nowadays, another American victory, eh?" He turned to Twombly. "What will be left of our poor language once you Yanks have finished with it?"

Twombly grinned, happy to help McGonagle deflect W.C. from the scent and eager to butter up the bishop, to earn what he would doubtless call Brownie points. "Ah, but that's unfair to us. We're a repository over there, Father. We've preserved words and whole phrases and old meanings that've disappeared over here. As for 'wireless,' the word has recently reappeared on my side of the Atlantic, where it refers, I think, to cordless phones. But take the word 'presently,' as another example . . ." And he was off, in full Twombly lecture mode.

Poor W.C., the wind taken out of his sails, dropped his chin to his chest, becalmed, so to speak, in the doldrums. As Twombly went on and on, so convinced he held our interest that he looked not at us at all but at Hogarth's portrait of Mistress Pettigrew's dog Bowser on the wall opposite him, McGonagle's eyes began to glaze over. Bastien, officiating at the devotions of who knows what imaginary company, made the sign of the Cross over first the salt and then the pepper shaker, and thereafter shifted his attention to his pudding spoon, the butter dish, and his napkin ring. McGonagle removed a heavy gold watch from a waistcoat pocket and glanced at the time, ostentatiously winding the stem. Bastien directed the sign of the Cross to the chandelier above our heads. From W.C.'s lips spluttered a muted snore. And still Twombly talked: "The preposition 'up,'" he said, "when added, I'm tempted to say adverbially, to the verb 'to knock,' produces in America a meaning at odds with . . ."

But I've told you enough about that ghastly meal. Like everything else, good and bad, it eventually ended. Belinda Scudamour came to fetch the major at ten-thirty; he, dear fellow, had slept through pudding, port, and coffee. That broke things up. Thankfully, thankfully.

Before he retired for the night, McGonagle told me he would have to be off betimes in the morning—he was pledged, for his sins, to play golf at a fearsome course near Ross-on-Wye—but a serious matter had come to his attention and he would be obliged if I would attend him at breakfast—"shall we say at six o' the clock?"—in his room. Perhaps I would be kind enough to apprise Mrs. Moriarty of his early departure. The usual would suffice: mixed grill and eggs, toast, a pot of tea—she would certainly remember his simple tastes. Father Fred here would join us. Behind him, Twombly tried in vain to suppress a smug grin.

*

Of that breakfast and its immediate aftermath I shall tell you anon. I want to speak now, albeit briefly, of the extraordinary mood that descended upon me during the dinner I have just described, a mood not unlike, I daresay, the kind of cloud of invisibility in which a Homeric god enwraps a favored mortal, thus shielding him, at least for that day, from the well-aimed spear. It was not that

I felt invulnerable, exactly—I am, as McGonagle himself meanly noted, "a bundle of not-exactlies"—it was that I felt that I no longer cared. I looked about me and wondered how I came to be where I was. Now, I don't mean I was experiencing the ordinary feeling of alienation familiar, I suspect, to most introspective people: "What's it all about, Alfie?" as the popular lyric once had it; or, "How on earth did I get from there to here?" Besides, what I have written so far is an effort, in part, to explain how it is that I am where I am. No, what I felt was something quite different.

I was the host at dinner, to be sure, and in that guise I was able to perform all appropriate duties. But a guise it was, and beneath that guise I enjoyed invisibility. I wanted desperately to leave, not just from the dinner table, but to leave for . . . where? And so I looked about me at all of the "corbies"—for the major too was dressed in black, his sense of irony perhaps having induced him to don formal evening attire—at dear W.C., more orthodox a Catholic in his atheism than a coven of popes picked at random, a kind of Don Quixote who boldly attacked what no sane man any longer defended; at glib and egocentric McGonagle, grown stout in his sinecure; at Twombly, eaten up with mean-spirited envy; at poor Bastien, foul-smelling, decent, compassionate, and on the brink of dementia; and even at Maude, who long has loved me and who, even today, would, I am almost sure, throw her own body between me and the bullet. And I found them all alien, utterly alien, to me. I was of a different species. What had I to do with these people? I felt an overwhelming desire to tear the collar from my neck, destroy the icons of my apostasy. There, I've said it. And I am shocked for the moment, Jew that I was, Catholic priest that I am supposed to be, into embarrassed silence.

☙

Solomon Falsch, not yet the Ba'al Shem of Ludlow, also ate among the Christians. He claimed to have derived from a kabbalistic analysis of Leviticus a series of numbers that, arranged in the form of the Star of David, produced a wonder-working blessing. (In Hebrew, as perhaps you know, numbers are represented by letters of the alphabet.) At any rate, he had only to pronounce this blessing over whatever the forbidden food—yes, even over pork itself—and at once it became acceptable fare in the eyes of God. Similar analyses produced other useful blessings. For example, he discovered a long string of numbers that when arranged in the form of King Solomon's Seal revealed a blessing rendering toenails a satisfactory substitute for the foreskin as a sign of the Covenant between the Lord and His Chosen People. No wonder, granted also his mesmerizing personality, he was able eventually to number among his disciples quite a few Christian converts—more converts, perhaps, than disciples actually born to the People of the Book.

The principle that animated his numerous innovations in traditional Judaism, as he explained in various ways to his disciples and as he noted more than once in his *Table-Talk*, was a pious desire to "sanctify the unholy," to "wash clean the unclean," to "reveal the heavenly spark of Creation lying at the heart even of unmalleable clay." The Almighty, blessed be He, had, in His infinite goodness, His unarguable wisdom, made man in His own image, but He had fashioned him out of dust, out of loam, out of dung. In the six days before the Almighty, blessed be He, rested, the Divine Afflatus blew through all things, leaving traces throughout Creation of Its passing. Created Nature, in obedience to the heavenly will, gave place to Creating Nature, and kind perpetuated kind. But in all succeeding generations of life and matter the original heavenly spark of Creation remained, yea, even in the merest clod. How better, then, to sanctify the Name than to celebrate the paradox, to find the spark of goodness at the heart of evil, the permitted at the center of the forbidden? "Thou shalt not . . ." was not as simple as it seemed.

Falsch arrived in Ludlow in 1758 after eight years in Bamberg. In Bamberg he had married again, this time, one suspects, rather more for money than for love, a woman known to history only as

Ugly Sarah, widow of Reb Jakob Graetz, moneylender to the bishop and to local lordlings. By 1756 Falsch was once more a widower. Ugly Sarah had died gorging herself at a Purim feast, eating without pause from six in the evening until shortly after one the next morning, when she fell face forward into a gooseberry tart. It was from Ugly Sarah's example, Falsch later claimed, that he learned the virtues of an abstemious diet and was inspired to write his *Treatise on Digestion*. At any rate, it was with gold jingling in his pocket that he arrived by post chaise in Ludlow, putting up at the Angel Inn. He immediately sent word by messenger to Beale Hall, informing Sir Percival of his whereabouts and then, after "tea-ing," as he puts it, undertook the exploration of the town. What he saw pleased him well.

The following morning Sir Percival himself arrived, full of hearty cheer, from his saddle scattering farthings and ha'pennies in the inn yard for the local urchins—as much as a shilling's worth by some reports—and insisting that Falsch remove himself to the Hall, which he was to regard as his own home until he found suitable accommodation, either here in town or in the country. "No, not another word, sir! Demme, sir, I insist!" The Angel was all very well, a fine inn, and Sir Percival would not hear a word said against it, but for a man of Falsch's distinction and learning, it would not suit, sir, not suit at all.

Falsch stayed a few months at the Hall, during which time he prepared a fintuq or two of Sir Percival's special medicine and managed to win the affection of Lady Alicia, whose beauty Gains-borough captured so delicately in the portrait now hanging in the Long Gallery—won it so certainly, in fact, that one wonders whether his departure from the Hall reflects Sir Percival's alarm. What we do know is that in March of 1759 Falsch acquired a lease on a house at the foot of Old Street, just uphill from Lane's Work-house and Asylum. Here he began by offering various remedies "to increase the beauty of fair women," hanging a shield before his house showing Helen upon the battlements of Troy, with Paris and

Menelaus below crossing swords in mortal combat. Maude says his remedies are perhaps as useful as any advertised today on the telly, and while I suppose her to talk tongue in cheek, it might not be amiss here to show you an example or two of what brought highborn ladies to Ludlow from a seventy-five-mile radius.

How we may take off red Pimples.

Beat two Eggs well together, add as much juice of Lemmons, and as much Mercury sublimate: set in the Sun, and use it.

How to correct the ill sent [sic] of the Arm-pits.

Pownd Lytharge of Gold or Silver, and boyl it in Vinegar; and if you wash those parts well with it, you shall keep them a long time sweet: and it is a Remedy, that there is none better.

By 1760, he had expanded his offerings, advertising that year in the Ludlow *Messenger* to teach "th'authentique Tongue wherewith Jesus spake the Sermon on the Mount." Soon after, having perhaps acquired a surer sense of what was wanted in Ludlow, he advertised in the *Messenger* and the *Bugle*, promising to teach the language that Adam and Eve, "the World's first and most perfect lovers," spoke in Eden. Build a better mousetrap, the Americans say, and the world will beat a path to your door. Falsch had clearly been onto something. He had sniffed the air and discovered a need. He was a success. More than that, he was in due course to become the Ba'al Shem of Ludlow.

⌒

I knocked on the door of the Garsington Room at precisely six in the morning. Twombly, I was confident, would not be there. Down the corridor an American wall clock (an exquisite Jeremiah Wilberforce in polished cherry wood, Boston, 1841) bonged the hour.

"Come in. Ah, do come in, my dear fellow. A good, good morning to you." The bishop turned floridly from the window and waved a welcoming hand. "I was admiring the view. You can just make out Ludlow Castle over there, one of the towers, at any rate. Magnificent against the sky, noble. Looks like rain, though, black clouds on the horizon. Never mind, never mind." He was dressed in tweedy plus-fours that descended directly from his frontal rotundity. Above he was swathed in a greenish cable-knit sweater, a turtleneck—and indeed the man himself looked something like an upended turtle.

The room smelled cheerfully of breakfast, a smell that caused saliva instantly to flood my mouth, for I had not yet eaten. On the table before a window sat the remains of McGonagle's "usual"—Maude had clearly managed to be up betimes. A large silver coffeepot stood on the sideboard, together with a pair of unused cups and saucers. McGonagle waved generously in that direction. "Help yourself, my dear fellow. Don't stand on ceremony."

I helped myself. McGonagle, meanwhile, furled umbrella in hand, practiced his golf swing. Swish! Swish!

I slurped my coffee a trifle too loudly, interrupting thereby an imaginary putting shot. The bishop looked up at me in mild rebuke.

"You'll pardon me for reminding you, but you wished to be off early this morning, Bishop. And, I believe, there was a certain matter of importance you wished to raise with me before leaving. Should we not perhaps begin?" The formality of my utterance bespoke my nervousness.

McGonagle glanced at his watch. "Where the deuce is Twombly?" he said. "Let's give him five more minutes." He took another swing with his umbrella, but his heart no longer seemed to be in it. "Between you, me, and the lamppost, his superiors across the ocean describe him as something of a pain. Inclined to get his knickers in a twist at the slightest infraction, choirboy on duty failed to polish the ciborium, that sort of thing. Fifty lashes, if he could. Disciple of Torquemada, eh? Still, he claims to have discovered a serious irregularity in your bailiwick. Probably nothing. Usually is, with chaps like that. Got to look into it, though. My responsibility, at the end of the day. Friend of yours, is he?" "I've known Fred Twombly since our graduate student days. We read English lit together." McGonagle chuckled. "Good reply. Don't think he means you well, though. I'd watch out if I were you."

What, more than anything else, motivated McGonagle was a desire for the peaceful life, the good life, the unrocked boat. Still, I was beginning to understand that this trait of his might work to my advantage. I might end up liking him, if only because of his attitude toward Twombly. Of course, not much shrewdness was required to see through the hypocrisy of my old enemy. But many wiser than McGonagle succumb to the blandishments of the sycophant because, as is well known, the sycophant praises in them what they believe most worthy of praise. Something in McGonagle had resisted. An elective inaffinity? Or a random one, in the manner of Martial's epigram: "*Non te amo, Sabidi* . . . I do no not love thee, Sabidius, although I cannot say why." In any case, the good news was that—once he had stoutly covered his broad rear from a potential headquarters' attack—McGonagle was to be found elsewhere than on Twombly's side.

A knock at the door and in rushed Twombly, unshaven, his white hair, what there was of it, in disarray, the collar of the very jacket His Holiness had spat upon untidily turned up. He clutched a folder to his chest.

"I'm sorry to be late, Bishop. Truly, I can't understand it. Ordinarily, I'm punctuality itself. Ask Edmond."

McGonagle looked dubiously at his watch. "Well, I don't have much time. I must be off in a minute. Most inconvenient. There's coffee over there if you need it. If there's time for it, I should say."

"I set the alarm for five A.M. The clock was an hour off, as I now know. When I awoke, it said four fifty-five; luckily, I glanced at my wristwatch, which said five fifty-five. I got here as quickly as I could. I can't imagine what went wrong."

What went wrong was that I had turned off the electricity in the old stable block from 2 to 3 A.M. Just my second line of defense, really. My first was a lemon named Fred on the desk in the Music Room, stabbed and hacked to pieces by my new letter opener, the gift of the Joliet, Illinois, Knights of Columbus, a letter opener that I honed last night by the light of the moon. I had faith in Falsch, to be sure, but I thought he would benefit from a backup.

"Yes, yes," said McGonagle impatiently, "let's get on with it."

"At once, Bishop, at once." Twombly extracted a sheet of paper from his folder and handed it to McGonagle. It was, as I could see, the page torn from Popescu's catalog, the page Twombly had sent me a copy of, the page marked extravagantly with a red circle, underlinings, question marks, exclamation points. Twombly looked at me and smirked. "Note the provenance of the item I've marked, Bishop. 'Library. Beale Hall.' Then note the item itself. A book of sonnets, presumably by William Shakespeare, and in an edition otherwise unknown to scholarship. Its worth is incalculable, millions upon millions, pounds, dollars, you name it; its presence here at Beale Hall would put the Library on the map, right up there with the Huntington and the Folger." Twombly pursed his lips prissily.

"And if W.S. is not William Shakespeare?"

"Well, sure, that would reduce its value some. But we're still talking big bucks here, Bishop. This is a unique edition. No other library in the world has a copy. No bibliographer has even heard of it. But I'm willing to bet anything we are talking Shakespeare."

"Anything, Fred?" I said. "Not your immortal soul?"

"An expression, is all. I'm not worried about my immortal soul."

"But isn't that what each of us is supposed to worry about?"

"Gentlemen, gentlemen, we've long left the school playground. Have you actually seen this book, Father Twombly?"

"Just the entry in that catalog page there."

"Is this a catalog page, then?" said McGonagle doubtfully.

"Don't be fooled by the print, Bishop. It's an affectation of the house, a French house, quite well known in the trade. The proprietor is this sleazy guy, Aristide Popescu, proof that scum floats to the top. I wouldn't put much past him, but if the Beale Hall Shakespeare's in his catalog, he probably bought it fair and square, bill of sale on demand and so on. Popescu, by the way, is an old friend of Edmond's, here. But, hey, I'm not making anything of that."

"But you haven't actually seen the book, you say."

"No, not the book itself. As I said, just the catalog entry."

"Then it may not exist."

"Oh, it exists, all right. Popescu wasn't fooling around."

"You know him too, then?"

"At least as long as *I've* known him," I said, interrupting. "Fred had dinner with him in New York recently."

"Friends?" said McGonagle.

"Heck, no," said Twombly indignantly. "We met by chance. I hadn't seen him for eons, not since my student days in Paris. Even then, I could tell he was what the French call a '*mal de type,*' a bad lot."

"Thanks for the translation," said McGonagle sarcastically.

Twombly missed the tone entirely. "That's okay. Anyway, he was lonely in New York, he said. He begged me to join him for dinner. I thought of it as my Christian duty. Our Lord Himself," he added primly, "went out to eat among sinners."

This was too much even for McGonagle to take without a snort of derision.

"It was over dinner that he showed me the catalog sheet."

"Father Music," said McGonagle, looking impatiently at his watch, "what have you to say about this painful business?"

"I hardly know what to say, Bishop. The book, if it exists, is not to be found in any of our library listings or in any records of library purchases or sales. There is no reference to it among the

Beale family papers. As soon as I received Father Twombly's alarming letter, I instituted an immediate and thorough search. To be sure, the catalog of the Library's holdings was, before my time, haphazard and far from complete. The process is ongoing. I hope to complete cataloging the manuscript collection before I die, the last redoubt, and then my work here is done.

"Next, I went to Paris, intent upon confronting Aristide Popescu. He would, I am sure, have shown me the 'paper trail' from Beale Hall to his catalog. But he was not to be found. He was off somewhere, said his son, who is his partner in the firm, Budapest, perhaps. The son claimed to know nothing of the book or of the catalog."

"That much is true," said Twombly. "The son has given me the same runaround. Popescu *père* seems to have disappeared."

"In short," said McGonagle, "there's nothing to be done until this foreign fellow, this . . . Popinjay? . . . resurfaces. Was that when you were supposed to have been killed, Father Music? I vaguely remember some sort of stir. It wasn't you, it was some other poor chap in your car. You were in Paris, am I right?"

"That's it, Bishop. That was me. And here I am, the bad penny. But as you yourself have said, until I can speak to Popescu, there's nothing more for me to do."

"Quite, quite. I understand entirely." McGonagle handed back the catalog sheet to Twombly as one glad to be rid of it. "Anyone with an old typewriter could have banged out those listings. Perhaps someone's pulling your leg, Father."

"That's it?" squeaked Twombly, as one appalled. "End of story? Nothing to investigate?" And then, in desperation: "Hey, I'm not one to make anything of this, but Edmond here is the proud owner of a new car, a Rover. Leather seats, all mod cons. The price tag has to be forty-five thousand pounds, minimum. That's a lot of spondulicks on a priest's salary, even if the priest in question is director of an institution. Something to think about, yes?"

"No, it's not," said my hero, Bishop McGonagle, perhaps

defending his own turf. "Our director's source of private funds is his own affair. And that of the Inland Revenue," he added, chuckling, perhaps to lighten the mood. "Besides, the car may belong to Beale Hall."

"No, it's mine," I said. "In fact, the Rover was a gift. I badly needed a car after my old Morris was smashed up."

"A gift?" said Twombly bitterly. "And very nice too. Who from, may I ask? Maude Moriarty, perhaps?" His voice dripped acid. He meant, of course, that I was lying. He hadn't a clue that he was spot on.

"It was a gift from my father," I blurted out, unable, of course, to tell the truth.

"Your father?" said McGonagle, amused. "He must be older than Methuselah."

"No, no," I said. "He's long dead. But he made some money after the war, reestablished himself in business. He left me a modest inheritance."

"Oh, sure," said Twombly.

"Well, I must be off," said McGonagle. He put on a jacket that matched his plus fours and covered his head in a tweedy cap. "How do I look?"

"Like a winner," I said.

"Your friend the major has an odd sense of humor, wouldn't you say?" said McGonagle. "Perfectly nice chap, and all that, but, well . . ."

"Major Catchpole is fighting his faith, old soldier that he is. It's a battle he cannot win. In truth, I don't think he wants to win it. But he's not ready yet to surrender. It's not us he's fighting, Bishop, it's himself. We must be patient with him."

"Oh, must we?" said Twombly nastily. "I know Catholic bashing when I hear it."

"Not that, I think, Father," said McGonagle, "but jolly bad taste at the dinner table." He grinned. "No pun intended, eh?" He looked about him. "Now, where's my brolly?"

I handed it to him.

"Ah, good, good. Keep me informed, Father Music. Find this Popinjay if you can."

"That's it?" said Twombly once more, this time resignedly.

"Yes, that's it," said McGonagle, making for the door. "Have someone send down my bags, there's a good chap, Music. Enjoy your stay here, Father Twombly. 'Scribble, scribble, scribble,' eh, what?"

And he was gone.

⌒

I saw my father again in 1975, a full twelve years after the previous, disastrous encounter. A telegram arrived at Beale Hall—yes, a telegram!—addressed to "Musič, the Priest" and signed "Mummi." My stepmother had found me, I later learned, by stopping a Carmelite nun in a cobbled street in Yafo and asking her for my whereabouts. The startled nun had directed her to the local librarian of her order. "Get thee to a nunnery," so to speak. And there I was, in an appropriate directory. As for the telegram, it was a model of succinctness: "Edmond. Come look your crazy pappi. Come quick."

Much had happened, I learned, since last I saw them. The family had fallen on hard times. Moshe, my half brother, had been blown up, a raw recruit, in the Yom Kippur War. What mincemeat could be scraped together had been given a hero's burial. Daphna, my half sister, had thrown herself screaming into his grave. Later, she had walked (and still walked in 1975) a seafront beat before the Dan Hotel, eager only to please her Russian-born pimp, a roughneck, according to my stepmother, who was seven-eighths not Jewish. Mind you, "Mummi" was herself in no condition to cast the first stone. The House of Musič might have furnished a Hogarth with a series of narrative paintings.

The Musičs had moved from what I now understood to be a desirable neighborhood in northern Tel Aviv to a flea-infested slum not far from the main bus station. The very air stank of rotten vegetables and diesel fuel. When she came to the door, my stepmother was a bedraggled figure in a striped dressing gown. Her cosmetics had melted grotesquely down a sweating, sickly face; her thin hair was in disarray. "*Now,* you had to come?" Behind her, in what I took to be the bedroom, an Arab in a cheap business suit was arranging his keffiyeh on his head. He peered at himself in the mirror and smoothed his thin mustache. As he made for the door, I stood aside to let him pass.

"You were wonderful today, baby," she said to him despairingly, her gold teeth glinting. "Today, you were a bull."

He frowned angrily. "Shut up," he said, and he pushed past me.

"Tomorrow, baby? I can hardly wait."

"Be quiet, can't you? I told you to be quiet. You want a good beating, is that what you want?" He put up a hand to hide his face from me and hastened out to the teeming street.

She smiled a smile of cynical weariness. "He's outside, your pappi, in the garden. Go and talk to him." She pointed a route through the filthy flat. A torn curtain flapped greasily at a glass door to the outside. "I'll make some tea."

The "garden" was a dirt patch in which two stringy chickens performed their brainless staccato motions beneath the white blaze of the sky, pausing with claw aloft and peering alertly about them at one moment, dipping their beaks to the dust at another. A faded awning supported by two wooden poles of different heights stretched a short distance from the rear wall of the building into the dirt patch and created some shade. Beneath it sat my father, in a colorful garden chair made of aluminium and of interwoven plastic strips. Beside him, a small, upturned supermarket crate served as a table.

"Take a chair," called my stepmother from inside the house. "There they are against the wall. Take two, one for me. Make yourself comfortable."

I took two chairs into the shade and arranged them around the crate. "Hello, Father," I said.

If he was surprised to see me, he gave no sign of it. Instead, he looked at me slyly and pointed to the chickens. "Tee-hee," he said. "Tee-hee."

My father was gaunt again, as he had been all those years ago in Orléans. His sweat-stained clothes hung from him; he badly needed a shave. On his sandaled feet, black flies clustered undisturbed. From where I sat, I could smell his sour smell. And yet he seemed well enough, if demented. At long last his pallor was gone; he had achieved the Mediterranean skin color of his wife.

"Well, what do you think of him, your pappi?" My stepmother emerged bearing a bread board upon which she had arranged two steaming glasses of tea, some slices of lemon, a small pitcher of honey, and some sticks of cinnamon. She placed the board very carefully on the upturned crate and sat beside her husband. "He doesn't want tea," she explained. "He doesn't want anything. All he wants is to watch the chickens."

"Tee-hee-hee," said my father slyly.

"He has sores on his arse like a crossword puzzle from that chair, haven't you, baby?" And she accompanied her words with a cruel poke to his ribs that brought tears to his eyes. "He feels nothing, he does nothing, he says nothing. He just sits and laughs at the chickens." She picked up a stone from the dirt at her feet and threw it at the birds. A look of alarm passed briefly over my father's face.

"What happened to him?"

"Have some tea. Here, like this." She dropped a slice of lemon into one of the glasses, poured in a little honey, and stirred the tea with a cinnamon stick. "Here, here, drink." She handed me the glass and prepared the other for herself. "What happened to him? What happened to him is he discovered one day he was accursed of God. Once he discovered this, he realized there was no point in doing anything at all. And so he sits." She sipped her tea. "Do you see the thumbprint of God on his forehead? No? He does."

"But what made him think himself accursed?"

"Let's see. Could it be because his first wife, your darling mother, was a lesbian who found his gropings repugnant? No, that's not it. Because he abandoned wife and child to the Nazis? No, again. Because his first son, your holy self, became a priest, an insult to the untold numbers of martyrs your church has slaughtered? Because his second son, my lovely Moshe, burst into bloody fragments in the Sinai? Because his daughter, my Daphna, opens her legs for whoever has a ten-pound note, a twenty-dollar bill? No, no, and no. Not for any of these does he know himself to be accursed."

Her educated eloquence in Hebrew surprised me. To my shame, I had supposed her an illiterate, superstitious primitive, a North African hardly out of the desert tent. Certainly, she could now bear to be in my presence without benefit of a charm to ward off the evil eye. Perhaps, in the intervening years with my father, she had learned that the evil eye is not so easily averted. The wind, after all, bloweth where it listeth.

"Your pappi knew himself to be accursed because he fell off a ladder and broke his leg."

My father glanced from his wife to me and nodded with indecent vigor.

She picked up another stone from the dirt and threw it viciously at the chickens, hitting one of them squarely in its upturned anus. It leapt into the air squawking. "Bull's-eye!" she said cheerfully and poked my distressed father once more in his ribs. "Caught up in the narrative, Edmond?" she said to me. "You're forgetting your tea."

Obligingly, I took a sip.

"Yes, it's almost five years ago now. He was building a *sukkah* in the garden. Not here, not in this filth, but in our old place. You remember, Edmond? You saw with your own eyes what a wonderful home we had then. Anyway, he was up the ladder, banging nails into this and that, when, before you know it, down he tumbles—crash! bang! What d'you know, he's broken his leg! Meanwhile, he hits his head with his hammer and makes a dent there at the left temple. Look, you can still see where the idiot made a dent. So apart from the broken leg, there's also blood spurting all over the place. 'I'm dying!' he screams, this hero. 'Save me, Nurit!' "Well, a broken leg they can set. A bleeding head they can stitch up and bandage. But his craziness they can do nothing about. While he's lying in bed waiting for his wounds to heal, he has time to think. Pardon me, Edmond, but your father's head was not designed for thought. This is what he thinks: 'I'm up a ladder building a *sukkah*. In other words, I'm performing a *mitzvah*, fulfilling a commandment, a good deed. This is when the Almighty, blessed be He, hurls me to the ground and pokes a hole in my head. Why does He do this? To show me that I am accursed, to show me that no good deed of mine is pleasing in His sight.' The logic of what follows from this has a certain beauty, hasn't it, baby?" Another wicked poke in her husband's ribs. "Why, concludes this Hungarian Einstein, do anything at all? And that's why we're here in this shithole of a place, that's why he sits here tittering at his chickens, that's why Fouad comes here three or four times a week."

She pointed to my drink. I took another sip.

"Fouad's not too bad. He pays the rent. Besides, a woman needs a certain stimulation, even at my age. Your pappi was no Samson, even in the days when he showed an occasional interest. Fouad takes a little work, a little careful attention to get him going, but once he's up, he's up, and he stays that way. The trouble is, he likes the back passage at least as much as the front, and that can be painful. I've no shame, you see. I tell it all. Besides, you're a priest. You must have heard many confessions. Nothing can shock you, I daresay. I tell my neighbors Fouad's here to talk business with your pappi. Do they believe me? Who knows? With an Arab involved, we could have a riot here. The religious are beginning to get violent. My neighbors have enough trouble putting a crust of bread in their children's mouths. They don't want trouble. Better to look the other way. Among the poor, there's a kind of freemasonry.

"It's funny when you think of it. He's the one accursed of God, but look at him: he's happy with his chickens. Now look at me." Hastily, she drew her robe over a naked, white breast that had just flopped into sight. "He is ground zero and I am made sick by the fallout. Do you know the story of Job? Sorry, of course you know it. In order to test Job, God did dreadful things to Job's family. But what had they ever done to be so afflicted? *They* weren't being tested. Had God no feeling for them, no love, no thought for the pain of Job's wife, Job's children? Well, we know the answer to those questions, don't we?"

There was no comfort I could offer her. I would not insult her by trotting out the platitudes designed to whiten the sepulchre, to hide the corruption within. Besides, she sought no comfort from me; she perceived herself to be comfortless.

"I don't know why I asked you to come. He's my responsibility, not yours. But he's your pappi. I thought you ought to know what's happened to him. How long can he go on like this? His muscles are shrinking, his mind is gone. He keeps on losing weight. I think he wants to die."

I returned to England via Switzerland, where I arranged for a monthly stipend to be paid to Nurit Musič in Tel Aviv. I never heard from her again. Nor did I ever again see my father. In late 1989 my bank informed me that the payee was deceased.

Part Five

If you tickle us, do we not laugh? If you poison us, do
we not die? And if you wrong us, shall we not revenge?

—*The Merchant of Venice,* 3.1.63

In matters of religion and matrimony I never give any
advice, because I will not have anybody's torments in
this world or the next laid to my charge.

—Lord Chesterfield, Letters, 1765

The day after McGonagle's departure, Twombly himself, reduced now in my presence to a walking sneer, left for a week's "original, hands-on research" in the loci of Shakespeare's youth, not merely Stratford, but the surrounding villages of Snitterfield, Shottery, Wilmcote, Aston Cantlow, Tiddington, and Alveston. He was hot on the trail of a William Shakeshafte, whom he believed to have been the poet, forced to change his name somewhat because of his recusancy, and who was for a brief time a schoolmaster in Lancashire among adherents to the Old Faith.

"Why not go to Lancashire, then?" I said hopefully.

"No doubt I will." But before I could sigh my relief: "Not this year, but perhaps next."

Ah, well. "Shakeshafte's an interesting variation, I'll grant you that," I said. "But have you ever thought that when he changed the name of his fat knight from Oldcastle to Falstaff, he was punning on his own name—'shake-spear,' 'fall-staff'—and acknowledging ruefully that he was having trouble keeping it up?"

For a moment, I had him. He slipped a notebook and pen from his pocket and began to scribble. But then what I had said penetrated his understanding. He blinked decisively and put them away. "Very funny, S.J.," he said nastily. "You know something? You should go on the stage. You really should. You're more fun than a barrel of monkeys."

"Wilderness," I said. "'Wilderness of monkeys' is the phrase you want."

Meanwhile, I was granted a respite and could turn to other pressing matters. I had thought of going to Paris again, but an exploratory phone call assured me that a visit at this time would be futile. It was to the younger Madame Popescu that I spoke, herself now a middle-aged woman, but one thoroughly Parisian, which is to say still a stunner. "Poor little Yvette" was in temporary charge of things, she said, her laughter along the wire betraying her nervousness. It appeared that Popescu *fils* had gone to Budapest in pursuit of Popescu *père,* only to learn that her "naughty, naughty father-in-law"—"ah, what a nuisance!"—had left Budapest for Moscow—or was it St. Petersburg?

"Is everything all right, Yvette? You can tell me."

"Of course, of course. What d'you think? You know Aristide Popescu. He must have caught wind of some rare edition. He sniffs the air—'sniff-sniff'—and follows its perfume with the eagerness of Casanova in pursuit of a new conquest. And is my Gaby any better?"

There was the story of a marriage in her allusion.

"Then I need not worry," I said. "When Aristide returns, please tell him I need to talk to him urgently."

"You and a hundred others." She could not mask her sob. "Pray for him, Father. Pray for them both." And she hung up.

It's obvious that Aristide is in some sort of trouble, he and his son. Well, he had always sailed pretty close to the wind. I was looking for help from one who might well need it himself.

I know rather more about W.S.'s *Dyuers and Sondry Sonettes* than I have so far admitted. I know, for example, how it came to be in the Beale Library. And because I know, I am forced to wonder whether it is genuine or counterfeit. Sir Percival acquired the book from Solomon Falsch in exchange for a Hebrew Haggadah printed in Dunaharaszti in 1609. That much is attested to in Falsch's private papers, papers I keep under lock and key here in my desk in the Music Room. (He wrote in many languages, did Falsch: Hebrew, Latin, German, French, Italian, English, Dutch,

Hungarian, to name the ones he used most frequently, and, except in those works actually published, he used a hodgepodge, a medley, switching back and forth in a single jotting among those tongues that best expressed his exquisitely nuanced meaning. Still, the records he wished to keep inscrutable to the uninvited eye he wrote in English, but an English cunningly written in Hebrew characters. It is astonishing how successful this simple code can be. I have been using it myself, but with my own small refinement: While Falsch wrote from right to left, the proper ordering for Hebrew, I write my Hebrew letters from left to right.)

The eighteenth century was a century of Shakespeare idolatry, in some respects more so than is our own. How the Western world, especially the British, who had a national, proprietary claim, longed to discover hitherto hidden Shakespeare manuscripts, hitherto unknown Shakespeare documents, hitherto buried whatever that might have some bearing on the Bard, his life, his work, his genius! Some genuine gold was in fact mined from the accumulated dust, some new light shone on a man, now become a god, who had sought but failed to achieve the rank of gentleman, but who had left a trail glimmering, albeit dully, through the law courts of the land. Still, not enough gold, not enough light, not enough to satisfy what swiftly became an English passion. After all, did not England's finest actor, David Garrick, inaugurate at Stratford in 1769—alas, five years too late for the bicentenary—the first Shakespeare jubilee? He did. And was not Sir Percival Beale caught up in the national fever? He was.

Sir Percival was a man of many parts, most subsumed under the phrase he himself preferred, "naturall Philosopher." He was an eager astronomer, botanist, and mathematician, with interests in many other fields of scientific inquiry. To be sure, he was an amateur, but he lived at a time when gentlemen amateurs did more serious work than was usual of scholars at the universities. He was, of course, a Fellow of the Royal Society, and he contributed many a paper to the *Transactions* of that august institution. His correspondence with such associates as Cavendish, Barrington, Benjamin Franklin, Euler, Linnaeus, and Montesquieu reveals an engaging, eclectic curiosity; much of this correspondence survives in the three-volume selection edited by his descendant Sir Corydon Beale, inventor of the self-cleaning chamber pot, and privatelv printed in 1902. Sir Percival's Catholicism did not interfere with his pursuit of scientific truth. Boswell attributes to him the quip, "Render unto Newton the things that are Newton's, and unto God, &c., &c." In his *Sapientia Rustici* (1783), Sir Percival himself wrote,

'Tis a dangerous thing to engage the Authority of Scripture in disputes about the naturall World, in opposition to Reason; lest Time, which brings all things to Light, should discover that to be evidently false which we had made Scripture assert.

Nevertheless, throughout his long life he remained a faithful Catholic. One hesitates to guess what he might have made of Darwin.

As you already know, Sir Percival was a great traveler and collector of curiosities. Indeed, Sir John Soane, the architect, told Lord Greville that it was Sir Percival who had first inspired him to become a collector, "the old gentleman" giving to Sir John, then but a boy, a few shards of Roman pottery and a broken, six-inch clay model of the Egyptian god Thoth. He was, said Sir John, "the mildest, gentlest, most obliging of men."

The Dunaharaszti Haggadah is a marvel of the bookmaker's art. It, too, is here, locked in my desk. Sir Percival acquired it in 1765 from the monastery at Vatra-Neamt, high up amid the whirling clouds of the Carpathians. He was on his way to the Gulf of Burgas on the Black Sea, where he had been told he would find some interesting Roman ruins, and had stopped off at the monastery to escape for a short while a fierce and bitter wind that had been blowing for days, to rest himself, his donkeys, and his guide (in that order), and to avoid murderous bandits, whom his guide had caught sight of approaching the very pass through which Sir Percival must go.

How the Haggadah had found its way to this remote monastery the abbot, who had only recently taken up his duties there, was unable to say and—Sir Percival recorded in his daily notes—seemed reluctant to ask, lest he appear ignorant before his subordinates. The Englishman rested in Vatra-Neamt for several days, during which time he was drawn again and again to the Haggadah. In truth, he coveted it. On the day of his departure he gave his host five golden sovereigns, a munificent sum anywhere in those days, let alone in that wild eagle's nest in the Carpathians, and begged him to pray for his guest, a sinner. The abbot insisted that Sir Percival take with him the Dunaharaszti Haggadah since he seemed so interested in it, since it was superfluous to the monastery's needs, and since no one in Vatra-Neamt could make out its characters. That, at any rate, is what Sir Percival told Falsch upon his return to England, when he showed his friend his new acquisitions.

On the other hand, he might simply have slipped the volume into his pocket.

It is my belief that the sight of the Dunaharaszti Haggadah in Sir Percival's library was for Solomon Falsch a turning point in his life. It marked the moment a trimmer turned toward genuine piety. For Falsch recognized the Haggadah. As a small child he had held it, trembling with awe, in his own hands, allowed so great a privilege as a reward for posing an intelligent question about the flight from Egypt at the Meyerbeers' Seder table. He could no longer recall his question, but he could still see his father's look of pride when old Meyerbeer called the boy to the head of the table and invited him to hold the book, to turn its pages, to look at its pictures; he remembered the heat in his own plump cheeks and the old man pinching them.

At that time the Haggadah was already well over a century old. It had been commissioned by the patriarch Reb Reuven Meyerbeer at the beginning of the seventeenth century from Gershom Shahor, the Prague master. What the boy Falsch saw then and what the man Falsch saw again when Sir Percival returned from his travels—on the title page, centered beneath the words הגדה של פסח, "Passover Haggadah"—is a picture of Dunaharaszti's wooden synagogue and tiny figures making their way to it across the square. The page also has a Gothic ornamental border that includes figures of Adam and Eve, Samson with the gates of Gaza in his arms, and Judith clutching the head of Holofernes. It is one of the most beautiful of early printed editions of illustrated Haggadoth, and it is extant only in this Beale Hall copy.

What Falsch felt upon seeing it, we can only imagine. Sitting comfortably and amicably with his patron in the exquisite oval library, as we may suppose, a glass of hock and soda water at his elbow, the turrets of Ludlow Castle barely visible beyond the estate's richly cultivated acres, he must suddenly have felt himself thrust back into a milieu he had long forgotten. He was perhaps reminded of his own lost innocence, of his people's stubborn belief, of family warmth, of his mother's cooking, of her face bathed in mysterious serenity as she lit the candles and welcomed the Sabbath. How had this Haggadah made its way to a remote monastery in the Carpathians? What did its removal there imply about the fate of the Meyerbeer family in Dunaharaszti? Its reappearance in his life struck a nerve and gave him an immediate purpose. Almost certainly, he reasoned, for the book to have left Jewish hands Jewish blood must have been spilled. Very well, he would rescue the Haggadah, he would wrest it from the tainted grasp of the *goyim*. In a handwriting whose near illegibility attests to his passion, he notes that he intends to win back this book for the Jews, by fair means or foul. He willingly and eagerly undertakes this task, which he regards as a "sacred duty."

What follows might well be called "an imaginative reconstruc-

tion." Still, it is solidly based on the written record: Falsch's jottings, and odds and ends culled from Sir Percival's papers.
Falsch began with guile. Encountering Sir Percival emerging not quite steadily from Peg Thumper's Palace of Pleasure in Pye Lane one late afternoon that spring, he greeted his patron warmly. "What ho, Sir P.! How do you? And how does milady? I beg you, convey to her my most cordial obligations. And what of you, my dear sir? You are well, I hope"—here I imagine Falsch nodding meaningfully at the polished door of Peg Thumper's establishment—"No recurrences of old problems, I'll warrant."

"None, I thank you. And you, sir, how do you?" Sir Percival tottered a little, and Falsch put out a restraining hand. "Demm' loose cobbles!" said Sir Percival. "Will you walk with me? Left my mount at the George."

"I had thought you left her at Peg Thumper's." This was doubtless said with a wink.

Sir Percival chuckled. "You rogue, you! Mean my horse."

"Medon, the skittish one?" You might have thought Falsch could tell one horse from another.

"No, Amycus. Medon is witherwrung." Sir Percival named all his horses after the most celebrated of the Centaurs.

"Ah," said Falsch very wisely, the word "witherwrung" being quite new and incomprehensible to him. "Have your stableman pulp some carrot and then sieve water through it into Medon's pail. Let him drink of that. I do not doubt his swift recovery." Carrot, in any case, could not hurt.

They turned the corner into Old Street.

"You that way," said Sir Percival, "I this way."

Falsch was not yet well acquainted with the Bard and did not notice the allusion. He would soon become very familiar with him, indeed. Meanwhile, however, "Will you not take some tea in my humble dwelling, Sir P.? Would you condescend? You would thereby bestow great honor."

"Why, yes," said Sir Percival. "Much obliged. I am not yet as steady on my feet as I could wish." He belched and waved a lace handkerchief fussily before his mouth. "And will your pretty housekeeper, Polly, have some of her hot scones for me, the currant scones? And gooseberry jam?"

"Rest assured she will."

"Ah, pretty Polly!" said Sir Percival lasciviously. Polly Plum was seventeen at this time. She had lewd eyes, a trim waist, and pouting breasts.

"Her name is Sarah now," said Falsch. "I've Judaized her, as I have all of my retinue. But her scones and jam are unchanged."

"Ah." The disappointment was evident in Sir Percival's tone. Judaized, Polly had become for him a species of alien nun.

Once Falsch had got Sir Percival settled, refreshments convenient to hand, in a comfortably furnished back room overlooking the garden, he raised the subject that now obsessed him, raised it with all the casualness suited to an idle thought wandering through a sleepy brain and by chance arriving at the tip of a tongue. "That Hebrew book you brought back with you from . . . where was it? a monastery in the Carpathians?"

"Vatra-Neamt, in fact. Best gooseberry jam in the shire!" Sir Percival conveyed a morsel of scone and jam to his mouth and patted his stomach with sticky fingers. "Better than anything I've had in London, let alone Beale Hall! What about the book?"

"I shall have Sarah—Polly that was—send a quantity to the Hall. No, no, I insist, my pleasure, my pleasure. The book is not worthy of so distinguished a library as your own."

"Why, man, what's it about?"

"A species of cookery book, suited to the kitchens, useful, perhaps, if your cook were able to read Hebrew. But my objection is to its commonness. Europe is flooded with it. It is to be found in every Hebrew household on the Continent."

"Colophon on my copy says 1609. Besides, it is not only ancient, 'tis also a very beautiful book."

"La, Sir P.," said Falsch, laughing lightly, "for all we know it was printed no more than twenty years ago. It would bear the same colophon. Your Hebrew printer and his reader are interested only in the year a book first made its way into the world. All subsequent editions would bear that first date. I had thought you knew. It is a peculiarity of the Jews. Pay no attention to the colophon." And he laughed again. Fictions tripped easily from his tongue.

"But the book *looks* very old. By gad, sir, it must be old!"

Falsch shrugged and smiled. "Let me relieve you of an embarrassment, Sir P. It may be of use in my household, where I am instructing Sarah in the Hebrew tongue. English in any case she cannot read, poor child, having been raised in utter ignorance."

"The illustrations are very fine."

"Shall we say one shilling? Nay, two! I shall give you a florin for the book!"

It was Sir Percival's turn to laugh. He waved a hand dismissively.

"You drive a hard bargain, Sir P. I shall offer you one guinea, and there's an end."

"I don't drive any bargains, Falsch. Not a tradesman, demmit! You forget yourself." There was a touch of iron in Sir Percival's tone, and a measure of distaste. He rose to his feet brushing crumbs from his waistcoat.

"I beg you to be seated, Sir P.," said Falsch, alarmed, rising himself to his feet. "I spoke but in jest. Forgive me. See, see where Sarah comes, bearing tea freshly brewed, warm scones—and more gooseberry jam, I'll be bound."

And in she came with a laden tray and exchanged the exhausted old with the brimming new. Pretty she assuredly was; Sir Percival had the right of it. Jewish Sarah retained the mischievous eye and the flirtatious flounce of the once vaguely Methodist Polly. She dimpled before the knight and curtsied for him.

Sir Percival sat down again. "Harrumph," he said.

Falsch sighed his relief.

And Sarah left the room bearing her tray and the reawakened lust of Sir Percival.

"Jewess now, you say?"

"Aye, sir."

"Quite, quite."

A species of nun she might seem to be to this natural philosopher—or, since he was also a classicist, a species of vestal virgin—but that very fact tickled a nerve of sexual perversity in him. Because he supposed her forbidden to him, he now found he desired her the more. She had no doubt already entered his realm of private fantasy: "Ah, if only I had encountered her at Peg Thumper's!" That sort of thing.

Falsch, who understood men, recognized the gleam in his patron's eye. Besides, was that not an inordinate bulge in Sir Percival's breeches? It must have occurred to Falsch that Sarah was a possible route to the Dunaharaszti Haggadah. If so, he did not act upon that thought. As we shall see, he had other plans for Sarah.

"Charmin' girl," said Sir Percival, pronouncing "girl" to rhyme with "bell."

"If there were some way I could acquire the cookery book for her without offending the noble gentleman to whom I owe so deep a debt of gratitude . . ." The obsequiousness must have cost him something, though.

Sir Percival actually snickered. "What though it's worthless, eh?"

"Worthless to you, Sir P. Consider: a pitchfork has great value to the farmer, if none to you; a common cookery book has value to a cook—to Sarah, who makes such splendid gooseberry jam. I venture only to suggest that neither pitchfork nor common cookery book should disgrace your splendid library."

"The sly knave doth protest too much, methinks," said Sir Percival as if to himself, but content enough that Falsch should hear him—another allusion to the Bard wasted on Falsch.

"You'll not part with it, then?"

"Not I," said Sir Percival. "With all your skimble-skamble,

you have but convinced me of the book's rarity." He got to his feet. "Seem to have left m' clouded cane at Peg Thumper's." He winked. "Have to stop off there again, alas, on m' way back to the Hall."

They parted amicably enough. Falsch swallowed his disappointment. He would have to try again, but by a different route.

᠙

I think I am able to understand something of Falsch's attitude toward the Dunaharaszti Haggadah, his determination to wrest it from its Christian prison, because of my own experience all those years ago in Rome. You will remember that I had been summoned there by the chief librarian of the Vatican Library and offered an assistant curatorship of the Hebraica holdings. "Offered" I say, but "bribed" I mean. The idea was to undo a key element in Kiki's endowment; in short, the idea was to get me out of Beale Hall. Father Rocco Marinaccio had even trailed before me the bestowal of an honorific "Monsignor." But I've already told you that, haven't I? The old tend to repeat themselves, and I, unfortunately, am old. Sorry. "Lead me not into temptation," I should have said to him sternly, the words coming to me only when it was too late. (The truth is, had they come to me in time, I would not have uttered them. I would not have dared, not as a mere priestling in the corporate headquarters of the Church. I am not built in the heroic mold.)

At any rate, I was given a lightning tour of the vast and largely secret collection, surely the richest in the world, far richer even than what is openly cataloged in the British Library and on display or available for examination in its museum, pausing only at particular treasures, highlights, so to speak. Torah scrolls dating back to the Dark Ages, the holiest of books written piously by the scribe, letter by letter, copies of the complete Talmud from both before and after the invention of printing, the comments and commentaries of centuries of Jewish sages, and as for Haggadoth, why, the earliest I can remember dated from the twelfth century and southern Germany, a Haggadah in which the faces in the illustrations have been deliberately distorted to conform with the biblical prohibition of graven images. But there were examples from every century, from manuscript to print, from hand-painted illustrations in brilliant hues and gold leaf to exquisite drawings in copperplate. The People of the Book, one might think, had devoted their lives to stocking this library. (In a bitterly ironic sense, I suppose they had.) But there were also other kinds of treasures, treasures in silver and gold, finely wrought. Torah breastplates and finials and delicate pointers, spice boxes, exquisite structures for housing the three matzos on the Passover table, a cornucopia of sacred and social artifacts. The collection, it seemed to me, covered acres. My guide, a young French priest with pink cheeks and clear blue eyes who knew nothing of my history but whose position on the still lively matter of Dreyfus could not be doubted, told me proudly that there was far more here in the Vatican than all the Yids in New York or London or Buenos Aires or even Tel Aviv could hope to put together. *"Pas mal, hein?"*

I was overcome, priest that I was and priest that I intended to remain, by a kind of nausea. It was as if I had been raped or, to descend a step, had returned home to find I had been robbed of all that I held most dear. But why, since I had abandoned it all? If I could have organized a kind of Entebbe raid to retrieve the entire Vatican collection for Israel, I would have done so. Well, that was my fantasy. The greater part of the holdings—who can say how much? Ninety percent? Ninety-five? Ninety-nine?—was stolen, and stolen over the centuries not without the slaughter of Jews. These were not items, most of them, to be acquired from Jewish merchants on the open market in the ordinary manner of trade. At best, the Vatican merely received gifts from those who had picked up Jewish property while murdering Jews, a sort of serendipity. That, as I say, was at best.

I suppose that the distinction between me and them I have

only recently recognized myself making has its origins in that experience. So strong was its manifestation the other week when Bishop McGonagle came to dinner that it verged on being a revelation, if not, in the Joycean sense, an actual epiphany. The tour of the Hebraica collection all those years ago must have awakened some sort of atavistic element in my soul, scratched, so to speak, a Jewish gene. At the time, what I did was buy a biretta.

(True, with the passage of so many years, I no longer remember whether I was actually told that much of the collection was stolen, its presence in the Vatican unacknowledged, or whether I deduced it, building on rumor. No, no, I *was* told it. I *must* have been. Why else would the memory of that day in all its details have remained so vivid for so long?)

What I have never told of that visit to Rome, not to anyone, not even to Maude, certainly not to W.C., was of a late-night discussion with my old friend Castignac and my guide to the Vatican Hebraica collection, the young, anti-Semitic priest. His name, long forgotten, popped into my head just moments ago, bursting to the surface like a gas bubble through the turgid bog of memory: Dominique Pomier!

We had gone to a restaurant in the Piazza S. Maria in Trastevere, where we had dined long and well and where we had drunk a strong *vino da pasto* rather too long and rather too well. We then repaired, unsteady on our feet, to the Via Emilia, a stone's throw from Villa Borghese, where Pomier's globe-hopping parents kept a flat that he had the use of. There, Pomier produced more wine, *vino da bottiglia*. We lounged and talked, and because we were young, we talked of sex. Yes, still young, the blood pumping hotly through our veins, we questioned the sex-negativity of Augustinian Christianity and the cruel imposition of celibacy on the priesthood. We ran through the time-honored, clichéd arguments as if we were the first to think of them. Castignac and I admitted to our sexual indiscretions, although, gentlemen to the core, mentioned no names. Pomier, for his part, claimed membership in a different sexual club, one in which Socrates, Oscar Wilde, and André Gide were honored members. "But, gentlemen, our numbers are legion, not merely today but throughout history." Castignac and I exchanged glances.

"As for me," said Pomier, slurring a trifle his words, "I prefer beautiful boys who are just on the cusp between asexuality and adolescence. I want to see fuzz, but no more than fuzz, on the upper lip and around the untried prick. I want to see rosy lips eager to encircle me and a clean, rosy anus eager to admit me."

Even in our drunkenness, Castignac and I made noises of dismay.

"You don't approve?" said Pomier. "Just follow nature, says the philosopher."

"Which philosopher? What they are is children," said Castignac. "It is not that they are boys. It would be a shameful abuse even if they were girls."

"Consider what such traumata might produce when the child becomes an adult," I said. "There can be no excuse for taking advantage of the innocent."

"Innocent!" Pomier laughed. "Is that how you think of your own childhood? Such experience is only traumatic if the adult world makes it so. Consider, I beg you, the practice of the Sambia and Etoro peoples of New Guinea. Among them, boys between the ages of seven and ten, and continuing to puberty, wank and suck off older males to orgasm and swallow the come. Why? Because these people believe that without swallowing semen boys can't become men. In their view it's analogous to breast-feeding; it's nourishment for the growing child. It would be a cruel abuse to deny these boys the opportunity to swallow adult male ejaculate." He winked at us.

"But we don't live in New Guinea," said Castignac. "It may be that attitudes toward sex among humans are relative. Perhaps there are no absolutes. But our society—I say nothing of our religious belief—condemns such behavior, condemns it without equivocation. The abuse is less the act than the effect of the act upon the child now grown, the psychological damage."

"Rubbish! They love it."

"So it would please you to think," said Castignac. "But your entire argument has to do only with the question of power, who wields it, who submits."

"You're right," I said. "And in that regard we are looking at an analog of the Vatican itself. We would like to believe that spirituality directs the pontificate, but we have evidence aplenty to conclude that it is directed by power."

"Be careful how you step," said Pomier. "You're on shaky, some might even say heretical, ground."

And so our drunken discourse was turned away from the uses and abuses of sex, its pleasures and varieties, to the conflict in Rome between the heavenly and the earthly kingdoms. We must have thought ourselves the last word in sophistication and daring.

Still, why is it that whenever I think of Twombly nowadays I am reminded of that foolish and drunken debate all those years ago?

༄

Bastien tells me that Twombly is back, has been back for three days already. My period of grace is over. Can it really be a fortnight since he set out in pursuit of a Catholic Shakeshafte? The time passes so quickly now, so very quickly. He has kept out of my way, I'll say that for him. But what his lying low might betoken, I am yet to discover. Possibly no more than embarrassment at a failed quest. He is digging in a field, after all, every inch of which has been dug up before, dug and redug, and by superior tools, to boot. Bastien reports, moreover, that Twombly is keeping to his quarters, avoiding his fellow scholars, using the common room only in midmorning, when it is empty, taking his meals alone. He is sulking, says Bastien, or, possibly, ailing. He looks yellow. Perhaps it is the jaundice, he suggests gleefully.

Well, in a week my old enemy will be on his way back to Illinois—not that I'll be rid of him even then: *Dyuers and Sondry Sonettes* is a bone that this dog will not easily let drop. But at least he won't be lurking behind corners. I plan to suggest to him before he leaves that next year he should go straight to Lancashire, much as we'd miss him here, waste not a moment in the hunt for Shakeshafte. What a coup for our side, after all, if he, Twombly, should demonstrate to an amazed world that Shakespeare was a kind of Catholic Marrano, devout in his faith, but discreetly worshiping only in secret. Perhaps the sympathy he shows for the despised Shylock and the reviled Othello, I could imagine myself telling Twombly, reveals a personal understanding of what it means to be the Other. Yes, from his own experience as a secret Catholic, Shakespeare would surely have known how it feels to be a secret Jew. William Shakespeare, S.J. Oh, it was an argument too good to miss.

☙

I find myself wondering what can have prompted Aristide to place *Dyuers and Sondry Sonettes* in his wretched catalog in the first place—now, after almost half a century of discretion. Was he suddenly in need of funds? Can he have forgotten whom he was endangering? My guess is that none of the works on the list was for sale. Each of them must have been acquired by dubious and murky means. Aristide may simply have printed the catalog for his own amusement, a record of his "private stock," or to flash before the envious eyes of others in the trade or of private collectors, his old clients. That he offered the catalog to Twombly on their ill-fated meeting in New York had more to do, I suspect, with the free flowing and excellent Pomerol than with anything else. Aristide, like Twombly and me, has grown old. He is perhaps not so sharp as once he was, less alert to danger, prone perhaps to bouts of forgetfulness.

☙

Falsch waited five years before broaching once more the matter of the Dunaharaszti Haggadah to Sir Percival. True, Sir Percival had spent three of those years in India, much of it in the company of Robert Clive, "a deucedly decent feller, let me assure you," and he had returned, this natural philosopher, this gentleman who despised lowly trade, with considerable treasure—plunder, one might say, if he wished to be unkind—as the Pondicherry Room at Beale Hall so splendidly attests. But Falsch had in any case determined on a five-year wait, five being the number of points on Solomon's Seal, the Pentagram, like the circle a line with no beginning and no end. Besides, the number 5 had many other associations, among them the fifth of the Seven Heavens, the Fifth being Refuge, where, it is said, ministering angels sing hosannas by night, and by day are silent in honor of Israel. In honor of Israel, Falsch wished to give refuge to the Dunaharaszti Haggadah.

The two men had changed in five years. Sir Percival had lost his right arm to a tiger, or if not to the tiger, which had horribly mauled it, then to Clive's surgeon, "drunk by night and blind by day," who had sawed it off. He wore his frightful injury with a certain panache, the sleeve of his coat gallantly pinned up, but he confessed to Falsch, as to his doctor, which, historically, Falsch was, that Lady Alice had fled the marital bedchamber in horror when, at a climactic moment, he had lost his balance and his stump had bruised her breast. She now refused him her conjugal duties, and he was not a man to force her. She spent most of the year in Jermyn Street, in London, in the house her father had bequeathed as part of the marriage portion. He had heard to his sorrow that young Lord Ullswater, the notorious rake, was often seen in Jermyn Street, and many another young spark. Had Falsch, perhaps, some potion that might induce Lady Alice to return?

Of course, there was for Sir Percival always the relief that Peg Thumper's establishment afforded, but in the absence of offspring he feared the Hall would pass to his brother, the odious Humphrey, and his ignorant brood. Sir Percival called upon all his classical stoicism, but to little avail. The joy had gone out of his life. The word that best described him now was "glum."

Solomon Falsch, on the other hand, had never felt better. Five years before, he had come to a fork in the road and made his Herculean choice. He felt no regret for the chicanery of the past and made no apologies for it. He simply made his new way with ever-stronger stride and ever-increasing joy. That part of the enterprise which today is to be found in the health and beauty aids aisles of the supermarket and the chemist's shop, he allowed quietly to die, still mixing his harmless potions for a few old customers, dowagers for the most part, those of them, at any rate, who still felt the itch in the blood. But he sought out no one new and charged no fees to the few he still served; he stopped advertising his "specificks" in the Ludlow papers, and he no longer kept a booth on market days in the Castle Square.

As for his school, it had become a genuine *beth ha-midrash*, a center for serious religious study. Those males whom he had once "Judaized"—using his somewhat (shall we say) unorthodox numerological justification—by clipping their toenails, he did not disabuse, thinking such heartless enlightenment the greater sin, a cruelty more displeasing to the Lord, blessed be He, than the original error. If a man believes himself to be a Jew, he reasoned, what Sanhedrin has the right to say him nay? As with Falsch's amended ritual circumcision, so with his numerological easing of the dietary laws. Here, all he could do was modify his own life and hope to influence his earliest English disciples by his example. While it was possible to circumvent the laws, he told them, the higher Judaism adhered to them strictly. Still, not much went on now in the way of conversion. And even in the heyday of Falsch's proselytizing, by far the greater number of his converts were female.

And so we come to Sarah, or Polly Plum that was. At about the time of Falsch's first attempt to wrest the Dunaharaszti Haggadah from Sir Percival, he had already thought to elevate the girl, given her obvious and lively intelligence, to the position of housekeeper. Besides Sarah, his household then included Abraham, Arthur Bum that was, who cared for the garden, undertook what heavy work was required indoors, and—when washed, combed, and neatly dressed—was, however clumsily, prepared to act as footman; and Leah, Bess Truman that was, who made fires and hauled water and swept floors and did whatever tasks she was called upon to do. As for Sarah, pretty, plump, and asweat with youth through her very pores, why, he had thought she might, as housekeeper, share his bed. And, shortly after his failure with Sir Percival but just before his arrival at the fork in the road, Falsch both raised her to her new position and let her raise him to new heights of pleasure.

Once he had chosen his route, Falsch began by considering anew the 613 commandments enjoined upon him and his coreligionists. He acknowledged the simple division established by a third-century sage into 365 prohibitions, corresponding to the number of annual solar days, and 248 mandates, corresponding to the number of "limbs," as reckoned in the ancient world, in the human body; he saw the value of the traditional simple division into positive and prohibitive precepts; he admired the more sophisticated assignment of the precepts to the headings of the Decalogue; and he appreciated the attempts of Maimonides and his school to apply Aristotelian logic to their classification. What Falsch was after, however, was a new classification, one that brought the precepts into the modern world and took account of certain facts, many of them unfortunate. For example, how was the Jew to see to it that the Temple was guarded at all times, since the Temple was destroyed, most recently in 70 C.E.? How, too, was the Levite to perform his special duties in it? How, after cleansing, was a leper to bring a sacrifice to a temple that was no more? And that is merely to consider anomalies relevant to the Temple. The 613 commandments concern much, much more.

It was while he was rearranging the commandments according to his own brilliantly original classification, one never printed although here in manuscript in Beale Hall, a classification that was nevertheless the subject of lively debate in the late eighteenth and early nineteenth centuries, that Falsch paid special attention to the precept traditionally numbered 218: he who violates a virgin must marry her and never divorce her. Sarah, once Polly Plum, fitted precisely under that rubric. The truth is, Falsch was more than happy to offer his hand in marriage, and Sarah was coyly delighted to accept it.

In my mind's eye, I see him on his wedding day, clad all in white, a white silk surcoat and white silk pantaloons, white silk stockings and white kid shoes, a hat of white ermine on his head. I see him standing beneath the wedding canopy in his garden, holding the hand of his bride. She, too, is clad all in white, a gown of white lace studded with pearls, slippers of white brocade peeping beneath her skirts, a circlet of white flowers banding her brow, her abundant hair braided in pearls. She blushes in her joy and modestly abases her eyes. "Behold!" says Falsch. "Behold, thou art consecrated to me according to the Law of Moses and of Israel!" He says these words in triumph, first in Hebrew, then in English. "Rise up, my love, my fair one, and come away," Falsch continues. "For, lo, the winter is past, the rain is over and gone, the flowers appear on the earth, and the time of the singing of birds is come." Sarah cannot contain her joyful laughter; her eyes flash fire. If she were a contemporary athlete who had just won a gold medal, she would pump the air with her fist in ecstatic victory. "Yes!" she would cry. "Yes!" As it is, she flings an arm with ease around her husband's neck, for he is no taller than she, and plants a lingering kiss upon his lips. "How fair and how pleasant art thou, O love, for delights!" says Falsch when she releases him. The wedding guests clap and laugh and shout "Mazel tov! Good luck be yours forever!" The May sun shines brightly on this union.

Actually, I have no idea whether there was rain or shine (or both) on Falsch's wedding day or whether the ceremony was conducted out of doors. I do not know that he quoted the Song of Songs or that Sarah kissed him boldly beneath the canopy. That's all poetic license, so to speak. It captures, I think, the spirit of the occasion, the joy that bride and groom may be supposed to have felt—in view, at any rate, of Falsch's unabashed words in the prefatory chapter to his (unpublished) *Treatise on Marriage*.

I am certain about what they wore, however. Falsch ordered his costume from a Jewish tailor in London's Petticoat Lane. As his accounts book records, it cost him £5.7.8 3/4. His boots came from Nicholas Smart, Ludlow's premier shoemaker, at a cost of £2.18.0 1/4; his hat, made to his own design, came from James Jamieson of Edinburgh, "Hatters to the Court of Schleswig-Holstein," at a cost of £4.19.11 1/2. Clearly, he had spared no expense. As for Sarah, her gown, her slippers, and her braided pearls were the property of Lady Alice, who had lent them for the occasion, condescending, in Sir Percival's absence—insisting, one is tempted to say: "My pleasure, dear little Sarah, my pleasure entirely. Nay, do not disappoint me." It is my belief that Lady Alice was eager to have Falsch safely married. Only then, according to the curious social customs of her class and age, could she honorably hope to enjoy a sexual liaison with him. Hence, her ladyship's presence at the wedding itself, a fact that Falsch does record.

I know, too, that there was a wedding canopy, one held aloft at its corners by four of the groom's male convertites, each of whom received 2/6d for his trouble. I know that among the wedding guests, apart from Lady Alice, was Lord Parfitt, her distant cousin but in Sir Percival's absence a close visitor at Beale Hall; Sir Jo[s] Turnbull, who had assured Falsch that he would turn Jew if Pitt the Elder were to remain Lord Privy Seal; the students of the *beth ha-midrash*, currying favor and enjoying a festive meal; Abraham and Leah, the rest of Falsch's household; and, wonder of wonders, three genuine scholars, pale and bearded, one from London and two from Amsterdam.

In the years when Sir Percival rummaged with Clive in India, the *beth ha-midrash* began to flourish. Students came not only from communities in many parts of Britain but little by little from Europe as well. Falsch began to publish his own biblical commentaries; the learned sought his opinions on many matters of religious consequence; his application of the Gordian knot solution to numerous Talmudic problems won serious attention in the wider Jewish world, sometimes condemnatory; his attempt to reconcile closed tradition with the open ethos of the Enlightenment created a stir, winning him friends and enemies. Bliss was it in that time, he might have said, to be alive. Some of his most devoted students were already calling him, at least among themselves, the Pish.

It was the Pish rather than Solomon Falsch who now visited Sir Percival, whom he had not seen in five years, a full twelvemonth since the baronet's return from India. Sir Percival was unaware of any change in his old acquaintance, except perhaps in his costume, which had become rather sober, not to say dreary, rather like that affected by a minister in one of the rabble-rousing Protestant sects so beloved, so dangerously beloved, of the lower orders.

Of course, he knew that Falsch had married; Lady Alice had written him an amusing letter detailing the extraordinary rites she and her cousin Lord Parfitt and his friend Sir Jo^S Turnbull were privileged to witness. "Had you but *bin* there, my deer Husband, I do not *doute* you would have larfed a Fortnight *sanz intervallum* and *dyn'd out* on the Tale *a full Yeer* arfter." The letter had arrived while Sir Percival, a bottle of brandy in his belly and his teeth breaking on a bullet, suffered that loss of a living limb of which we spoke, sawed off clumsily by a butcher-surgeon more drunk than he. The letter, therefore, did not much amuse him.

Readers of Maude's fictions may recognize in what follows whole passages and much dialogue stolen and adapted from her bestselling romance, *The Constant Cuckold*. I make no excuse for the theft, even as I acknowledge it. My firm belief is that she got much of the material for that book from pillow talk, from what I told her in the wee hours of my researches. Certainly, the situation of the fictional Sir Digby Savile is very much like that of the real Sir Percival Beale. Sir Digby, poor fellow, had suffered a terrible wound in the groin from a French musket ball while serving under General Wolfe in the conquest of Quebec. Maude is rather coy, as I suppose she had to be, about the exact nature of the wound. Sir Digby apparently could still function sexually. But the appearance of his "manhood," healed though it was by the time of his return from Canada, was so ghastly that his wife, Lady Charlotte, fled first their bedchamber and then Sir Digby's "ancestral pile," Beltraven. In London, Lady Charlotte quickly became the season's toast, but scandal followed hard upon the heels of fame. In Beltraven, Sir Digby smote his breast and grieved. And at this low ebb in his fortunes, he was visited by his old, kindly tutor, Ebenezer Stump, a man of no experience who brimmed with good advice. I do not believe that I shall much harm the truth if I flesh out the pitifully few facts available to me with Maude's florid but pertinent fiction.

Who can doubt that Sir Percival was envious of Falsch's lot? He had in the past year thought often of Sarah, who in his conceit remained Polly Plum. He had undressed her in his mind, stroking with his remaining hand his plump, reluctant member, his copy of Cleland open beside him. Why, the girl could not be to this day above eighteen. He saw her face, blushing and sweet-featured; he saw her ripe breasts, finely plumped out in flesh, but withal so firm that they sustained themselves in scorn of artificial stays; he saw their rosy nipples, pointing different ways; his gaze looked below and followed the delicious tract of her belly to the parting, scarcely discernible, that seemed modestly to retire downward and seek shelter between two plump, fleshy thighs—a parting or a rift whose front was o'erspread by rich, curling hairs, surely the richest sable fur in the universe.

But before he could introduce himself, so to speak, into his fantasy, sighing, he would come, his half-erect cock spurting its thin gruel onto his belly. Why should the Jew have her when he, a baronet, could not even have his own wife?

Still, like most sane people, Sir Percival drew an untroubled distinction between his fantasy life and the life he lived. Fantasy was best served by Peg Thumper and her like. The life he actually lived, however, was rendered miserable by his wife's revulsion and her departure for Town.

Sir Percival was rather hurt that Falsch had not come to see him upon his return. Was this how Jews showed gratitude? It was beneath his dignity, of course, to seek out the Jew. What one might do in Egypt, after all, one would not do in England. Falsch must come to him. And after a five-year interim that is what he did.

"So good to see you, my dear fellow! And how doth Benedick, the married man?" Sir Percival had thrown away another allusion.

"I was truly sorry to learn of your misfortune." The Pish nodded in the direction of Sir Percival's neatly pinned sleeve.

"Took you until today to tell me so, nevertheless. No, no, not a word. Understand perfectly. A newly married man, especially a man married to so dainty a morsel as our plump Polly—nay, forgive me, I mean Sarah—knows feelingly where his best interests lie. What? Eh, what?" Sir Percival winked and pointed to his crotch.

The Pish winced.

It was now that the natural philosopher told the man he thought of as his doctor the unhappy story of his marital woes and begged him for a potion that might overcome Lady Alice's disgust at his injury, cause her to renounce the rakes and profligates who were now her constant companions, and return with eagerness to his bed. From ill-mannered bawdiness to desperate self-pity in a matter of moments: such was the measure of Sir Percival's misery, torn between genuine affection for his wife and deepening worry about his manhood, *amour-propre* often vanquishing mere *amour*. His thoughts were no longer suited to the cold and lucid inquiries of the Royal Society; his thoughts were hot and murky, and they burst like fetid, oily bubbles upon the roiling sea of sex. A tear rolled down his cheek.

It would have been easy for the Falsch of old to take advantage of his patron's evident vulnerability, easy to consult his books of ancient recipes, easy to concoct a harmless potion from roots and herbs, and offer it in exchange for the Dunaharaszti Haggadah. But the Pish would no longer purvey any medicine in whose efficacy he had no trust.

"There are herbal remedies and charms and amulets," he said. "There are words that may be recited beneath the crescent moon and spirits to be plucked howling from the underworld. All these are recorded by the Ancients, as many of the books in your excellent library bear witness. But we number ourselves among the Moderns, Sir P., and in the contest between the Ancients and the Moderns, we know on whose side we bear arms. Are you not, as it were, a bright light, a luminous orb, shining the truths of natural philosophy upon a superstitious world? Are you not an honored member of the Royal Society? You are. Like Sir Francis Bacon, whom we may think of as our Great Founder, we grant all honor to the Ancients. They were giants, he said, and we are but dwarves. Yet if we dwarves busy ourselves to stand upon the shoulders of those giants, we shall see farther than they.

"Besides, the greater part of all such heathen recipes intend the capture of the male by the female. What does the legend of Circe tell us but this? What else do we learn from Omphale's capture of Hercules? Or to step from pagan myth into history, what would the Lord, blessed be He, wish us to understand from Samson's fate at the hands of Delilah? And is not his blinding a very sign and symbol, so to speak, of his blindness? No, Sir P., as Moderns we must accept an obvious truth: women have natural charms aplenty to augment and to surpass any charms they may purchase from a cozening apothecary. But we men, alas, what natural charms have we?"

"Then is there no hope for me?" Sir Percival pulled a snotty cloth from his coat pocket and dabbed his eyes and blew his nose.

"Why, have you forgot your own creed, my good sir? It is not my place, forgive me, to remind you of your Trinity of Virtues, Faith, Hope, and Charity, of which, in your belief and in mine, the greatest is Charity. To be without Hope, however, is to be without Salvation."

Sir Percival smiled, despite his misery. "And thus we see the Devil can cite Scripture for his purpose."

The time was fast approaching when no such allusion to the Bard would pass by the Pish unrecognized. But that time was not quite yet. "You do not suppose me the Devil, I hope. And what, apart from your good, can be my purpose?"

"Only a minor devil, not *the* Devil at all." Sir Percival chuckled.

"Falsch, Falsch, what can you know of true religion? We Christians are bound to hope for our salvation, yes. For that, our Lord suffered agony upon the Cross. Remember, what finally damned Faustus was loss of hope." Sir Percival had in mind Christopher Marlowe's play, unknown as yet to the Pish; the Pish, for his part, knew the legend of Dr. Faustus from his years in Germany. "A fellow might hope, as a child," Sir Percival went on, "to leap unaided above the moon. He won't be damned if, as an old man, he lose that hope. Faith and Reason are not always at odds. It may not be unreasonable, and it is certainly not damnable, for me to lose hope of Lady Alice's return. You had been my hope, Falsch, and you say there is no help."

To the Pish's embarrassment, the baronet blubbered into his filthy square of cloth.

"Come, come, sir, be a man! Hope there is, my dear Sir P., but its source is not in magic, black or white. Short of asserting your rights by main force and creating a scandal, two possible routes lie before you. You can strive to win back the Lady Alice by making her jealous, by going up to Town and flaunting a mistress or two, in the Vauxhall Gardens, say, or in a box in Drury Lane. Let her see that her absence from your side concerns you not at all, nay, rather advances your pleasures. Or you can woo her once more, flatter her, pester her with *billets-doux*, pursue her with all the ardor at your command. Those vows were sacred that made you man and wife; remind her of them, albeit gently. Of the two routes, the greater wisdom is to choose the second. But bestir yourself, my dear Sir P., bustle."

"Gad, sir, I'll do it!" Sir Percival's eyes were rimmed with red, but he managed a broad smile, a smile so broad, in truth, that it revealed how severely the bullet he had bitten had chipped and cracked and broken his canines and molars. "Faint heart never won, et cetera, et cetera." He leapt from his chair, stuffing the unsightly, damp cloth back in his pocket, and pulled a sash on the wall. "Oh, I shall have her back, my dearest Alice, ah, I feel it here, here in my heart's heart." He pulled the sash again. "Where is the damned fellow? I'd rip his balls off if he had any. Chunter! Chunter!"

"I am here, sir, at your service." The man had entered on silent feet. Periwigged and rouged, he bowed low before Sir Percival, so low that his bow bordered on insolence. (In *The Constant Cuckold* Bellows, the sinister footman, plays the role of Chunter.)

"Ah, there you are. Good, good. Pack my trunks, Chunter. We're off to London."

"Very well, sir. May I ask how long we are staying?"

"Why, what's that to you, man?"

"The better to know how much to pack, sir." Chunter verged on a smirk.

"Hmm. How long d'you think I'll be, Falsch?"

"Impossible to say. You should, I think, pack for a long stay. If happily the stay be short, why, what's unpacked can readily be packed again."

"Pack it all, foolish fellow, pack it all."

Chunter bowed and withdrew.

"You've given me hope, Falsch. By gad, sir, you've given me

hope. How can I ever repay you?" Sir Percival was ebullient, he laughed out loud.

"The return of Lady Alice would be payment enough, were payment even called for. But I confess, Sir P., I came here today to plead once more for that book you brought back with you from your adventures in the Carpathians."

Sir Percival turned as if by magic to stone. "You people never give up, do you?"

The Pish ignored the insult. There was, in any case, nothing he could do about it. "Whether in the marketplace that book has great or little value, I confess I do not know. Its value for me, however, cannot be measured. You are a baronet, Sir P., and the marketplace is not for you. I understand your noble aversion, believe me. Very well, I propose that you tell me what you would accept in the book's place. If I can acquire it for you, why, then, we are both satisfied. Think, Sir P., only think."

Sir Percival had no desire to think. All he wanted at this moment was to be rid of the grasping Jew-fellow. Was this to be his reward for casting countless favors in the wretch's way? On the other hand, Falsch was undoubtedly clever and had certainly proved his worth, most notably in Alexandria. And he was persistent, as witness the present occasion. His people had ever cast their net about the world and pulled in what fish they wanted. Why not set him a task, then, that, if accomplished, would outweigh a thousandfold the loss of any other book, let alone a book he could not hope to read, a book acquired casually, serendipitously, as a gentle tramp picks up a farthing from the cobbles?

"Very well, Falsch. I'll exchange it for some new thing by the Bard, some authenticated thing: a manuscript in his hand and bearing his signature; an as yet unknown play; perchance, an edition of a work not to be found in any library. Find me such a thing and the so-called cookery book is yours."

"I shall do it," said the Pish immediately. "Which bard had you in mind?"

"Which bard?" Sir Percival laughed in scorn. "You have little hope of success if you must ask such a question. *The* Bard, man. The supernal genius England can boldly field against any champion of Greece or Rome. William Shakespeare, the Swan of Avon. Heard of him, Falsch?"

The Pish was a man of broad culture, in his rebellious youth a devotee of classical literature. In Greek or Latin, he could easily outquote Sir Percival, and probably many an Oxford don. Frankly, he doubted the likelihood of his patron's confident assertion. He had, of course, heard of Shakespeare, had heard of him first in Germany, where he was much admired. In the years he had lived in England, years in which the native Shakespeare idolatry grew apace, he would needs be deaf not to have heard of him. He had even seen an indifferent performance of *Julius Caesar* at the theater in Mill Street, the new bridegroom anxious to please a bride he must soon wean from love of such low and irrelevant entertainments. (It is curious that Falsch, himself an obviously accomplished actor, had so little interest in the theater.) But Sarah had begged him to take her to see Mrs. Wharton in the roles of Calpurnia and Portia, a doubling the great actress had introduced to thunderous applause two seasons before in London. In his *Notes*, Falsch remarks that the play had "some good lines in it," but they were "poorly spoken," the actors "striking attitudes more suited to the statues in the Roman Forum than to ordinary humanity." As for Mrs. Wharton, "I would give a score of her for my Sarah." And then, grumpily: "The play lasted too late. This kept us up, and spoiled our supper, for we did not get home till half past eleven o'clock." Still, Sarah thanked him for his indulgence of her in a way that pleased them both.

"I shall need to lay down a foundation for my inquiry, Sir P. May I in your absence make use of the library at Beale Hall?"

"I shall so instruct the servants. Start with Dr. Johnson, let him guide you. Stay here in the Hall, if you wish, you and Sarah. I'll leave word. Oh, and, Falsch, I've been meaning to tell you: be more generous henceforth in your meting out of syllables. I am everywhere known as Sir Percival, not as Sir P." "As you wish, sir. Please forgive my unwarranted liberty." He smiled ingratiatingly. The baronet's rebuke, after all, had no power to sting, for did not the Pish as good as hold the Dunaharaszti Haggadah in his hand? And so began a study that, alongside his religious texts, gave the Pish pleasure for the rest of his life.

⌒

Major Catchpole, my dear old W.C., is dead, and I must weep for him. He was old and frail and not very well of late, but he need not have died, not yet. It was Fred Twombly who killed him. The kindest, the most decent of friends is no more, and back to Joliet has slunk the guilty wretch who caused that once great heart to crack. "The major's gone to a far better place," says Maude, with no special knowledge whatever. But the cliché comforts her and is meant to comfort me.

Like many a tragedy, this one too grew from comedy—a comedy of errors, in fact—some aspects of which would have delighted W.C., providing him with fresh ammunition for his war on the Church. He had been feeling somewhat poorly, a bit wobbly in the knees, declining his well-loved tramp in Tetley Wood with his "significant other," alias Belinda Scudamour, even begging off our weekly chess game. "Not in the mood," he said, "off my feed." Belinda asked Dr. Twitcher to call in at Benghazi. The doctor recognized a nonserious ailment of which there was an awful lot about and recommended bed rest, aspirin, and plenty of liquids. He had also noted a slight enlargement of the neck glands; to be on the safe side he would drop off a prescription for an all-purpose antibiotic at the chemist's in Tower Street.

Bed rest was precisely what W.C., in his enfeebled state, needed. But since he still thought of himself as a limber fellow, he fretted. Belinda did what she could to entertain him. Because she knew he liked to look at her gorgeous breasts, she unbuttoned the top of her blouse and leaned over him frequently, ostensibly to rearrange his pillows, her perfume rising; because she knew he would sneak a look up her skirt if he could, she wore her shortest skirts, crossing and recrossing her legs as she sat at an appropriate distance from his bed and read to him from the exasperated *Independent* or the truculent *Guardian*. She is a good girl. It was a measure of his enfeeblement, not of her charms, that his attention had slackened.

How else might she amuse him? She found in the cupboard beneath the stairs a large cardboard box of photographs that, it turned out, had belonged to Imogen, his wife, left behind with the silver dining-room bell and one or two other odds and ends when she ran off with her would-be-Iberian lover. For the most part, they interested him not at all, but he found among them a series of photographs, bound in a thin rubber band that broke as soon as touched, taken in the Marais in Paris in the 1930s. Imogen, the major knew, had spent her summer holidays in France late in that decade, perfecting her French. But the photographs had some artistic merit—not snapshots at all—and he doubted that she with her Brownie box camera had taken them. They were the work of a clever photojournalist who perhaps had a degree in anthropology or sociology, and they depicted Jewish life and Jews, sympathetically but wittily, and with a Gallic twist. They interested W.C. only because he thought that among the Jewish subjects, caught on the fly, as it were, unposed and unaware, might be my parents. And in one photograph there was a plump little boy that he thought might even be me. He said as much to Belinda, adding, "Father Music must see these."

When the boy arrived from the chemist's with his medicine, W.C. had Belinda summon him to his bedroom. "What's your name, young man?"

"Brian," he said aggressively. He picked at a pimple on his chin. "Brian Throstle."

"Well, Brian Throstle," said W.C. grandly, "how would you like to earn a pound?"

"A quid? You must be joking. Oh, I shall faint, I really shall."

"Why don't we just phone the Hall?" said Belinda, who stood at the bedroom door. "Why do we need a messenger?"

"Well, then, five pounds, I'll go so far."

"No problem," said Brian sarcastically. "Who d'you want me to kill, then?" He winked at Belinda, who covertly gave him the reverse victory sign.

"Do you know Beale Hall?" said W.C.

"Gawd!" said Brian, insulted.

"Good boy," said W.C. "Go there, and ask Father Music to come to Benghazi when he has a spare moment. Tell him Major Catchpole has something interesting to show him. Can you manage that, Brian?"

"Gawd!"

What Brian actually said when he got to the Hall was that the old geezer at Benghazi was sick in bed and wanted a priest.

As ill luck or fate would have it, Maude and I had gone up to London, she to consult an osteopathic surgeon in Harley Street, a Mr. Adrian Sprott-Wemys, and I to hang about waiting for her. And so Brian delivered his message to an elderly priest he met emerging from the arched entrance to the old stable block. That priest was Fred Twombly.

Twombly insists that he came looking for me before taking matters into his own hands. "There was no time to be lost, you must see that, Edmond." But this was an opportunity he must have thanked the Holy Trinity and all the blessed saints for. Oh, the Power and the Glory! He was going to be able to exercise one of his priestly functions! Oh, the joy of it, the sheer, aching joy! An academic almost on the point of retirement, he seldom got the opportunity to officiate sacramentally anymore. But extreme unction, the best and most necessary of them all, giving the dying a last opportunity to square themselves with heaven!

He dashed to his room, picked up his bag of needments, a sort of priestly first-aid kit, and hurried over to Benghazi. Belinda was up on a ladder at the back of the cottage deadheading the roses that climbed to the roof; she did not notice his arrival. She had left the front door open, airing the downstairs, which still smelled of the curried Indian take-away Tubby had brought with him last night when he went off duty. Through the bedroom window she saw that the major had nodded off, his lips twitching as if in amusement. Meanwhile, Twombly, already indoors, paused before the hall stand only long enough to kit himself out and peek approvingly at his reflection in the mirror. Then he ascended the stairs in stately wise, bearing before him Cross, book, and travel-size container of unction. He entered the sickroom already intoning in Latin. Belinda, seeing him through the window, shrieked her surprise.

The shriek awoke W.C., who saw a priest bearing down on him holding aloft a Cross and reciting the hated mumbo jumbo. He turned purple in his rage. "How dare you! Get out! Get out!" He heaved himself up in the bed and pointed with trembling finger at the door. "Get out!"

"But you sent for a priest—"

"Are you mad?" shouted W.C. "Get out of my house, you, you stupid git, you, you wanker, you, you . . ." Suddenly, he seized up, the frail body jerking, his face seeming to collapse, his eyes rolling sightlessly, and he fell back motionless upon the pillows.

Belinda had rushed to the bedroom as quickly as she could, and she witnessed W.C.'s massive stroke from the doorway. "Oh, what have you done?" she wailed. At the bedside now, she felt for signs of life. "He's gone. You've killed him."

Twombly's face was ashen with fear. He seemed, said Belinda, to shrivel into himself, like the wicked witch in the fairy story. What had he done, in fact? He sought to defend himself. "Now, hold on, young lady, hold it right there. You're talking to a priest. I was sent for. The guy knew he was dying."

"The major wasn't dying, any more than the rest of us," sobbed Belinda. "The doctor saw him this morning. He had the flu, that's all. And he certainly didn't send for you. He said you were a 'sniveling prat.'" Merely quoting W.C. seemed to cheer Belinda a little. "He said you were a 'pompous bum-sniffer.'"

A spot of color came into Twombly's cheeks. "The kid from the drugstore, he said the major had asked for a priest. You want to phone up and check?"

"The major wanted to see Father Music, but as a friend, not as a priest. He had something he wanted to show him."

"Well, I'm not clairvoyant. And I'm not going to stand here and take abuse. You're not a Catholic, I guess."

"Not anymore, I'm not." She remembered some more invective. "He said you were a 'bloody hypocrite,' an 'arse-licking pillock.'"

"He was a Catholic, even if lapsed. I must pray for his soul. He would have wanted that." He held up his container of sacramental oil. "And I can still anoint him. It can't hurt. The unction was blessed by Bishop Farley in Joliet before I left for England, and as a precaution I asked Bishop McGonagle to bless it again the other week when he visited Beale Hall."

"Haven't you worked out yet what he wanted? What he wanted was you out of his house. You heard him yourself." The tears began to fall now in earnest. "Why don't you show him that much respect? Just go. Please?"

"You should be phoning the doctor, not arguing with a man of the cloth going about his sacred duty." Twombly turned on his heel and sought to make a dignified exit. But he dropped his Cross and in seeking to recover it dropped his book. He left on legs made weak by his ordeal. The word "Arsehole!" followed him down the stairs.

As I've said, she's a good girl, is Belinda.

⌒

A tale is told among the *Tales of the Ba'al Shem of Ludlow* of a visit
to the Pish of the learned Rabbi Izaak Spiegelman, Gaon of
Cricklewood. The Pish made his guest welcome, pressing upon
him an abundance of food and drink, and they sat talking into the
night. But an hour or so after they had retired, the Pish was awakened by moans emanating from the Gaon's room. He flung open
the door and rushed in.

There, standing at the head of the bed on which lay Rabbi
Spiegelman, was Death. "What a nerve!" shouted the Pish.
"How dare you! What are *you* doing here? Who invited *you*?
This man is a guest in my house! He is under my protection!
What shamelessness!" So severely did the Pish berate the
Angel of Death that he folded his black wings over his head
and ran away. Then the Pish placed his right hand on the
rabbi's forehead and, lo, he was cured. However, lest the
Angel of Death return in his absence, God forbid, the Pish
stayed by the rabbi's bedside until it was day.

Later, the Pish explained that he would not ordinarily
interfere with the Angel of Death going about his lawful
business. "After all, he has his job and I have mine. Perhaps
I acted a little too hastily, surprised to come face-to-face with
the Angel of Death when there had been no earlier sign of his
presence. And so I interfered, speaking from my grief." *The
words of the wise are as goads* (Ecclesiastes 12:11).

⌒

The question that troubles my mind is whether W.C.—had
Twombly not burst in upon him unsummoned, unwanted, and, in
the guise of Death's harbinger, shocking him into death; had he
lived out his allotted span, by now in any case close to its end; had
he possessed, in short, some inkling that the end was now truly
nigh—whether, I say, he would have from what he knew to be his
deathbed called for extreme unction, made his peace with the

Church, whose essential truths he had long sought to prove (or so I suspected) by attacking its gross absurdities and painful hypocrisies. If so, the Church in the person of Father Twombly denied him that death the Church presumably would have wished him to have, a sinner, contrite, reconciled, made fit for eventual salvation.

I wish he were alive today; I miss him. How he would have enjoyed shaping and polishing the story of his last encounter with Twombly! "And another thing," I hear him saying, "why did the bloody twit have his death juice blessed a second time? Had some of the original blessing evaporated since he left America? Was he merely topping up? Was he trying for a double-strength brew, a sort of American 'all-new, improved version,' a concentrate?" No, a living W.C. would have welcomed death in the heat of such a battle, wielding aloft his sword of truth, a hero to the end, not a captured soldier suing for mercy and wondering why he had fought at all. And for that I am grateful.

Part Six

No viper so little, but hath its venom.

—Thomas Fuller, *Gnomologia*, 1732

If Philip [II of Spain] possessed a single virtue it has eluded the conscientious research of the writer of these pages. If there are vices—as possibly there are—from which he was exempt, it is because it is not permitted to human nature to attain perfection even in evil.

—John Lothrop Motley,
History of the United Netherlands,
1868

he wretched Twombly did not return as promised to Joliet, Illinois; instead, he went first to Paris and from Paris to St. Petersburg, and all in a calculated attempt to bring me down. And who should we suppose paid for this expensive lark of his? Not the Knights of Columbus, who had more than done their bit on his behalf; not, rest assured, his piddling college; not (I am *almost* certain) the Church. Then who? Twombly must have dipped into his own modest reserves, the nickels and dimes saved over a parsimonious, churchly lifetime and kept, I would imagine, in a post office account; the proceeds from the sale of his mother's belongings, his share, at any rate, from the division among seven greedy siblings; that sort of thing. His quest is an extravagance that serves only to lay bare his single-minded obsession.

In Paris, Twombly learned that Popescu had been caught attempting to smuggle national treasures out of Russia and was now being held in a prison in St. Petersburg. The son had gone out to rescue his father and had himself been detained as a probable confederate.

Twombly burst into Popescu's office like the Grand Inquisitor. There he found Mme Popescu the younger, who had been left in temporary charge. He besieged her with a barrage of questions, and in no time at all he had reduced the poor woman to tears. *"Du calme, madame, du calme. Soyez tranquille, je vous en prie,"* he said in his execrably accented French. He poured her a glass of water from the carafe on the desk and waited impatiently for her sobs to subside. "Now let us begin at the beginning."

Her husband had enjoined her to say nothing to anyone of his father's plight, she said. The firm's reputation, his father's good name, these must not be jeopardized. Rescue must come discreetly, from friends in the government and in the diplomatic corps. Meanwhile, the son had left Paris to offer his father what comfort he could. "With what terrible result, you now know, *Père.*"

Mme Popescu was beside herself with anxiety. She crossed herself in Twombly's presence and fell to her knees, begging him to join her in a prayer for intercession to Saint John of God, patron saint of booksellers. After praying with her, Twombly detained her on her knees for a few more moments. "I wish to see your files, madame. I'm looking for a certain bill of sale."

"But my husband instructed me to keep the files locked during his absence. His words to me are sacred. I cannot disobey him."

"It may go worse for him if you don't," threatened Twombly. "I am a man of God going about God's business."

"Even so, *Père.*"

"Very well. Then I must ask you to show me a certain very rare volume of English poetry, one whose ownership is in dispute."

Mme Popescu put out her hand and Twombly helped her to her feet. She smiled, went over to her desk, and picked up the telephone. "Claire? Please ask Monsieur Boucheron to come here for a moment."

Twombly was still on his knees, his smirking face bowed over his clasped hands, apparently praying anew.

After a discreet knock, the door opened. M. Boucheron proved to be the *portier,* a giant figure, a retired wrestler, bursting from a uniform of goose-turd green that sported gold buttons and gold trimmings. "Madame?"

"Monsieur Boucheron, the reverend father is about to leave. Please escort him downstairs and, should he need them, give him directions to his hotel."

Twombly glared at her with naked malevolence. But he had succeeded only in stiffening her spine.

M. Boucheron caught Twombly beneath his elbows and lifted him, still kneeling, from the floor. Before Twombly's feet could touch down, the *portier* had him out of the office. *"Au revoir, Père,"* said Mme Popescu sweetly, closing the door.

"So what?" Twombly said to me from Paris a day or two later. "It makes no never mind. Gives me a reason to go to St. Petersburg. Always wanted to follow Raskolnikov's route around town. Let's see whether a few months in a Russian prison have softened Popescu up some."

"You'll do what you can to help him, I'm sure."

Twombly chuckled. "Could be. But don't worry, Edmond, whatever happens, I'm gonna pluck out the heart of this Shakespeare mystery. Just wait and see."

⌒

At first, in my panic, I thought I would follow Twombly to St. Petersburg, perhaps even get there before him and . . . and what? There was the rub. I had no plan of my own, no possibility of a plan, merely the need to frustrate his. But how? Denounce him as a spy to what was left of the KGB? For that I had no need to travel farther than the telephone. A discreetly anonymous tip to the Russian embassy in London should suffice. At least, it would if information gleaned from Cold War spy novels held true. But the truth is, I no longer have the stomach for such chicanery. Yes, I'm willing to cast the odd spell, mix the occasional compound, enjoying a kind of half-belief engendered by my readings in the Falsch papers. But that's about all the deliberate villainy I can manage these days.

Besides, I have been very much involved in Maude of late, in her hospitalization, and in her alarming return to the faith. There had been signs since the bishop's visit of a Catholic renewal in her, signs which I chose either to ignore or to explain away. Not that

McGonagle had wrought the change, I hasten to add. His visit merely provides a *terminus a quo* for my observations. But it was the night of the dinner, the night that I experienced so strong a feeling of alienation from Catholicism and all its adherents, whether bound fast or hanging loose, and it was after McGonagle and Twombly had retired that Bastien and I found Maude on her back on the kitchen floor, snoring away, an empty bottle of gin in her hand, another empty bottle lying in an immodestly suggestive position on her lap. In her sleep, she had vomited over herself. She was disgusting. Bastien cleaned her up, kneeling beside her, cradling her head in his arm, wiping her with clean cloths, mumbling comforting sounds when she moaned. He was good at that sort of thing. Then, enfeebled as we both are by age, we nevertheless managed between us to get Maude's gross bulk to its feet. We discovered then that she had also lost control of her bladder. Slipping and sliding in the mingled vomit and urine on the kitchen's flagstone floor, we nevertheless managed to propel her to the couch in her butler's-pantry office. We could never have managed the stairs. Bastien covered her gently with a coat he found hanging in the cupboard and we left her to her stench and her snoring.

Maude and I have never spoken of her appalling drunkenness that night; our discreet silence about her shame forms another brick in the wall between us. But she has not had a drink since. I think she has taken a vow, a serious one, I mean, a Catholic one, on her ancient knees and in despite of (or perhaps welcoming) the pain in her hip, before one or another of the holy statues in the chapel. How she was able to get up betimes on the morning following her debauch and prepare for McGonagle his "full English breakfast" is a miracle (and perhaps a miracle following hard upon her vow, and thus a confirmation of the Old Faith).

W.C.'s recent death in the very act of screaming vituperation at a priest may have stirred in her the long dormant or deliberately suppressed terrors of Hell. And I have found myself wondering whether her boozing in recent years had begun as an attempt to drown her guilt, to deaden her fear, or whether her guilt had directed her to the bottle, a "saintly" self-destructiveness, a sick form of redemption. But there are other signs of her reawakened belief. She regularly attends early Mass in the chapel now—well, not *now* exactly, *now* she's in the hospital, as I'll explain in a moment. (We don't speak of Mass, either; for all I know, she's been going to confession, too—not to Bastien, whom she would regard as one of my confederates and hence a mocker of all things holy, but to one of the visiting scholar-clerics Bastien has put on the devotional roster. Two more bricks in the wall.) And there has appeared in her office a triptych rather like a vanity mirror, in the center Christ wearing his crown of thorns and morosely displaying his wounds, his right hand, punctured, raised in benediction; in the left panel Mary and in the right Joseph, both on their knees, both haloed, both with hands posed in prayer, both gazing in mute adoration at the sunburst around "their" son's head. Three votive candles stand before the triptych. As yet, I do not think she has lighted them. But to have such a vilely rendered and cheaply commercial object as this horrid triptych in one of England's great houses, one stuffed, so to speak, with works of art, exquisite and divine, suggests that Maude is far gone on the road to trashy, bargain-basement Romanism.

Of course, despite the life she chose to share with me, there is a sense in which Maude never left the Church. She had never really questioned the credibility of its teachings. In her view, we both stood on very tickle ground, ground that would inevitably open beneath our feet and swallow us up. We were doomed, oh yes, no doubt of it at all, at all; we had exercised our God-given free will and opted for sin. She had weighed love and sentiment and pleasure against the never-doubted truths of her faith, and found that in her moral weakness the former had the greater weight. But she had never denied the Church's claim to be a trustworthy teacher of constant doctrine. My own blasphemies she used to regard as the foolish blather of a cheeky boy. But then she grew old, and love and sentiment and pleasure shrank in proportion as her body grew stout and her flesh sagged and incontinence threatened. And she was in pain from her hip and in shame for her drunkenness. And then she was to go beneath the knife and Hellmouth yawned before her.

"You're horribly out-of-date," I tried to tell her. "You're still back with Dante and Hieronymus Bosch. That's not what Rome is putting out now. Not a bit of it. Hell's not a *place* anymore, an actual *locus* of endless physical punishment. The wasps are not going to sting you for all eternity. You're not going to freeze in ice or burn in fire. That's all metaphor, mere poetry. His Holiness will tell you that himself; you've no need to rely on me. Hell's a state of being. What the damned suffer from nowadays is the deprivation of God, the total alienation from all that's good and loving."

"Metaphor, is it? Mere poetry, is it?" she said scornfully. "That's rank Protestantism you're spouting. A Prod might have his conscience pricked; a Catholic is pierced by real nails."

"Well, why doesn't the soul in Hell ask a merciful God for forgiveness?"

"It's too late, you old fool. If you're damned, God denies you the ability to offer up the prayer."

"So according to you, God's to blame. But the Church says otherwise. It's the sinner himself who's chosen to reject God's grace. God is not punitive; the damned themselves elect their punishment, the ultimate exercise of free will."

"You're far worse than W.C. ever was. I'll not listen to you."

"Why do you suppose the Dies Irae has been abandoned? When did you last hear it sung at a funeral? It's gone from the liturgy not because it's cruel but because it's embarrassing. The tortures of the damned are drooled over in psychopathic detail."

But the Vatican's effort to bring the Church into the twenty-first century, even as the twentieth century slipped away, was wasted on Maude. For her, the substitution of English for Latin in prayer and hymn and ritual deprived them of authenticity. In her view, Catholicism was not to be fiddled with, not even by those sitting in the highest councils. Certainly, nothing was to be discarded. She knew what was true religion and what was not. One did not have to practice it to know it. It resided in the letter of the old law, not in the vaguenesses, the hesitations, and the uncertainties of Vatican II.

Her willingness to put up with *me* for the sake of *us* was fast ebbing. A love that had once burned brightly with romantic and sexual passion had long since cooled, its flames guttered, its substance reduced to a hardening pool of irritable familiarity. Need she be damned through all eternity for this, the dregs of a love we had both outlived? Such, I imagine, must be her thoughts.

Ah, but had not Christ died for her, too? It was not too late. She would not now commit the greatest sin of all, the sin of despair. No, even at this eleventh hour, her Church offered her redemption. She was contrite, she would repent, she would be saved.

She is in hospital at the moment recovering from her hip operation. Even in this, her return to the fold has manifested itself. She was fully prepared to go to a private institution, she had told Mr. Sprott-Wemys, her Harley Street surgeon—cost was not an issue in her case, God be praised—but she was sure she would be more comfortable if the institution were Catholic.

Nothing could be easier, he assured her. He would have her admitted into St. Cosmas and St. Damian's just outside Leominster—"splendid views, grounds running down to the river Lugg, a noble pile, my dear Miss Moriarty"—yes, the Saints had served his patients well, most recently Sir Patrick Spens of Dunfermline, scion of a Catholic family that traced its roots beyond the Conquest. Perhaps Miss Moriarty had heard of him? As for himself, Mr. Sprott-Wemys was a devout adherent of the C. of E., but one perched on so high a branch of that noble tree as to be only a whisper away from accepting the bishop of Rome as primate of England. His dear mother and his dear sister were both members of an Anglican order, the Sisters of Margery Kempe, their convent beautifully situated near Diss. They, at least, were the guarantors of—if she would permit him the pun—his bona fides. For such reasons, at any rate, Mr. Sprott-Wemys believed himself uniquely qualified to acknowledge the prime importance of the spiritual dimension to physical and (dare he say it?) *psychological* healing.

٩‮‬

Aristide Popescu finds himself in prison in St. Petersburg because his travel agent in Paris failed to acquire for him a Russian exit visa. So minor a slip and so major a consequence! Without an exit visa, he was prevented from boarding his plane. Aristide, old, bowed, but still vigorous, fulminated against all things Russian; he screamed and waved his fist; he stamped his foot; he told the impassive, uncomprehending official behind the desk just where she should shove St. Petersburg, spires, Winter Palace, and all. In fact, he made such a fuss that two security guards were summoned. They took his passport from him and led him off—"frog-marched him," said Twombly, chuckling at his own pun—to a windowless interrogation room and ordered him to calm down. They gave him a filthy glass of tepid, clouded water and a miniature bottle of vodka and locked him in. One of them stood outside the door while the other went to report to their captain. The captain glanced through the passport. "French," he said. "He travels a lot. Let him enjoy an hour or two more of our hospitality. Meanwhile, take a close look in his luggage. You never know."

Between a cashmere sweater and a heavy silk dressing gown was found a neatly wrapped parcel made of corrugated paper. Within the parcel, swathed in bubble wrap, was a dark green leather box about the size of a standard box file. The box, only slightly scuffed with the passage of time, was richly chased in gold leaf: a central baronial escutcheon, beneath which was the name de Kaimovsky, and a border of asterisks. Within the box reposed a manuscript of *Boris Godunov* written in Pushkin's own hand.

Beneath the title page was a letter, dated June 7, 1824, dedicating the work to Natalya Vaginova, an actress who is known to history only because Pushkin was for a very short while madly in love with her. On the verso of each sheet in the box was an official stamp: the silhouette of a three-masted sailing ship surrounded by the words "Leningrad: United Workers' Library." Obviously, Aristide had some serious questions to answer.

Baron Leopold de Kaimovsky, a friend of Disraeli and the French Rothschilds, was a fabulously wealthy Jewish industrialist and bibliophile. He was granted his title and the prefix "de" by a grateful French government when, within a decade of the Franco-Prussian war, he single-handedly underwrote the cost of what today would be called a "feasibility study" aimed at building an impregnable line of defense between France and Germany. Back in his native St. Petersburg he built De Kaimovsky House, an exquisite structure, almost a palace, on *Angliyskaya naberezhnaya,* the English Quay. Its sole purpose was to house his library, which in due course he proposed to donate to the nation. Events overtook him. In 1919, two years after the revolutionaries marched on the Winter Palace, the nation stole its inheritance. De Kaimovsky House was occupied by a squadron of the Red Army cavalry that quartered their horses on the ground floor and raped what women they could lure to the first and second. The chandeliers they used for target practice. It took the personal intervention of Comrade Lenin in 1920 to save the house and the collection from utter destruction. He had the members of the squadron arrested and marched to the woods outside Vsevolozhsk, where they were lined up and shot. De Kaimovsky House then became the United Workers' Library.

The curator of the collection is a certain Nikita Krivchun. His is a plum job since it includes a gracious apartment beneath the raised ground floor, what in England is called a maisonette, albeit in this case a rather large one, which also enjoys access to a beautiful neoclassical garden. (You might be tempted to think of him

as, in superficial ways, an Edmond Music *in piccolo.*) He was curator before the breakup of the Soviet Union and remains curator
under the new dispensation. His days, however, may be numbered.
Like many a manager of state-owned enterprises under the
Soviets, Nikita Krivchun supposed that with the sudden switch to
capitalism, what once he had held in charge for the people was
now his to dispose of for private profit. Luckily for the St. Petersburg Rare Books and Manuscripts "Little" Library (formerly the
United Workers' Library), he had only recently acted upon his
misunderstanding and only a few items had been sold. In any case,
Krivchun utterly denied having sold even so much as a paper clip.
His denial is complicated by the fact that Aristide Popescu, when
arrested, had in his possession a bill of sale for the Pushkin manuscript that the curator had apparently signed. "Lies! Forgeries!
The Yids are at the bottom of it!" screamed Krivchun.

Twombly phoned me from St. Petersburg. "Just to touch base,"
he said.

"How is Aristide bearing up? Have you seen him yet?"

He ignored my questions. "Same pattern as before," he
sneered. "Bills of sale for what shouldn't be bought and sold.
Popescu likes to cover his ass. This time, though, he may have
inserted a suppository. Could be we'll see him hoisted by his own
petard!" Throughout the elaboration of this vulgar metaphor he
was suppressing a mirth that burst out now into an open cackle.

There are political complications and ramifications. Krivchun
has an older brother, Dmitri, who is and who has long been Deputy
Minister of Culture. Dmitri Krivchun has, like his brother, managed to straddle the divide between communism and capitalism.
Moreover, he enjoys the ear of the President, with whom he frequently wassails. This deputy minister wields power and influence
out of all proportion to his remit; he knows many secrets, and
he has a trunkful of IOUs. But he also has powerful enemies.
There are whispers of secret Swiss bank accounts, of money laun-
dered through the Isle of Man. He, too, blames the Yids, who, he

says, fearful of attacking him directly, have hawked their AIDS-bearing phlegm at his innocent, scholarly brother, a bibliophile who has devoted his life to the preservation of the nation's heritage. Aristide is being held in prison, it would appear, because certain politicians want to compel his sworn evidence against Nikita as a means of weakening Dmitri Krivchun. Let Nikita be shown to be corrupt, then questions about Dmitri's financial dealings abroad become possible. On the other hand, these very politicians have to consider how Dmitri Krivchun might retaliate. The result is a kind of political stasis.

Poor Aristide experiences this stasis as a species of Dantesque Limbo. He is guilty before the fact: as a distinguished European dealer in rare books and manuscripts, a man with half a century of experience, he cannot claim ignorance of laws having to do with national treasures. He must have known he was breaking the law when he bought Pushkin's manuscript and attempted to leave the country with the precious text concealed in his luggage. And even if he knew nothing of the law, his ignorance of it does not excuse him. Still, the authorities might let him go with a hefty fine and a caution if he cooperates. (Of course he will cooperate; he cannot wait to cooperate.) The problem is the anti-Krivchun forces, who are not yet convinced that they can safely attack. Meanwhile, Aristide languishes in prison.

"Well, is Gabriel getting anywhere with the authorities?"

"Popescu *fils*? A lightweight. Useless, trust me."

Gabriel Popescu is being held as a hostage, a goad to "encourage" his father's cooperation. He is not allowed to leave the city, and he is followed wherever he goes. His communications with the outside world are monitored and when necessary censored. He is allowed to visit his father and his father's advocates; he may go freely where any tourist may go. Best of all, he occupies a suite at the Astoria, a world-class hotel. "Not like the Rus, which is the best I can afford," said Twombly bitterly. "If I were a layman with a layman's petty hatreds, I would want my enemies booked into the Rus." The sword hanging over the son is another means of keeping the father malleable.

⌒

I am forbidden to visit Maude. It is three weeks now since her hip operation, four weeks since she entered the hospital. I have been driving up to St. Cosmas and St. Damian's almost every day to see her, no mean feat, and at the time of the actual operation spent three uncomfortable nights at a bed-and-breakfast in Leominster. And now I am forbidden!

She is being kept in hospital well beyond the time ordinarily allotted to patients who have undergone hip operations. The reason is that she has developed a curious blister on her inner thigh, a blister that refuses to drain. She showed it to me on what proved to be my last visit. "Close the door, Edmond," she said, "and come and look at this." Daintily, she lifted the skirt of her nightie, carefully keeping hidden that most private part which once she had flaunted before me. The blister was ghastly to look upon, perhaps nine inches long and three humped inches wide, and pointing like an arrow to her quim; it was deathly white, whiter than the white thigh upon which it sat.

I was taken aback. To mask my disgust, I attempted a little joke. "Better watch out," I said. "It seems to know where it's going."

She looked at me with hatred and disdain. Quickly, she covered herself. "You can open the door again."

"It was only a joke."

"The door, Edmond."

"The visits upset the patient," Mr. Sprott-Wemys fluted over the phone from his London office, "and calm is so important to her recovery. We're willing to admit, we scientists, that calm's the best medicine in the world, don't y'know. We do what we can at the Saints, painkillers (when necessary), physiotherapy, tasty meals, cheerful surroundings, dedicated staff, flowers and fruit in every room, and so forth, but at the end of the day, it's psychological peace that heals best, inner calm, far better than anything we can achieve with pills—and, of course, the availability of what I like to call the spiritual dimension. I'm sure you'll understand, Father."

"Well, I don't. I don't understand at all. Miss Moriarty and I have been colleagues at Beale Hall for almost fifty years; we are more than colleagues, we have long been friends. I think you'd be wise to consult first with your patient before laying down the law in arbitrary ignorance. If I fail to turn up, you'll soon discover how upset she can be. And if it's the spiritual dimension you value, need I remind you I'm a priest?"

"It pains me to inform you," said Mr. Sprott-Wemys, clearly enjoying himself, "that the request comes first from Miss Moriarty herself, only secondarily from me." Then he tried for a jocular, we're-all-men-together sort of tone. "Both of us in our different professional capacities, Father, have encountered never-married ladies of a certain age who develop peculiar ideas, a kind of sexually frustrated mental miasma that addles the brain."

"Is that what you think's wrong with Miss Moriarty?" I said coldly.

"Not at all, not at all, Father!" Mr. Sprott-Wemys backtracked quickly. "Dear me, no. But I *do* think that now, in her time of trial, we should indulge her little whims, don't you? You'll have her back at the Hall in, at most, three weeks, as good as new. Her hip is mending nicely; she is well along in her course of exercises; and we are attending to her blister. It's her psychological health we must concentrate on now. Meanwhile, you can phone the Saints and get a daily progress report. Only, please don't phone the patient herself. Respect her wishes. The wise physician must acknowledge that sometimes the patient herself knows what's best for her. I imagine you find that to be true in your line of work, too."

"Not in *my* line of work, no," I said, but he had already hung up.

Well, I might have read the writing on the wall, graffiti that point to much of what divides us. The kind of Catholic in-jokes I have always made that used to please or mildly shock now anger her. She has no patience with my cynicism, and finds me sarcastic when I suppose myself merely ironic. She has said she will pray to Saint Jude of Thaddaeus in my behalf, Jude, the patron saint of desperate cases and lost causes. At one time, such a promise would have been a loving little joke between us; now, I fear, she is in earnest. And I know I upset her dreadfully on my last visit. It wasn't just the foolish remark the sight of her ghastly blister brought unbidden to my lips. No, in my ill-conceived effort to amuse her, I told yet another joke, a joke I had first heard years ago on the top of a bus, a joke about the nonsensical doctrine of papal infallibility, hoping to bring a smile to her lips, for she looked more than a trifle down.

But, of course, her room at the Saints was no place for such a joke, as I should have realized. Christ is twisted upon his Cross on the wall above her head and reflected in the mirror on the wall opposite so that she can see him. On her bedside table, there is a missal and a selection of what look like a fanned hand of playing cards but what upon closer inspection prove to be prayers for various occasions. Nuns flit in and out of the room with pills or thermometers or magazines or pots of tea for two with biscuits, all but curtseying before my dog collar. Through the window, we can see rolling, well-tended lawns and a rendering in the manner of Jacob Epstein of Michelangelo's *Pietà*. In short, she is being cosseted by Catholicism. And onto this smooth surface I clumsily skipped my stone.

"You'll not have forgotten, Edmond, that when a pope has it in mind to teach on matters of faith and morals, he is protected by the Holy Spirit from error."

"Naturally, you'll want me to ignore already acknowledged errors," I said, and perhaps there was a touch of sarcasm in my voice. After all, she knows well enough where I stand on such matters. "It's probably best to forget about such fallible infallibilities as the use of torture to suppress heresy, the embarrassing defense of slavery, the horrid teachings about Jews and Judaism, the doctrine of 'no salvation outside the Church,' the prohibition of lending money at interest, the refusal to believe the earth moves around the sun—shall I go on?"

"You are a wicked, hateful man," she said. "You have picked up where your friend the major left off. With your every utterance you pierce afresh the tortured body of Our Lord. Like the major, you will roast in Hell for it. I'll not listen to you more." She was in earnest. There were tears in her eyes.

"Maude, I'm sorry. I would not have offended you for the world."

She reached beneath her pillow and found a rosary. "I'm tired, Edmond. I think I'll sleep. Go now." She began silently to mouth her Hail Mary.

I left, of course.

‹ⱺ—

Twombly has managed to see Aristide. Popescu *fils* and his father's lawyers succeeded in persuading the authorities to grant limited visitation rights to the prisoner's lifetime "spiritual guardian." Aristide is being held in Kresti Prison, a gloomy complex of dark red brick on the eastern outskirts of St. Petersburg. It was built at the turn of the century to house an endless stream of the Czar's enemies and slipped easily into the role of detention center for political dissidents in the heroic age of Stalin's purges, remaining for the balance of communist rule a convenient way station to the gulags. Guard towers, heavily armed guards, and ferocious dogs have not softened its aspect in the new era. Conveniently close by is the KGB building with its four underground floors of torture cells.

"The good news is the view *from* the prison," said Twombly in a reverse-charges call from St. Petersburg. He was "touching base" once more. "'Kresti' means 'crosses' in Russian, did you know that, Edmond? Probably, it refers to the building's shape? It's in the form of a cross? But here's the irony: right across the Neva River from the prison is this beautiful convent, the Smolny Convent. If

Popescu pushes his bunk under his narrow-slit window and stands on his toes, he can actually see it. Gosh, that stunning cathedral dome, Edmond! Those four supporting cupolas! The golden orbs that top them! Wow! If I were your friend Popescu, I'd spend my time looking out the window. So I said to this lawyer who was taking me to the prison, I said, 'Well, you've got willing prisoners on one side of the river and unwilling prisoners on the other.' I was thinking of 'Nuns fret not,' Edmond, get it, Wordsworth? Anyway, this lawyer says most of the 'nuns' are divorced women, not in Smolny by choice! Russian Orthodox, I guess."

Kresti Prison, I gather from the evident *Schadenfreude* of Twombly's report, is a kind of hell far more daunting and hopeless than anything Dante imagined for his Inferno—more daunting, perhaps, because it is real, palpable, visible, not a metaphor or symbol of anything, certainly not merely an imaginary place where a poet might pay off old scores by locating his enemies. At Kresti, a cell is no more than sixteen meters square, and it is shared by forty inmates and countless cockroaches. The prisoners have to sleep in shifts since there are not bunks enough for all of them. Buggery is a casual fact of life; a scream in the night might issue from one of the demented or from a victim of rape. And the stench is enough to turn the strongest stomach. Meanwhile, on any given day, groups of women can be seen outside the prison walls, wives, mothers, sisters, girlfriends, waiting through the endless hours in the hope of catching a glimpse of a loved one, a face in a window.

Of course, Aristide's case is not so desperate as that of an ordinary prisoner. Well, he *isn't* an ordinary prisoner, not yet. He is only being "held" in Kresti, not imprisoned there, a vital, not merely a semantic, difference. He has not yet been tried, after all. Indeed, his presence in Kresti might as easily be due to an unfortunate bureaucratic cock-up as to the machinations of Dmitri Krivchun's political enemies. In fact, Popescu's lawyers are striving to get him transferred, at least until his trial, to more salubrious quarters. "The rich are different from the rest of us, Edmond," said Twombly, so bitterly and with such conviction one might have supposed the insight was his own.

Aristide has a cell to himself, four meters by four, and his son was granted permission to supply the prison's sagging military cot with a new mattress and clean bed linens. Aristide has meals delivered to his cell three times a day from Le Moulin Rouge, St. Petersburg's ritziest new restaurant. Apart from a cot, the cell boasts a small table, a three-legged stool, a slop bucket, and on a rough shelf in a corner a pitcher and bowl of dented, rusting tin. A bulb of low wattage behind a grille in the ceiling is perpetually on. Every morning, a trusty swabs out the cell and empties the slop bucket. The authorities have showered other privileges upon him—for example, two books, one, a copy of *Bleak House* in Spanish, the other, a guide to Paris in Russian. And he is allowed visitors: his lawyers, his son, and now his "spiritual guardian." True, he is locked into his cell and allowed out for only forty minutes a day, when he is required to walk alone in a tight circle in one of the yards, terrified of the snarling dogs straining at their leashes while their witty masters pretend to lose control of them. True, his cell, like all the others, is overrun by cockroaches. True, the stench in his cell, while somewhat muted, is enough to make his visitors blench. "But compared with the others," said Twombly merrily, "the guy is living in a luxury studio apartment. I kid you not."

Aristide is far from his former confident and dapper self. In the two months of his incarceration—two months in this unspeakable place!—he has, in Twombly's vile phrase, "let himself go." His once fine clothing hangs listlessly on his shrunken body. He has aged, or, rather, his age has abruptly caught up with him. He is unkempt, his nails black and torn. His skin gives off a clammy, yellowish sheen; he exudes fear through his pores. His eyes are never still; they dart everywhere, as if danger might appear at any moment from any direction.

When Twombly was admitted to his cell, Aristide did not get up to greet him. He remained where he was, sitting cross-legged on the floor, his back against the far wall. "Have you come to rescue me, Fred?" he chuckled. His eyes roamed the room restlessly. "I've come to pray with you," said Twombly with all his customary pomposity. He went over to Aristide and knelt before him. "Come," he said. He took him by the elbow and helped him to his knees.

Aristide took in his hands the cross that dangled from Twombly's neck and stroked it as if it were Aladdin's lamp. He glanced all about him nervously and whispered, "Have you any news for me?"

"News? Well, I bring you your daughter-in-law's greetings from the rue du Faubourg Saint-Honoré and your son Gabriel's from the Hotel Astoria."

"Please, I beg you, don't toy with me, Fred. Very well, it's true, when we were young fellows, students, we didn't care much for one another; all right, but that's ancient history, I hope. My case is desperate now. You cannot imagine what it's like to be locked in here, what I suffer. Have you seen the sculpture, the one across the river? Take a look at it. It will help you understand. So I beg you, tell me the news from Paris. Is the government involved yet? The consulate here? These Russian lawyers they've given me are worse than useless. They're probably working for my enemies. They should have had me out of here by now. Touch my cheeks, look, they're wet, d'you see? Only touch them. And what's my son doing all this while? Has he forgotten me? He hasn't been here for two days, two whole days! For Christ's sake, Fred, stop screwing around, what news have you for me?"

His voice had risen from a whisper to a strangulated shout. Suddenly, the metal cover to the window grating on his cell door slammed open and the face of a guard appeared there. It was a young face, flushed with the bloom of adolescence, a face that had not yet known a razor. The boy looked at them sternly; he possessed "ravishing eyes of a limpid, Slavic blue." Twombly waxed lyrical in his description.

Aristide raised his voice to a level well above what was comfortable for his visitor. They were both still on their knees, and Aristide was barking into Twombly's nose. "Yes, Father, I'm being very well treated. I've no complaints at all. How could I have? The staff are showing me every courtesy." Meanwhile, he blinked his eyes and gave his head short jerks to indicate the presence of the guard.

("I don't mind telling you, Edmond," Twombly confided, "his breath stinks abominably. A sewer! It was all I could do to stop myself from turning away or showing my disgust.")

The door over the grating slammed shut.

"I have no news other than the Good News, the Gospel. I came all this way to offer you spiritual comfort, to pray with you, to help you find the strength you'll need to survive your time of trial."

Aristide raised his restless eyes to the ceiling. "Oh, Fred," he croaked, "I shall go mad!" But then he turned savagely on Twombly. "You devil! You came here not to help but to torment me!" He took hold of Twombly's cross, tore it from his neck, breaking the chain, and dashed it to the floor. Then he began to laugh; he clapped his hands and roared with laughter. The tears streamed down his face. He beat his chest, he tore at his hair, he laughed and laughed.

Twombly picked up his cross and kissed it. As quickly as he could with his aching joints, he got to his feet and nervously made for the cell door. "I'll be back," he said, and knocked on the grating for the guard. "Take a day or two to calm down. Remember, the greatest sin is despair. Meanwhile, I'll pray for you, I can promise you that."

His answer was more mad laughter.

"I shall let him stew for a bit, and then, Edmond . . . to him again," said Twombly cheerfully. "I've got him by the short and curlies, and that's a true fact, as my students say." Twombly phoned me right after his ghastly visit to the prison, reversing the charges, of course. "Just wanted to keep you abreast."

"I can't believe my ears! 'The short and curlies'? Are you the Fred Twombly who is an ordained priest in the one true Church, humble servant of a compassionate Savior, wielder of the Power and earnest of the Glory, or are you an impostor, a servant of Satan? Can it be that Father Fred Twombly exults because he holds our old friend's testicles in his hand and can, if he wishes, squeeze them? Is that the power? Then wherein lies the glory?"

"It's just an expression, is all," said Twombly huffily. "Words. Air."

"Like the Sermon on the Mount?"

"Give me a break, Edmond! Christ is less concerned with the words we utter than with those we inscribe on our hearts."

"Equivocation, Fred?"

"That's a doctrine that's saved many of us over the centuries in times of trial."

"Precisely. But equivocation is the privilege of the accused, not of his judges."

Twombly made no effort to mask his irritation. "We both know Popescu to be a swindler. You may choose to overlook it, but you know it. Well, I'm the first to leave to Caesar the crimes committed against him, but I am Christ's advocate in matters pertaining to Christ. That hitherto unknown Shakespeare text belongs to Beale Hall. Popescu has it, and he must not be allowed to profit from it. That's the bottom line."

There was no point in arguing with him. "Did you see the sculpture across the river?"

"What sculpture?"

"The one Aristide told you to take a look at."

"Oh, *that*," said Twombly impatiently. "Yes, as a matter of fact, I did. It's an abstract bit of rubbish created, as you might expect, by some Jew or other, a madman who spent some time in one of Stalin's gulags. Chomsky? Chimpsky? No, Chemyakin. All it is, is a barred prison window, and you look through it at Kresti, across the river. Oh, and there's this sphinx on each side of the barred window; they're sort of facing one another. And the side of each sphinx's face that's turned to Kresti is a skull. That's about it, except for some plaques inscribed with quotations on democracy, tolerance, and peace by Sakharov, Akhmatova, and so on. Talk about gloom and doom."

"Perhaps sculpture's not your cup of tea," I suggested sarcastically. "It obviously spoke to Aristide. I suppose he thought it would speak to you. Perhaps in the West, we take our freedom too casually."

"Give me a break. I know art when I see it. My guide told me the guy's living in New York now. Where he belongs. Another Jewish success story."

What was the use? "What are you planning to do next?"

Twombly read total capitulation in my question. I was the one he was after, remember, not poor Aristide, who merely served his end. "Well, I'm going to offer him a choice. Either he will instruct his daughter-in-law to give me a copy of the Shakespeare volume's bill of sale and a photocopy of the volume in question, in which case I will get the Vatican to become engaged in his behalf, perhaps the Holy Father himself making a plea, or I will inform the Russian authorities that Popescu had perpetrated a similar outrage in the United Kingdom and who-knows-how-many others elsewhere."

"But surely *you* don't have any influence at the Vatican?" I said, amazed at his effrontery.

"Right. None whatever. But Popescu won't know that. He'll happily clutch at straws."

"Have you no conscience? Will you even evoke the name of His Holiness to buttress your lies? Aristide is *in extremis,* man. Will you squat over him and void your bowels?"

"Spare me your moral assessment, S.J. I say nothing of your unsavory metaphors. The point is the return of Catholic property to the Church. Let's get that done first. Only then let us indulge our combative faculties on questions of what's right and what's wrong."

"But what if he won't cooperate? Surely you wouldn't denounce him to his tormentors? He's in enough trouble without your interference. You'll not add to his grief."

"Oh, won't I?" said Twombly chuckling. "Well, well, perhaps I won't. But Popescu doesn't know that. I told you I'd get to the bottom of this Shakespeare mystery, Edmond, and one way or another, I will."

٩—

But "this Shakespeare mystery" and Twombly's determination to solve it were quite pushed from my mind by a desperate if not entirely unexpected event at Beale Hall. It grieves me beyond measure to report that Bastien, my faithful donkey, my oldest friend, has at last gone over the edge. He is a lunatic—but, of course, being dear Bastien, an utterly harmless one.

One of our cleaning ladies, the aptly named Mrs. Mopp, had entered the Great Hall intent upon her dusting-and-polishing duties when she noticed what she took to be a new work of art, a life-size sculpture of a Christ pinned not to the Cross but seemingly to the wood paneling beneath the Knigge portrait of Cardinal Taittinger. As she drew closer to the statue, she noticed certain oddities about it, oddities that she took to be sure signs of the artist's up-to-date symbolic intent, incomprehensible, of course, to her. For example, Christ's head, which rested on his right shoulder, was encircled not with a crown of thorns but with a chaplet made of intertwined and color-coded telephone wires. The palm of each outstretched hand held not a cruel, piercing nail but a purple plum secured in place by the thumb. Around Christ's loins was arranged a tea towel, a garish souvenir of the Tower of London. A corkscrew hung from ordinary string tied around his neck. But oddest of all, as she was now able to see, was Christ's body, for it was not the body of a man tortured to death at the vigorous (and perfect) age of thirty-three but that of a man more than twice that age, a body well advanced in decrepitude. Finally, she noted that the sculpture gave off what she would later call "a horrid pong."

Mrs. Mopp stood for a moment examining the work of art, her feather duster poised for action, when Christ opened one eye, looked at her, and then deliberately winked. Mrs. Mopp gasped. But far worse followed. Christ pushed himself forward, lifting his arms toward her as if intending an embrace. Now the poor woman found her voice and screamed; and she ran shrieking through the rooms and galleries, through the former servants' quarters, through the kitchen and the scullery, and out the tradesmen's entrance, collapsing on a bench beside the door.

Meanwhile, Christ, or, rather, Bastien, had taken it on the lam, dashing out of the man-size entrance cut into the Great Door, hopping painfully across the forecourt's gravel—ouch! ouch!—and then, with an ever slower and more wobbly gait, making for Trafalgar Hill and the victory column. He fell to his knees just short of the plinth, rolled onto his side, and lay panting. "Here wast thou bayed, brave heart." He was found an hour later by one of the groundkeepers and PC Whiting, the latter summoned from his late-morning tea. (Yes, it was still PC Whiting. Tubby had failed his examinations and was thinking of leaving the force.) It proved impossible to unwind Bastien from his fetal pose. They wrapped him as best they could in Tubby's oilskin raincoat and trundled him back to the Hall in a wheelbarrow.

I had been in Ludlow all day—for no particular purpose, merely idling, avoiding, I suppose, the myriad niggling duties that fell on my shoulders in Maude's absence—and did not see Bastien until the evening, long after the departure of the doctor that Tubby had had the wit to summon. Tubby had also summoned Belinda Scudamour, his "very own private nurse," as he winkingly called her, and she had awaited my return. There was nothing physically wrong with Bastien, the doctor had told Belinda, granted his age. Oh, he had a deviated septum, to be sure, but that was about all. "No, what he needs," Belinda reported, imitating the doctor's plummy tones, "is what we medical chaps call a 'trick cyclist,' know what I mean?" He had left his telephone number in case Father Music should wish to call him for a referral. "I'd sponge him down, if I were you," the doctor had concluded. "And let a little air into his room. He's a bit ripe."

Bastien's room in the converted stable block was spartan, a monk's cell, if ever there was one. There was a simple Cross on the wall above his cot, a footlocker, a hard wooden chair, and a small chest on which stood a photograph in a frame, a smiling woman, his sister Joséphine, her hands holding on her shoulders a yoke from which depended milk pails. The window was open; on its ledge was a container of perfumed deodorizer spray, left there, no doubt, by Belinda. The room smelled pleasantly of heather.

Bastien had not answered my knock. When I entered his room, he had turned from me in his cot. I went and sat beside him there and patted him on his haunch.

"How goes it, old friend?"

He reached blindly behind him and grasped my wrist with surprising strength. "Oh, Edmond, I am so ashamed."

"Now, now."

"Who was it I frightened?"

"One of the cleaning ladies. Mrs. Mopp. I've spoken to her. She understands."

"What can she understand? Oh, what have I done, Edmond? They'll put me away. Mrs. Mopp, you say. Do I know Mrs. Mopp? Which one is she? The fat one who always wears her hat when she cleans? No woman is safe. What might I do next? It just came over me, Edmond. I had to do it."

"Don't exaggerate, old fellow. You only acted out what many of us, particularly us priests, have had drilled into our imaginations from our earliest days: 'What must it have been like for Him?' 'Think of His agony, of His pain as the nails tore into His flesh, as His very weight pulled at his wounds.' That sort of thing. It was just bad luck that someone interrupted your . . . experiment."

"Do you really think so?"

"I don't doubt it."

"I don't remember anything of the kind. I think I thought it would be something of a lark, dressing up as Him, I mean." He cackled so hard he began to cough. "Not dressing *up,* dressing *down.* I deserve a dressing *down* for *un*dressing. But men don't wear dresses, only priests and women, not men." He scratched his head, his hair wild upon his pillow. "And my skin itched so. I couldn't bear my clothes a moment longer. Poor Mrs. Mopp."

"You've been under something of a strain, I imagine, what with Maude away."

"It's a blessing she's away! Not that she's in hospital, I don't mean that. But it's a blessing she wasn't here to witness my shame. It doesn't bear thinking about. Promise me that you won't tell her, promise me, Edmond."

"If that's what you want, why, yes, I promise. But this is Maude we're talking about. She's known you as long as she's known me."

He turned toward me for the first time since my arrival. His grip on my wrist tightened. I had been sitting too long in a slightly twisted position. My back ached and the hand whose wrist he grasped tingled painfully.

"Don't let them put me away, Edmond, don't leave me to the Church. I don't want poor Castignac's fate!" His eyes, I saw, were red-rimmed; his cheeks were wet. "Send me to Jojo, my sister." He released his grip and pointed to the photograph. I stood up. "Let Jojo come and get me."

I gave him my word.

He turned from me again and gave a great shuddering sigh. "I'm tired. I think I'll sleep."

"Good night, good Bastien."

I was answered by his weeping.

You would be forgiven if you deduced from the dialogue recorded above that poor Bastien was (by and large) sane. He had experienced what we might call an aberrant psychological "episode," a brief period in which his mental gears had slipped. But everything was back in place again now. After all, he understood quite clearly what he had done. The retrospective shame he felt was entirely appropriate. His fear of incarceration in some Catholic institution for the terminally incurable was reasonable enough: the form his madness took, after all, was not one the Church would want to have bruited about. But I have omitted a significant element from his speech, its obscenities. He punctuated almost every sentence with nouns in triplicate ("piss, shit, fuck," "cunt, prick, arsehole," "pillock, twat, sod," and so on), as casually, mildly, and meaninglessly as another might use "as it were" or "to be sure," mere fillers, rhetorical grace notes.

Had you heard him, you would not have thought him sane.

⌒⥈

The Bard was proving elusive. Authentic Shakespearean works as yet unknown to an eager public seemed impossible to come by. The Pish now knew enough about his quarry to mock the breezy assurances he had once given to Sir Percival. Over the years, he had cast his net wide. He corresponded with agents, booksellers, and antiquarians around the world. Occasionally, he got wind of something promising, only to have his hopes dashed. The "finds" were spurious, clumsy forgeries that would have taken in only the most ignorant of bardolaters, those begging to be fooled. Or if not spurious, then useless.

For example, a certain Ambrosio de Aguilar, a New Christian of Portuguese origin, wrote to him from Recife in Pernambuco, Brazil, offering a copy of the plays of Aristophanes, the Greek text "purified and rendered inoffensive to Holy Church" by Fra Danielo Donatelli, in a unique edition published in Lisbon in 1563 solely for the library of his ancestors, "may they rest in peace." De Aguilar perhaps reasoned that a play was after all a play, whoever wrote it; what he was offering was an edition of undoubted rarity.

In fact, the Pish bought it in hopes of adding it to a small collection of bibliographical rarities he was assembling. If all else failed, Sir Percival might be willing to exchange the Dunaharaszti Haggadah for other attractive additions to his library at Beale Hall. But when after many months the book at last arrived, it proved to be a book no longer. The heat and humidity of Recife, together with the voracious appetites of its insects, had transformed the work into a pulpy brick. There were no pages to turn.

In all this while, the Pish had become something of an expert in Shakespeare. He had begun by devoting an hour a day to the study of the plays and poems. But an hour soon seemed too little, and so he doubled the time allotted to his profane studies, and added to it whatever few extra minutes he might snatch from his other duties—to his prayers and religious observances, to his students and the exegesis of Torah and Talmud, to his voluminous correspondence and his many other writings, and of course to his beloved Sarah, beautiful, blossoming, and still thumpingly audacious in the marital bed.

And he read not only deeply but also broadly. He read in Dr. Johnson and other worthies of Shakespeare's life and achievements. He read what he could of England's history during the reigns of the first Elizabeth and James. He read other poets and playwrights of that Golden Age: Sidney, Spenser, Marlowe, Jonson, Donne. And with the passage of time, he began to develop his own thoughts about the plays and the poems, their meanings and significances, and the psychological complexities they lay bare. It seemed to him that a genius with so profound an understanding of human nature and withal so evident a sympathy for his fellow creatures must be Jewish, could *only* be Jewish. And he spent what he himself called "many fruitless hours" trying to find evidence in the works for what his "very soul" told him must be true. The study of the Bard and his joy in the works became his secret and subsidiary vocation, and the Bard himself provided the Pish with his excuse: "'Tis no sin for a man to labour in his vocation."

But all his efforts to acquire some piece of Shakespeariana that the world at large knew nothing of seemed doomed to failure. The years passed, his beard grew white, plump Sarah became fat and garrulous, and still there was no reward for his devotion to the search—other, of course, than the sheer pleasure and intellectual rigor his "subsidiary vocation" granted him. By the time he first held *Dyuers and Sondry Sonettes* in his hands, he must long since have given up hope. It was surely a miracle. Unless . . .

Unless, as I suspect, the book is a fake, a counterfeit, a travesty the Pish himself, in his desperation to win back for Jewry the Dunaharaszti Haggadah, brought into being. After all, both he and Sir Percival were now old. Either of them might die before the Haggadah could be ransomed. This possibility must increasingly have gnawed at the Pish. As for me, I have never seen the Beale Hall *Dyuers and Sondry Sonettes*. There was too little time between Aristide's finding of it in the library and Maude's selling it to him. But my suspicions are, I think, reasonably based. First, I have found among the Pish's miscellaneous papers a fragment of a play purporting to be by the Bard but written in the Pish's own familiar Hebrew script, as follows:

From

THE LAMENTABLE TRAGEDY OF PRINCE ESAU;
OR, ALL IS TRUE

By

WILLIAM SHAKESPEARE

Scene Two. Isaac on his Death-bed. Noon.

ISAAC: Who's he that stands without my chamber door?
Come hither, sirrah; speak, reveal thyself.
For know, these orbs that once beam'd forth their light—

Yea, look'd upon that Angel bright that stay'd
My father Abr'am's hand what time he held his knife
Above my heart—are now burn'd out. Speak loud,
For 'tis thy voice must tell me who thou art,
And I am somedeel deaf. Such is mine eld.

JACOB: 'Tis I, your son.

ISAAC: Which of my sons art thou?

JACOB: Oh, father, dear, your Esau speaks to you,
Your first-born son. Obedient to your wish,
I here have brought a well-stewed dish of game,
That you might eat and eating gain the strength
Which heartless age hath robb'd you of. 'Tis Esau
Bids you eat.

ISAAC: Come near and sit beside me.

JACOB: Forget the blessing not you promis'd me.

ISAAC: Nay, in good time, but tell me, Esau, first,
How is't thou hast so fast accomplishèd
The task I set thee?

JACOB: The Lord your God, I trow,
Granted me good fortune. The chase was swift,
The kill was clean, and to my tents I hied,
Your fav'rite spicy *Gulyàs* to prepare.

ISAAC: God grant it may be so. I fear some ill.
Come close, my son, come close that I may feel you—
Whether in truth you are my son or no.
He goes to him.
The gentle voice is the voice of Jacob;
Yet Esau's hands are hairy, as are these.
Like crested wave I stand in doubtful pause
Whether to make for shore or back retire.
And yet I'll try once more. Come closer still
And kiss me, my good son, that I thy clothes
Might smell and thus may learn the truth of it.

Art thou my Esau, as thou sayest?
JACOB: I am.
He kisses him.
ISAAC: Ah, the smell is the well known smell of Esau.
Near death I am, and purblind I may be,
But with my nose I feelingly can see.

Perhaps the Pish began to write a "Shakespeare" play on an Old Testament theme in a foolish effort to demonstrate the Jewishness of his new hero; perhaps he abandoned it because he felt inadequate to the task. Whatever the case, he soon tried his hand at the Elizabethan sonnet, and with the short lyric he had found his genre. A number of the sonnets survive among his papers, grouped together under the general title "To Serena," which name I assume to be Sarah poeticized. One example should serve to reveal his skill (or, if you please, his lack of it):

Say that my loving mistress smile at me,
Or say she frown and stamp her pretty foot;
Whether her kiss from bondage sets me free
Or anger foul in prison doth me put—
Whate'er she does, I swear she hath such grace
That manhood's self in me she makes to grow;
Thus manhood has its source in female's face
And in those other parts I've come to know.
This paradox all reason doth defy
And to philosophy the fig doth give:
That in her spicy nest I, living, die,
And, dying, rise again, once more to live.
Thus do I live in hope but to expire,
And in my death burn with a lover's fire.

To this evidence I would add a remark the Pish makes in quite a different context in his *Table-Talk*. He is speaking of English surnames, which often strike him as amusing, and offers as one among many a certain Guido Honeybone, a printer well known to him who kept his establishment in Bristol. The Honeybones had been printers there for many generations. "Honeybone, now, what can it signify? Not a question I would want to ask the dear lady, my wife!" But he amplifies his story by adding that the current possessor of the name once made a remarkable discovery. Guido Honeybone, for unexplained reasons, once chose to break through a wall in the family cellar and found an alcove behind it six feet by six that housed a printing press, fonts, and a quantity of folio sheets, "all perfectly preserved, all dating from the time of Good Queen Bess." Possibly, the Elizabethan Honeybone was caught up in the religious controversies of the day, a Protestant sectarian who thought that Bishop Jewell and the rest had not gone far enough in stripping the English Church of its Roman impurities. Perhaps he had bricked up his press to escape the authorities.

And my final piece of evidence is an item unexplained and otherwise inexplicable in the Pish's household accounts: "To G. Honeybone, Bristol, £51.10s.0d." This was no piddling sum in Honeybone's day. What might he have done to earn it?

I am confident that these clues have led you to the simple conclusion to which they have already led me. The Pish was the only begetter of the volume *Dyuers and Sondry Sonettes*. If that is so, the book still has value. It is a unique copy of an eighteenth-century forgery. It is a forgery perpetrated by the Ba'al Shem of Ludlow, no less. It is a volume of poems that may have their own merit. It is a fine example of pre-Romantic Shakespeare idolatry. And so on. But it is not quite so heavy a club as Twombly believes.

Should I speak up now, before the wretched man revisits Aristide in Kresti? To do so would be to admit I know such a book came from Beale Hall. And that might implicate Maude. She would surely speak up to save me, with what consequences to herself I dare not think. I am thus faced with an intolerable choice, a conflict of loyalties. Aristide or Maude? Aristide is in the lion's den. His need is great. But Maude is Maude. And so, you see, there is only one possible answer to the dilemma. I must sacrifice Aristide in defense of the woman I have lain beside for half a century. And yet, is my conscience perhaps posing a false conflict of loyalties here? Were I to call off the hellhound Twombly from his current prey and offer myself to his rapacity, thereby almost certainly implicating Maude, would Aristide be much helped? Help him I would if I could. But he, like Laocoön, is caught in the coils of monstrous political serpents, crushed by issues far beyond and irrelevant to his undoubted crime. His rescue thence, if it come, will be the result of jockeying among powers both national and international. From this point of view, my "confession" to Twombly would be a truly futile gesture.

⌒

Well, that woman, it seems, wishes to lie beside me no longer. Two days before the day I had expected to bring Maude home from the Saints in my still new and wonderfully comfortable Rover, I received a call from Angie Mackletwist telling me that "for the time being" Ms. Moriarty had decided to move in with her. In fact, she was already there.

"What on earth for?"

"She'll still need looking after, Father. A woman's touch for a woman's intimate requirements . . . Need I say more?"

"A great deal more! I've got a private nurse laid on, twenty-four hours a day, for as long as she's needed. Whatever's wanted, *I'll* supply. Beale Hall will, I mean. Ms. Moriarty's a valued employee." I heard Angie's intake of breath and hurriedly changed my tone. "So kind of you, so kind. Still, you've a business to run, God love you. It's too much to ask of you. But you'll have garnered up treasure in heaven, I can assure you, simply by being willing. I'll come by and pick her up now, shall I?"

"And then there's Ludlow District Hospital just around the

corner, easy access to a physiotherapist, doctors aplenty, emergency hours, trained nurses to change the bandage on her . . . on her . . . well, you know, Father, her upper leg, limb, I mean. What could be more convenient, I ask you?"

"But—"

"No need to say it. My pleasure, I assure you. Well, we've always enjoyed a bit of a natter, Ms. Moriarty and me. And think of the stairs at the Hall! Alfie, my nephew, he's brought over a camp bed he uses for his ma-in-law whenever she deigns, you know, lives in Poole, ever so comfy—the bed, I mean. He's put it in the front room, brought in the telly from the kitchen, all mod cons. She'll be well looked after, don't you worry."

"I'd like to have a word with Ms. Moriarty, please."

"Ah, poor soul, she's resting now, Father. Bit of a trauma—have I got that right? Trauma?—the excitement, the ride in the ambulance, and that."

"I'd still like to have a word with her, if you'd be so kind."

"Try her tomorrow. She'll have a bit of her strength back." And the beastly woman hung up.

Well, rather than phone Maude again, I went the very next day to see her, armed with a large bunch of flowers for the convalescent and a small tin of Licorice Allsorts for Angie Mackletwist. Angie lives in Martyrs Lane, a stone's throw not only from Ludlow District Hospital but also, and perhaps more important, from Holy Cross Roman Catholic Church. Martyrs Lane is a drab street of pebble-dash terrace houses built shortly after the war to replace a clutch of squalid hovels. The pay-and-display box was on the blink and so I had to park two streets away. It had begun raining on the drive over from Beale Hall, a fine, penetrating rain, more like mist than anything else, and I was soon soaked, not having had the wit to equip the car with an umbrella. I splashed through the puddles in my trainers, my poor bunions rubbed raw.

Beside Angie's front door and protected from the rain by the overhang was a holy-water font together with a picture of the

Sacred Heart made red by an electric bulb. My own ordinary heart sank. It was going to be an uphill battle.

Nevertheless, I rang the doorbell. It was answered by a priest with a wizened, crab-apple face and the stature of an emaciated second-form schoolboy. "You'll be Father Music," he told me. "Come in out of the wet, do." And he used a handshake to pull me over the threshold. He was surprisingly strong. "I'm Father Phipps, Philip Phipps, at your service. Alias 'Old Pip-Pip' to the naughty boys and girls in the choir over at Holy Cross, God love them." He smiled a smile that caused his eyes to disappear into the multiple creases of his face while it revealed yellow teeth flecked with foam.

"I've stopped by to see Ms. Moriarty."

"Of *course* you have. No less have I. Here, let me have your wet mac. I'll hang it up on the hook there, shall I?"

It was a business getting my mac off. We stood in a tiny entrance hall in a space barely enough for the two of us. Before me stairs ran up to the first floor; beside them a short, dim corridor led, I suppose, to the kitchen at the rear. I put the flowers and the tin of sweets on the stairs and let the little fellow help me with my mac. On a small shelf beneath the tinted hall mirror were displayed a plastic figurine of Our Lady rising from a base that said "Souvenir of Lourdes"; on a wire stand, an upright saucer depicting in lively colors the martyrdom of Saint Sebastian; and a framed, "colorized" photograph of Pius XII smiling thinly. On the wall opposite was affixed the miniature brass head of a deer, its size about that of a clenched fist, and from its head sprang several hooks, to one of which, by standing on tiptoe, Pip-Pip was even now hanging my mac.

"This will be the front room, then, I expect," I said, making for the door beside the hall mirror.

He caught me by the arm. "We can't go in there just yet. My own visit was interrupted." He glanced at his watch. "I'll have to be gone in a minute or so. There's no end of Christ's work to be done." He stood on tiptoes, put his hand beside his mouth, and whispered in my ear. "The nurse from the District is in with her now. Dressing the wound, you know. It won't heal, they say. The doctors are baffled. It's a stigma of a sort. Mark my words, it may reside rather more in our bailiwick than in theirs." He winked extravagantly; his yellow teeth bubbled with foam. His breath had a hint of the Eucharist and the half-remembered scent of the machine oil I used on my bicycle in the old days.

We stood in awkward proximity, he gazing up at me expectantly. I was tempted to pat him on the head.

"It's odd we've never met," he said. "I've been up at the Hall a number of times over the years. You're something of a recluse, I suppose, sunk in scholarly matters. Still, I heard you once at the annual Cardinal Newman lecture series. You introduced that American chap, Father Trimble, was it? Father Trembly? Something like that. It was years and years ago. He was talking about G. K. Chesterton, I think. No, God forgive me, I tell a lie. His lecture was on Hilaire Belloc; yes, I remember now. It was called 'Belloc, an Unacknowledged Apostle of Tolerance.' Very interesting, too."

"I never attend the lectures."

"I'd have seen you more often, else. No, up at the Hall I've had to make do with that other Frenchman, your second-in-command, Father Bastien. Nice chap, salt of the earth. But between you and me"—and here he twiddled a forefinger above his left ear—"I'm not sure his lift still reaches the top floor."

"Father Bastien retired a fortnight ago. It was all getting a bit too much for him, good soul that he is. He's back in France, living peacefully on his sister's small farm and drinking the untroubled wine of their own cellar."

"Is there a vacancy at the Hall, then?" he said eagerly. "If there is, may I ask you to think of me? I'm just the chap for the job."

"Things are at sixes and sevens at the moment, Father, what

with Father Bastien gone and Ms. Moriarty still on sick leave. But their absence helps me concentrate the mind, no doubt of it. I'm having a bit of an organizational rethink, trying to accommodate Beale Hall to the new millennium, however late in the day. But I'll keep you in mind, never fear. You're at Holy Cross, then?"

"For my sins." Here he chuckled, spitting foam. "An old joke," he explained. "Where would we be without a bit of laughter, eh?"

"The Gospels often tell us that Jesus wept; nowhere do they tell us that He laughed," I said sternly.

He looked at me askance.

Now I *did* pat him on the head. "There, there," I said. "Nothing but another old joke."

"Ah," he said, relieved. "And a good one, too. Makes you think, though. It's quite true, after all. He never *did* laugh."

"Not even once. 'Sorrow is better than laughter,' Ecclesiastes advises us. Tell me, who's running the show at Holy Cross nowadays? Not Father Manning?"

"Good gracious, no! He was before *my* time, even. I think by now he may be dead, God rest his soul. After him came Father McBrien and that shameful scandal in the sacristy, may he find forgiveness in heaven. And then the present incumbent, young Father Pinfold. He came to us from a parish in the East End of London, and he's right on the 'cutting edge,' to use one of his own ultramodern phrases. Wants everyone to call him Kevin, or, better yet, Kev. A bit difficult for some of the pious old dears who dust and polish and arrange the flowers, that. His preferred attire's blue jeans and a T-shirt." He looked at me keenly to check my reaction. I merely nodded, which told him nothing. "And why not? The disciples themselves, I venture, didn't patronize ecclesiastical tailors, eh? Mind you, he's achieved wonders, has our Kev.

"I've always been on the social-services side of things, something of a peaceful backwater, hitherto. The government, you see, have the programs, the funds, and the personnel. What I could do was visit the housebound, the elderly and infirm. Offer the faith to those who already possessed it. But Kev has pushed me out into midstream, where the current is swift and the rocks are plentiful. Now I'm 'into' substance-abuse counseling. Not only that, I'm 'proactive.' I don't sit back waiting for them to come to me. I go out and find 'em. That's what I'm doing here, actually. I've been told Ms. Moriarty has a tiny problem."

"Nonsense," I said loyally. "She'll take a drop now and then, just to be sociable, even as you and I."

He looked at me slyly. "Then you knew I was talking about alcohol abuse?"

The little bastard! "Who told you this nonsense?"

"Miss Mackletwist was worried about her friend, God bless her, and told Kev. Kev told me. And here I am." He looked at his watch again. "I've a seminar over at Holy Cross in five minutes, mostly teenagers, who'll leave if I'm late. Please make my excuses to Ms. Moriarty and assure her I'll be back as soon as I'm able." He picked up my hand and shook it briskly. "Delighted to meet you at last, Father Music. Do please remember my interest in the Hall. Well, you've given your word. That's good enough for me." He inched around me in the narrow space, opened the door, and— poof!—he was gone.

I stood and dithered for a moment or two, wondering whether I should perhaps come back at another time, when the door to the front room opened and a nurse in full World War I nursing regalia appeared, calling cheerfully over her shoulder, "Back in three days, then, hen. Remember now, do your exercises like a guid girl, lest ye turn into wobbly jelly. Lord love ye." She turned and saw me standing in her way. "Where's the wee man that was here to see my patient, the wee priest?"

"He had to leave. I'm Father Music, his replacement."

"See that she walks around the room a bit. And if she wants a wee cup of tea, let *her* make it. She needs to move about. But *you* carry the tray for her. She'll need her walking stick for a while, d'y'see. Can ye remember all that, Father?"

The nurse and I were of a size. I had to step out of the house in order for her to get past me in a seemly way.

It was no longer a surprise visit. Maude had heard me speaking to her nurse. "Edmond, is that you?"

"None other, my dear." I picked up the gifts from the stairs where I'd left them and went into the room. "A few flowers to cheer you up, Maude, and some sweets for Angie—or for you if you'd prefer. No, please don't get up."

She had lost quite a bit of weight since last I saw her; she was almost slim. She wore a new, floor-length bathrobe tied neatly at the waist. Her thinning hair was drawn back and caught in a velvet ribbon behind her head. It was easy to see the lineaments of the young Maude. She sat down again in a chair that had evidently been placed for her near the window. Through it, she could see what passed for a parade in Martyrs Lane.

"You're looking absolutely smashing," I said.

She gazed out at the murk and drizzle beyond the panes. "You shouldn't have come, Edmond."

"Shall I put the flowers in a vase for you?"

"Oh, do what you like," she said irritably. "Put them in the kitchen sink. Angie'll take care of them." And as I turned from her: "Angie doesn't even like licorice—nor, as you ought to remember, do I."

In the kitchen I threw flowers and sweets into the rubbish bin.

We sat for a while in a silence that was anything but companionable, she still gazing out the window, I, on a small chair covered in a plum-colored moquette that matched the small settee adjacent to it, looking about me. The front room itself was small, perhaps ten feet by ten, and fussily appointed. The walls and ceiling were stippled, but painted over in glossy cream. There were French doors with frosted panes in the wall opposite the window, leading, I suppose, into a dining room. A Carver chair upholstered in flocked pink velvet stood at a precise angle in each of the corners bracketing the French doors. Opposite me was a small fireplace with an electric fire embedded in it. On its mantel, organized by size, was a neat line of little glass creatures, the largest in the middle, a horse, rearing its head six inches into the air. Above the mantel hung a two-tone, paneled mirror shaped like an open fan. Beside me stood a small, highly polished cabinet. On it, atop three crocheted doilies each of an appropriate size, were arranged a lamp with a tubular glass stem and a tiny, fringed shade, an empty cut-glass decanter, and a framed photograph of a nun raising her arms as if in benediction over a group of grim girls in gym slips, some of them holding field hockey sticks. On the wall behind me and reflected in the fan-shaped mirror was a framed print of Versace's *Christ Throwing the Money Changers out of the Temple*. Of the camp bed and television that Angie's nephew Alfie was supposed to have brought into the front room there was no sign.

I have given so precise a description of this wretched room to make clear the great gulf that separates it from the glorious surroundings in which Maude had spent most of her life. Never mind the grand, semipublic spaces of Beale Hall and their magnificent appointments, the art and artfulness that greet the visitor at every turn—why, the very room she calls her "office," the erstwhile butler's pantry, is exquisite in the comparison, ample, wood-paneled, comfortably furnished, with a view from its windows onto the smaller of the rose gardens. I say nothing of the bedroom we have shared for so many years, the Mrs. Curricle Room, named after the Shakespearean actress who was a mistress of George IV. The very kitchen upon whose flagstones Maude passed out is more attractive than that front room. It pained me to see her sitting there.

I looked covertly at Maude and saw her face in profile. She was frowning, twitching her lips, drumming her fingers on the arm of her chair, deep in some argument going on in her head. Perhaps it was with me. She had certainly blocked out the fact that I was physically present.

"Come home with me, Maude," I said.

"Where's Father Phipps?" She spoke sharply, as if I were keeping him from her. But she did not turn her head to look at me.

"He sends his apologies. He had to leave. But he promises to return as soon as he's able." I tried for a jolly tone, hoping to change her mood. "A funny little chap, decent, no doubt. Godly, even. But for the absence of a beard, he reminds me of one of dear old W.C.'s garden gnomes. Still, you don't want Holy Cross, Maude. It offers everything you can't abide. Why, from what I hear, it makes Vatican II look like the High Middle Ages. Heavy metal, reggae, rap, all that's most appalling in contemporary popular music shunted onto the fast track for Christ. Next Sunday's feature for early Mass is a new group from London, Pontius Pilate and His Nail-Driving Five." Well, all right, I took some liberties with the truth in the interests of lightening the mood, but I nevertheless built a reasonable edifice, I think, upon Pip-Pip's hints. Of course, I took just the wrong tack; I succeeded only in making things worse for myself. "'The chief honcho,' as he is known to some of his parishioners, wants to be called Kev, and perhaps he ought to be. No doubt he himself calls Jesus 'Josh.' It's a high-tech world, after all, and it behooves the Church to be user-friendly. But you don't need Kev or Pip-Pip, Maude, you've got me."

"You!" She gave a bitter laugh. "You're the problem, not the cure."

"Angie told me she'd fitted out the room with a bed and a television for you."

"That's it, Edmond. Typical. Change the topic. Avoid at all costs talking about anything that matters." She had turned to face me. A tear ran down one cheek.

"When are you coming back to the Hall, my love? When are you coming back to *me*? I mean. There, is that matter enough?"

"I'm an alcoholic. You know that, even if in your harmful decency you've never confronted me with the fact. Of course, your looking the other way may have meant nothing more than your usual self-centered pursuit of the peaceful life, not decency at all, at all. You're a great one for inaction, you'll grant me that at least. 'Avoidance is nine points of happiness,' you've said more than once. I used to think you were joking, being witty and all. The point is, I'm now a *recovering* alcoholic—at least, I hope so. Father Phipps has had some success with the likes of me. Angie put him in touch. He runs what he calls a 'seminar' over at Holy Cross."

"Who's avoiding the question now? Why can't Phipps visit you at the Hall? Or if you have to attend the seminar, if that's part of the therapy, why can't I drive you in to Ludlow for it?"

"Merciful hour, but for a smart fellow you can be terribly stupid! It's our living together has done me in. What could a woman do worse than spread her legs for a priest? Every day since first we met my conscience has tossed a few grains of guilt at me. Why d'you think I've been dousing myself in gin? But gin won't wash the guilt away. I'm up to my neck in sand, Edmond; it'll smother me."

"But we haven't done it for years. I'm not even sure I can anymore. And then there was your hip getting in the way. No need for guilt, none at all. Look, I'll move to another room. Or if you like, we can have a bed moved into your office. Why not? That way, you can avoid the stairs and keep my dastardly, bestial lust at bay at one and the same time."

"I'm not supposed to avoid the stairs. That's why Alfie took back his camp bed. Mr. Sprott-Wemys was quite clear about that. I must take what exercise I can, always doing a little more than I want to. I sleep upstairs in the second bedroom."

"Another good reason to return to the Hall. We've got stairs all over."

"You're not listening, are you? You never listen to me, Edmond. And you never did. I'm not coming back to the Hall, not ever. Try to understand. I'm finished with all that. I'm finished with you." And here she began to sob. But when I rose to go and comfort her, she shrank from me and waved me off, as if my touch would defile her.

I waited for the sobbing to stop. "Shall I get you something, a glass of water, a cup of tea?"

She made an impatient gesture. She wanted nothing from me.

"What about your work at the Hall? What about all your gear?"

"I'm retired. As director, consider yourself duly notified. Have someone pack up my gear. Angie's Alfie will fetch it for me." These words emerged as if rehearsed, and perhaps they were.

"But what brought this on so suddenly?"

"There's nothing sudden about it, it's been coming on for years. Not that you noticed or could ever see me as anything but a convenient extension of yourself. What's different now is I made a holy vow, a sacred vow, to Mary, Mother of God. I swore that if I came safely through my operation, I'd amend my life, I'd give up the booze, I'd try to live in a way more pleasing to the Lord."

"You made a bargain with Heaven, is that it?" I said sarcastically.

"It was nothing like that, you wicked man, you mocker of all that's holy. When I think how I used to admire you, would hang on every blasphemous word, I could vomit! I did not beg to live longer. I've lived quite long enough. I merely vowed that in the time remaining to me I would strive to diminish my daily shame. What I would beg for was forgiveness."

I gestured to the room in which we sat. "And this is where the penitent will sue for grace? If it's a hair shirt you want, you've chosen well."

"What's wrong with it, you blethering snob? Infra dig., is it? Well, I daresay coming from such noble quarters as you do, those wonderful, airy apartments above the shop in the swanky Marais district, where milord slept in splendor alongside the dear duchess, his mother, all this must be painful indeed to your eye. But here, and especially in this room, I am reminded of the home in which I grew up, only Angie's a better housekeeper than was my poor, sainted mother, God rest her soul. I'll stay here, if Angie will put up with me, at least until my blister's healed."

"Ah, yes, your mysterious post-op blister." I was hitting out wildly. "Father Pip-Pip believes it may be miraculous, an example of the stigmata that lead to sainthood. Of course, he, innocent fellow, doesn't know its exact location, that it's to be found on the smooth white flesh of the upper inner thigh, mere inches from the holy of holies, or that it looks not in the least like one of Christ's wounds but rather like a condom sheathing His engorged prick."

But in my anguish, I had gone too far. I knew it even as I spoke the dreadful words. How could I have been so crude, so cruel?

Her face held a look of extreme horror, as if the Devil himself stood before her. She screwed up her eyes tightly and held up both her hands, palms toward me, as if to fend me off. "Go!" She almost gagged on the word.

"Maude, I'm so sorry, I didn't mean—"

"Go!" she screamed.

"Forgive me, Maude, I—"

"Go," she whispered, "please go."

I went, of course. And as I went I heard her, poor misguided soul, begin to stumble through the Act of Contrition. "O my God . . . I am heartily sorry for having offended You . . . and I detest all my sins . . . because . . . I dread the loss of heaven . . . and the pains of hell, but most of all because . . . they offend you, my God . . ."

<2—

"When sorrows come, they come not single spies, but in battalions." The Pish chose these words as the epigraph to his (unpublished) *Conflict 'Twixt Faith & Reason Resolv'd.* They are, of course, the words of Hamlet's uncle, the fratricide; but as the Pish himself has elsewhere noted, "the Bard, that Great Cham of Irony, often gave his most profound utterances to his villains and fools."

I had heard nothing from Twombly since he told me he planned to return to Kresti Prison only after letting poor Aristide "stew" in his terror for a short while longer. Twombly had sounded so confident of triumph that his failure to get in touch began to alarm me. After enduring a week of silence I phoned the Hotel Rus in St. Petersburg, only to be told that "the holy father" had left somewhat abruptly a few days before. And so I phoned the Hotel Astoria. There, the concierge adjusted his voice to match his news. M. Gabriel Popescu had left that morning. He was embarked upon a most melancholy journey, the accompaniment of his dear father's body back to their native France. *But what had happened?* Alas, he was not at liberty to say.

After that, I phoned the younger Mme Popescu. She told me she was beside herself with grief. Ah, what a disaster! Ah, what a cruel blow! She would pray for his soul; she hoped I would do no less, a prayer from a priest being perhaps more efficacious in such a case.

"But what is the case? What happened, madame?"

"Suicide. Ah, the horror, the misery, the knowledge that he is already suffering the unimaginable pains of hell!"

"How was it possible?"

"A classic case, Father, as you must know: despair. He was an old man, long accustomed to the good life, the ample rewards his business acumen had brought him. And what a fall he had, from luxury to a stinking Russian prison cell! It must have turned his mind, poor soul."

Aristide, it appeared, had managed to lean his iron cot upright against a wall in his cell. Then, perhaps strengthened by his desperation, this enfeebled old man had succeeded in climbing to the top, standing for a moment teetering on the rim while he secured his hands in his trouser pockets, and then had plunged backward, headfirst, to the stone floor. The distance he fell was not great, but it was enough.

"The irony is that powerful forces were already stirring here in Paris. The President of the Republic was ready to intervene in my father-in-law's behalf. That very day, Gaby had asked the American priest, that awful fellow, to convey the hopeful news to the prison. My husband himself could not go; he was engaged in marathon phone sessions with the authorities in France. You would think that such news, conveyed by a priest—by any priest, even the American—would have been enough to calm Papa's restless spirit. They surely prayed together, he and the priest. But his months of cruel confinement must have driven him quite mad. Within an hour after his visitor left, Papa was dead." She sobbed for a moment into the phone, then blew her nose. "And now, Father, he turns for all eternity upon a spit in Hell!"

"Calm yourself, my child. If he was mad, as you say—and who can doubt it?—he will not be held responsible for his act, either in this world or the next."

"Ah, is it true, Father?"

"But you have my word. We will pray for his soul, petition Heaven for mercy. In the fullness of time, he will sing among the angels."

"Poor Gaby will be lost without his father. He adored him."

"Gaby will find his strength in you."

"Ah."

"And in his faith."

"Yes, Father."

"And how is the widow faring? Bearing up, I hope."

The glibness learned for such occasions during my tenure as a young priest in the Kensington parish had clearly not been lost. One comforts the bereaved by suggesting that the loved one has gone to a far better place and by gently implying that to wish otherwise is a species of selfishness. The priest stands aloof from ordinary human suffering, from genuine empathy, even, for he possesses, as it were, the larger picture. The clichés roll out unstoppably; all is well. And the truth is, merely to utter them is comfortably to disengage myself from fellow feeling.

"The widow? Ah, yes, the widow." She laughed bitterly. "Bearing up very well, I should think. She's in Buenos Aires staying with her billionaire friends. She would not return even when she was told her husband languished in a Russian gaol. Nor will she return for his funeral. 'There will be time enough to mourn next month when I'm back in Paris as planned, once the season here is over. What difference can it make to Aristide now?' My charming mother-in-law has a heart of ice and no soul at all."

"Judge not," I said fatuously. "Leave her to Heaven." But what a bitch, in any case!

And yet, in truth, what difference *can* any of it make to Aristide now? She has it right, the bitch. His story is like a medieval lament on the fickleness of fortune and the certainty of death. He is a figure in a danse macabre. As are we all. What matter now that he climbed so successfully the ladder of this world or that, legally speaking, he did not always cross his *t*'s or dot his *i*'s? And what do we really know of the elder Mme Popescu, or the nature of the marriage, their private understandings or agreements or compromises, his infidelities, or hers, or whether the boiling passion of their love first cooled and then grew cold in the ordinary drafts of merely living together in the house of time, or whether for him or for her love was locked in or locked out? We know only that he chose to die. In that, he lords it over most of the rest of us. He himself might say that when the Russians refused him an exit visa, he issued one to himself. Then I see him winking, and smiling his cynical smile.

It is a comfort of sorts to suppose he chose his moment of death. But like all comforts offered the bereaved, it is as empty as the infinite void into which all the dead tumble, the unrelieved and unrelievable blackness, the total absence of sensation or thought, utter annihilation, a condition more terrible to contemplate than medieval visions of Hell itself, where unbearable pain is at least an earnest of feeling. The divine Dante's *Commedia* is a whistling in the dark, a granting to airy nothing of a local habitation and a name.

How free is the choice of any suicide? What physical sufferings urge him on? What psychological demons? What dreams of glory, of heroic self-sacrifice? What delusions of martyrdom, of an afterlife? What loneliness, what fear, what despair? And who might have whispered in his ear? Twombly returned to Kresti Prison to turn the screws on a man already reaching his breaking point. I cannot doubt he said nothing of the hopeful news Gabriel Popescu had asked him to convey to his father. Twombly did what he told me he would do. He offered Aristide, quite without warrant, assurances of the Vatican's intervention if he would only cooperate, and he threatened the direst consequences for the ingrate if he would not. Perhaps he gave this desperate man until the following morning to come to a decision; probably he said a hypocritical prayer over the cowering wretch, urging him to examine well his conscience.

It may be that Aristide, out of a romantic sense of honor, of old-fashioned gallantry, refused to betray Maude, whom he remembered as the young beauty he had seduced into selling him a valuable item not in her power to sell and into forging a signature to render the buyer blameless; it may be that he refused out of loyalty to me, out of old friendship; it may be that he remembered Twombly well from the old days and despised him. And it may be that in his old age and his physically and psychologically weakened condition, the new complications Twombly heaped on him proved too much for him to bear. Whatever the case, his freedom of choice lacks a certain . . . freedom. Twombly visited Aristide, and then Aristide killed himself. Sometimes, *post hoc ergo propter hoc* is a sound argument.

In a way, Twombly has scored an own goal. With Aristide dead, what hope has he of running down *Dyuers and Sondry Sonettes?* What danger does he pose to Maude or to me?

What can I say about Aristide? I knew him when we were both young. The truth is, I always liked him, despite his chicanery. Perhaps because of it. There are better ways to die.

៚

Nosce te ipsum, the Ancients kept on urging us, know thyself. "He hath ever but slenderly known himself," says Regan of her father,

Lear. And can I so little have understood not only Maude but myself? We had loved each other and lived in the closest intimacy, and yet remained strangers. We knew everything about each other, and yet knew nothing. Unable myself to believe, I had not gauged the depth of her religious longing. I had been aware of her distemper but not of its magnitude or of myself as its cause. Why could she not have told me? Why could I not have asked? I am a very foolish, fond old man. I miss her more than I can say.

The first time I phoned to apologize, Angie Mackletwist answered and hung up as soon as she recognized my voice. The second time, she told me that Ms. Moriarty would not speak to me. "And about time, too," she added. "Oh, the shame you've brought upon that poor woman. And yet—can you believe it?—she won't hear a word said against you. Mum's the word with her, not a word of complaint. But anyone who had anything to do with Beale Hall knew what you were getting up to, no need for a gypsy with a crystal ball. You might as well have taken out an advertisement."

Little could she, Angie Mackletwist, have imagined such depravity as was mine. That a priest, a man who had renounced the flesh with the most solemn of vows to the Son of God, a man who possessed not only the Power but also the Glory, the means to succor the helpless and cleanse the sinner of his sins, a man whose special privilege it was to administer the holy sacraments—that such a man should have debauched the virtue of an innocent young woman and kept her for the rest of her life in sexual bondage to his vile demands and, through the misused authority of his office, in a spiritual wasteland—such a one places the crown of thorns once more upon the brow of Our Blessed Lord, hammers once more the cruel nails into His tender palms and feet, mocks and derides Him as He hangs once more upon the bitter Cross. (Of course, I paraphrase.)

"If it was up to me," said Angie, "I'd have told it all to Father Kev, all your filthy wickedness, and he'd've been on the blower to the bishop toot sweet, no doubt about it. But I promised Ms. Moriarty not to harm you. 'We are all sinners, I no less than him,' she said. 'Leave him to Heaven and to his conscience.' Well, all right. But I've got a conscience, too. Thanks to you, she's an alcoholic; thanks to you, she lost her way. But as sure as I hope for my own salvation, if you give her any more bother, anything at all, I'll report you to the police."

"I'll not call again, I promise you. Just tell her that Aristide Popescu is dead, a suicide. No, no, don't tell her about the death. It will only upset her. Just tell her that if she has poison for me, I'll drink it. Gladly. Yes, just tell her that, please, Ms. Mackletwist."

Part Seven

Doth any man doubt that if there were taken out of men's minds vain opinions, flattering hopes, false valuations, imaginations as one would, and the like; but it would leave the minds of a number of men poor shrunken things, full of melancholy and indisposition, and unpleasing to themselves?

—Sir Francis Bacon, "Of Truth,"
Essays, 1597–1625

In the affairs of this world men are saved, not by faith, but by the want of it.

—Benjamin Franklin,
Poor Richard's Almanack, 1754

I have been getting my news of Maude from Father Pip-Pip, late of Holy Cross, now of Beale Hall. His courtship of me has paid rich dividends for him. He learned soon enough that he was my only reliable conduit and that he could turn the spigot on and off at will. Like a woman whose goal is marriage and whose only assets are her sexual favors, Pip-Pip revealed, so to speak, a portion of bosom here, permitted, again so to speak, an eager hand to caress, outside the satiny skirt, a plump thigh there, reserving total surrender until the wedding night. Once he found himself, through my efforts, safely ensconced at the Hall, he held no news back.

"She's in New York," he told me, "staying with cousins in the Borough of Queens, good people called Dowd, serious Catholics, from what she says. She drops me a line from time to time, you see, just to let me know how she's getting on."

"Ah, yes, the Dowds. Boozers to a man, I shouldn't wonder. She's mentioned them from time to time over the years. Great supporters of the IRA and the gunrunners. They have a pub in— what is it? Kissena Boulevard? Yes, I think I'm right, Kissena Boulevard. The Green Harp, it's called. They live above it." I glanced at him speculatively. "Not the best place, perhaps, for a recovering alcoholic. I hope you're advising her to return here with all deliberate speed."

Pip-Pip had the indecency to laugh. We were in Benghazi, which I was even then transforming into my retirement cottage.

Dear old W.C. had left it to me in his will, you see. I shall tell you all about that in due course. But little by little, in advance of the formal announcement of retirement, I was putting my stamp on the place. And what I mean by the phrase "putting my stamp," I shall also reveal. But for the moment we were lounging in what was still recognizably the major's sitting room. Pip-Pip had popped over to the cottage, he said, to lend me a hand. Now he poured himself a second stiff brandy, raised an inquiring eyebrow at me, the decanter hovering over my glass, and laughed, or perhaps sniggered.

"I would not have thought it a laughing matter, Father."

"That generation sold the pub years ago and retired to the 'owld sod,' fulfilling the romantic dream of many an Irish-American. But in the meantime the Green Harp helped them produce Wall Street lawyers and 'money managers,' a fair sprinkling of priests and nuns, and in recent years the leader of a rock group. Maude is staying with her cousin Patrick Dowd and his wife. He's a city councilman from Queens. Maude has actually been to dinner with the mayor, a good Catholic like herself. So I don't think you need worry about evil influences."

"Good, good," I said.

"Indeed it is. I've been in touch with Father McKeon, who's priest in the parish where the Dowds worship." He seemed a trifle embarrassed. "Well, what with all my years in the social-services side of things, I got into the habit of following through, you see, referrals and so forth. It would not hurt, I thought, if Father McKeon were made aware of Maude's special problem. He tells me that a more devout lady he has seldom met."

I grunted. For a little fellow, he could certainly put away the booze. I saw him eyeing the decanter again. It was a very fine brandy, part of the major's dwindling stock. "Well," I said, getting up, "it's time we were back at the Hall. There's Bastien's filing system still to unravel and the accounts are in arrears. We might have to hire a temp or two."

Would you believe it, he poured himself a double shot of brandy and swallowed it in one! "Right, Father," he said cheerfully. "Let's go."

It is three months now that Maude's been in America. News still dribbles in, mostly of a churchly sort. I already know more than I wish to of Father McKeon's goodness, of the ladies of the Salve Regina Society, a charitable organization that has kindly made her an honorary member, of the neorococo splendors of St. Sebastian's and the amiable simplicity of its St. Jude's Chapel. When I offhandedly asked Pip-Pip whether Maude ever mentioned her friends at Beale Hall, he said, "Well, yes, to be sure. She never fails to send her best regards to all at Ludlow and environs."

Not much, you'll admit. But yesterday he rushed in to see me, all excited. Maude had enclosed a sealed letter for me in her latest to him. "She's signed up for a reading group at St. Sebastian's," he told me eagerly. "They're working their way, those who have the Latin, through the writings of the Early Church." He hovered over me, expecting no doubt that I would share my letter's contents with him. But I waited until he had left me, his disappointment pleasingly evident, before slitting the envelope open with my Knights of Columbus dagger. It contained a copy of the complete Latin text of the "Homily on the Sinful Woman," the winsome work of Ephraim the Syrian, one of those texts, no doubt, that her reading group was tackling, and her own translation of it. At the top of the first page, Maude had scribbled "EM, FYI, MM." Here is a brief excerpt that well conveys the flavor of the whole:

> She bound her heart, because it had offended, with chains and tears of suffering: and she began innerly to weep: "What avails me this fornication? What avails this lewdness? . . . Fearlessly, I have robbed merchants of merchandise, and yet my rapacity was not satisfied . . . Why did I not win to myself one man, who might have corrected my lewdness? For one man is of God, but many are of Satan."

Maude had gone over certain passages throughout the work with the orange ink of a marker pen, the better to impress upon me the radiance of Ephraim the Syrian's thought. Much, for example, was covered in the excerpt above: "What avails me this fornication?," "I have robbed . . . merchandise," and "many are of Satan." That last clause was obviously directed at me. There's no point in quibbling that Maude has misconstrued the Latin. Yes, the schoolgirl winner all those years ago of the Donegal Latin Prize has got it wrong. She understands Ephraim's grieving woman to mean no more than a relatively mild complaint: "Many men purpose [sexual] evil; they are the agents of Satan," and Edmond Music, by implication of the orange ink, is one of these. But in fact, as my own translation makes clear, the woman means that had she had but one man, in a union presumably sanctified by Mother Church, she would have been bonking with God's blessing. But as a harlot she has known many men, and these can only have been sent to her by Satan, for they have filled her eager purse in more senses than one. God, in short, frowns upon unsanctified sex. (The "I have robbed merchandise" is, of course, spot on.)

And this paltry bit of Early Church palaver—Ephraim the Syrian, for pity's sake!—is what, after so long a self-imposed silence, Maude chooses to communicate to me. She is an old woman; it is no longer a breach of gallantry or etiquette to say so. But I fear that she has not accumulated wisdom with her years. She is berating an old man for having led her astray half a century before, when both were young and fire burned in their loins. In blaming me, she betrays her sex, for she accepts implicitly the view of woman, promulgated by the Early Church, as a creature driven by her vaginal urges, but as one who may yet be saved from damnation by Church-sanctified, marital swiving. Of what we both once thought of as love, Maude has nothing whatever to say.

I wrote back to her, of course. The homily she had sent me gave me leave. But I said nothing about the "sinful woman." I forbore pointing out to her the error in her Latin translation or the implication of its correction: that she had had many men in her time. To my knowledge, I was her first, as the watered-silk chaise in the Music Room at Beale Hall bore shocking witness on that first wonderful day. The tentative reaching out of her gentle hand to the gross swelling in my priestly trousers is a memory that I treasure even now. In the years that followed, I would willingly swear upon my life to her sexual fidelity. No, I wrote as cheerfully as I could of life in Beale Hall; of my closeness to retirement and of Benghazi, my unexpected inheritance; of Bastien, out to peaceful, well-deserved pasture; of Pip-Pip, more efficient than Bastien but less a desired friend. I asked her whether she was still writing her memoirs and if her muse still whispered romances in her ear. And I begged her to return to me, for without her my life was a void, and into it I stared as into nothing, nothing, nothing at all.

Days and days, a week, a fortnight, a month now, all have passed, and I have had no reply.

Ours is a situation fraught not merely with irony but with paradox—from its beginnings a staple of Christianity. I, a priest in the Church, have lost my love *to* the Church. A piety she never manifested in youth now has her in thrall. She is possessed— not by the Holy Spirit, but by what she supposes to be the Holy Spirit. Of course, she has always been a believer, and, because a believer, consciously a sinner. But, after all, in that condition she is scarcely distinguishable from most sophisticated Catholics in the Western world. And *they* bloody well get on with it. No, Maude is cursed with a sort of Catholic fundamentalism—not with the spirit of the merciful Jew Jesus but with that of the uncompromising *goy* Savonarola.

And so we come to the greatest paradox of all. Maude is bewitched by Mary, but bewitched by which? The Gospels offer a plethora of women who bear that "grand old name." Is Maude bewitched by Mary, the mother of Jesus, or by Mary Magdalene, the enigmatic Mary? How many Marys were there, in any case? A sinner called Mary comes and anoints Jesus' feet. A Mary is the sister of Martha and Lazarus. Seven devils—count 'em—are exorcised from a Mary. A Mary stands at the foot of the Cross. The risen Christ greets a Mary in the Garden of Gethsemane. The Orthodox Church has held on to an extravagant triplicate of Marys: the sinner, the sister of Martha and Lazarus, and Mary Magdalene. We in Rome, unexpectedly parsimonious, have reduced them to one. Even the name of Mary Magdalene has its problems. It may mean that she was from Magdala or that she had curly hair, in those innocent days a sure sign of the adulteress—or, through happy-go-lucky false etymology, that she was virginal, Mary the Maid. Which of these Marys possesses Maude? I suppose it scarcely matters which; it matters only that Maude is possessed. And because she is possessed, she is in need of an exorcist.

But no priest of the Church can be the appropriate exorcist of a woman thus possessed. She is invested, after all, with a spirit of which the Church heartily approves. Is the only alternative, then, the Devil? Must we turn to Satan, invoke the powers of Hell, to exorcise so debilitating a spirit, one so destructive of human happiness? If so, it must be the Satan of Job, the ancient, honored Adversary, the power who had not yet become the demonic personification of later, watered-down Judaism and ever-watery Christianity.

⁂

The Pish performed an exorcism once, as his private papers make clear. He performed it at the behest of Sir Percival Beale, who, despairing of his wife's return, supposed her possessed of an evil spirit. Shame kept Sir Percival from approaching his own confessor, the process of exorcism in the Church being extraconfessional and therefore not bound by secrecy. True, the Lady Alice's behavior in London was far from secret, but a kind of honor among adulterers and cuckolds prevailed on that sophisticated level of society, and in Shropshire, at least, a man might maintain without mockery the fiction that his wife was in London for her health. An exorcism in the Roman rite, on the other hand, would provoke a scandal of such dimensions that ballads about it would be sung, for all Sir Percival's wealth, upon the streets of Ludlow.

The knight had followed the Pish's advice. He had gone up to London and there had sought to court his wife anew, sending her many an ardent *billet-doux,* many a virginal rose, many a poem he had hired a poet-of-the-moment to compose, many a love ballad sung by a skilled lutanist beneath her window. And all to no avail. Then Sir Percival had pursued the second route the Pish had recommended to the lady's heart. He had turned up at his box in Drury Lane in the embrace of two bodice-bursting doxies; he had attended, masked and in the guise of Paris, the infamous Libertine Ball thrown annually by the notorious Lucretia, duchess of Pinner. And he had been seen slouching through the scarlet door of the Debauchers' Club in Conduit Street, guided to that wicked place by a complaisant debauchee. And still to no avail. All that Sir Percival had achieved was a daunting case of the pox. He concluded that the Lady Alice was possessed, and, ordering the odious Chunter to pack his trunks, he returned to Beale Hall.

The Pish was one of a select group, the Ba'alei Shem, and hence was qualified to exorcise an evil spirit, or "dybbuk," as he was bound to call what possessed the Lady Alice.

"Go, my dear fellow," said Sir Percival. "Set her free."

Accordingly, the Pish kissed Sarah good-bye and took the post chaise to London, putting up at the Crown in Furbelow Street. "Fish pie, landlord," he said, "and greens of the season. Bream braised in autumn ale and Whitechapel cream. Plum duff. Hock and soda water."

Lady Alice was delighted to see him. She had from his earliest days in Ludlow cast a lascivious eye on Sir Percival's "sweet, incony Jew," but circumstances had deprived her of that consummation for which she so devoutly wished. It was said that Jews had huge battering rams of Devil's horn, implacable, and hangers like twin leather moneybags, heavy with gold. It was said that their frequent eruptions were volcanic, filling a lady's thirsty pleasure channel again and again with love's all-devouring lava. Why, merely to think of the Jew had caused Lady Alice to demand of Sir Percival, in the days when she and her husband still shared a bed and he had anointed his member with Maimonides' medicine, that modest satisfaction he was able to provide—and in the days when he was abroad and no other help nigh, to seek privately induced, inferior gratification, the digitation that produced both calm and shame. And—heavens!—now her maid Lucy told her that a Jew-gentleman from Ludlow waited below! It could only be he!

"Ah, yes, he is Sir Percival's physician. A man of extraordinary learning. 'Tis best I change into my night attire. He comes to cure me of my . . . er, of my exudations."

"What exudations, my lady?"

"Those that you know not of, Lucy. La, child, how you prattle! First help me to my boudoir and into my peignoir of Irish lace, the one Lord Kilkenny was kind enough to send from his foreclosed estate; then, let the Jew-doctor come to me."

To be brief, the Pish was successful in his adjurations, and by way of proof Lady Alice returned to Beale Hall, but his notes on what occurred in the lady's London boudoir are sketchy. He identified the spirit possessing Lady Alice as that of Lilith, Adam's first wife, who was created from the earth at the same time as Adam and who balked at imposed inequality, disputing the manner of their sexual intercourse, preferring to be on top. Lilith was a demon not easy to dislodge. She laughed at spells based on kabbalistic numerology; a powerful demon herself, she mocked the invocation of lesser powers. The laying on of hands, it seemed, made her more tractable, but she refused to cede her conquered territory—the Lady Alice—who writhed under the conflict of competing armies.

But once the Pish learned that Lilith had pitched her tent *in utero*, had there unfurled her banner, he knew, alas, that physical force alone could evict the demon from her seat. "Forgive me, my lady," he said, and hurled his battering ram at the portcullis. There, repeated assaults gaining ground, the Pish lifted aloft his flag and summoned his reserves: "Once more unto the breach, dear friends!" And lo, victory was his. With a cry of anguish and the fierce crepitations of a Chinese dragon, Lilith made haste to depart through the posterior gate. And the lady made haste to return to Ludlow.

$\sim$

Maude has vouchsafed me a second communication, this time putting my name on the envelope. In short, it came directly to me. A step forward, perhaps. The message, alas, was identical with the last: "EM, FYI, MM." But this time she had scrawled it on the top margin of an article she had snipped from the Cambridge *Herald*. The article was of considerably more interest to me than any homily of Ephraim the Syrian. Its heading announced, "Retired Cleric Bares All!" The subheading narrowed the focus: "Elderly Priest, Crazed by Remorse, Repents in the Buff." The subsubheading told more: "Self-Flagellation on Steps of Hospice." Well, have you guessed? Yes, it was Father Fred Twombly, late of Holyrood College, Joliet, Illinois, who had finally snapped.

It appears that Twombly had made his way on his knees through the iron gates and along the short drive leading from Howells Street to the front steps of the Sisters of the Five Wounds. He was fully clad at the time and carrying a stiff briefcase which served him as a crutch for his painful progress. Once atop the steps, he extracted from the briefcase a short whip of many thongs, each tipped with a metal aglet. He now undressed himself, folding his clothes on the steps beside his briefcase. He retained only his black socks, held neatly in place by old-fashioned suspenders. Back down on his knees, he picked up the whip and began, at first vigorously, to beat himself about his shoulders and back, soon drawing blood. Then he began to falter, falling forward onto one supporting arm, gasping for breath and in pain. He had been observed so far only by Gavro Pavelić, a recent immigrant from Croatia, who was raking the hospice's leaves into a mulch pile. Pavelić was delighted by what he saw, crossing himself many times and falling to his own knees. Later, through an interpreter, he told reporters that this was the first act of genuine piety he had witnessed since his arrival in America.

Farce has ever seemed to attach itself to Fred Twombly. It chanced that Sister Beatrice Joseph, the mother superior of the Sisters of the Five Wounds, was even then accompanying a departing visitor, an important benefactress, to the front door, which she opened with a flourish, preparing her favorite and highly dramatic "God love you!" farewell. What she and her visitor saw was a bloody, naked, scraggly old man struggling to his feet, his horrid, empurpled genitalia hanging alarmingly, and he was gesturing at them with his whip. This sort of behavior might well be acceptable, the mother superior was aware, in, say, Montepulciano or La Coruña on an appropriate Church occasion, but in Boston? Never! The distinguished visitor, quite rightly, shrieked; Sister Beatrice Joseph slammed fast the door, picked up the hall phone, and called for the police.

The police arrived in the persons of Officer O'Toole and Officer Mahmood. It transpired that the madman was a priest from out of town, a threat only to himself. He gave up his whip without demur and sat himself down quietly on the steps, shivering with cold and faint with shock. A kindly O'Toole sent Mahmood back to the police car to fetch a blanket. Mahmood grumbled but complied. He wanted to take Twombly to the station and book him. "A guy like that should be emasculated," he is reported to have said. (More likely, as Tubby later, with apologies to the cloth, assured me, Officer Mahmood had said that the "fuckin' motherfucker should have his nuts ripped off." Tubby is an enthusiast of American television, especially of inner-city police drama.) O'Toole, good Catholic that he was, thought otherwise and had a word with the mother superior, who admitted that here was a skeleton perhaps better returned to the closet. Twombly agreed, quite affably, to admit himself to the Sisters of the Five Wounds for examination, evaluation, and possible treatment.

I would be less than human if I did not admit that Twombly's travails caused me to celebrate a little holiday in my heart. But why had Maude sent me the clipping? In part, no doubt, because we had for decades shared a dislike of the man. But to admit to such a mutuality in the past is to point to a similar mutuality in the now. Was this a calculated admission, however subtle? I allowed myself to hope so. She need not have bothered, after all. She might easily have deprived me of guaranteed pleasure.

For a moment, I wondered whether Twombly had perhaps felt remorse for his role in the sudden seizure of W.C. and the suicide of Aristide Popescu. One cannot know the motivations of another's soul, of course, but I decided that Twombly had, in those two deaths, long since declared himself innocent of blame.

I summoned Pip-Pip and asked him whether by chance we currently had an American scholar in residence. Yes, he told me, we had a Father Peter Agnelli—on the faculty, as luck would have it, of Cardinal Spellman College, Providence, Rhode Island. I then mentioned to Father Agnelli, to whom I offered a glass of Puligny-Montrachet 1963, that Beale Hall had certain fellowships in its gift for which he might qualify, particularly if he were armed with a reference from the director general; and I casually suggested to him that he might be willing to use his contacts in New England to find out the truth for me about a certain Father Fred Twombly, a frequent visitor to Beale Hall and recently an inmate at the Sisters of the Five Wounds.

Within a week Father Agnelli was able to tell me about Twombly, "a painful case." The diocese in which Father Twombly had taught was currently being sued by seven of his former students, all male, now married and middle-aged, who accused him of a sexual abuse that had scarred their developing lives. The suit implied that there were other former students unwilling as yet to come forward. The then undergraduates had been offered high grades in exchange for sex. He had not actually *done* anything to them, they readily admitted. While Ravel's *Bolero* played on Twombly's gramophone— "Yes, he was *that* corny," said Agnelli— a student was required to undress before him and stroke his own member. During this exercise, Twombly wanked off. That was it.

"Odd, you might think," said Agnelli, but a Jewish woman he had met once in New York at "some book party or other," a woman of immense psychological insight, had said to him with devastating matter-of-factness that "everybody does *some*thing." And she had looked up at him and smiled ironically. At any rate, Twombly's ex-students claimed that their subsequent sex lives were gravely impaired, resulting in frequent periods of impotence. Their wives, Agnelli understood, were filing a separate complaint.

Twombly had denied everything, but that was to be expected. His retirement, certainly, was swift, and no doubt the principal of Holyrood College had urged it upon him. But had he truly cracked under the pressure of accusation, or had he cunningly chosen to place himself beyond the range of official inquiry? Whatever the case, he is now imprisoned with Castignac, my old friend and his old enemy.

⌒ᴗ

I begin now to consider my end. At my age and in my condition, this is a reasonable, not necessarily a morbid, undertaking. The grave yawns hungrily before me. Why pretend otherwise? The horizon, once far off, is nigh. I stand, as it were, on the brink of the abyss, with neither courage nor fear, indifferent, certain only that death, "a necessary end," as the Pish's beloved Bard so eloquently puts it, "will come when it will come." My circle grows ever smaller, a concomitant of age. Those whom I knew best, those whom I loved or hated, are gone from me, hidden from my sight by death, despair, derangement, or distance.

What has moved me to these teleonomical lucubrations is, I suspect, the news, conveyed to me by Father Pip-Pip, that Maude, my Maude, is on the point of marriage to a certain Tim O'Flaherty, longtime widower, father, grandfather, great-grandfather, former district attorney in the Borough of Queens, president emeritus of the Loyal Sons of the Emerald Order of Erin, and lay pillar of St. Sebastian's. She actually wanted Pip-Pip to let her know whether she should inform her putative fiancé that she is a recovering alcoholic.

Well, well.

"Is it not a wonderful thing at their age?" Pip-Pip wanted to know. "May we not say that the Spirit moved within them?"

"Something, it may be, moved within them," I said, pretending to no more than a polite interest.

We were sitting together once more in Benghazi. I have now officially retired, and Pip-Pip is running the show over there at Beale Hall. At the moment, he is merely the *acting* director, but unless he bungles a rather undemanding position—or undemanding as it will certainly be once he has a competent staff in place—I daresay he has found his sinecure. Good for him. I bear him no grudges, I.

Pip-Pip thought it better to move the subject away from Maude. "Shall I top you up?" he said and raised the decanter toward me. I shook my head, pointing to the brandy still filling my glass, and he attended to his own needs. This was not W.C.'s rare brandy, never fear; for Pip-Pip's visits I now kept a decanter filled with Tesco's own. "Is the cottage to keep its old name, Benghazi?" he wanted to know.

"Why ever not?"

Belinda Scudamour and I were the major's sole beneficiaries. The solicitor's letters caught us both by surprise. Belinda had inherited all my old friend's investments and banking accounts, his accumulated liquid and liquefiable wealth, a fair sum; I had inherited the cottage—and at a most convenient juncture in my life, too, a moment at which I felt I could not stay where I was and yet had nowhere to go. Bereft of Maude and Bastien, Beale Hall had become a mausoleum, its spaces echoing with my various losses.

"Well," said Pip-Pip, "Benghazi is a word that had special meaning to Major Catchpole. He was in the North Africa campaign, after all. But what can it mean to you?"

"It means the major to me; it means my friend." What does Pip-Pip think I ought to call the cottage? Le Marais? That most assuredly has meaning to me. Le Vel d'Hiv?

Now, now, never mind. Let me not be carried away. Pip-Pip means no harm.

Bishop McGonagle, writing on behalf of the board, had thanked me for a lifetime's faithful service and offered to sponsor a farewell dinner, "a slap-up affair, my dear fellow, do say yes." (Of course, I said no.) He professed himself happy to hear that I was to remain in the vicinity, within, as it were, his purview. He remembered my late friend the major very well, a dear-dear man, a man of sound Catholic principle, no matter what roguish opinions he might have expressed—witness his gift of the cottage to me, a gift the good-good man no doubt surmised might ultimately find its way back to the Church. Meanwhile, I was to consider Beale Hall as still my bailiwick. There would always be a place at table for me. "Use us, my dear chap, use us. You'll find us not ungrateful."

I watched Pip-Pip sipping his drink. I swear he looks, despite his wizened face, no more than fourteen. I know his age is forty-eight. Still, I was tempted to tell him that too much alcohol would stunt his growth. "So you think she's going to marry this O'Flaherty fellow?"

"Yes, I think so."

I looked beyond his head to the de Kuyk portrait of the Ba'al Shem of Ludlow on the wall above the mantel. As I've already hinted, there are a few items I have brought over here from the Hall, choosing to interpret McGonagle's "use us" quite loosely.

The de Kuyk portrait, for example; the Curse; all the Pish's writings, in manuscript or print; most of the Hebraica, a few related odds and ends. I have even affixed what must have been the Ba'al Shem's *mezuzah* to my front door, a genuflection, as it were, to sentiment. Well. I know that I am not a Catholic. Am I perhaps a Jew by default?

What am I to do?

⌒

Yes, I still have the Dunaharaszti Haggadah with me. I used to keep it, you may remember, locked in my desk in the Music Room. How could I leave it in Beale Hall? I could not. How could I leave anything touched by the Pish in that stronghold of the plunderers? And I do not use the word "plunderers" idly. You may have wondered, given the proposed exchange between Sir Percival and the Pish of the Haggadah and *Dyuers and Sondry Sonettes*, how it came about that *both* unique books were to be found in the Beale Hall Library.

(As an aside, I must tell you that the Shakespeare volume, whether genuine or, as I surmise, forged, has disappeared from the face of the earth—or so I conclude from young Popescu's written response to my inquiries. He claimed that he could find no record of such a work, neither the book itself nor a bill of sale, nothing whatever. Ever since his father's tragic death in the hands of Russian barbarians, ugly rumors had begun to circulate in rare-book circles that not only impugned the integrity of the firm but cast unwarranted shadows on his dear father's memory. He was confident that I would not wish to participate in calumny; as a man who had dedicated his life to the holiest of truths, I would not wish to sully my soul by circulating lies. He trusted I would agree to accept his most distinguished salutations.)

Lady Alice died in 1783 of a cancer in her left breast, or rather, most immediately, of the shock following her breast's removal. The operation was performed in her boudoir at Beale Hall. Before she went under the knife, she suggested, with brave irony, to Sir Percival that she and he might soon offer themselves at some show or other in London, perhaps at Tom Tiddler's in Covent Garden, as new-hatched wonders, he without an arm and she "without a titty." Sir Percival had canvassed the Royal Society in search of a surgeon possessed of the sharpest skills and the most up-to-date methods. He found his man in Mr. Lemuel Sprott, B.A., M.A., Cantab.; M.D., F.R.C.P.S.; F.R.S.; and choirmaster of the Chapel Royal. Mr. Sprott was assisted in his butchery by a Mr. Andrew Fielding, B.A., King's College, New York, a loyalist who, to his credit, had fled his native land when some of his countrymen took up arms against their king. The odious Chunter kept a firm grip on Lady Alice's feet; her maid Lucy and Mrs. Dorcas the cook each pinned down an arm. Also in attendance were Sir Percy, Father Hugh Fairchild of Holy Cross, and the Pish, the last there at Lady Alice's particular request.

In the event, Sir Percival fled the room; Father Fairchild lost control of bladder and sphincter and collapsed, fainting, in his own wastes. (The first and second gardeners were summoned to bear him away.) The medical men, the house servants, and the Jew remained at the bedside. The poor woman's screams, it was said, were heard as far away as Ludlow. Once she lost consciousness, she never recovered it. Toward three in the morning, the maid Lucy asleep from exhaustion, her hand enclosing that of her mistress, and the Pish alone in prayerful attendance, Lady Alice breathed her last.

Sir Percival survived his lady by fourteen years. During that time he published his modest *Ephemerae hominis miserrimi* (1787) and his monumental three-volume *History of the Welsh Marches* (1789–92), and he made daily, postprandial visitations, no matter the weather, to the mausoleum he caused to be erected to house her remains, a structure that grimly overlooks the lower lake. He met a violent end. His cantering horse Eurytion reared suddenly as a garter snake crossed its path, catapulting Sir Percival from his saddle. He narrowly missed becoming the Stuart Oak's first victim; instead, he zoomed headfirst into a nameless walnut tree, the arm and hand that might have reduced his momentum left behind, as we know, years before in India.

As for the Pish, he had died on Christmas Eve of the previous year, 1796. Sir Percival had comforted the widow as best he could, assuring her that while he lived she would want for nothing. The only account that survives of the Pish's death is to be found in the notoriously unreliable *Tales of the Ba'al Shem of Ludlow*, a collection that panders to the credulous. A nameless narrator tells us that he had "heard all this from Rabbi Harvey Fried of the holy community of Ilkley, who passed away in the Holy Land."

The Pish was surrounded by his disciples and by many a sage steeped in the wisdom of the ages. He told them that he felt weak. "Soon I will be with God, blessed be He."

In the middle of the night a servant came into the bedroom, and he heard the Pish saying, "I'll agree to a contest. You've no need to cause me pain."

The servant said, "To whom are you talking, master?"

And the Pish said, "Look there, look there. Can't you see the Angel of Death? Once he ran from me in fear, his wings hiding his head in shame; now his chest swells and fills with joy. Whichever of us first errs is the loser." And he ordered his servant to bring him some barley water in a large glass, for he felt weak. But the servant brought barley water in a small glass, and the Pish said, *"Man has no power on the day of his death;* even my servant will not obey me."

Then the Angel of Death exulted in his triumph: "You are the first to err, for the words in Ecclesiastes are these: *Man has no power over the day of his death,* not *on.*"

The clock in the corner stopped at that instant. The servant placed a feather beneath the Pish's nostrils and so learned that his master had passed away.

What we do know is that Sir Humphrey Beale, Sir Percival's younger brother, succeeded to Beale Hall. Sir Humphrey had no use whatever for the Jews; in fact, he despised them. He is the author of that wretched pamphlet *Perfidicae Iudaicae* (1802) that provoked the Kilburn Riots of 1803. It transpired that the Pish's home in Old Street, where he had conducted his *beth ha-midrash,* the stone building cheek by jowl with Lane's Asylum, where the indigent and the wicked were then corrected, was owned by the estate. Sir Humphrey knew what to do. Within a week of his arrival in Shropshire, the disciples were dispersed throughout and beyond England, the Jewess Sarah and her Jew-servants were out on the cobblestoned street, and the complete contents of the house "reverted" to the estate. That's how it came about that the vast collection of Pishiana, including the Dunaharaszti Haggadah, ended up in Beale Hall.

I hold the Haggadah with trembling hands. Considering its great age and its tumultuous travels, it is still in splendid shape. I am overwhelmed by an emotion to which I cannot give a name. I look at the central illustration on the title page yet again, at the little figures hurrying across the square in Dunaharaszti, making for the wooden synagogue. Among them are my forebears; in my anachronistic fancy, perhaps even my young parents, not yet married. Might that minuscule figure not be the future Ba'al Shem of Ludlow himself, here still a boy, not yet bar mitzvah? I turn the pages. Here are the pictures of the four sons, the wise, the wicked, the simple, and the one who does not even know that there are questions to be asked. The wicked son is clean-shaven, he gnashes his teeth, and on his head he wears a hat that is something like a miter. I turn more pages. Here are pictured the plagues that the Lord God visited upon Pharaoh and the idolatrous Egyptians. Across this page in an arc sweeping from frogs to boils and on to locusts is a disfigurement of speckles, now a dingy brown. Wine or blood? Given the history of my people, they could be either, or both.

"*My* people" I have written. But in what sense mine?
Not to worry; let it stand.

⌒

I have settled without fuss into Benghazi. You would think that
after nigh upon half a century, the move from the magnificence of
Beale Hall to the simplicity of the cottage might prove . . . what?
troublesome? Not a bit of it. You would think that after nigh upon
half a century of living with Maude, living alone might prove . . .
what? unbearable? Again, not a bit of it, trust me. I revel in my
retirement!

I am beginning to think, though, that Pip-Pip had it right, that
Benghazi is not what I should call my home, no matter my loyalty
to the major. The name I'm toying with is Dunaharaszti.

Belinda and Tubby visited me last night. They're emigrating to
Canada, to London, Ontario, to be precise, and they wanted to say
good-bye. Tubby has a job with the rank of sergeant in the local
police department and Belinda has been offered a position in the
Queen Mary Geriatric Hospital. I wished them well.

"But what if you don't like Canada, Belinda?"

"Well, America is just south of the border, and besides, we can
always come back here."

They can afford to experiment. The major's gift makes it
unnecessary for Belinda to work at all. And as for Tubby, he is
Belinda's besotted adjunct.

"If you go to America, you can look up Maude," I said bitterly.
No, I didn't actually say it. I thought it, though.

Perhaps *I* should go to America. Why not? That might sway
her, woo her back. Old Lochinvar has come out of the East . . .

Perhaps I exaggerate my contentedness.

⌒

I received a packet in the post the other day. It was addressed to
me at Beale Hall. Father Pip-Pip was kind enough to cycle it over.

"It's from Maude," he said eagerly, hovering over me. "Look, there's her return address. And here, see, the customs tag says 'Printed Matter.' It's a book, I daresay. I wonder *what*, exactly . . . Perhaps one of her romances."

"Well," I said, tossing the package casually onto my in-tray, my heart pounding, "I'll defer the pleasure." I indicated the chaos of papers on my desk. "I'm sorting my correspondence, a task I've been putting off for years. No excuses now, though."

He tried to mask his disappointment. "I'll be off, then. Don't want to interrupt." He paused. "I'd be grateful for the stamps, if you've no use for them. I've a nephew who's a keen philatelist."

I saw through that ruse at once: tearing off the stamps would perforce open the packet. "I'll see to it you get them, never fear."

Of course, I tore open the packet the moment I saw him through the window cocking a leg over the saddle of his bike. I'm still trying to come to grips with the packet's contents.

There was a book, all right, and with it a letter. The book was *Dyuers and Sondry Sonettes;* its title page was stamped 'Library. Beale Hall.' In the letter, she sought to explain herself.

She had bought back the book from Aristide when, months ago, she had read Twombly's original letter. She had seen it by chance one evening on my desk in the Music Room, while awaiting my return from Benghazi. She apologized for reading my correspondence, but she had absorbed the letter's content before she could avert her eyes. At any rate, she had made contact with Aristide immediately, luckily just before he disappeared into Eastern Europe. She had paid him what he had paid her, plus the signature advance from her latest novel, in its genre to be another bestseller, *Get Thee to a Nunnery!* Aristide had driven a hard bargain. Afterward, he had admitted to her that he had long had his doubts about the book's authenticity. But their initial agreement had hedged him in, and he was, after all, "a man of honor." In short, he had been unable to consult the relevant experts. In the end, he had been pleased to receive "a reasonable return" on his investment.

As for Maude, she had intended to present me with the book upon my retirement, to do with it as I wished. If before then any questions had been raised about it that might have threatened either of us with harm, why, she could have produced it at a moment's notice. She had never supposed that the idiot Twombly posed a real danger, and now, of course, as he was a self-certified loony, no one would pay the least bit of mind to any of his ravings. Well, then, Father Pip-Pip had written to her about my retirement. She was pleased that I had supported the good man's candidacy as my replacement. It was time for me to receive my retirement present, and here it was.

What her apologia fails to explain is why, if Aristide had wiped his slate clean, Twombly still posed him a threat. I am reluctant to excuse Twombly of Aristide's suicide. Aristide, obviously, cannot be questioned. Nor, for that matter, can Twombly. And as for Aristide's son and heir, Gabriel Popescu, he has claimed ignorance of the whole matter (and it may even be that he is telling the truth).

Beyond that, Maude's letter had a dreadful note of finality to it. She had taken to America as a child to a sweet shop and thought that she would stay. It was a grand place for the Irish, simply grand. Besides, she had met a very fine gentleman, a good Catholic, who had asked her to marry him. She would be lying if she said she was not tempted. She would not deny that she and I had once "got it on," as they say in Queens; less prosaically, we had heard the glorious harmony of the spheres, or so we thought in our youthful, wicked passion, mistaking for heavenly what she now knew was diabolic. She hoped that for the sake of old rapture I would leave her now in peace, no longer importune her with letters that tugged at her heart and moved her to tears of sorrow and pity, and yes, of anger. "Let it be, Edmond, let it be." She was sure that I wished her all happiness, even as she wished it me.

I'll not be going to America after all, it seems. Old Lochinvar is not wanted.

൧

To use a word Pip-Pip taught me when first we met, I have not lived a "proactive" life. Quite the contrary. And on that very day, that damp and weepy day when my bunions had been rubbed sore in my sopping-wet trainers, Maude told me—this was in Angie Mackletwist's sitting room, or "lounge," as I think Angie called it—that I was "a great one for inaction, that I was." And she quoted me: "Avoidance is nine points of happiness." She might have added, "When in doubt, don't," another of my well-worn watchwords.

It's all true, I'm timorous, hesitant, not in the least self-assertive. Certainly I'm not shaped in the heroic mold. Well, not many are. But I carry inextremity to extremes. During that time she thought me witty, my weakness and ineffectuality were excused. I was acting a part, striking a pose. Perhaps I was. Well, in due course, Maude came to see through me, a man, in any case, not truly opaque. Besides, if I was indeed playing a part, the adopted role soon became the reality. Rather than proactive, my modus was reactive or, more usually, inactive. How otherwise explain my continued presence in a church in whose beliefs I disbelieved and of whose wickedness and chicanery, particularly toward my former coreligionists, the bleeding pages of history I know to be a testament? Well, in my retirement I have left that hypocrisy, theirs and mine, behind me. I have left behind in Beale Hall, destined for my successor or for the rubbish tip, everything related to my years in what I might justly name the wilderness, from bell, book, and candle to my yellowing dog collars. But why did it take so long?

Inertia, in part. An unwillingness to rock a relatively steady boat. The lure of the familiar. My attractiveness first to Kiki and then to Maude, a perverse attraction engendered, I supposed, by the cloth, the lure of the taboo. The comforts and perks of life at Beale Hall. The passage of years. The fact that others determine who we are. And so on and on.

But perhaps Freud, the discredited Jewish doctor, might point to my earliest years, when I lay beside my mother enjoined not to move, only to keep still. Certainly, I learned there the prized virtue of immobility. And thus if in my later life I failed to act, I was merely earning my mother's approval. "Edmond is such a good boy!" Perhaps. The likelier truth is that I have emulated my wretched father, the accursed of God. Certainly, I might as well have spent my life sitting on an aluminum-and-plastic garden chair and watching the mindless scrabbling of the chickens.

や

I've had the leisure to examine *Dyuers and Sondry Sonettes* closely over the last few weeks. My suspicions (and, as I have learned from Maude, those of Aristide) were well founded. The book is an eighteenth-century fake. Moreover, I can prove that its author was the Pish and that he left in it certain (deliberate?) clues to his identity. That the collection stems from the eighteenth century is shown by a number of (deliberate?) anachronisms. For example, here is the second quatrain of Sonnet LXII:

> My love, who loves me not, hath lover new,
> Whom in her closet she hath lately kiss'd—
> As when the God of Fashion this law drew:
> "Let quadrille be the rage! Away with whist!"

As every schoolboy once knew, quadrille was unknown at the dawn of the seventeenth century, and it ousted whist (and ombre) as the card game of fashion only at the end of the eighteenth.

Elsewhere, the sonneteer reveals (deliberately?) that he is a Jew. Take Sonnet LXXVI as an example. The lover complains, in true Petrarchan fashion, that his mistress is compounded of impossibilities and contradictions. Here is the climactic, the concluding couplet:

As well mix fustian with the finest silk,
Or in one meal devour both meat and milk!

This lover, please note, keeps kosher! The last sonnet identifies (deliberately?) the lady herself. Her name is hidden under the flimsiest of disguises. There are 105 sonnets in the sequence, but the last of them is numbered not, as we would expect, CV but DV, not 105 but 505. Here is the first quatrain:

> Three hundred kisses for the fairest she,
> Is yet two hundred short in true love's game;
> For but five more will put in hand the key
> That will unlock the myst'ry of her name.

Three hundred? Two hundred? Five? These numbers, of course, add up to 505, or DV, the unexpected number assigned this final sonnet. Our kabbalistic Pish, we may surmise, enjoyed playing with numbers. In Hebrew numerology 5=ה, 200=ר, and 300=ש. ה+ר+ש=שרה; and שרה is "Sarah" in Hebrew graphology. The sonnet is, then, a genuine love poem, the Pish in praise of his wife.

Dyuers and Sondry Sonettes clearly belongs with the Pishiana. What will happen to the Pishiana when I am gone, the books, the manuscripts, the scribbled notes? Perhaps I'll leave it all to the Tabakman Museum in Tel Aviv, the museum to which, years ago, I offered in loan the Beale Hall Talmuds. It is but a small redress of the balance, but there is an irony in the very thought of it that brings a smile to my lips.

I wish I had the gift of poetry. *Maude, bawd* and *board* and *bored, cord* and *chord* and *clawed* and *cawed, ford* and *floored, Gawd!, hoard,* and *whored, implored, jawed, lord* and *laud, gnawed, pawed* and *poured, roared, soared* and *sword* and *scored* and *stored* and *snored.* It's a good rhyming name is *Maude.* Besides, you don't need rhyme nowadays. No, but you *do* need ability. I'm no Pish, let alone a Byron.

⌒

What am I? A man whose parents were Hungarian and who was born in France, even though he has lived most of his life in England. I am what the neo-Anglican and neo-Royalist poet T. S. Eliot sniffily condemned, the deracinated Jew, "Chicago Semite Viennese." Unlike the rooted great man himself, of course: London, (anti-)Semite, St. Louisian.

I am not a Catholic. Can I be a Jew? What I am is a man at the end of his life, who is, for a' that and a' that, a man.

⌒

I have a very comfortable bed here in my cottage, here in Dunaharaszti. (The postman professes he's unable to pronounce the new name. He'd had enough trouble learning the old one, he said. Why couldn't people use decent English names, no offense, sir, no offense in the world? "Like what?" "Well, Dunroamin's very popular, if you want to begin with a *D.*") But comfortable or not, it has taken me a while to become accustomed to the changes. The first floor, for example, is much closer to the ground floor than it was in Beale Hall, where even the attic has twenty-foot ceilings. The bedroom itself is much smaller here; the walls press in. Then, too, the cottage abuts onto Tetley Wood, from which, through my open window, the sounds of nocturnal creatures enter: slitherings, squeaks, swoops, screams, hoots, warbles, rustlings, shiftings, anything but silence. After half a century, changes in the most ordinary things take getting used to.

For most of my life, falling asleep never proved a problem. I would assume my normal sleeping position, close my eyes, and drop off. Now, though, I enter first a drowsy twilight, a kind of Keatsian condition, neither sleeping, nor waking, a dreamy state in which, it seems to me, the conscious mind shapes the images of the unconscious, or in which, perhaps, the images of the unconscious inform the conscious mind. I rather like it, and I strive to prolong the twilight. Last night, as I lay drifting, drifting, I became aware of Maude entering the room. She supposed me asleep and moved as quietly as she could, unwilling to disturb me. I deliberately snored a little but watched her through narrowly parted lids. America had been very good to her. She seemed to have shed years and pounds, and she moved with a sprightliness that she had not enjoyed for years and years. I watched her undress and carefully fold her clothes, humming quietly to herself "The Spinning Wheel," an old Irish air she used to sing in moments of contentment. Can you imagine the joy I felt, the boundless happiness! My eyes filled with tears. I lay quietly while she got into the bed beside me, muffling my sobs, unwilling to spoil her surprise. But I could not contain myself for long. "Maude," I said, "Maude, you've come back to me!" But it wasn't Maude at all. "Be quiet, Edmond, not another word. Lie still." It was, of course, my mother.

ACKNOWLEDGMENTS

It is at once a pleasure and a duty to acknowledge the great contribution to this novel of Dr. Gideon Meyer of London, a friend of many years. For what I know of Tel Aviv in the 1960s and of St. Petersburg today, I am almost entirely in his debt. He cheerfully answered my niggling questions, and when (in the case of St. Petersburg) he was occasionally himself in doubt, he went to the loci and looked about him, and he asked pointed questions in that city of those who know.

For any errors that may have crept into my writing he is, of course, entirely without blame. For whatever worthwhile there is here that has captured the flavor of these two cities, he deserves the credit.